A WYATT
BOOK *for*

W

— ST. —
MARTIN'S
PRESS

Also by Douglas Unger

Leaving the Land
El Yanqui
The Turkey War

VOICES FROM
SILENCE

DOUGLAS UNGER

A Wyatt Book *for*

St. Martin's Press ❧ New York

The epigraph on page ix is from *The Selected Poetry of Rainer Maria Rilke* by Rainer Maria Rilke, edited and translated by Stephen Mitchell, copyright © 1982 by Stephen Mitchell. Reprinted by permission of Random House, Inc.

Design by Junie Lee

Library of Congress Cataloging-in-Publication Data

Unger, Douglas.
 Voices from silence / Douglas Unger.
   p.   cm.
 "A Wyatt book for St. Martin's Press."
 ISBN 0-312-13204-2
 I. Title.
 PS3571.N45V65   1995
 813'.54—dc20   95-2825
                                                  CIP

First edition: August 1995

10 9 8 7 6 5 4 3 2 1

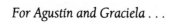

For Agustín and Graciela . . .

The author gratefully acknowledges and thanks Mirta Arlt for her liberal permission to make specific references to the novel *The Seven Madmen,* by Roberto Arlt (David R. Godine, 1984; translation by Naomi Lindstrom). And a debt of gratitude is owed to Andrew Graham-Yooll for his book *De Perón a Videla* (Editorial Legasa, S.A., 1989) and the crucial information it provides about current events and police files during the era 1955–1976 in Argentina. Thanks also to Christopher Towne Leland and Osvaldo Sabino for helping me to stay as objective and sane as possible over the years spent writing this book, and for their own invaluable creations.

. . . But listen to the voice of the wind
and the ceaseless message that forms itself out of silence.
It is murmuring toward you now from those who died young.

—Rainer Maria Rilke
"The First Elegy"

Contents

VOICES FROM
SILENCE

First News

September 4, 1983

My beloved Diego:

Years have passed in which we have searched for you, written everywhere we might find news of you, to your mother and father, and to the last address we had for you. Our letters must never have arrived, because never have we had a response.

We have had great need of you. The ████████████████ after Perón has killed Alejo and Miguel. Miguelito was shot in bed. Alejo disappeared without a trace, and we have given up hope. Martín Segundo is living in exile in Paris. ████████████████
██
██

[These lines were censored.]

We two Beneventos who remain are still looking for our Diego of Arenales Street, the boy who came to live with us once and who called us Mamá and Papá. When Miguel and Alejo could no longer call us Mamá and Papá, we had great need of you.

What must have happened all these years? The last we knew, you had graduated from university and were leaving on a trip. You had promised to visit us, as soon as you got your brother off the streets of New York and under a doctor's care again. I answered every letter you wrote in those days, until Papá and I were also arrested. All the time of my detention I thought of you even as I thought about the others, afraid something might also have happened to you. It's strange now to keep writing to you, so many times, but equally a joy for me, because Papá and I remember so much of you and feel sure you remember us. I'm not going to tell you now the horrors that happened in this country, the massacres, the concentration camps, the tortures, because I don't know ██ ██████████████████████████████

[The next page was missing.]

and this has been a particular ordeal for us. We're still being watched. We still don't get some of our mail.

Please write to us as soon as you can. Now that we will soon have a democracy again, I can pray with some hope that one of our letters will reach you, and yours might reach us. Papá has need of you. He's saddened with Martín so far away, and he has fallen into a depression even as he tries to lead a normal life again, going every day to a new office he's started. One of the things that makes him suffer most is never knowing about you. He's tried to telephone your family but we lost the number long ago and it's unlisted. Nothing gets through. We hope and pray ██████████ will leave us alone and we won't have to go on in silence.

All we wish is a long letter from you telling us what has happened with you, so we can send you news of us. We don't have

much money anymore, the ████████████████████████
██
which is also a grief to Papá. But even in this terrible economy, we
might be able to bring you to Buenos Aires to see you again. That
would be a miracle and a blessing for us, but most of all please
write. You will always be our son.

> Go with God, wherever you are.
> Mamá

Patterns of Movement

WE WERE ALL on top of each other, with tearful hugs and kisses, almost from the moment we were greeted at the door. What struck me first, glancing around over their embraces, was that their apartment was so small now, shockingly tiny compared to my memories of the grand Parisian building on Arenales Street. I recalled from the year I had spent as an exchange student with the Benevento family, fifteen years before, that their home had taken up a whole floor of the building. That elegant flat had contained a dozen large rooms, a spiral staircase up to a library, a separate apartment at the back for the maids. It had marble balconies, intricate iron grillworks, high tooled wooden doors as heavy as colonial fortress gates.

My family now lived in four small rooms in which a few scarred pieces of Spanish furniture remained from the past. Too many books were stuffed into two modest bookshelves near a loveseat-sized couch. A dining table took up most of the living room. Many of the artworks on the walls were familiar, but in the reduced living space that was my family's now, the paintings and lithographs covered almost every square inch of the walls. The walls were so crowded with paintings that they looked from a distance like colorful but messily overplastered pages from a stamp album. The visual memory, the shock from the past that struck me next, was that these same pictures had once been as tastefully arranged as in a palace.

We broke off our embraces. Mamá and Papá Benevento looked gray and worn. As they led us through the short entryway, I could see how slowly and carefully they moved, and that maybe this wasn't only from the effects of aging. My wife and I were led into the living room, where we sat down. Just in front of us were two small framed photographs of Alejo and Miguelito that had been set out on the coffee table.

"This is how they look when we last see them," Papá explained to Betty Ann in his accented English.

My wife and I had talked long and often of this moment, of how it would be, of what might be possible to say. We had had a year and a half to think about it, the time it had taken for us to save up the money and find a way to make this trip. We knew what had happened to my Argentine family from letters and from a few quick words in phone calls just to hear their voices. We had resolved that our place in their lives for the two months we would be visiting would be to be strong, even cheerful, a balance to their grief.

Betty Ann started to cry. Mamá quickly sat down on the loveseat next to her. The two women who hardly knew each other fell into a long embrace.

Mamá was a tiny, delicate woman. All her features, and her

beautiful clear face, seemed perfect and in proportion but for their tininess. Her skin was so white it was almost translucent. This effect was sharpened by the black lace shawl over her shoulders, and her dark hair piled on her head with a Spanish comb. As I watched her, I saw again how rigidly she carried herself, her body as though locked up in places. She moved with the careful stiffness of people recovering from hard falls or automobile accidents.

As the women held each other, I looked over and saw how Papá Benevento just stood there, looking at them with a sad, helpless expression. I got up off the couch to stand next to him, meaning to say something reassuring, then we were suddenly embracing each other like father and son. That was when I felt myself about to go, too, fighting off a wave of grief that rose up out of the center of my chest. I started saying to Papá Benevento in long racking breaths of Spanish how sorry I was, sorry, so sorry that I hadn't been there to help, that I had been gone from the family when they most needed me.

Mamá struggled out of Betty Ann's arms with a sudden hold on herself and a bitterness in her voice that cut through us all. "It's not your fault," she said sharply. "You couldn't have done anything. None of us here is to blame. When certain things happen to you in life, you learn what really matters. A son has come home to us, alive and well this night. He's brought us a new daughter. That's what matters now."

She moved across the small space and joined her frail arms in a hug with her husband and with me. The three of us were bound there in her embrace, part of what she had left of her family reunited in a tight clinging mass of emotion. She let go then, kissed my cheek, and said, "Translate for your wife now, my son. I don't want her to feel lonely."

I dug out the bottles of whiskey and cartons of cigarettes I had brought as gifts, American L&M's and Johnnie Walker Black,

Papá's favorite brands, which were so prohibitively expensive in Argentina. I set them out on the coffee table in a small gesture of celebration. Papá gave me a strong squeeze around the shoulders, kissed my cheek, thanked me. He went to the kitchen for a bucket of ice. I saw with some relief that he was moving better now, with quick, clicking steps over the tile floors. He was a man always impeccably dressed, in crisply ironed shirts, in slacks with tight creases, his mustache neatly trimmed, his thinning gray hair combed precisely straight back on his head. There was a correctness to his every gesture that I could see might be unchanged. It was an uprightness in his posture, in his being, that sense of the proper Argentine gentleman. He had once been an important lawyer for international businesses. In his movements there was still an awareness of the power and position he once held in the world. He brought in the ice, opened one of the bottles of scotch, then filled glasses for all of us except himself.

"I gave up smoking and drinking years ago," he explained. "It had reached a point where my whole system was running on nothing but poison. God knows I would have smoked myself to death by now with all that's happened. But on the drinking, well, I've only given up my little whiskey until the year two thousand. After that, I plan to be the healthiest man in the cemetery."

I sat down again. I looked at the lines of dark amber bottles with their fancy black labels with a strange and lonely feeling that even in this, too, I had failed him. I raised my glass and finished it off in one long swallow.

Mamá wouldn't sit still. She got us all back on our feet again and proudly showed us around the tiny apartment. She led the way, Papá following with Betty Ann, trying to make conversation with her in his rusty English. I agreed too enthusiastically with Mamá that it was a nice apartment, surely all the space they needed. She picked up small objects or pointed out certain paintings and lithographs—this little statue, this leather-bound book of history, this cubist print, the torn panels of a painted screen of *Gregorian chants*—reminding me of their presence in our lives when I had lived with them. There was an odd dreaminess in her voice and gestures. It had been a long time since she had indulged in something as simple as the pleasure of nostalgia.

I watched and listened distantly. I had the sense that this was a person I no longer knew. Where was the society girl who lingered in bed each morning with her breakfast and telephone brought to her on a tray? Where was the class act who ruled over a palace and servants, who dressed to the nines and concerned herself with art and culture and filling up her social calendar with the very best? Where was the grand señora I remembered? Not that this person—this new person—wasn't in many ways better, somehow, and I could sense this, for what she had been through. The radical change from the affectations of the bourgeois princess, the Argentine grande dame, many of which I had never liked, was simply so marked. There wasn't one trace, not one gesture or intonation of her voice, left of that in her being.

Mamá led me into the one guest bedroom. I was struck by the small Spanish-style fold-out bed with its blue checkered bedspread, and by the closets in which, still, there hung a collection of young man's clothes. I recognized them at once as belonging to Alejo. Mamá just opened up the wardrobe and chest of drawers, and it was clear whose they were. She had saved everything she could. She kept the room arranged as if Alejo might come through the door at any moment to toss himself on the bed and prop himself up to read through the siesta. I particularly remembered two posters, now mounted and framed. One was a Russian cartoon that showed a paunchy Lenin standing on top of the globe with a broom, sweeping fat caricatures of the ruling classes out of his country, and a slogan in bold Cyrillic letters underneath, *Tovarich*

Lenin Ochichtayet Zemlovo ot Netchisti. The other poster was a famous Magritte, the one of the figure in a bowler hat shown from behind as he stares out at an open seascape. Next to him is his own silhouette, as if cut out of a surreal rendition of sky, sand, and beach or a sculpted pane of glass. Suddenly, I could hear young Alejo explaining to me on the day he had purchased that poster at a street fair, tacking it up in his room on Arenales Street, his voice filled with an excited sense of the discovery of magic and revelation, *the man is looking at the ocean, and so we are being made to see the ocean through him. . . .*

Alejo always searched in this life for the ideal and the visionary. Under the military dictatorship, that alone would have been cause enough to be disappeared.

"Somehow we have managed to keep the things in Alejo's room the same way he left them," Mamá said. She had noticed how I was staring off into the posters.

"I know, Mamá," I said. "There's no need to explain."

"No. I feel there is," she said. "It's . . . curious, to do this. It . . . I was in a detention camp. Your Papá was in and out of detention two times. When we finally got back to the apartment, everything was smashed to pieces. We lost that home later, but I won't go into that now. That was after the military squads broke in and robbed us three times. But the furniture had been left, turned over and broken, just the way it was the night they took us to prison. At least one of our neighbors put a new lock on the door. They were afraid to go in and try to clean up. But Alejo's room, you remember, the one with the biggest window, and the balcony with the beautiful jacaranda tree outside, even though the military ransacked it and carried off so many of his books, for some reason they left his room almost just like this. You would think they would have torn down this poster of Lenin as proof that we were all communists, just as they used my collection of Jean-Paul Sartre as evidence to keep accusing me. But they didn't. They left most of the things in his room. So here it all is," she said. "But enough of this now. There will be plenty of opportunities to talk about what has happened. This is the room where you're going to stay, my son. Our house is your house, as always," she said.

We joined Papá and Betty Ann, who were sitting down again in the living room. Papá was saying in broken English, "But every-theeng it change-a . . . when . . . democracy. New *presidente* . . . a good man . . . we vote for him . . ."

He turned to me with a look of frustration. He said in a rapid, angry streak of Spanish, "Translate for your woman that I learned about democracy with a gun pointed at my head. Three times, a gang of sons of whores dressed in jungle fatigues broke into my home. They put a pistol to my head and made me tell them about my politics."

Mamá threw herself out of her chair as if she were launched by a cannon, something hysterical and desperate in the way she moved. She rushed into the kitchen. Papá rose quickly and followed her in to help.

"What was Papá trying to tell me?" asked Betty Ann.

"He, ah, well, he was just trying to tell you how glad he is about the new democracy," I translated.

Betty Ann was in a shaky condition. She was filling the whiskey glasses again, but her hands were trembling. She spilled a little. I grabbed up some napkins and mopped at the spill. Betty Ann held out a glass to me. "I really like them," she said. She smiled, tensely, as if trying to reassure me that the evening was going well enough. "They're such good warm people," she said.

Maybe it was just at that moment, as I nodded, yes, surely, to my wife, that I picked up the whiskey glass with an intense clear desire to wipe out every cell in my brain. Drinking seemed like the only solution. Tomorrow was time enough to consider a new life. In the meantime, I could drink until sense and vision were all washed out, until drinking became a kind of forgetting, and a punishment, body and brain so sick with drink they barely felt alive.

Something was burning in the kitchen. Mamá and Papá were chattering away at each other urgently. By the time I got to the kitchen to try and help, Mamá had an apron on and was already carrying in a tray of overcrisp canapés. "Since our maid—do you remember Isabelita? Since she retired, I'm the one doing most of the cooking," Mamá said. She waved away my clumsy gestures to lend a hand. "When you move in and we get a routine of life set up, then you can help out, my son. We'll all work together and pitch in. Everything has changed in this house. What do we need a maid for now?"

"The maid didn't leave because we couldn't pay her," Papá was quick to add. He, too, was wearing an apron. It was absurd and out of place, a sight impossible for me to accept. I had always thought of Papá Benevento as the grand señor, the don, the patriarch. I recalled the way he used to hold court as if his study were a senate chamber. We four boys would all stand reverently before him, answering his strict but kind questions like litigants before a judge's throne.

Papá tossed the apron aside quickly as he left the kitchen, as if it was second nature by now to tie and untie the strings. "We can still afford a maid," he said. "We just never hired a new one after we had to ask poor Isabelita to leave. The military terrorized her. She was crazy, toward the end. We couldn't trust her to be stable enough even to answer the telephone in case one of the boys called in. But we didn't just toss her out into the streets. We made sure to set her up with something comfortable for her retirement, before we were arrested."

"She was the closest to Miguelito," Mamá said, beginning to serve the tray of canapés around. "You remember. They were almost like mother and son, those two. When Miguelito disappeared, she was like a madwoman all over the neighborhood. She could have gotten all of us killed. She was crying out on the neighbors' doorsteps and in the streets, '*Mi Miguelito! Mi Miguelito! Mi pobre Miguelito!*' And we just couldn't have that. It was hard enough on us without the maid making it worse. Anyway, I have her address, if you want to see her."

"We're on the same subject again," Papá broke in, shaking his head slowly. I was about to say sure, I would visit Isabelita. I had good memories of the tough old Galician maid. Sure I would visit her and bring her a little gift, but I said nothing. Papá chewed a canapé as if it were poisoned. "It's always the same thing in this house," he said. "We can't get away from it for a minute. Always the same conversation."

"It's going to change from now on," I said. "You'll see." I turned to Betty Ann. "Isn't that right, honey?" I asked in English. She nodded yes, smiling nervously. She hadn't understood more than two words of what had been said.

"We're going to have some good times in this house," I continued. But my voice was just a bit too highly pitched with frantic Spanish, and I saw that my hands were moving a little too wildly through the air. "We'll move in. We'll help. We'll sit and listen to music just like we used to do, Vivaldi, Albinoni, you remember? Here," I said. I dug into the plastic bag for the small stereo tape player and headphones, another gift for the family. No one moved to take them from my hands.

"Your Papá hasn't listened to music in years," Mamá said after a moment. "His records reminded him too much of the boys. The way you all used to sit in his study with him and listen. Then the military stole his stereo during the third break-in and interrogation. So why bother to listen to music? After that, we had no way to play music anyway."

The evening went on like this, almost never off the topic of what the family had suffered during the years of silence. I kept thinking back at the many times I had written without reply, my letters vanishing into nowhere, until, finally, I had stopped writing. The first few years when there had been no news I made repeated inquiries through the United States State Department and its special Office of Human Rights. I asked contacts I made with the press to try to find my family. Still, there had been no information. The names of each one of the five members of the Benevento family were added to the long lists of the disappeared that were read into the *Congressional Record* on the floor of the United States Senate. After that, I gave up trying. Seven years had passed without any news. Then there had been Mamá's first censored letter, forwarded through so many old addresses that it was a miracle it got through. Anguished telephone calls had followed, then letters, and messages through friends, all during the long year and a half until I had finally been able to make this trip to visit them. And here they were now, fifteen years since we had lived together, and it was hard to imagine they were even the same people.

We chewed on canapés and drank whiskey around the coffee table. Mamá went into her bedroom and brought out a large poster tacked on a staff. It was a huge, out-of-focus blowup photograph of a sharp-featured young man, his long nose raised in the air proudly, an expression in his almond-shaped eyes and on his face against a foggy background of trees as if he had just won a lottery. We all agreed it was a happy face, an intelligent face. It had an expression full of hope and good spirits and dreaming. It was the face of their son who read books and composed songs, their poetic son. Under the photograph, there was a bold, handwritten legend, *Alejo Benevento—19/11/76.*

Mamá showed us the white scarf that had the same name and date embroidered on it, and that she wore on her rounds with the other mothers of the Plaza de Mayo. That was the one protest march the dictatorship had never been able, under the eyes of the world, to put down or crush or kill, the hundreds of mothers who, every Thursday from three in the afternoon until five, had slowly marched around the center of the plaza, the altar of the nation, making known to anyone with a conscience on this earth that their children had disappeared.

I looked on as Mamá made the meaning of all this clear to Betty Ann, partly in French, the only foreign language Mamá knew, and partly with hand gestures. Betty Ann spread the embroidered scarf out gently in her lap, stroking it in a way that made me think she had had too much to drink.

"Here we go again," Papá said. The tone in his voice was gently scolding, directed at Mamá, and at her scarf and her sign. "The same subject, even tonight, when we should be celebrating. With Martín Segundo married and back from exile, and now with our Diego and his wife here, it's like we're a family once again. It's a miracle! We should be happy!"

"Yes, Martín, maybe you're right," Mamá answered slowly. She took her scarf back from Betty Ann's lap. She folded it neatly, then held it in both hands the way a soldier's widow holds the flag pulled from a coffin. There was a strange, hypnotic quality in her voice. She didn't look at any of us, but off somewhere a great distance from the room. "Yes, we might be a family once again," she said. "But just look at us now. We're no longer like the parents of the family. The way we are now, the way we've been living, it's as if our children have given birth to us."

A long, sad silence fell like a shadow. We sat there, staring into our empty plates. The dinner had long ago burned completely, then been politely forgotten over snacks and more whiskeys. Finally, Papá got up to start clearing plates, and Mamá politely excused herself to help him. I was about to get up and offer to wash the dishes, but Betty Ann pulled at my arm and stopped me. I settled back into the couch. She drew closer and asked me in a voice low enough so Mamá and Papá couldn't hear, "Where's Miguelito's scarf? Where's Miguelito's photograph and name on a sign?"

I also suddenly noticed that absence, and didn't know what to say. Certainly, no one was going to ask. I checked my watch. It was hard to believe so many hours had gone by. I realized that I was also very drunk. The tiny apartment was starting to look for brief moments like the deck of a ship in heavy seas. My tongue was thick enough with scotch that I was pronouncing Spanish with a lisp, like a Castilian with a speech defect. I had to work hard to be understood, and it was getting embarrassing. Too much had happened for one evening. It was time to go.

We weren't supposed to move in with my family on the first night. I had learned to be careful about that kind of thing, to check first and make sure there was no chance of an imposition on others, or on myself. I had used the excuse of the long and uncomfortable flight and the need to recover from it for a day, to get our bearings, before making any move. I had informed the Beneventos that this was what we were doing. So, a few hours before the reunion, we had gotten off the plane and checked directly into a modest hotel.

"It's getting late," I announced too abruptly to Mamá and Papá, unsteady on my feet as they came in from the kitchen. "Maybe we should go now," I said. "We should take things one step at a time."

"Tomorrow!" Mamá let loose in a high, shrill voice. It was as if she had forgotten the arrangements. "You're moving in tomorrow! Of course you're moving in tomorrow!"

Mamá rushed over to me and pressed so close that she had to tilt her head back to look up into my face. I grabbed at her

15

awkwardly, pulling her small body tightly against mine, squeezing her hard, her head tucking neatly just under my chin.

"Tomorrow," she said more quietly. "We can take care of you much better here than in any hotel, my son. The room is all ready. We can expect you tomorrow?"

"Tomorrow, Mamá," I said. And we stood that way, holding each other as though we wouldn't let go. I looked over her shoulder at Betty Ann. Her head was leaning sleepily against one high cushion of the couch. "But in the afternoon," I said. "We'll be here late in the afternoon. It's no use being all tired out. We don't want to be any burden. We want to be a help around here."

"We have great need of you here," she said.

Then we were all suddenly moving for the door in a whirl of coats and borrowed umbrellas and reassurances. It was raining, hard, in the streets outside. Papá was telling Betty Ann how much he liked her, what a boon and treasure she was to the family. In the middle of the final hugs and kisses in the doorway, he said in English, "And our Diego. He was such trouble, he should tell you. But how much we have missed him! Alejo and Miguelito loved our Diego too much!"

I thought Papá Benevento had probably meant *so* much. But for hours and days and months, that one parting phrase would echo in my brain. It would go off at times like a bomb in my ears. *Too much,* as though perhaps they really had. *Too much,* both boys too devoted to and even worshipful of my own rebellious manners back then, to my growing my hair long, to my radical politics, and to my troubles with the police in the year I had been an exchange student living in their home. And it was suddenly clear to me that, sure, it had been too much of setting the wrong example for their boys, as an admired and elder brother often can. But was that really too much? Was that really true? It was an irrational feeling, no question, but no less sure or true for that. And it struck me like

16

a siren shriek inside my head, with the weight of premonition, and with a sharp, certain clarity I could never get out of my mind again. Once put into words, it was too late. I, too, for their untimely deaths, must bear my own full measure of responsibility.

We made our way out the door, slowly, an eternity of hugs and tears and parting words. "Good night now! Until tomorrow! Good night! Don't get wet! Good night! *Hasta pronto!* Sleep well, children! Good night! Take care! Good night, dear children!"

The next morning, there were moments when I was sure I was losing my grip. Or was it the city around me that had suddenly gone crazy? It was a foggy, wintry day. My hangover made things even foggier. The sun only burned through the clouds for a few minutes about midmorning. The gray sky was like the lid of a massive kettle that tipped up to let the light in and the pressure escape. Nothing else I saw made sense until I could discover the cause.

Almost no one in Buenos Aires stayed very long at his job that morning. Lines at banks stretched out and circled city blocks, becoming disorganized mobs that spilled into the streets. Near the markets and the department stores and gallery emporiums, people were rushing around with boxes and net bags and even suitcases. These were being stuffed full of goods as fast as possible. Cigarettes were the first to go, stripped off the shelves of the corner kiosks and stalls. Supermarkets were the worst. People crowded around the checkout counters, pushing and haranguing each other. It was like a feeding frenzy. Cooking oil was gone by noon. So was almost every staple canned item, every bag of rice and flour, every liter of long-life milk. Wine and soft drinks and just about anything else that could be stockpiled without spoiling were soon sold out. Money was gripped in fat sheafs of colorful bills, then scattered around like all the leaf storms of autumn wrapped up in a single day.

17

Announcements were in the news. The official inflation rate had finally broken the dreaded "rationality barrier" of 1,000 percent. Added to this, the stock market was crashing faster than the exchange rate of the peso. The panic was on. Factory workers were walking off the assembly lines. Offices were closing. All over the city, people were desperately getting their pesos out of banks or out from under mattresses and trying to spend them, fast, on anything they could find. Or they hunted for someone to sell them *los verdes,* solid yanqui dollars called simply "the greens." One of the bellhops at the Gran Dorá Hotel caught me in the lobby on my way out. He stealthily passed me a business card with nothing but a telephone number and a first name printed on it. He said in a low voice, "You want to change dollars, *che,* you get the best black market rates from me. Ask for Jaime. I make one phone call and give you the price down to the minute."

It was that way all over the city. The price of yanqui dollars was actually changing by the minute. Police were called out to markets in the poorer districts to shut them down and keep people from rioting. I ranged around the city center, walking off my hangover, and the more I became aware of what I was seeing, the harder it was for me to believe.

I picked up the daily papers at a newsstand. For a moment, I resisted the strong urge just to begin to walk in the direction of the Plaza San Martín, then turn down the posh Avenida Santa Fe, retracing the steps I had abandoned so many years before until I reached Junín and turned toward Arenales and the ornate facade of the building I had once called home. I wanted to do this but was held back, feeling it was about to rain again, also the weight of the package of medicine in my hand that was wrapped in colorful paper and tied with string like a precious gift.

During the night, my wife had come down with a head cold and cough, a common reaction to the climate change. I turned back in the direction of the hotel. But for the first time, I felt the sense of familiarity with the city that I had expected all along. This sense was in a particular smell on the air, the sounds and rhythm of movements of traffic and people. Even in the panic of the economic crisis, there was still a proud arrogance of face and gesture in the people passing me on the sidewalks, a particular aggressive self-centeredness that in many ways defines Argentina. It was in the solid Parisian architecture rising up over the streets. It was in the way bus and taxi drivers made hell-bent for intersections in defiance of the traffic lights. It was in every move of the well-dressed men and women hurrying with that quick Buenos Aires walk to the banks and the money exchanges with briefcases and purses stuffed with cash. Watching this all around me, I began to think that little had changed. I remembered how I had called this my city once. It was in my blood, and here it was all around me, even in the sensations of the ridged tile sidewalks through the soles of my shoes. I thought of the verse of the famous tango and what it said, that once one returned to Buenos Aires, there would be no more troubles or forgetting.

By afternoon, it was raining again. Toward winter in Buenos Aires, there is sometimes a ground fog that billows in off the river and accompanies the rain with a bone-numbing chill. Out on the street, I covered Betty Ann with my coat, telling her she was foolish to be out at all today. We had to think about the move to the Benevento apartment, and we should both be at our best.

She was in a happy mood. We window-shopped like tourists a few blocks from the hotel. I tried to calculate the prices of fine shoes and leather jackets and fur coats in dollars rather than the hundreds of thousands of pesos listed on the black felt boards with easily changeable numbers. Some of the windows had chalkboards. Store clerks were hastily erasing the prices, raising them between morning and afternoon. I felt in my pockets for the wads of colorful bills from the money I had changed at the airport with some sense that they were worth far less than just yesterday. I wondered what it would be like to adjust to that kind of inflation, what it was going to mean to our daily lives.

There was a restaurant down the street, a traditional Argentine grill, or *parilla*. Enough beef to feed an army company was barbecuing on skewers set up around a huge open hearth that took up almost a whole row of picture windows. The coals of the mammoth orange sleepy fire made the place look warm, and through the windows, the white jackets of the waiters glowed as they moved back and forth through a dim romantic light. We came in out of the rain, hungry and hopeful, happy enough to find such a warm-looking place.

I was chattering away. There were very few cultures that revolved as much around food as did Argentina. The richest and most flavorful beefsteaks in creation were only the beginning. There was the quality of the salad greens, as fresh and full of sweet life as flowers. There were the pastas, the breads, the pastries, the wine, the fruits of the seasons, all so incredibly abundant and, at least as I remembered things, within reach of everyone.

We shared a menu, and I translated. We ordered filets of beef so tender they could be cut with the edge of a fork, shredded carrot and onion salad, fried potatoes, red wine. We settled in and got ready to enjoy ourselves. But as I looked around, something was missing. The waiter, for example. He was in an obvious bad temper, was even rude as he took our order. He openly sneered at the wine I selected and remembered as a good Cabernet from *bodega* López, and that cost only a few thousand pesos.

We took in the impressive scene of the huge, cavernous, and mostly empty *parilla*. Tables stretched off into the smoky distance, which seemed to echo with the slightest noise as in an abandoned gymnasium. There were only a few small groups of mainly older souls in the place. They were huddling over clean linen tablecloths, gray faces reflecting the firelight as if each table were a lonely hearth cut off from the others. The expressions were too subdued, too sad-looking. It was as if they didn't know of the time when the streets of Buenos Aires had been full at this hour, raining or not, the all but sanctified hour of lunch. Nor how almost every night, crowds of happy people would pack themselves into the brilliantly lit Lavalle Street, like a kind of glitter gulch for movies that showed continuously until dawn. They didn't remember how the live theaters on the Broadway-like Avenida Corrientes would let out at ten, how the sidewalks were as mobbed with enthusiastic faces as a political convention that had chosen a winning candidate.

The way I remembered Buenos Aires, the restaurants were jammed all day with happy diners, the theaters were packed, and later on, nightclubs played jazz and pop and folkloric music until early morning, then after-hours clubs in the port sector called La Boca poured out whiskeys and tangos that never stopped. It was a city that halted in its energetic life and round-the-clock entertainment only on Sunday mornings for dawn mass before it went to sleep for a few hours, or far more likely, headed off in tribal hordes for the soccer stadiums.

Once again, as I looked around the restaurant, I saw nothing of the city I remembered. The faces were tired-looking, tense, disturbed. Surely it was the economy, that great lead weight oppressing the world. I watched closely as a table of elderly gentlemen tried to figure with pocket calculators the value according to the latest black market rate for the U.S. dollar of the many tens of thousands of pesos their beefsteaks and salads and wines were going to cost them today. I had the sense, again, that I had stepped across some unforeseen boundary of memory into a new and unknown country.

Still, we were trying to enjoy ourselves. It had been rare in our marriage to have the freedom of only each other's company. We were a happy couple, generally speaking. But most of the time, our energies were focused and fueled by the need to take care of others. When we married, Betty Ann already had a five-year-old daughter, Heather. We were doing the best job of caring for and nurturing her that we knew how to do. Then there were our extended families—I had a schizophrenic brother who had needed constant support ever since he had come back that way from Vietnam, and she had an alcoholic brother-in-law who had lived with us on and off in the early years until he had finally dried out. Or one of my wife's sisters would turn up occasionally, sometimes with a kid or two dragged along. Or her older sister's grown-up daughter would turn up with *her* kids and move in with us. We were always the ones pitching in for a family member bounced out of a job, a marriage, or a home. Even the year we had been in such trouble ourselves that we changed apartments and crap jobs nine times, we were there for our families. We were always the ones who were called on to help.

Somehow, through all of this, we had both finished graduate school. We believed in education more than anything else. We were convinced that if we worked hard, studied hard, and did the right things, a good life would come to us. Just about the time we had given up believing this, after rattling back and forth so many times across America in search of God knew what, maybe just a place to rest up by then, our convictions proved out, and our lives did change. I found some success with books and writing. I was offered and accepted a teaching job. The best newspapers in the country started giving me assignments. I wrote a few literary and topical "essays" for the news on Public Broadcasting. Betty Ann landed a part-time teaching job and began giving private lessons in her fields of acting, speech, and movement. Nothing could stand in our way by then. We had even bought a house, something we had at one time given up dreaming would ever be possible.

Across the table at the restaurant, I could see my wife was feeling worse. She nearly tipped her chair over from the force of trying to suppress a cough, not wanting to let me know. She drank her wine, fast, after trying not to cough, and with something like the same expression as when she tossed down drinks to fight off her fear of airplanes. But she kept praising the flavor of the huge rich steak she was feeling too queasy to eat. She loved the wine. She said over and over again how much she loved me. Then she finally did cough, recovered, and said, "Oh, God, I'm sorry. This is our time. And look how I'm ruining things."

I took her hand and said it wasn't her fault. Going from eighty-five degrees in New York straight into a humid River Plate winter was a shock to anyone's system. We were quiet for a long time. I knew what she was thinking. I was thinking the same. We had a long and busy day ahead of us. I was going to meet my Argentine brother Martín Segundo, for the first time in years, the first time since he had returned from exile. She was going to do the job of getting us packed up and ready for the next move. Neither of us had a clear idea of what we were getting into, what was going to happen.

"Oh, look!" she said suddenly. I turned my head quickly in the direction she was pointing. I drew in my breath. A single ray of sun had suddenly appeared through the half-open milk-glass door of the restaurant, like a bright streak of sulfur slicing through a blue fog. "That's so beautiful," she said. She was the kind of woman who tried to put the best face on everything. She was smiling, full of energy again, something that lifted my worries. "Maybe we'll get some sun after all," she said. "Don't you think so?"

Years can pass and people can look just the same, perceived through the eyeglasses of certain memories that never age. Martín

Segundo looked outwardly to be the same sturdy, blond young man, casually dressed in an Argentine businessman's uniform of blue jacket, gray slacks, and prep-school tie, almost exactly the same uniform we had both worn every day when we were students together at Colegio San Andrés, an exclusive Catholic school. The only thing missing was the crest on his pocket, the simple crucifix of St. Andrew, a blood red X. Martin was a lawyer now, as the family had always planned for him to be, hoping he would follow Papá Benevento into practice. Seeing him that day, I recalled how rough it had been between us at times, but I had an immediate sense that his years in exile had changed him. His manner was no longer that of the spoiled boy I had known, but rather of a man who now considered all implications, and paused to think before he spoke. He carefully measured his words as though giving testimony, as if anything he said could or would be used against him.

The purpose of our meeting wasn't only to see each other. Martín wanted to prepare me, and warn me. He was very concerned to get the facts straight about what had happened. He had only just returned from exile four months ago. Only after two years of elected government had the Benevento family considered it safe for him and his wife and their baby to come home.

"These are the facts," he said. "Alejo is a classic example of the disappeared. After the death of Perón, Alejo and I were both active in the opposition movement, the Montoneros. We wanted to fight back against the corrupt government of Isabel Perón and her minister, López Rega, who was a shameless gangster and maybe even a genuine witch, if you believe in that kind of thing. Isabel went crazy. She was hallucinating and hearing voices. That gangster was running the country in her name. And what else were we going to do? We were naive enough to think we could change things. Then the generals, the comandantes, threw her administration out of office and things really got bad.

"That's when Alejo and I went underground. We took an apartment together, as a safe house, out in a remote corner of Villa Urquiza. Our involvement with the militancy was still nothing too serious. We had meetings. Just as we used to when you were living with us, we went out painting slogans on walls at night. We talked about guns and bombs and urban guerrilla war against the tyranny of the state, but it was all just talk for us. In other groups, well, some people went out and planted bombs. But Alejo wouldn't have done anything like that. By that time, he had joined a public employees' union. He was a law clerk at Tribunales, the main courthouse building here in the capital. He was trying to organize his local of the union into a group to agitate for higher wages. He had a ditto machine and was publishing some newsletters and pamphlets for them.

"Alejo had a girlfriend at that time, who was also in the resistance. She was a nice girl, but I had a bad feeling about her, like she might be the kind to talk too much at clubs and at parties. This wasn't any time, I told him, to get stupid over a girl. Alejo must have made the mistake of calling this girl and making a date with her that gave an exact address and time they were to meet. He knew as well as anyone that he wasn't supposed to use the telephone that way, not with anyone else who was in the movement. That was November 19, 1976. No one ever saw him or the girl again."

We were sitting in an expensive *confitería* called Young Men's, on the Avenida Córdoba. Waiters in bow ties and red jackets moved ceremoniously back and forth through a crowd of mainly middle-aged and prosperous people chatting over their coffees, whiskeys, and sandwiches. Meeting with Martín Segundo in such a posh atmosphere was strange. Young Men's was very different from the smoky student bars and pizza joints that I remembered us hanging out in so many years before, in which the talk was mainly of soccer and girls or how to fudge our way through difficult exams for which it seemed no one had studied.

Martín and I had been too competitive with each other then, too critical, too quick to judge. It was with Alejo that I had formed a close and brotherly friendship. Alejo, with his arms loaded down with novels of fantasy and adventure we passed back and forth, discussing them late into the nights. Alejo, who was always off in some other world of his imagination, so spaced out that he hardly looked at traffic when he crossed the street. I used to watch him do that and shut my eyes. It was nothing less than a miracle each time he made it, still unaware that a *colectivo* bus had nearly run him down. He was a kid who had to be reminded to change out of his rope-soled peasant shoes for school, whose rumpled schoolboy's jacket was always stuffed with heels of bread which he constantly pulled out of his pockets and devoured the way other kids might have eaten chocolate bars.

I thought of him then, seeing him vividly, Alejo, who was so promising and intelligent, the kind of privileged-class youth for whom stale bread was better than candy. The facts of his disappearance, especially in such a bourgeois atmosphere of luxurious illusion as was Young Men's, with its leather-covered booths and expensive woodwork and large bubbling fish tanks lining the room, everyone sitting there looking so rich, suddenly struck me deeply. In those surroundings, his loss was much more real.

Martín Segundo took a long swallow from his beer. He took large messy bites from the tray of dainty English-style sandwiches, wolfing them down as though talking about his brother's disappearance had caused in him a compulsion for food. I reached a hand across the table and squeezed Martín's forearm, needing to touch him that way, solidly, reassuring. Martín nodded once. He grasped my forearm and squeezed back in that same kind of gesture, something primitive and tribal in it, that masculine clasping of arms.

"It's a miracle you're still here," I said. Martín Segundo set down a partly devoured sandwich and nodded his head again. He looked around the room through his tortoiseshell glasses and motioned to the waiter for another beer. By Martín's silence, his uneasy shifting around in the booth, I felt I must have said something wrong. "It must be so hard for you," I said. "Something like the responsibility of all three sons is yours alone."

"Maybe so," Martín said. "But that's not what I've been thinking. I've been thinking that it's a bitch to be back in this country at all. I had a pretty good life going in Paris. Another two months and I would have been the owner of my own travel agency, with the good apartment, the good car, the good wife, everything. Now just because I was born here and Mamá and Papá would never consider leaving, I have to be the one to come home and give them at least the chance to see some grandchildren. I was never their favorite. I know that," he said.

Martín looked across the table with a full sense of his own irony. It was hard to remember if we had ever liked each other. Yet now, with what had happened, that didn't matter.

"There are circumstances, too," Martín said. "You should know them before you move in. Papá thinks that Alejo was tortured. I'm not so sure. When Alejo didn't come back to the apartment that night, I packed up my things and got out before morning. We had a rule. Everyone in the militancy had this rule. We took an oath that if we were caught, we were to stand any torture for twenty-four hours. That was to give those living with you, and those in the same cell, enough time to escape. You understand, the rule was that after a day, you were free to spill your guts. You weren't expected to take it any longer.

"So I got out of the apartment and went into hiding with friends. Later that week, I contacted Mamá and Papá and told them. Mamá made the journey out to Villa Urquiza to the apartment to see about clothes and things we had left behind. She still had some hope that Alejo would be there, or might somehow have left some message. No one had touched the place. Lists, names, pamphlets, posters, everything was just the same as when we left. The police would have come, surely, if Alejo had told them where it was. As far as anyone knows, none of the others in Alejo's union cell were ever captured.

"So that makes me believe that Papá is wrong. They didn't torture Alejo. He was too smart for that. I think he must have tried to run or maybe he did something else to make sure they shot him. I think he must have died like that. In the very first hours, on the first day, before they could make him say a single word."

Martín dug into the tray of sandwiches and finished them. There had always been a sense about Martín Segundo, a narcissistic impulse he followed. He consciously and with almost illicit pleasure indulged himself, his comforts, his appearance, his body. He drank beer and scooped handfuls of peanuts from the plates and ate sandwiches with evident indulgence. It struck me as good to see this now, and the way Martín would every once in a while find the mirror, in front of which stood a fish tank, in which to admire himself, check his handsome features, run a hand through his hair. He examined his reflection as if it were a kind of reassurance. His intelligent face shone clearly superimposed against the black and yellow and tiger-striped predator fish darting around, jabbing their ways through the bubbling tank with their antennae. He straightened his tie. He smiled at himself, checked his teeth, pushed his glasses higher on his nose. I thought back with regret at the times I had thought badly of Martín Segundo for this quality of self-admiration, the times when he would flex his muscles in front of mirrors and pat his hard stomach, calling himself such a macho. It was different now. I was sitting across from a man who had learned the value of even the simplest good thing in his life, in himself, in his surroundings.

"Cortázar wrote somewhere that they did experiments with fish tanks," I said. "They put a glass divider in the middle of the tank. They left the fish for a time, getting used to their one side of the aquarium, circling around in there. When the glass was removed, it was like they didn't know it. They never would cross over to the other side. They just kept swimming around and around in that limited space."

"Sure. I remember reading that, too," Martín said.

We sat for a long time, staring into our reflections through the whirling, abstract patterns of colorful fish.

"Well, so there it is," said Martín Segundo. "That's the story of Alejo. That's all we know about him. The case of Miguelito is different. You might even call it something more Christian," he said. "But maybe not. To know or not to know what happened, which is worse? What do you think? Which one?"

"It's not for me to say."

"No, go on," he said. "Which one?"

"I'd want to know," I said. "I do want to know."

"That's one way to tell an idealist from a pragmatist," he said. "In Paris, there were so many exiles that we formed our own soccer league. We met all the time. Most of us took the opposite position from yours. After all, what use is it to know what happened? How is that going to help you put bread and wine on the table?"

I nodded in answer to his question.

"All right then, you know where I stand," he said. "After Alejo disappeared, Miguelito really went wild. He started going around armed with a pistol and then later with a machine gun. Papá and Mamá kept trying to find him at the houses of his friends and get him into line somehow. They wanted to send him immediately out of the country. Then Miguelito went underground. Nobody knew where he was or what he was doing. He didn't even tell me where he was going. Banks were being robbed back then. There were assaults on police stations and on the prisons. At night, there was shooting in the streets like regular fireworks.

"During that time, Miguelito disappeared. After the first few months of not hearing of him, Papá was of course adding his name to all the legal work he was doing on behalf of Alejo and others of the disappeared. He filed for habeas corpus. He got the best-connected lawyers in Buenos Aires to petition the military and the courts, to make declarations. He tried to find at least one federal judge with enough balls to demand a release or at least a report about what had happened. Of course, any judge like that was arrested. Or his own family was threatened. So, again, no word, nothing.

"About a year later, Papá received an anonymous phone call informing him that Miguelito's body was in the city morgue. The police claimed he died in a gun battle, shot by one of his own militant friends. But that's a big lie. The police showed Papá photos of Miguelito shot in his bed, in an apartment that wasn't anywhere near where we later found out, through one of his friends, he had been hiding. The wounds didn't look very recent. There wasn't a trace of blood on the sheets. The police record showed the date of his death was December 8, 1977, but who knows when it could have been? By the time they told Papá, a year later, it was too late to determine precisely when he had died. But at least, after another two months spent filing papers, the police gave Miguelito's body over to them and Papá and Mamá could see him buried. That was in February of 1979, long after Papá and Mamá had themselves been arrested the first time.

"So that's what happened. That's all they know. Sometimes I think it would be better if they didn't even know that much."

"It's not for me to say," I said. "But I don't think they want to turn their backs on what happened."

"Don't you see how they are? What's happened to them? It's Miguelito's case that's coming up at the trials. There are some things Papá won't talk about, not to me or even to Mamá, matters relating to the testimony he's supposed to give in court. He had to go out to Chacaritas Cemetery and exhume Miguelito's body for evidence. I'm telling you now so that you'll know. You won't have to ask them too much about it. It's not a good thing to mention around them, especially around Mamá, unless they're the ones who bring up the subject. Do you understand what I'm saying?"

"Sure. Sure I do," I said. "I'll be careful around them."

"Things will come out when you talk to them. But in my opinion, the less said about what happened, the better it will be for them. They're very emotional right now. Especially Mamá, with you coming. The both of them are going around telling everyone that they have a son who is coming home. Do you understand me? Can you see how important this is to them?"

"I understand," I said. I didn't know what else to say. I nodded yes, surely, and drank my beer straight down.

"This is an expensive place," said Martín Segundo, changing both the subject and his mood. He was gazing around at the wealthy and established-looking customers at the tables. "It's a good thing you're paying the check," he said. "The way things are with me now, I don't think I've had a beer in a place like this for months. In Paris, well, they were better days. You can imagine how hard it was to leave the nice life it took me years to build.

31

Even my wife was working, in computers, and the baby was learning French. I don't know. It all seems like a dream now. Here. Here she is," he said.

Martín Segundo reached into his jacket pocket for his billfold. He pulled out a color snapshot of a bald, smiling baby held aloft by a tall, beautiful woman, both of them in scant bathing suits, on a Mediterranean beach. I told Martín he had landed himself a woman more beautiful than he deserved. He laughed and shrugged his shoulders.

I pulled out my hip-pocket wallet. I opened it to the picture of my stepdaughter, Heather, already a leggy teenaged girl, her sweater about three sizes too tight for her as she thrust herself at the camera as if trying to show the world she had beyond doubt become a young woman.

"Such a pretty girl," Martín said in his accented English. Then he said something in French that I didn't understand. I asked for a translation. Martín laughed and said, "The effect of it is that you are going to have a lot of boys around."

"That's already true," I said. I examined Heather's photograph. I thought of how many times we had uprooted her and dragged her around the country. Only in the past two years had there been any stability, and she was flourishing in it. Just a little normalcy was all she had needed. She was popular in school. She had boyfriends. "When she first started dating, I swear I felt like strangling any boy who took her out. Even the nice ones. Maybe the nicest ones most of all," I said.

"Oh, no, I can't even bear to think of how it will be when my daughter gets to that age," said Martín Segundo. "Jealousy," he said. "The first time I ever felt that was when you moved in, the big-shot exchange student, like a special person in our house. I'm sorry. I was a real *boludo,* a first-class asshole, that year."

32

I started to say something to object. Martín raised a hand to stop me.

"No. It's true," he said. "But it's different now. Exile in Uruguay. Then in Brazil. I made it all on my own in Rio, begging money like a *negro* on the beach. Then I got my refugee pass to Paris and I worked at any kind of shitty job I could find. I lived like the hippies. I even sold souvenirs to the tourists."

"Really? You?" I said. "The famous rugby champion? The same guy who threw a fit until he could get just the right maroon sash and tie to go with his new tuxedo?"

"You're right. I'd forgotten that," he said.

"Those must have been tough times."

"No, no! That's not what I'm saying! You're always so fucking intense about everything! Lighten up for once!"

"Now you're right," I said.

"But don't you see what I mean? I really loved Paris! I loved *that life!* I wasn't any angel before I left this country. Neither was Alejo or Miguelito, or most of us in the movement. . . ." He grew quiet for a moment. He looked off around the room. Then he turned, looking me directly in the eyes, and added in a low voice, "Maybe, really, I should have been the one who died."

Suddenly, I wanted to shout at Martín. I wanted to reach across the table and shake him by his collar to stop him from talking. It wasn't out of any generous spirit toward him but somehow to save myself. I saw the need that Martín was sharing with me. At the same time, memories were passing through me like a blinding rain of welder's sparks. We had never been friends, but at least we had fought like brothers. The superlit tropical fish in the large aquarium beside us swam on, turned, swam on in circles, never touching the glass, as though the exact dimensions had been memorized even in their cells. We were in there with them, washed over by a salt tide of words. They were hurtful words. They made us remember too much, not only the brothers who were gone, but our own absences and failures as long as arteries. There was a pain in all this that made me speechless. It was a deep and pure pain at the center of my chest. And I felt it growing, fast, like a laboratory tree I had reported on once, a tree that was made to grow faster by a series of increasing electric shocks.

"I didn't die," said Martín Segundo. "That didn't happen. What could I do about that? And when that didn't happen, there had to be some way for one of us to save himself, isn't that clear? What I want to say is that from then on, it wasn't easy, no, but it wasn't hard exactly, either. I had girls. I had cars. I fell in love and got married. Every day was new. Each morning was like a hope that one good thing, one really good thing, just might happen. That was my life. That was the life I loved. So, well, now I'm back in this country again, shuffling papers and filing motions in court for Papá's new law firm. I'm wearing worn-out pants and even corduroys to court sometimes because his practice isn't earning enough millions of this worthless money so that I can afford a decent suit. That's the situation. Papá and Mamá are walking around with broken hearts and empty pockets. Without me here, they would feel they had nothing."

"Come on, you don't have to explain . . ."

"Shit!" He slapped the table. "Let me finish!" He gave me such a look of frustration that I wanted to curl into nothing in my chair. "Look," he said. "What I'm trying to tell you is that sometimes I don't give one shit about them or about what happened anymore. Sometimes I don't care about anything but my own life, and my wife's, and my baby's, and to hell with this country and everyone else. That's me now. That's who I really am. Do you understand what I'm saying? Please don't misunderstand. I'm glad you're back here. Me more than anyone. We're all glad you're back. We love you. We're happy to see you. So welcome home, brother. After so many years! Welcome back to Argentina!"

We were due at the Benevento apartment at five o'clock. After we made it down the hotel elevator and out onto the sidewalk with enough gear for a safari, there was a strange little incident. I ended up stiffing the bellhop who had struggled with our bags. I couldn't find any bills in my pockets of the smaller denominations; every one of them was a fifty thousand, and the only "greens" I had were hundred-dollar bills. I showed the gay-looking paper pesos to the bellhop. The poor man shrugged his shoulders. "Don't worry, señor, you'll take care of me next time," he said. "It's just the crisis. Always the same in this country. They think the trouble with inflation is there's too much money. But the truth is that there's never enough in the right quantities. You'd better ask the taxi driver if he can handle a big bill, señor, so you don't drive around all day looking for change."

Mamá Benevento was waiting for us with the table set for an English-style tea. We discovered that did not mean that we would actually sit down to drink tea. Nor would we eat the hot croissants or little cakes and sandwiches Mamá had managed to get from the bakery before the shelves were stripped clean. The moment we arrived, bag and baggage, a frantic activity took over the Benevento house.

There were long minutes spent in the doorway, with me interpreting between Mamá and Betiana, as the family had decided to name her, before we could even set down our bags. Betty Ann had coughed just once. Mamá determined from me that she had caught a cold. I explained that it was really nothing, she was feeling much better already, but Mamá got the sudden idea to dig out a heating pad from somewhere deep in a closet. She placed it in Betiana's hands before she had even taken off her coat. Just at that moment, Mamá remembered that tea was set. She called us to come in and take off our coats and sit down.

After one sip of tea, Mamá jumped up out of her chair as if stung by an insect. She rushed off to the bookshelf in the living room to look for a list of words she had left there, written in Spanish, so that I could write out their English equivalents and begin to teach Spanish to Betiana. Just as Betty Ann was getting the general idea of what that was all about, Mamá urgently insisted that we both get up from tea and follow her around the apartment. We set down our cups and sandwiches.

Mamá led us on a tour, making Betiana practice the Spanish words for important things and showing her what they were, the shower curtain, the clean towels, the refrigerator, the bread box, the cupboard where the coffee was kept, then the clothes-washing room with its system of clotheslines strung up on pulleys. We were happily beating our way through a jungle of hanging wet laundry when Mamá suddenly discovered a houseplant she had left to soak in one of the laundry sinks the day before. She scolded herself about the plant. She hurried off with Betiana in tow to try and save the plant immediately, leading her through the apartment to the small balcony off the living room. In all of this, I noticed that Mamá Benevento was moving differently than she had the night before. She no longer seemed so fragile, so stiff and careful with every step. She now flung herself around so suddenly and carelessly that I had to fight off the reflex to reach out and catch her.

The two women were soon up to their elbows in potting soil. Then the telephone rang. Mamá Benevento dropped everything and ran back to answer it with an air of emergency. Betty Ann and I stood waiting tensely, bracing ourselves for bad news. I overheard what I could and translated for my wife. It was a gossipy conversation about the Argentine art world. Mamá was complaining that the Radical Party was denying some government grants and postings to *peronista* painters and writers. I recalled the time when Mamá had been away so much in high society at galleries and openings. I watched her now as she gripped the telephone hard against her ear, chattering away, nervously raking one of her earthy hands through her hair and over her face, leaving dark streaks on her cheek and forehead.

"What should I do?" asked Betty Ann. She was in an awkward position, standing there in a half-crouch, propping up a partly repotted, drowned-looking begonia in a planter the size of a wash-tub. There were so many other smaller plants crowded in it that it looked as if the begonia would smother them. "I think Mamá wants it planted here," she said. "But I'm not sure what to do with the other plants. Can you ask Mamá what I should do with this?"

"To tea! To tea!" Mamá shouted out happily from inside the apartment. She clapped her hands and called out, "Come on now, children! Come back inside! Come along right now or it will get cold!"

I managed to prop up the sulking begonia with a stick. Then we came in obediently from the balcony and sat down again at the table. We lifted our cups and took a sip of tea that had gone cold. I raised a crisp, buttery croissant to my lips and took a bite. Mamá was out of her chair and off like a shot. She made rapid urgent hand gestures at Betiana to follow her at once. We pushed our chairs back and got to our feet. We trailed after Mamá Benevento, dragging along as many of our bags as we could.

"This is your house! You're in your own house!" she sang out cheerfully. She led the way into Alejo's bedroom, which would be our room. "This is it," she said to Betiana, with me translating. Mamá was singing away like a bird in the sun. "No need to rush to get settled in. You can relax now. Do anything you please. You're on vacation now, my daughter. Relax here, if you want. Come on now and relax. Come on into your room and sit down. Come in now to sit down and rest and relax!"

She stood at the center of the room, waiting, nervous. Betty Ann coughed. This reminded Mamá of illness, and she was off again in a rush to the bathroom, where she clattered around, then reappeared carrying a tray so loaded with medicines it looked like a bizarre thirty-course meal. She handed the tray to Betty Ann. "Quickly now, we should make up the bed," she said.

She banged through a closet looking for clean linen. The twin bed was made of heavy iron and had a pull-out second bed stored underneath. I busied myself with setting the bed up, pushing the two twins together to make a double bed. "Translate for your woman, my son, that before this was Alejo's, it was the first marriage bed for your father and me. I know it doesn't look like much now." She was spreading out the clean sheets and tucking them in around the rough-looking iron frames. "But we were so young then and so happy," she said. She rose up on her toes to get close to my ear and added in a lower, conspiratorial voice, "Tell your woman that I conceived my first two children in this bed."

She arranged and laid out a sickroom for Betty Ann in a few minutes. She made up a concoction from several medicine bottles that looked like a foaming pink Bromo and insisted that Betty Ann drink it straight down. The gas heater was lit, put out, lit again in demonstration. Mamá discovered the heating pad again, plugged it in, and had Betty Ann hug it to her chest as she lay down in the bed. I translated insistently for Betty Ann that she was feeling better, there was no need to bother so much, but it was no use. By that time, Mamá Benevento had noticed how crowded the closets were in the room.

Wardrobe doors flew open and we were at the center of a whirlwind of flying clothes. She was gathering armfuls of the family's summer clothing and rushing it to another closet somewhere down the hall. I noticed that she left Alejo's hanging clothes just as they were, in the other wardrobe.

Our baggage was piled up in the bedroom doorway. Coming in and out, Mamá was stepping gingerly over the bags. Before I could move them, she insisted on demonstrating the French blinds. She pulled the cord and revealed the window. Outside, there was another small balcony like a secret garden, stuffed full of an impossible number of plants. She quit talking about the French blinds. She noticed a forlorn-looking twiglike plant in a black mud pot on the balcony. She asked me to forage out there and get it in for her, which took some acrobatic twisting around, pushing my way through snapping foliage, shoving heavy treelike things aside to make enough room to move. Mamá lamented that one of her plants had died. But wasn't this a beautiful pot? The *indio* designs on the pottery etched into the black clay?

"Since you're feeling better, my daughter, maybe you and I can work for a while with the plants. It will do us both good," Mamá said.

Betty Ann gave me a confused look, as though she might have missed something with the language difficulty. I shrugged my shoulders. Mamá reached for her hand. She tugged Betty Ann forcefully up from the bed and heating pad. Both women were out the door in a hurry, Mamá leading her double-time back out to the mess of planters and potting soil on the balcony off the living room.

The afternoon was a chaos of bedroom arrangements, baggage, planters, soil, medicines, and sips of cold tea whenever we passed by the beautifully laid-out table. For the first time, I began to understand the effects of what had happened to Mamá Benevento. She was now a woman who could not stop moving. She jumped up and fluttered around the apartment like a frightened sparrow. She lit cigarettes and stubbed them out after one puff. Or she left them forgotten and burning in ashtrays as her attention suddenly shifted to yet another project, action, compulsion to keep herself busy. All at the same time she typically had two pots cooking on the stove, items of clothing pulled out with seams to sew and cuffs to raise, clippings to cut out of the newspapers for her expatriate friends. When the telephone rang, she answered it in a voice filled with urgency. She was up to date on the Argentine art world, and on the movement for human rights. She hung up from these conversations out of breath. She wrote notes to herself on small scraps of paper which were scattered all over the apartment.

Her pattern of living was to devote one minute out of every ten minutes to each of the ten projects she had going all at once. She could not settle down. She was everywhere on the run, from one task to the next, even as pans billowed up with black smoke, newspaper clippings mixed and whirled and scattered to the floor, unfortunate plants sagged and then drowned under flowing water taps. She kept mixing up names and personal messages in the letters she was writing. She would never sit down and finish one letter. She laid out stationery as if in a tandem series on the living-room desk. She would write a sentence or two on one page, then shift her pen over and write a different sentence to someone else, keeping four or five letters going at once until she made a mistake, scolded herself, crumpled up the page, and started all over again from the beginning. By that time, she was smelling smoke. She rushed off to the kitchen to keep the house from burning down.

As I watched her movements, I thought of how the effects of a trauma of such grief and terror were different for different people. I had read with great interest the Amnesty International studies out of Amsterdam on the victims of torture, and also the Holocaust accounts of psychologist Bruno Bettelheim, of Primo Levi, and others. Some people withdrew, grew quiet, shrank away like wounded animals into dark and lonely hiding places. Others found solace only in violent thoughts or actions. Anger helped them to recapture the independence of the human spirit from the imprisonment of grief. They recovered themselves in acts of revenge or in social causes. Some starved themselves, in every way, from the guilt that they were the ones who survived. Others couldn't control their eating or drinking, or ever learn again how to plan as far ahead as the next day.

In college, before I met Betty Ann, I had lived with the daughter of an editor for Radio Free Europe, Zdenek Czerny, who had been in the Auschwitz labor camp. He told the story of how for many years, he carried a spoon in his jacket pocket. When he passed restaurant windows or sidewalk cafés, he sometimes couldn't resist the compulsion to sit down and finish what people had left on their plates. Other survivors adjusted to the effects of state terrorism by means of a continuous and obsessive pattern of movement. They became nervous wrecks. They were not able to concentrate on a single task or idea for more than two minutes, and they couldn't stop moving. Like these others, if Mamá Benevento ever stopped moving long enough, she would begin to remember. And so the jumpy, manic energy everywhere around her and about her being was in some way an effort at forgetting.

An ambulance passed by on the street below with the jarring, alien sound of its electronic siren. Mamá pressed both hands to her ears and sat down on Alejo's bed with an anguished look, fighting off panic. Only long after the sound was gone could she lower her hands and start to breathe again. "There were years when sirens like that were going off all the time," she said. "I began to imagine each time that it was meant for us. We never knew who it would be next carried off to the grave."

She leaped up suddenly and rushed out of the room. She was back in an instant with a box of tools and nails and screws. She told me she was going to take me up on my offer to help around the house. She needed me to fix a few things. It was something to keep going with, a new list of projects and details to scatter the mind. I hauled in an old rickety ladder from the laundry room. With Mamá's instructions, I climbed up on it and was about to drill a hole in the plaster wall so it could hold a metal collar and a screw.

The telephone rang. Mamá took off fast enough to catch it by the second ring. She rattled off a few quick phrases and was back again to hold the ladder. "That was your father," she said. "He's going to be late for supper. He was at the bank all morning. Then he worked all afternoon taking depositions for the trials. Remember Father Vargas?"

I said yes, I remembered. Father Vargas was in charge of the charity mission in the shantytown slum on the outskirts of the city. Whenever we students at Colegio San Andrés cut up or got into trouble, which was often, we were suspended from school and had to work off our demerits with bricks and mortar and ditch-digging. We spent long days under the supervision of Father Vargas, helping to build his school and community center in the slums. I had put in two weeks with the priest and his crew of delinquents.

"Six priests from the charity missions of San Andrés were disappeared during the dictatorship," Mamá said. "Father Vargas was one of three who survived. The monseñor himself, the horrid bishop who once got you into trouble, it was he who turned his own priests in to the military. They were preaching the theology of the liberation in the slums. They were taken away without a word of protest from the church. The official charge against them was 'subversion against the Argentine way of life.' That's the way it was under the military. Even our priests were targets," she said. "Your father, I'm afraid, doesn't have a very tough shell anymore.

He wants to go to the movies for a while to clear his head."

We both dropped the subject, and concentrated on the placement of the hole I was supposed to drill. I thought these fix-it chores around the apartment would be good for us both, considering her condition. There were dozens of projects that needed doing. Working on them together would be a new beginning.

"Translate for your woman that since we moved the fourth time, I just haven't been able to put this house together," Mamá said. "The house you knew, the beautiful home on Junín and Arenales, that one I put together when I was young. We lived there thirty years. I just haven't had the energy to work properly on this one."

"Tell Mamá that my mother has a saying," said Betty Ann, her voice strangely muffled inside the large suitcase she was unpacking. "It's Irish, I think. 'Three moves cleans you out the same as a fire.' "

I translated, and Mamá nodded very seriously in agreement, missing Betty Ann's effort to make light of the situation. I was almost finished with the hole-drilling project, working away on it, when Mamá suddenly had me abandon doing that and move the ladder into the living room. She asked me to climb up and change a lightbulb in the ceiling fixture. Dust and dead insects spilled out of the glass. I brought down the frosted globe, and Mamá ran off with it for cleaning. She brought a broom back with her to sweep up the mess. She discovered that the handle was loose. Our project together became hunting around the house for the epoxy and gluing the broom handle back in place. And before the light fixture was back together, why not sweep up the plaster dust from the hole drilling?

It was enough to drive anyone crazy. But a rhythm was being established between us. Martín Segundo had his own house, and a baby to worry about, and was working too hard. Now here was someone she could count on to drill holes for screws strong enough to mount a new wall heater. I could jimmy around and unstick the bathroom lock so the door wouldn't keep popping open. I could take a set of French blinds apart, unscramble the cords, oil the machinery, and put the blinds back together again. I could carry a ladder from one end of the house to the other, back and forth, back and forth, as in some absurd, sped-up silent movie, careful not to swing around and smash anything. I could shift heavy potted plants and small trees from one side of the jungle balconies to the other, endlessly, until Mamá decided for at least one moment they were in the exact positions for the light to save them. No matter how frustrating the scattered movements, I started not to mind. A more primal language was exchanged between us. Her house was in need of a son.

Later, Mamá was scolding herself for how late supper was and how she had just let a pan of potatoes and carrots burn. Papá Benevento came cheerily through the door. As if he had known dinner would burn, he carried a large package of empanadas, the rich meat, cheese, and vegetable pies shaped like little half-moons, the Argentine convenience food. "Hello! Hello everybody!" he called out in English. He stepped into the kitchen and moved pots and pans around. "Hello!" he called out again. "I bring empanadas! Is anybody hungry? Empanadas solve all the problems!"

Papá was in unusually high spirits, considering what Mamá said he'd been through, and the tension of the economic crisis. While the women were still busy in Alejo's room, Papá signaled to me, secretively, to accompany him to the living-room desk. He was carrying several legal-size salmon-pink folders under his arm. He unlocked a desk drawer and filed them inside. I was about to ask what was in the files he treated so carefully, but it was clear Papá had something else on his mind. He reached into an inner pocket of his sharp gray lawyer's suit and came up with an envelope stuffed with currency.

"How are you fixed for money, my son?" he asked in a low voice. Before I could answer, Papá had turned and pulled a large book out of the bookcase. "If you ever need money, this is the family bank," he said. He separated the currency, most of it yanqui hundred-dollar bills, but there were also about a dozen dark blue bills, German marks in denominations of one hundred, along with some French twenty-franc notes. "This must seem like madness to you," he said. "This terrible inflation has reached the point where it no longer fits inside my head. It was a mess out there today. Nobody knows anymore what anything is worth. Here's the whole nest egg, every peso it was possible to move into hard currencies. The way it works in this house, everything goes into the same pot, right here. So now you know where it is. There are also some pesos—just take as many as you need each day," he said.

Papá showed how the currency fit neatly between the fat book's pages, volume two of the glossy color edition of *Enciclopedia de la historia argentina*. He slid it back into its place on the shelf. "We're really very lucky," he said. "Most people don't know what to do. I've seen this coming, and have been stocking up for weeks. There's enough to get us all through the month with something extra for any emergency."

I started to tell him I had plenty of yanqui dollars of my own, that Papá should change any pesos he needed with me, it would be a convenient arrangement for everyone. But the women were coming out of Alejo's room before I could finish. Papá shushed me quickly. "Let's change the subject, my son. Talk about the economic crisis makes your mother feel physically ill."

We all sat down to a happy supper. Papá showed off his high spirits. He smiled and laughed and struggled with his English, making Betty Ann feel welcome. Mamá only leaped up five or six times. We ate the hot empanadas and a salad. We shared a fine bottle of Cabernet from Mendoza that Papá brought out especially for us, serving it with a voyeuristic pleasure in the drinking of others. He and Betty Ann settled in to chatting pleasantly about movies.

"What was the Father Vargas deposition like today?" Mamá asked sharply, and as though no one else at the table were talking. She had been eating fast, and quickly drinking large glasses of wine. She was using her fingers, peasant-style, to eat her empanadas, letting the warm oil run over her hand and down her wrist. Seeing this was strange. I remembered how she had always sat at the head of the table, quoting from the fastidious rules and etiquette she had learned from her education with French nuns. She had been a tyrant about table manners, laying down the law for her family until every utensil and gesture was in its place. Now she was eating empanadas with her fingers, chewing her food as roughly as a dock worker. "What about it?" she asked, chewing. "What did Father Vargas say?"

Papá quit eating. He pushed his plate aside.

"Nothing much. He was very eloquent. He'll make a good witness. Admiral Massera himself once inspected the cell where they were keeping him. Father Vargas spoke clearly and to the point. He didn't waste time."

I leaned close to Betty Ann, in a whisper translating what Mamá had asked, and what Papá had been doing that day.

"Who is Admiral Massera?" Betty Ann asked.

"Comandante of the navy. They have torture center," Papá answered in English, then turned to me and said in Spanish, "Translate for her that Admiral Emilio Massera is the one responsible for the concentration camps run by the navy. He's going to be on trial for his abuses. Father Vargas was tortured by the navy," he said. His voice had a lawyerly tone, as though he had little emotional attachment to his words.

"What did Father Vargas say that upset you?"

"What was that Mamá just asked?" Betty Ann said.

"It wasn't so much what Father Vargas said. It was just that I didn't know that he had been so disfigured. They burned him very badly, with the electric prod. And, well, you might imagine what they did to him."

Betty Ann wanted to get every word Papá was saying. As I translated, I could see the effect this was having. It wasn't as though she didn't know she would hear such things. Still, there's nothing that can prepare anyone for hearing the words so closely. Her face took on a shocked look of incomprehension.

"How disfigured is he?" she asked.

I didn't answer. She kicked me under the table.

"Father Vargas is a priest," I said finally. "After they were through with him, physiologically speaking, he was something less than he used to be as a man."

Papá Benevento did his best to smooth over what had been translated by excusing himself from the table to begin clearing plates. Mamá asked Betty Ann for a cigarette. Betty Ann looked stuck to the seat of her chair, the change in mood overwhelming. I was about to go join Papá in the kitchen to help with coffee. Mamá tugged at my sleeve and stopped me.

"Translate for your woman, please, that I'm very sorry to bring up bad news at the table. I forget that people don't have such tough shells," she said. "Your father, I'm afraid, doesn't have a tough shell anymore. He hears certain stories and still gets upset and can't sleep. But that doesn't happen to me. No matter how horrible the testimony is, and I have heard many, many terrible stories, all I keep thinking is good, very good, thank God for the miracle this person is alive so that people can know. I'm the tough one in this house. I'm hard enough by now to hear anything, and I mean anything, and all I feel is hatred."

The family settled into a more subdued pattern with one another after the meal. The women went in together to Alejo's bedroom, where there was a television set. Betty Ann sat with Mamá in front of a situation comedy as she dragged out clothing to mend, working at an easy communication over the domestic chore. While doing this, Betty Ann saw how much Mamá's back and neck were hurting her, her muscles locked. She insisted on giving Mamá a back rub and massage, and I was called in from the living room to make her meaning clear. The two women went into Mamá's bedroom.

I joined Papá again in the living room, where he quizzed me about our lives over the years. I talked about how we had met in graduate school, then the years of moving around the country, working at anything we could find. Papá Benevento urged me on, delighting in the details of how our lives had turned around, and what I was writing, especially for the newspapers I had done articles for, since he knew and had read some of them. I was about to rummage through one of my suitcases to bring out some clippings I had brought along. Sounds came from the bedroom. We stopped talking.

From the living room, we listened to the sound of Mamá weeping. Over this weak and pitiful expression of pain was Betty Ann trying to help her by saying, "Let it out, let it out," in English, over and over again, "Let it out." I explained to Papá what must be happening. Betty Ann was a master at fixing backs and necks. Her thumb and hand pressure knew exactly each muscle and bone, and how to massage out the pain. We sat together and listened. The sounds grew steadily in intensity, with a ritual tone and rhythm, then they stopped.

There was a long silence. Then the sound of Mamá's voice calling out to Papá and me. We went into the bedroom. Mamá was undressed and under the covers of the bed, Betty Ann sitting beside her, both women's cheeks marked with tears. Mamá opened her arms out wide toward Papá and hugged him. Over his shoulder, she said, "Translate for your woman, Diego, that she's a very loving and tender person. I'm very happy to have her as my daughter. Tell her that I say you're a lucky man to have her. I never would have thought it when you first lived with us. You were an interesting boy, don't get me wrong, but you didn't have a very good way with girls. So it's a real surprise to me that you've had such luck with a woman."

The family had a good laugh at my expense. We all hugged and kissed good night. After scurrying around, brushing our teeth and turning out lights, Betty Ann and I were left alone in our new little room which looked like Alejo's room. We had unpacked, off duty now, it seemed. I sneaked out and into the kitchen to look for a second bottle of good wine and some glasses. I tiptoed past the bedroom of Mamá and Papá in a way that reminded me of a youth spent like a thief in my parents' houses.

We changed for bed. We drank the wine. We settled back and relaxed. Then we were kissing, falling deeper into each other, the wine running in our blood. Soon, pajamas and nightgown were tossed to the floor and we were moving, just right with each other, in a happy embrace. The iron bed frame started creaking and banging like a metal gate in the wind. We stopped moving. We shushed each other. Mamá and Papá's bedroom shared the wall against which the bed had been banging. We listened intensely for a sign we might have disturbed them. We lay there like two fugitives hiding from a close brush with the law.

A sharp ridge of the bed frame was cutting across Betty Ann's back. Quietly, whispering, we adjusted our position. We kissed again, letting ourselves go a little less. Our hands settled into the familiar patterns of exploring, and then she raised her hips up gently. I moved over her to find again just that right position, deep inside. There was a sense in our physical love, after so many years together, of comfort and tenderness and satisfaction. This was what marriage was about. We came through the doors from a hard day in the world and found each other home. The mattress was soft under her body. She kept sinking in and slipping to one side. The bed rattled. We stopped again. Groping awkwardly in the unfamiliar space, we tried to change positions. Rolling over, I was lifting her up and over my body when one of her legs kicked out sharply. She stifled a shout of pain.

I hopped out of bed and turned on the light. She had scraped her shin on the bed frame. An ugly gash ran from her knee halfway down her leg. The light was startlingly bright on her bleeding wound. I tipped my head back and shielded my eyes against the clustered glare of naked bulbs. I remembered that I had not quite finished putting this bedroom fixture back together. I quickly threw on my bathrobe and sneaked out in search of Band-Aids and antiseptic. I found some peroxide and gauze in the medicine cabinet, the metal hinges squealing loud enough to cause me to hold my breath. In the hallway darkness, I cracked my head against a wall. I sat on the bed and set to work cleaning up her wound.

"How could anybody make children in a bed like this?" Betty Ann asked.

"But you've got to admit it's got style. It's like a museum piece. Early Spanish Inquisition."

We laughed. I found a clean white sock for her, and she pulled it gingerly up over her shin. I poured what was left of the wine and we finished it off. I turned out the light, and we did our best to snuggle up together over the uncomfortable iron rails, pressed closely against the coolness of the wall. We lay there, holding each other. After a moment, I whispered to her that I was sorry. She shushed me. "Maybe this isn't going to be so easy," I said.

"Hush now. This is just fine," she said. "The only really weird thing about being here is you. I mean, think about it. When have you ever fixed anything around our house?"

We laughed again. We kissed good night. Then we lay there quietly until she fell asleep in my arms.

I was still aroused, and felt my heart beating. Lying there this way, I thought of how we had been when we first met, and I wondered just exactly when it was we had changed. My memories were vivid and passionate, of a tireless physical love when we first met. Over the years, the intensity of our attraction had changed, replaced by a settled quality, and tender comfort. I was afraid of that too comfortable feeling somehow, and she could sense this. Yet that familiar and rooted intimacy of our marriage was what I most counted on. I felt a warm and overwhelming love for her then, and thoughts like a sweet silent prayer that we would never lose each other. I kissed her sleeping head. I kissed her hair spread out on the pillow. When I was sure she was soundly enough asleep, I pulled away from her and rolled uncomfortably across the iron frame to my side of the joined beds. I was tired. I lay on my back and closed my eyes.

Several mufflerless *colectivo* buses exploded by in the street below. Later, a gang of drunk and noisy youths passed just under the window, singing loud obscene stadium songs and shouting out one another's names. In the dim and faintly blue streetlight that filtered through the cracks of the French blinds, Alejo's wall posters shone. Lenin looked like a witch's shadow with his broom. The clouds of the Magritte were black crows moving in the sky. I tried not to look at them. Across the room, a tall carved wardrobe of Spanish oak was still mostly filled with Alejo's clothes, cleaned and pressed and ready. I thought of them there, hanging empty.

I thought of the reality of Alejo being gone for senseless reasons and then of my blood brother Harry, who had gone off to a meaningless war and had come back crazy, had been repeatedly confined in locked hospital wards for almost fifteen years. The only thing I knew I had learned was that I was helpless in both situations. I thought regretfully of the many ways I had made my heart cold to the loss of my brothers. I had spent half my life pushing my real feelings aside and hiding them somewhere.

My mind was racing. I rolled over on my stomach and closed my eyes again. I tossed, trying to get comfortable, but my legs were too long. My feet stuck out over the bed frame at the ankles in a way that was making them go numb. I gave up. I pounded my fist into my pillow in frustration. I rolled to my back again and stared up blankly at the ceiling. I realized my hands were clasped over my middle on top of the covers. I changed positions quickly, startled at the thought that I was laid out like a corpse.

Thinking about that made me suddenly remember something, an *indio* myth I had read about once and then forgotten. It was from the writer Miguel Angel Asturias, from one of his trilogy of novels about Guatemala, *Los ojos de los enterrados*. Maybe it was just a chance passing belief from the jungles of Central America, or maybe it was a more universal superstition in Latin America, I wasn't sure. The myth was that when a murder is committed and justice is not done, the murdered one opens his eyes when he is buried. The eyes of the interred stay open like that, restless and searching, waiting for justice either human or divine.

It wasn't a good thing to remember that night. Now that this thought had invaded my brain like an unwelcome noise, I was sure I would be a victim of insomnia until I went psycho from lack of sleep. But it was too late. My imagination was trapped somewhere deep within the earth. There were stirrings, a rising anonymous murmuring of human voices, movements underground. For an instant, I felt sure my brother Alejo was watching me. There was a presence there in the room that was stronger and more solid than my memories. I was convinced for that moment that the dead do visit the living. I was looking and listening so intensely in the dim blue near-darkness that my eyes were burning and my ears were ringing with the strain. I was sure that if I could only just hear and see well enough, my brother's voice would tell me what had really happened to him, where he was, under what small mound of earth in this universe he could be searched for and then found and brought home.

It was just my mind playing tricks. I was imagining things, comforting myself with thoughts of even this much life after death, which was nothing but so much nonsense and superstition. Alejo was gone. No one would ever know how. He had disappeared without a trace, as simply as that. No one would ever find him. And justice? Here, in Argentina, it was the opposite of the common saying. Justice was not for the living but for the dead.

Trouble in the Streets

I SPENT MORNINGS that first week getting a press credential. One of the producers for the news program for which I had done three television "essays" had been kind enough to write me a letter of introduction and request for media privileges. Because of its very tight budget, the program was planning to cover the trials by means of occasional reporting by the anchors, edited from stories taken from the wire services. If something more happened, footage and commentary could be purchased from an outfit called VISNEWS, out of London and Amsterdam, that would have a full crew on the scene. Only under the most unusual circumstances, and if the program could somewhere find the money, would any thought be given to using a freelance correspondent from the steps of the courthouse. I was planning to send copy to the program anyway. I made arrangements with an Argentine wire service, Noticias Argentinas, to use its telex machines.

As is the customary process in many foreign countries, I took the letter to the U.S. consulate and waited while it was examined and checked for accuracy. Then a secretary for the press attaché wrote another letter, addressed to the office of the Secretary of the Press of the President of Argentina, requesting my status be granted as a *reportero gráfico* with the Argentine government. I needed sets of passport photos. There were forms to fill out at the office of the Secretary of the Press, located in one small wing of the Casa Rosada, on the Plaza de Mayo, the pink presidential palace and government house. The whole process took dozens of hours and many cab rides through the city until I had the red card covered with official stamps and signatures and sealed in plastic.

I left the apartment to pick up the finished credential early one morning. I hailed a taxi in a rush. The driver gave me a curious look when I stated my destination, "the government house."

He was a stocky, bald, Italian-looking fellow. His muscular arms embraced the steering wheel clear to his elbows. He looked back at me in the rearview mirror, and then forward into the traffic-clogged streets through a tangle of soccer pennants and a plastic statue of the Virgin on his mirror mounting. He inspected me again for a moment, looked me over suspiciously, then turned the flag down on the meter.

"The government house," he repeated. He extended the syllables of the words in a way that made clear his contempt. "Don't tell me," he said. "The Minister of the Economy is speaking today. The same shit as always in this country. Prices are going up. The currency is going down. His friends who are now running this economy from hell are going to get rich. The rest of us can go die of hunger, *che,* for all he cares. Isn't that true? Well? Tell me if it isn't. Democracy or not, it's all the same," he said. "Sometimes I think this country was better off under the military. Well? Isn't that true?"

The driver made an obscene Italian gesture with both hands cupped together that meant "Don't swell my balls"—he didn't want to hear any more fairy tales. He searched my face in the mirror with an intensity that demanded some kind of answer. I didn't feel up to the hotheaded argument it would undoubtedly lead to with this sympathizer for the military. I shrugged my shoulders in a slow, bothered way.

"Ah! I thought so!" the driver said. Without looking once through the windshield, he pressed his foot down on the accelerator to beat out a *colectivo* bus and nearly got us killed. "You know exactly what I'm trying to say," he said. "Even though you are a foreigner, which is obvious, I can tell you know something about this country. So here's my own personal view. This is the situation," he said.

The driver stopped talking for a moment, coming up against an impossibly snarled intersection. He made gestures toward me and then at the traffic jam as though it somehow proved the point he was making. "You see? All the fancy cars parked on both sides of the street? That's illegal, and that's the cause of this mess. But do you think there's anyone in this new democracy who will do anything about it?"

He rubbed his fingers together in a universal sign language that meant money, telling me that the city officials were taking bribes.

"That's how it is now with everything," he said. "Listen. This is the story. You want to hear the story? This is the story," he said. "When God made the world, one day, He reached the stage when He gave out all the riches to each different country. A lot of the best went to Europe, and to North America, the wealthy northern continents. But every place was left with its drawbacks, isn't that true? For example, down here in South America, in the country of Chile, our Creator decided to give them bountiful copper mines and a fantastic stretch of Pacific Ocean. Then as drawbacks, He gave that country harsh bare mountains with earthquakes all the time and soil that was really tough to grow things in without back-breaking work. Up in Brazil, God reached down a finger and made the Amazon, and then the rain forests. He filled the jungle with gold and emeralds and all kinds of jewels, and on the coast He made sure there was the easy living on the beaches, like in Rio and Bahia. Then He put down a hundred kinds of poisonous snakes, thousands of tropical diseases, and decided there would never be any oil to run their automobiles. Uruguay He left so many things out of that the people have to work like slaves in order to live. And Paraguay's so poor it's hardly worth mentioning.

"So then God got around to our beloved Argentina. Our beloved Argentina, *che*," he repeated in a way that made clear his frustration. "He gave this country the richest possible land on which to grow food. All a man had to do to eat was scatter a few seeds. Just let the cattle run loose and it was possible to get rich. He gave it so much oil and gas to run its machines that it will never run out. Then just the right temperatures, and rainfall, just the right amounts almost always. God gave it the best ocean, and the most beautiful mountains. The most beautiful women, too, that truth can't be denied, and along with that blessing, God gave us a few really great soccer players and musicians, so that life in this country would be just about perfect.

"So to make a long story short, God gave to Argentina the best from His supply of riches, and each one of the necessary blessings in all His creation. And when they saw this, the Chileans up there, and the Brazilians, the Mexicans and the Venezuelans and every-body else, like most good people do, they started complaining to God. 'What are You doing? Why are You giving so much to that one big country? You've given it so much that it looks like You must be depriving everywhere else!' And do you know what God told them? Do you?"

The driver was looking back at me again, with amusement, waiting for a reaction. I shrugged my shoulders once more. "God told them not to worry. 'After all, I am a just God,' He said. 'I have a plan for that rich country down there. My plan for that rich country is that I am going to populate it only with Argentines.' Only with Argentines," he said again. "That's the story. And isn't it true? Isn't that just what has happened?"

The taxi driver laughed at his own joke, loudly, and pounded his fist on the steering wheel a few times for emphasis. I hadn't heard the joke before, and laughed a little along with the man. But what was interesting was that he was telling such a story. A few years before, he would be extolling the military regime while lamenting bitterly the loss of the Malvinas/Falklands War in the fiasco with the British. He would be making excuses, blaming yanqui conspiracies, with a fervent and fascist national pride. Now he told his joke with a self-deprecating sentiment, a former nationalism that was turned in on itself, expressing his disillusionment even to a foreigner. With the trials of the comandantes soon to begin, and with the new democracy's failing economy raising so many questions, I was struck by how this kind of national self-criticism was everywhere in the streets.

There was a different kind of national criticism in the Benevento house. It was a bitter undercurrent to almost everything that was said. At times, I felt as if we had been taken in by my family, provided an outline of what had happened, then left to find out the full story for ourselves. Each day, new colors and details were filled in, sometimes so casually or in passing that they went along with "good morning" and "good afternoon," with a stark and brutal reality. Time had crumpled for my family. The past was folded over the present and became the future.

The family was busy. I was off getting my credential. Papá Benevento was out very early in the mornings to his law office, where he spent until noon working for his commercial clients to earn just enough money to keep going on. He devoted his afternoons to what he now called his "real work" of voluntary service writing briefs, filing motions, and doing legal research for the CELS human rights organization. Mamá Benevento and Betty Ann spent most mornings together. They shopped in the neighborhood for the day's provisions. They waited in the long lines made by inflation, spending all the pesos in their purses before the prices went up at a pace beyond belief. Then there were many other household chores and projects, including the cooking. Betty Ann was getting jumpy from having to run out to the kitchen just in time to keep Mamá's pots and pans from burning. She very discreetly suggested that she should take over preparing the family's big midday meal. Everyone was relieved when Mamá Benevento said yes.

For many, the traditional Argentine workday was divided into two equal shifts. From eight-thirty in the morning until half past noon was the first; then from three-thirty in the afternoon until eight in the evening was the second. The family gathered at one o'clock, after the first shift of our working day. We sat down and ate at the big table, and often, Martín Segundo would drop by for lunch with Papá instead of going all the way home to the Palermo district of the city. After the meal was over, while the rest of the family lay down for an hour's siesta, Betty Ann and I generally did the dishes, then took a long walk to one of the parks or along the posh Avenida Santa Fe, or up Avenida Pueyrredón to the fashionable Recoleta district for coffee at a sidewalk café.

Despite the chill in the river breeze, we enjoyed our outdoor double espressos in the sunlit afternoons. We spent two or three hours each day like this, strolling hand in hand, feeling like innocent teenagers on a first or second date. Betty Ann was picking up the language, surely and steadily. I was just beginning to show her a little of the city, its statues and fountains, its majestic Parisian boulevards, its elegant galleries of shops that were brimming with designer clothing, shoes, purses, leather jackets, and fur coats. Fired by Mamá Benevento's daily bargain-hunting, Betty Ann was becoming more interested in beating the inflation, was on the lookout for practical things to buy. In just three days, a pair of fine high-heeled winter boots she was considering and needed in the North more than doubled in price.

After shopping around like this, we returned home to an empty apartment. Papá was off at his afternoon work. Mamá generally volunteered her afternoons to helping at the office of the CELS. Or sometimes she took on paying jobs she was offered in her specialty as an authority on the history of Argentine painting and sculpture. She was a visiting teacher to classrooms in private schools and institutes, or she helped to prepare shows in private galleries. Betty Ann and I would set the table for an English-style tea by the time she came home. Over tea, we visited with Mamá, as much as we could with her scattered movements. Then we got ready for evening. After a light supper with the family, we went out to tango or folkloric music shows I had seen listed in the cultural section of the newspaper. Or if we stayed in, our family would sip drinks and chat in the living room before going to bed early. A daily routine was established. It was a comfortable pattern, an intimate rhythm. It was something that was beginning to feel very close to the warmth and centeredness of any normal, and at times even happy, home.

The trials began. There was a great outcry of controversy when the President of Argentina, Raúl Alfonsín, who, until the economic crisis, many had called *El Providencial,* the "Providential President," appeared on television. He made an angry speech claiming that his administration had uncovered a combined civilian and military effort to mount a coup d'état to overthrow the new democracy in protest of the trials. I held my tape recorder to the television in the Benevento home. I telexed a report to New York, and waited to see what might happen.

The day the trials opened, I made it easily through the packed hallways filled with electronic security checks and into the surprisingly small courtroom. The tribunal seated perhaps eighty people on the main floor, with space for eighty or so more in a balcony gallery that overlooked the proceedings. A large crowd gathered outside the central courthouse building, the Palace of Justice. It was a mass demonstration of thousands, held back by police barricades. The crowd raised signs and chanted slogans demanding convictions. All through the morning, as I watched the very slow, theatrical dance of the judges and lawyers, the sound of the demonstrators was like a rasping low growling in the distance.

In the press box, I sat shoulder to shoulder with the reporter from *Newsweek*. Correspondents were there from the *New York Times* and the *Miami Herald*. I assumed some of the Argentine reporters were stringers for the major wire services. But correspondents from the United States were most notable for their absence. There were at least a dozen French, Spanish, and Italian reporters. So many Latin American newspapers and television crews were represented that their numbers spilled over into the aisles. It was an important story for them. Depending on the outcome in Argentina, the governments of El Salvador, Brazil, Uruguay, and Bolivia, among the other new democracies, were considering trials of their own former military dictators for human rights abuses.

The first day was taken up with discussing a series of tedious written motions. Defense lawyers argued that the whole case against the nine comandantes should be thrown out of court on the grounds that it was a political trial. And shouldn't military men instead be brought up for court-martial by the armed forces, by right of their rank and service?

The president of the six-member court of appeals, seated high above the motions, was the head of the panel that would act as both judge and jury. The court president functioned like an Examining Magistrate, under the Napoleonic legal system of Argentina, asking most of the questions. He started reading off a list of names of members of the former government of Isabel Perón who would be called on to testify. It appeared he was going to see the trials began at the beginning of the years of "dirty war." Then he listened to the written motions read by the prosecution. By morning's end, he seemed in favor of their contention that, because of the brutal nature of their crimes, the tortures, murders, and disappearances of which they were accused, the generals and admirals had forfeited any rights to a military rather than a civilian trial.

After the morning session, I took a taxi to the offices of Noticias Argentinas. I wrote out a detailed summary of the first hours. I emphasized the tension in the atmosphere following the President of Argentina's warnings of a possible military takeover to stop the proceedings. Closing the piece was: "Not one of the nine defendants, who are represented by twenty-two lawyers, attended the trial."

I waited around until early evening at the wire service offices, smoking, drinking coffee, watching the always tense and energizing frenzy of the newsroom, dozens of reporters banging away at their computers until the very last second of their deadlines, the sharp sounds of the keys like a plague of clicking grasshoppers. I was hopeful about word from New York, sure that some of my copy would be used.

The telex with my name on it finally came in. I grabbed it up eagerly, then stood there reading it with stunned disbelief. On the evening broadcast, against what I imagined was a background projection of the porkchop-shaped map of the country, all that had happened was that one of the anchors had read off the TelePrompTer, in exactly fourteen seconds, the following text: *In Argentina today, trials began against the nine comandantes who ruled that country under the recent dictatorship. These trials mark the first time in the history of Latin America that a government has prosecuted its former military leaders for human rights abuses. The trials are expected to continue over the next several months until a verdict can be delivered.*

The press box steadily emptied over the next few days, until there were only a handful of foreign correspondents left. I heard a rumor among them that in the United States, only two of the three major network news programs had even bothered to mention the story. What was beginning to happen at the trials was a parade of victims before the judges and lawyers, each recounting a similar terrible experience of imprisonment, torture, witness to kidnapping or murder. I began to attend the trials mainly in the mornings, then only if there was someone important or unusual who was scheduled to testify. I collected pamphlets and tracts from the human rights organizations, previews and summaries of testimony in special editions of the newspapers. I spent hours reading through them carefully, highlighting items, writing things down. By the end of the second week, I had five shopping bags full of documents, testimony, scribbled notes. The general picture was emerging. Not that that was much help to my own growing need to discover more, something closer, what even in so many bits and pieces I might never be able to find out—the true story of what had happened to my brothers.

One afternoon, I got in early from the trials. Betty Ann was busy in the kitchen, filling the house with warm smells of garlic and spices.

Suddenly, Papá Benevento rushed in from his morning's work, hardly calling out a hello as he came through the door with both arms loaded down with salmon-pink legal folders. He made a beeline for his study, and I heard heavy cupboard doors banging open and closed.

At first, I wouldn't have thought this unusual. Bringing work home seemed a logical thing for a lawyer to be doing. But Papá Benevento had an expression on his face as if he had just robbed a bank. He was sweaty and out of breath. He seemed unusually nervous, his shoulders shifting around unnaturally under his suit jacket. He moved too fast. I followed him through the open archway from the small living room into a space near the window set aside as his study, a work area with a desk and files. Papá was on his knees, stuffing the legal folders into a heavy wooden cabinet that had locking doors. He didn't look comfortable again until he had turned the key and dropped it into his pocket.

The telephone rang. I answered. It was Mamá calling to say that she was delayed for lunch and would be on her way to an art gallery for the afternoon. She had left a box of slides on the desk in the living room. Could her Diego catch a *colectivo* bus and bring them to her after the family finished eating?

I took down the address of the gallery. I told Papá and Betty Ann that Mamá wouldn't be home for the midday meal. Papá relayed the message that Martín Segundo was also unexpectedly busy. He would grab a sandwich downtown.

I went into the kitchen, tied on an apron, and helped Betty Ann serve up her garlic chicken, parsley potatoes, and salad, the meal she had spent most of the morning shopping for and cooking. There was enough food on the table to feed two families. My wife looked disappointed by the empty places as the three of us sat down. Papá made small talk with Betty Ann in his stiff English, asking about her morning, her impressions of Buenos Aires so far, what she was planning to do that afternoon.

During a lull in the small talk, I changed the subject and asked in Spanish, "If you don't think it's indiscreet of me to ask, Papá, what were all those files you locked in the cabinet?"

"Nothing really," he answered in Spanish. "Routine business. Martín Segundo and I have been working at the CELS, the Centro de Estudios Legales y Sociales. We're helping to prepare documentation for the trials. The CELS office had another bomb threat this morning. But don't worry. That happens all the time. We have a system for bomb threats, worked out during the time of the dictatorship. . . ."

Papá Benevento was breaking bread, dipping it in the sauce of his chicken. His tone of voice was as if he were talking about nothing more than a seasonal nuisance in the weather. He was actually smiling, happily chatting on.

". . . Things got so bad that the military was murdering lawyers who had done nothing more than agree to defend leftists who were accused of murder. Evidence for the defense in these cases was regularly tampered with or stolen. The absurdity of the whole mess is unbelievable. Anyway, my son, our system is that when we are not sure that duplicates of our files and evidence have been received by our friends overseas, we make copies in the office. Say a bomb threat comes. Or a death threat to a particular lawyer. We put out an immediate call to our members and distribute the files all over the city. In my case, the files go into that old cabinet in the living room where I used to keep my guns before the military stole them. Maybe I should rent a big safe-deposit box at the bank to keep the files in. During the dictatorship, the military actually broke into safe-deposit boxes at banks many times, so are they really that much safer there? My feeling is that legal briefs and files are just as safe here at home," he said.

Papá suddenly noticed how hard Betty Ann was trying to follow the conversation. "There's no need to translate all of this, my son," he said. "It's just routine."

I translated the last sentence for Betty Ann. She kicked my shin under the table, demanding more, and I did my best to summarize.

"Oh, I see," she said. "They were so blatant as to go into banks and break into safe-deposit boxes? How could they get away with something like that?"

"It is clear now in our newspapers," Papá said. "All comes out now. Trials are very, very important just now. One officer, General Camps, he and his soldiers allegedly robbed many banks. Now all the country will know what the military did."

Papá Benevento turned to me in his usual tongue-tied frustration with English and rattled away in Spanish. "Tell your wife that they also robbed money from me, my property, everything. They were like gangsters. But I don't give a shit about the money. What's important is that I'm going to have my own chance to testify. Miguelito's case is coming up. We're not sure yet of the actual date when it will be presented. But tell your woman that I would like you both to be in the courtroom when that happens."

I was translating, simultaneously, as Papá was speaking, but I was falling behind. With the pressure of her sharp shoe against my shin, Betty Ann was urgently demanding to know every word. I was doing my best, but Papá was speaking so fast that he seemed to ignore, or run over, her obvious desire to understand everything.

"Maybe don't tell your woman this," Papá said. I stopped translating, reaching a hand over to put a little pressure on my wife's arm. "I don't think I want the women to know," he said. His voice had changed. It was dreamy and hesitant. His eyes glittered, filled with an emotion he was holding back. "It's strange, those files I brought with me today. Miguelito's case is in with all the others. There it is, locked away in the very cabinet he once broke into and I caught him playing with my guns. I didn't plan it that way. If I had arrived at the CELS office ten minutes earlier or later, a different stack of files would have been signed out to me. I can't help thinking about that, the way timing and chance happen to us all. There it is, his whole case come back home. But don't say a word about this. Especially not to your mother. She hasn't seen all the evidence yet. There are some pretty gruesome police photographs, and other testimony which might do her harm. She'll come in and see that the cabinet is locked. As always, she'll just assume the reason why. I've been doing this for years, so she probably won't even ask. So let's just agree not to mention what's there. Is that clear, my son?"

"It's clear, Papá," I said.

"Sometime, if you want to look at Miguelito's file yourself, we'll find somewhere else, just the two of us," he said. He looked over a little guiltily at Betty Ann, who was now staring down into her plate, feeling isolated, a prisoner of her own language. Then Papá said again, for emphasis, "I don't think either of our women should see it. Are we agreed?"

"Agreed," I answered.

"What was that you were just saying?" asked Betty Ann.

"Not important," Papá said, and smiled. "It was something between fathers and sons. This was a very good dinner. You are a very good cook, Betiana. And now, my pretty daughter, can I help you to pass the plates into the kitchen and we will all have dessert?"

Papá skipped his usual nap after dessert and left right away for his office. Betty Ann and I did the few dishes together in an atmosphere of her wounded silence. I tried to smooth things over, telling her that Papá Benevento had been telling me something personal between the two of us. But she knew enough Spanish that she wasn't buying that. She tossed a sponge angrily into the sink and pulled off her apron. "I've had enough of this," she said.

"Please, honey, it's not my fault," I said.

"Not your fault? Don't you know that Papá speaks English? When there are just the three of us, can't you even show me that much consideration?"

"Look. Can we talk this over later? I'm supposed to run an errand for Mamá right now. It shouldn't take long."

"Then go and run your errand. Do anything you want," she said. "But from now on, it's a new program for me. I'm not going to cook big dinners that nobody turns up for and then just sit there at the table, completely left out of the conversation. You're off all morning, or even when you're here, it's like you're lost in space. Well, okay then. I understand. This is an important time for you. But my plan from now on is to go out on my own. I did just fine traveling on my own in Europe when I was in college. I had adventures. I had fun. People made an effort to help me learn the languages. I saw a hell of a lot more on my own than I'm seeing here with you."

I followed her through the apartment and into the bedroom. She opened a wardrobe door and began to shuffle through her hanging clothes. "Maybe I'll meet a nice Argentine man who'll take the time to explain a few things like the Italians always did."

She shook out her best dress, black and corseted, the one that always made me think of taking her dancing. She stepped into it and pulled the straps over her shoulders.

"Honey, I'm sorry," I said. "Sometimes Papá says things that just shouldn't be translated."

"Well then, with me there, that's one hell of a rude thing to do," she said. She sat down on the bed and started to put on her good black nylons. She discovered a run from one ankle up to the thigh.

"He says things about the boys," I said. "About the way they disappeared. Things he doesn't want even Mamá to know. Because you're also a woman in his family, he's treating you the same way. It's a form of respecting you not to tell you these things."

She balled up her nylons and tossed them across the room. The anger went out of her body. Her shoulders slumped, and she pressed her face into her hands. "Oh, God, I'm sorry," she said. "Of course I know that. I could figure out that much. It's just that I hate that kind of treatment so much. It reminds me of the way my father used to act, like us girls were so useless to him."

I sat down on the bed beside her. I put my arm over her shoulders and pulled her body close. We sat there quietly like that for a moment, leaning into each other. "You're trying so hard," I said. "Everyone can see and appreciate how hard you're trying."

"It's getting late," she said. "Why don't you just go if you're going to go?"

"I promise I'll be back soon," I said. "I'll take cabs both ways. In the meantime, why don't you go have an espresso and a cognac at that place on the corner? You remember? The bar with the big red awning that we haven't tried yet? I'll be back by the time you're ready to pay the check. We'll just let everything go here tonight and spend some time on our own."

"Just get going," she said.

I kissed her on the cheek and stood up to leave. I told her again how quick I would be. I'd meet her at the bar down the street before she even missed me. I went into the living room and found the box of slides Mamá needed. I ducked into the bedroom once more to blow my wife a kiss. She was changing out of her best dress into something else.

The address of the art gallery was across the city, in the colonial district of San Telmo. San Telmo was becoming like the old Greenwich Village of Buenos Aires, the bohemian neighborhood, just now being gentrified. There were still many crumbling and abandoned buildings that dated back at least a century, taken over by families of the poor and transformed into slums called *conventillos,* with colorful laundry strung messily over the rotting balconies. But in between and around the slums, there were now renovated antique shops, art galleries, avant-garde theaters, Spanish courtyards turned into outdoor cafés, and underground clubs promoting the new and liberated wave of art and music that had exploded into life after the years of dictatorship.

It was taking longer than I had expected to get there by taxi in the heavy traffic after the midday meal. I realized too late that a combination of the subway and a *colectivo* bus would have been much faster.

The second shift of the day in Buenos Aires was about to begin. It was soon to be the time for the first strong espressos of the afternoon in offices, around conference tables, in shops, and at every kind of business. Feeling the frustration of being stalled in the afternoon traffic, I considered why the country was in such trouble. So many people in government ministries and businesses followed the traditional schedule. From eight in the morning until noon, the only real work ever got done. After that, everyone went home or to a restaurant for three hours of heavy food, wine, maybe a quick little nap. There was yet another rush hour in the city until it could open up again, slowly grinding into motion for the second time in a day from three-thirty until eight o'clock in a slow, heavy burden of paper shuffling, rubber stamps, ministerial duties, and attempting ENTEL phone calls that almost never got through. I had had a taste of the traditional work schedule in all the niggling bureaucracy involved with the press credential. How inefficient it was, I thought. How wasteful of time and energy and human resources. I had seen firsthand how the featherbedded government bureaus and offices would, after the midday meal, kick into what seemed to me now, stuck in gridlock, four more hours of avoiding real work in a sleepy digestive indolence.

How to save Argentina? That was a question in the streets of Buenos Aires almost constantly now, as it had been for the fifteen years since I had lived in the country. Stalled in the dense black fumes of traffic on one of the diagonal boulevards within sight of the Plaza de Mayo and the pink presidential palace, I fixed my mind on a definite solution. The way to save this country? Give only a half-hour break at noon, then demand that the workday continue. Shut the restaurants down by decree. Make everyone carry a sandwich in a brown bag if necessary. Somehow, some way, defy the tradition of so many centuries, eliminate one of the charms that made Argentina what it is, and once and for all declare the midday meal illegal.

As the cab finally broke out of the jam and the tires beat rapidly over the quaint cobblestoned streets of San Telmo, I was struck by a full sense of my own irony. All it had taken was the pressure of time and a traffic jam to turn my mind into something very close to a corporate destroyer of cultures, a yanqui fascist of the first water, a complete totalitarian in thought if not in deed. I realized how much I really loved and missed the Argentine sense of the world. Why hurry? Why make myself crazy? Why not take some time for food and family and a little relief in the middle of each day?

The gallery was a large ground-floor space with windows facing out toward Humberto 1º Street, the cobblestone mews that was just off the historic Plaza Dorrego. The plaza was filled with trees and had a colonial atmosphere heavy with the centuries. Old men and women sat on benches in the plaza, enjoying the sun. They looked out from the square at bohemian funky music clubs, bars

71

and restaurants, antique shops and art galleries in the newly renovated Spanish buildings.

The particular gallery I was going to looked unopened as yet, still in renovation. An elegant woman greeted me at the door. She introduced herself with a familiar kiss on the cheek, an informal greeting custom, as Ana María Cruz de las Heras, an aristocratic name. She was a woman in her early forties who had taken advantage of every kind of cosmetic and beauty treatment her wealth had allowed. She easily passed for ten years younger. Her strawberry-blond hair was perfectly cut into a pageboy style, the latest fashion from Vidal Sassoon, her high cheekbones and sharply announced features masked with a suggestive makeup that made her look as if she always dressed for evening.

Mamá Benevento and her friend Beatrice were inside the gallery. I greeted them with kisses, and they led me to a smaller back room. A slide projector and a screen were all set up. Ana María pointed casually to a chair that was meant for me. A maid in uniform came in from the Spanish courtyard and served coffee.

Ana María was trying out her English on me, which was a pleasant experience because of how perfectly she spoke it. She said she had been to New York many times and kept an apartment there. From what I could guess by a few dropped names, including that of Amalia Fortabrat, the famous concrete heiress and one of the wealthiest women in the world, Ana María had been making the scene with other rich Argentines at their regular luncheon table at the Tavern on the Green in New York's Central Park. When the comandantes first took over the mess left behind by Isabel Perón, reporters were invited to that table and told what a salvation the military was for the country. Later, during the Malvinas/Falklands War, it was said that secret payments were arranged over lunch there for emergency shipments of Exocet missiles. When the new democracy was declared, it was likewise celebrated with rounds of applause at the table and patriotic slogans over another round of martinis.

Mamá Benevento interrupted the conversation and explained how they were now setting up a show of Argentine artists who had been either banned or exiled by the military regime. I moved over closer to the projection table and gave Mamá the needed box of slides. In a low voice, I tried to explain how rushed for time I was, but Mamá asked me to sit down for at least a moment. She was the one really working here, holding the slides up to the ceiling light, making sure they were in the proper order. She wanted me to stay, and it was clear there was no polite way out. I would have to sit for a few minutes at least and watch the slides.

I sat down. The maid drew the blinds and the light went off. Ana María took the chair next to mine. I caught a sudden draft of an exotic perfume I hadn't noticed before. The first slide went up on the screen in a shock of colors. Ana María leaned in closer, resting a hand on my arm. I exchanged a confused and shadowy glance with her in the projector's glow. The voice of Mamá Benevento from behind us began to explain the artist's work in an assured and informative way.

The first series of projections was of the work of a painter named Noé. Mamá Benevento explained how they represented a time when Noé had been in difficulties. His work looked made out of all kinds of salvaged materials, bits of wood and rags, cardboard, perhaps linoleum. The slides were of collage-form constructions, colorful with acrylics on different surfaces but mainly on wood. All of them had a satirical political content. One of the best slides showed cutouts of a huge crowd of heads and shoulders, just what is seen from the point of view of someone in the middle of a street demonstration that is about to get tear-gassed by the police. Signs and placards were held up out of the crowd and broke through the lines of the painting into three dimensions.

Slogans were scrawled roughly on the signs. One was *Christ speaks on the moon*. Another said simply, *Women*. A third slogan, *Don't abandon us,* rose up over the crowd and broke through the frame.

The slide changed to the next construction, also a crowd scene, showing macabre police scattered among ghostly faces like nightmarish specters. Politicians were the subject of the next slide, smiling from the screen with shark teeth. I was reminded of the frescoes by Orozco in the government house of Guadalajara, Mexico. This work by Noé seemed to be from the same school. Both abstract and representative at the same time, the caricature quality of the political humor served to point up social injustice and violence. I remembered the way Orozco's massive and cartoonish representation of society was surrounded by a nest of snakes vomiting bayonets.

Mamá Benevento and her friend Beatrice were chatting away casually about how brilliant Noé was, and perhaps more pointedly for the benefit of Ana María Cruz de las Heras. Mamá said more than once how well-known Noé had become in Paris and New York, her tone of voice sharp with the implication that this was, unfortunately, the most important requirement for an Argentine artist to become famous in his own country.

I checked my watch and nearly went out of my skull thinking of the time. I had this image suddenly of Betty Ann sitting at a bistro table. Across from her was a very Italian-looking man solicitously courting her. This was no doubt a deferred kind of guilt I suffered. In the dark intimacy of the slide show, I felt a beautiful woman's warm hand on my arm. The art was now hard to concentrate on. Despite myself, I was feeling a strong attraction. The box of slides ran out. The lights went on and I blinked my eyes. I disengaged my arm from the perfectly manicured hand of Ana María Cruz de las Heras. I pressed the hand once in a gentlemanly way and stood up to leave. In a voice loud enough so that Ana

María and Beatrice could hear, I reminded Mamá Benevento that I had to go now, I had left my wife waiting for me.

"Don't be so bothered," said Ana María. "Let her enjoy the city on her own."

She had stood up when I did, and she leaned in close to my shoulder in a peculiar way. I felt speechless and confused, as I often did in the company of a beautiful woman. And here was an aristocratic, pretty, obviously very wealthy woman way beyond my league and class who was actually pleading with me to stay. There was sure to be trouble brewing if I made the wrong decision.

"I'm sorry," I said to Ana María Cruz de las Heras. "You know how it is," I said. It struck me that of course this woman would never have known how such things went. "My wife doesn't speak the language," I said. "Maybe I'll take her to a movie in English. It could be all she needs is to hear her own language again. But I'm late now, and I should be going."

"You go and take care of her, my son," Mamá said, still busy working with the projector. "Your woman is too much of a treasure to leave feeling lonely."

"What a shame and a pity," said Ana María. "Some other time then, you promise?"

She followed me to the door of the gallery to unlock it for me. On the way, she took my arm. I was like soft clay in her hands as she strolled with me through the unfinished exhibition rooms. She pointed out the high-tech light fixtures her architect had installed in the ceilings, and the first-rate arrangement of hanging spaces he had designed. I agreed too enthusiastically how tasteful they were. I stood there like an idiot, overexpansively praising the creativity with her space.

At the door, she gave me a business card from a box of them. Then she reached inside my jacket and pulled a pen out of my pocket. She wrote her home telephone number on the back of the card. "Call me anytime," she said. "Maybe we could get together for a little coffee. I'd really like that. I know what happened to the Benevento family. My heart goes out to them. But maybe, well, I could show you the other side of things."

"Sure. That would be nice," I said nervously. She smiled at me in a way that made me take a step back, my shoes scuffing awkwardly on the polished tiles as if my feet no longer knew where to take me. I thanked her and apologized again for leaving. Then in the doorway she took my hand. She stood up on the toes of her Guccis made of crocodile skin. Instead of giving me a quick kiss on the cheek, the custom between friendly men and women even on a first meeting, she pressed her lips quickly against my lips. The kiss was too fast. I couldn't react. It was open to many interpretations, surely, but I sensed something very strong in it, as disarming as the no doubt scientifically selected pheromones in the perfume she wore, exactly blended to match the chemistry of her body and skin. I breathed in the scent of this woman once more and then stepped out quickly into the street.

I began to search for a cab at the Plaza Dorrego. There, out in the crisp, neutral air, in the cool shadows of the trees surrounding the plaza, I tried to shake myself of the feeling that I had been the object of a strong flirtation. Then again, maybe I was wrong, I was reading too much into nothing. It just might be that a lot more had changed in this culture since I had lived in it, and since the years of military repression.

I was late, way too late. Then I was stuck again in traffic in a taxi, pounding my fist into the back of the seat every time the car lurched forward and made a race for a clear lane then braked at another bottleneck. It was nearly four-thirty in the afternoon before I was let off just up the block from the café with the red awning, the Rouge Rouge. There was an emblem next to the name, a pair of ripe red lips pressed into a kiss.

I rushed through the door and found Betty Ann seated by the window. She was searching the street, and didn't see me come in. She looked like she might have been crying. That shocked me, and I swallowed, hard. Then, as I drew nearer, I saw that it wasn't sadness. There was something very wrong. There was a wild and desperate expression on her face. She leaped up from the table and threw her arms around my neck as if I had just returned from the dead. "Oh, God! Thank God you're here!"

"Calm down, calm down," I said. "What happened?"

"Oh, God. Oh, God . . ."

I held her, at the same time looking around the café. The tables were deserted. It was a kind of pseudo-French place with hanging red crepe and Toulouse-Lautrec prints on the walls. The red kissing lips were printed on the windows, the menus, the ashtrays, everything. Most of the lights were turned off, and there was an unnatural darkness. My eyes adjusted. Hovering around in the shadows near the door to the back was a lone waiter in a dinner jacket who was looking at us as if he wished we would leave.

"Get me out of here, please, please," she said.

"What's the matter?" I asked. I freed one arm from holding her and reached out to the table for the check. I let out a low whistle. Even with the inflation, the amount was unbelievably high, more than all the pesos in my pockets. "Jesus, honey," I said. "What did you order?"

"My God, but you don't know what I've been through! I was followed! I had to keep ordering or they would have closed the place down! Jesus, I was so damn scared."

"Come on, baby, what are you talking about?" I said. I tried to guide her around the table and sit her down again, but she wouldn't move. I waved for the waiter, then pulled out my wallet for a credit card.

"I'm not imagining things," she said, pulling away. Her hands were shaking as she reached into her purse for a cigarette. "There were four of them. Four men," she said. "They were in a black car. The car was waiting there when I came out of the house. I started to walk down the street. The car pulled out and followed me, like at two miles an hour. I walked faster, and the car speeded up. One of them rolled down his window. He leaned out and leered at me the whole way, right beside me, just off the curb. I made it to this place and ducked in and thought, thank God. I sat down and ordered some wine. Then I saw the car pull over to the curb and men getting out. They came in here! Three of them sat down right there, at that table! My God, the way they stared at me! One of them unbuttoned his jacket so I could see his gun. You don't know what it was like! They were cruel, ugly, horrible men.

"I didn't know what to do. I was afraid to stay but even more afraid to leave. At least there were a few people in here. But when they saw what was happening, everyone left but those men. Even the waiter was scared. They said things to him. He came over and told me he had to close. But I said, bring me a menu, I'm not going anywhere, not me, no señor. Then I just kept pointing to things on the menu and ordering them. What did he expect me to do? He saw what was happening. Then all of a sudden, the three of them just got up and left. And I've been here ever since, just me and this waiter."

The waiter was standing by our table, back with the card and slip to sign, politely waiting for her to finish. I turned to him and asked him in a commanding voice if men had been bothering my wife.

"They keep me so busy in here that I don't notice anything," the waiter said. "But we had quite a crowd in here today," he added, a grimness in his tone and manner that said much more. He nodded his dark *indio* head just once, and that was enough said. "Please now, sir, we close this place at this hour of the afternoon. I have only kept it open out of courtesy to the lady."

I pulled several large bills out of my pocket and offered him a generous tip. The waiter looked at the money for a moment, then at the floor. He shook his head no. He reached into his jacket pocket and pulled out a set of keys, ready to lock the door behind us.

"He told you," Betty Ann said, out in the street. "You know I'm not imagining things."

It had turned into a crisp autumn day. The clean afternoon light was such a contrast to the somber interior of the café that for a moment it was difficult to believe what she had told me. Why would anyone do to her what she had said these men did? What had she ever done to attract that kind of trouble?

"Whatever happened, it's all over now," I said.

"What the hell do you know?" she shouted. "Where were you? Where? You weren't there! You have no idea what it was like!"

She made two fists and pounded them against my chest. I grabbed her, roughly, by the arms. I shook her once, and she froze there, glaring at me angrily. We stood like that for a moment. Then she put her arms around me and leaned into my chest with a heavy sob. I held her that way, bracing her. People passed all around us on the sidewalk. I was finally able to break us free of the embrace and lead her to the curb.

I held up my hand, and a taxi was there. We climbed in. I had no idea where to tell the driver to go, so I said just to circle around awhile until we could decide. We sat quietly in the backseat. I put my arm over her shoulders and watched out the windows. The cab took Avenida Pueyrredón in the direction of the river. Then it doubled around on the orderly residential streets past the tiny Plaza Paraguay with its hordes of small children and their housemaids out for a stroll. The cab took another turn and we were suddenly going down the street where we lived.

We were caught in the thick slow traffic of the afternoon on that narrow artery. Betty Ann was leaning into my body, calming down now, smoking one cigarette after another. We both felt in a daze, mindlessly watching out the windows at the tranquil, tree-lined street in the Barrio Norte district. The cab was slowly drawing up to the building where we lived. Betty Ann suddenly pressed up against the window. She waved her hands around with a wild urgency. "There! Right there!" she shouted.

I looked ahead, out the windshield, and saw what she meant. The street was packed on both sides with parked cars, but there it was, a black Ford Falcon. As we drew closer, through the rear window of the Falcon I could make out the heavy dark shapes of men sitting inside it like so many hunched-over bulls. A long whip antenna sprouted from the car's trunk, not the kind for any normal radio. I recognized the type of car at once. Argentina was the only country in the world still manufacturing this relic of the sixties, and the Ford Falcon was the national police car. It was a car that had a trunk large enough to hold the blindfolded victims of kidnappings and to carry off the bodies of the disappeared. Now here was one like so many others, stationed in a no-parking zone, waiting on the street. And it was sitting directly across from the entrance to our building.

I was out the taxi door and onto the sidewalk as fast as I could jump. I took out my wallet and dug for my press card. I was moving fast, blindly, seeing only that black car full of men. I came up on it from behind. I started pounding on the rooftop with my fist, pressing my credential up against one of the rear windows. Startled dark faces turned toward me. I thought I saw the movements of one of them reaching for his gun, but I didn't care, I couldn't stop now. I was shouting at them, every obscenity that I knew, pounding on the roof in a rage. "You bastards! You sons of whores!" I screamed. "I'll have your jobs! I'll go to the Minister of

the Interior himself! Who do you think you're fucking with now?"
I shouted. "Who do you think you are? Just who do you think you
are?"

A rear door on the car started to open. It looked like one of the
men would jump out onto the sidewalk and take me on. I took a
fighting stance and got ready, out of control, crazed. "You want to
kill me?" I screamed. Traffic was stopped now on the street. People
were leaning out their windows and watching. "Come on! Right
now! Right here in front of everybody! Do it! Let's go! Are you
cowards? Is that what you are? Cowards!" I shouted.

A large hand fell on the shoulder of the man in the dark suit
and pulled him back into the car. The door slammed and the
motor started. I pulled my notebook out of my pocket. I couldn't
find my pen. I patted my pockets frantically. As the car pulled
away, I stood there with my notebook open uselessly. I tried to
memorize the license plate. It was blank of city codes, clearly a
police number. None of the men inside the car was even looking
back at me. Like a small black whale, the car pulled out into heavy
traffic that parted for it easily, melding into the mechanical tides. It
moved slowly away from me down the street. The car turned at
the first corner and vanished out of sight.

I was left standing there, my empty notebook fluttering in the
breeze. What I had done suddenly struck me. Angry car horns
honked around and behind me. Betty Ann and the taxi driver were
leaning out their windows, calling to me. But I was frozen there. I
stood rooted, shaking, too scared to move.

Safe House

THAT EVENING, AFTER Betty Ann had been followed and harassed by what I was sure was the secret police, and after I had challenged them in the street like any fool who didn't know better, the last thing I thought we should do was to go back to the family's apartment. I had the cab take us about fifteen blocks away. We got out at a crowded, very public sidewalk café on the Avenida Santa Fe. I dialed Papá Benevento from a pay phone at the bar, using a number he had given me for the CELS human rights organization. When Papá heard what had happened, he said he was leaving his office immediately and to meet him at a *confitería* called the Tortoni, on the Avenida de Mayo. He said not to make any other moves until he got there.

The Tortoni was a historic place. Famous tango singers, artists, and writers of the twenties and thirties used to gather there in the afternoons. High Romanesque columns created an atmosphere of a temple to the past. Way in back, looking on from the tobacco-yellowed walls were gay caricatures and photographs of Carlos Gardel, Hugo del Carril, DiSarli-Florio, and other tango artists. There were portraits of the writers Roberto Arlt, Leopoldo Lugones, Ricardo Güiraldes, and other notable poets of a self-proclaimed immortal generation of art and music, "the last happy men," the writer Christopher Leland had called them. Their images were enshrined now in the Tortoni, captured in their joyous social and literary whirls, dancing tangos, playing guitars and accordions, looking out over the tables from a bygone era when Argentina had been powered by what seemed an inexhaustible store of forward-looking hope.

"Don't worry, children," Papá said. He arrived out of breath, and sat down across the table. He was speaking Spanish so fast I had to ask him to slow down so I could keep up in translation. "This kind of thing happens often to those of us who work for human rights. The men who followed you are probably secret police, or other agents of the military. They park, just as you have described, in front of our houses. Sometimes they follow us down the street. Nothing to worry about," he said. He smiled, waving a hand across the table casually, as if shooing away a fly that was annoying his coffee.

"Think of it as a kind of show," he said. "After all, there are more than one thousand police and army officers who took part in the atrocities of the dictatorship who are still on active duty. Many of their names are bound to come out at the trials. They're making attempts to intimidate those of us who know them. But we have laws now, and a real democracy. Few of us think they will be bold enough now to hurt anyone. It's not like before, when they could do anything they wanted. So our offices get bomb threats. They make death threats against witnesses scheduled to testify. Let's just say they're letting us know that they're still here. And think about it. We're not the ones who should be frightened. They're the ones who are running scared. . . . So, now," he said in English He gently took Betty Ann's hand across the table. "No worry. No danger," he said. "But we want you to feel safe. We have the place for that. San Miguel. We are going there this weekend anyway. It is a nice place. Do you like we should all go live at San Miguel?"

There was a firm cordiality in his suggestion, and a tone that implied we couldn't refuse. Moving to San Miguel, the Benevento family's weekend retreat in the suburbs, was the last thing I had imagined we would do. I began to see even more Papá Benevento's cultivated manners, his whole way of being. He covered things over in a smooth, even happy-sounding social conversation. He made the gallant gestures of a gentleman, full of reassurances, calming any worries or fears. But underneath that surface was another meaning. This time, he, too, was concerned, if not scared, by what had happened. I was struck then by the full weight of what he was saying. We were going into hiding.

"San Miguel is a wonderful place to live," Papá continued, noting my silence. "It's only an hour by train into Buenos Aires. I can get to work easily. Your mother can go off to her jobs. You children can take the train each day and still do all the wonderful things there are to do in this city. . . . So, are we agreed now? Do we have a plan?"

"Don't worry about me," said Betty Ann. "I'm fine. It's like a bad dream by now. It's hard to believe it even happened. It's Diego here who's half crazy."

"Whatever you say, Papá," I said darkly. We exchanged a long look across the table. He nodded once, letting me know he saw that I understood what he really meant. "When are we going?" I asked.

"It's all settled then," he said. "We'll pack up this evening." He outlined how we would all meet at the apartment, toss a few essentials into our bags, then set out on the late-night train. He explained what we were going to do quickly and pleasantly, the same way he might if he were taking his family for a happy weekend at the beach. He finished outlining the plan then and smiled. Everything was agreed on. Everything was clear.

He changed the subject. He settled back in his chair. He looked around the Tortoni for a moment and began to talk about the years of tradition the place meant for him, how symbolic it was of the great tango age. Papá was seeing the place with the eyes of his youth, when he would sometimes come in for a coffee after his classes at the law school and listen to the intense conversations about music and writing. As I interpreted his pleasant stories into English, I felt a sudden sadness in the place. The tradition he was vividly describing to us had vanished. The yellowed portraits looked on from the walls without meaning, without expression, most of them long ago forgotten. Overhead, the light fixtures flickered at the ends of their frayed and aging wiring. Around us, the chairs and tables were shabby and scarred. The waiters were ancient, creaking men, stooped gray figures who shuffled back and forth among the tables like so many ghosts.

San Miguel was a suburban town, spreading out around a bustling village center that on weekends took on the carnival atmosphere of a street fair and flea market. Large estate houses sat on elegant, walled-off acreages of lawns and trees. On the low, swampy side of the town, growing out on the other side of the Pan American Highway in what looked like heaps of industrial wreckage piled up into dwellings, there was a shantytown slum, a *villa miseria*.

Such shantytowns had been rare in Argentina barely two decades before. I searched my memory and couldn't place more than a few of them. The one outside San Miguel seemed to have a reason for its existence loosely connected to a nearby garbage dump for greater Buenos Aires. Inhabitants of the misery village picked through the dump for rags and scraps of tin and anything else they could salvage that might be used or sold. Both the dump and the shantytown regularly flooded in winter. The rising waters of the River Plate delta and the strong southeasterly winds scattered trash and wastepaper all over the flat mud plains and through the pitiful sprawls of shacks made of scrap wood, cardboard, and tin. The skinny bare trees on that side of San Miguel looked as if they had grown weird leaves of trash paper. Dirty plastic bags hung from the branches like huge postindustrial fruits, swaying and billowing in the winds.

The misery village was hidden from view on the other side of San Miguel, that district that was reserved for an exclusive suburban paradise. Walking along through the orderly lanes and streets of the wealthy estates was like a lesson in international architecture. There were Swiss-chalet-style homes built out of rare Brazilian woods, English-style stucco or brick country cottages with profuse rose gardens, modern Bauhaus German fortresses of concrete and glass and steel, and whitewashed Spanish Mediterranean villas, adobe over brick with high curving arches and red tile roofs. The houses sat on golf-green lawns the size of playing fields. Swimming pools stretched out through the distance like strings of glittering turquoise cubes. Just walking through this region of the lucky and the rich, I found it hard to imagine Argentina could be anything but one of the most prosperous countries on earth.

The Benevento family had a weekend sanctuary at San Miguel. Mamá Benevento had christened the four-acre estate Santa María de Lourdes, after the patron saint of the order of nuns that ran the strict boarding school in which she had spent much of her youth. Everyone else in the family called the big, hedged-off garden simply San Miguel. There was a small swimming pool, with lawn furniture set up around it. One end of the grassy open area had been marked off by the boys into about a half-size soccer field, with white arches for goals at either end. A red brick *asado* grill was built under the trees, a huge grated barbecue big enough to cook meat for a regiment. San Miguel was the place where the Benevento family could return to the style and grandeur of living they had once known.

San Miguel was what remained to them of the past. San Miguel was still thought of by Mamá and Papá Benevento as belonging to their boys. The trees the boys had planted just before they were disappeared were now nearly taller than the houses. The best memories of their sons had grown along with them. The last time that Alejo, Miguelito, and Martín Segundo had been seen together was one hot spring Sunday, spent kicking a soccer ball across the lawn. The soccer field had been left empty, unused since Alejo had disappeared. The white paint on the wooden goal arches was cracked and faded, the netting left to decay into a mess of hanging strings.

During the years before the harsh dictatorship, Papá Benevento had been earning a good deal of money from his law office. He had bought the estate from one of his wealthy clients. For tax reasons, the houses and grounds had been left on official documents in the client's name, under a gentlemen's agreement. Because of that, during the state terrorism of the comandantes, as long as the Beneventos took great caution about the family's movements, the secret police had no way of knowing that they owned the estate at San Miguel. The apartment on Arenales Street was often under surveillance. The phone was tapped. The mail was monitored and censored. Ford Falcons full of army thugs in civilian clothes were often parked outside. All three sons fled their home to live underground, with false names. San Miguel became the family meeting place. It had never been invaded by soldiers of the dictatorship, never robbed and violated by thieves and gangsters in camouflage fatigues. San Miguel was the family safe house. When Mamá and Papá Benevento were let out of their bare concrete cells in detention centers, alone, without their sons, San Miguel was as close as they could ever get again to feeling at home.

That night, after a quick, chaotic move out to San Miguel, I lay awake in one of the built-in twin beds. Papá and Mamá Benevento had settled us in the small but comfortable guest cottage. I had built a fire in the Spanish-tile fireplace. Betty Ann and I drank scotch and unpacked in a daze, then settled in to watch the logs until they turned to embers. We talked over just why it was we had agreed to come out there—maybe checking into our own hotel room away from the family would have been safer. But she knew what I wanted. Whatever they were living, I would live it with them, not only as a support for them, but to gain a greater understanding of what had happened. We kissed good night and went to our separate beds, not knowing what to expect, or how our lives had changed.

Even though it was a cold night, I lay there in a sweat. I stared up at an inkblot-like water stain on the ceiling that I could make out in the dim orange light. A strange metallic taste filled my mouth like a poison. I was suddenly enraged. My mind, heart, blood were boiling. I was cooking with rage from my insides. Why why why did we wind up in this situation? Why? How?

I'd be damned if I'd put up with it. That moment, for the first time, I fantasized about getting a gun. The names of many torturers and murderers were available on a master list. The list had been published for everyone to see in a recent edition of *Diario del juicio,* a tabloid supplement about the trials. So why not get a pistol and go out and do it? Why not be done with it once and for all?

In the newspaper that morning, there was a photograph of

allegedly one of the most notorious butchers of the military dictatorship in Argentina, one Teniente de fragata Alfredo Astiz. Three governments were getting ready to prosecute Astiz. First, he was due to face trial in Argentina. Then Sweden and France were both demanding he be extradited on charges of kidnapping and murder. Teniente Astiz was accused by Sweden of the disappearance of a sixteen-year-old girl, the daughter of a consular official, an unfortunate mix-up, the navy claimed, a mere case of mistaken identity. Not long after that, according to a delegation of lawyers from France, Teniente Astiz had entered the grounds of a church convent with his death squad. The nuns, French citizens of a charitable order of missionaries, were known for occasionally hiding small groups of political refugees until they could flee into exile. In front of witnesses, Teniente Astiz and his thugs had allegedly dragged the French nuns out into the street by their hair. Hoods were pushed over their heads. Their wrists were tied with wire behind their backs. The nuns were then tossed into the trunks of Ford Falcons. According to the French indictment, the cars drove off to a navy helicopter base. Teniente Astiz then allegedly loaded the nuns onto a helicopter. He personally supervised the operation as they were flown out over the River Plate and then pushed, one by one, out the open door. Inner circles of the military dictatorship had called this particular covert operation "the case of the flying nuns."

In the newspaper, there was a photograph of Teniente Astiz that told the rest of his story. Over the protests of two foreign governments, the notorious military playboy, the racecar driver and tennis enthusiast, had been released on his own recognizance, set free to walk the streets. Dressed in his Ray-Ban sunglasses and Ralph Lauren sports clothes, he was shown strolling down the sunny Avenida Santa Fe, smiling and eating an ice cream cone. And how could that happen? The people who recognized him, one or two who even challenged him on the street, why had none of them done anything to the man? How could he just walk right by out in the open without someone trying to kill him?

I lay awake, thinking how easy it could be. I saw every detail, and in my mind, I planned it out down to the second. From the legal file Papá had locked away in the apartment, I would get the name of the officer in charge, the man accused of the torture and cover-up of the murder of little Miguelito. I would find out the man's address, go there, and knock on the door at one o'clock in the afternoon, the hour the bastard would be lunching with his family. Right there, in his own front door, bang bang bang, then *ciao,* the whole thing would be finished and done with. But what would that really do? Wasn't it a coward's best reasoning to conclude, rightly, that a quick death from a bullet was too good for men like him? I was suddenly angry at myself for this whole line of thinking. Nothing wasted time and energy and spirit so much as thoughts of vengeance. But I couldn't help myself. I was hateful, rabid, tossing and turning with an unbearable and murderous rage.

Rage built up and powered me for days. I was short-tempered with everything and everyone. I went into the city to cover the trials on two mornings and grew furious at the tedious reading aloud of written motions before the court. I decided to stay the rest of the week at San Miguel, relying, instead, on the printed testimony in the *Diario del juicio.* No matter what I was doing, I sometimes had to break off, so filled with rage I hurried away from people and to the guest cottage, where I could be alone. But that was no escape. Finally, I just had to give in to a resigned, heated, steaming pattern of movements, barely keeping the lid on, most of my activity directed by Mamá Benevento as I helped her around the San Miguel gardens.

Mamá Benevento was a kind of abstract expressionist gardener, tossing bulbs and cuttings at the huge, fenced-in landscape the way some artists throw paint at canvas. I helped her plant a lemon tree one day, digging the hole deep, laying in the fertilizer. Over the next three days, she changed her mind about its location and asked me to dig so many holes for the tree and drag it around so much that it was nothing but a dried-up sheaf of bare limp twigs by the time we were finished.

We all kept busy as the days passed. Betty Ann was helping Papá in the big house with the project of repainting the living room and bedroom. As long as we were now living there, he had decided to take a few days off from his work to devote himself to that chore. The ceiling of the big house was a whirling labyrinth of spreading brown water stains from a leaking roof, which had just been fixed. They painted coat after coat of white chalky paint over the stains, which was an improvement, but the stained areas were still too damp to take paint well and the stains began to show through every new coat. Betty Ann kept climbing up onto a ladder beside Papá and attacking the stains with yet more buckets and brushes and rollers. They both wore funny peaked hats they had made from newspapers. They were getting along well, happy enough, it seemed. Meanwhile, I worked outside, digging, hacking away at the earth with a shovel, using it like a pickax on the invading subterranean tree roots. I imagined the heads of generals, colonels, and captains of the dictatorship under the sharp cutting edge of my shovel. I brought the blade down in swift chopping blows across their necks.

Six days after we moved out to San Miguel, the whole country came to a sudden halt. Inflation had been volcanically erupting to levels nearing 2,000 percent. The newspapers carried photographs of workers at factories on their lunch hours. Under pressure from the labor unions, some factories were now paying their workers in cash at noon each day. The workers then rushed out to the chain-link fences surrounding the plants, wadded up their fat sheafs of nearly worthless paper bills, and passed the rolls through the fences to their wives. The women rushed off to try and spend every last peso as soon as they could, before the prices changed.

The inflation had become madness. Suppliers for stores and factories and businesses quit making shipments because they could no longer collect their bills fast enough not to go bankrupt when they had to replenish their goods. Store shelves stood empty. When the banks suddenly closed, there was a special emergency televised address by the new president of the nation, the one some had nicknamed *El Providencial,* the Providential One. Lately, they used the name only with irony in their voices.

The president looked haggard, tired, with deep bags under his dark eyes. His voice was gravelly and low, hardly forceful enough to inspire confidence. He announced new measures to combat the inflation and declared a new currency for Argentina. The Argentine peso that had been the national money for 175 years was now going to be replaced by a new money called the austral, "the southerner," as it translated. People almost immediately treated this change cynically. They nicknamed the crisp new bills *pinguinos,* "penguins," after the flightless Antarctic birds. The austral was to be pegged at a value equaling exactly one dollar for one austral. The old worthless paper money in peso denominations was to be turned in to the banks for the new money. That was the plan. In the meantime, the banks would remain closed to avoid runs on them. Wages and prices were frozen.

Advertisements went out all over the nation that night, begging for popular support for the new currency. With all the fanfare, music, and jingoism of a recruiting drive for a war, on television and on radio and on billboards everywhere the slogan was blaring out, *The country needs its Argentines.* Then yet another foreign debt payment was announced, a sum in hundreds of millions of dollars equal to 45 percent of all the international trade earnings of Argentina for the entire past year. Even that much succeeded in paying only the barest fraction of interest owed on an amount which by then had grown to what seemed the unrepayable fifty-some-odd billions of dollars of debt to U.S. and world banks that the military dictatorship had left as its patriotic legacy until the end of time.

There was rage in the streets and rage in the trade unions. Voices of protest rose up from what remained of the demoralized military, who threatened to break out of their barracks in full combat gear, jungle camouflage paint on their faces. Scandals hit the newspapers about all the special interests which had taken advantage of information leaked to them by the new democratic government. They had cashed in on the currency change and the wage and price controls. Big merchant concerns had long before engaged in hoarding. State-owned telephone, gas, and electric enterprises had obviously known what would happen. This news was reflected in the huge bills almost everyone began to receive just days after the money reform that showed price hikes of an average of 130 percent. It came out that many individual speculators and managers of banks with friends in the new government had for some weeks been dumping old pesos for any hard currency they could find at almost any price, further deepening the exchange-rate crisis. Those well connected to government were emerging from the money storms as immensely richer men.

Papá Benevento was in a rage over these revelations. He tossed his morning newspapers aside with disgust. He paced around and around the lawn of San Miguel with curses on his breath. He sometimes stopped pacing and just stood out on the lawn, his head lowered, his shoulders slumped, overwhelmed by a dark and dejected mood. Like many professionals in Argentina, he decided to close his office for a few days, at least until the crisis eased up enough so it was possible to do business again. He had lost confidence in the new democracy of *El Providencial*. Papá now openly called it full of crooks, one more ironic spin of what seemed the unbreakable tragic cycle of government incompetence and corruption destroying the country.

The day after the currency change, I discovered that Betty Ann and I were suddenly now like almost everyone else in Argentina—without money. There was no place to change dollars, and nothing worth changing them for even if I could find a black marketeer somewhere in the trees. Nobody knew what the new money would be really worth. It certainly would not be nearly the official exchange rate the government had announced. With the new prices that had come down all across the nation, Betty Ann and I were left with hardly enough old pesos for the round-trip train fare between San Miguel and the city.

The whole Benevento family was in similar condition, and they were a family that had, in many ways, been prepared for the crisis. We had food, good books, chores to do, comforts. But where could we go now? What could we do?

I felt even more imprisoned behind the high fences of the safe house. I spent that day of crisis even more enraged than before, if that was possible. The weeds I was strangling with gloved hands and uprooting with violence were suddenly the throats of all the crooks, liars, cheats, greedy generals, speculators, usurers, and inside traders who had run the economy of this beautiful country with so many immense untapped resources and the richest soil on the face of the earth straight into the fiscal and spiritual trash heap that was now its history.

A strange seedling tree arrived at San Miguel, almost big enough to take up the whole bed of a pickup truck. It was a kind of tree called the *ombú*. Mamá Benevento had ordered and paid for the seedling many weeks before. The workman who delivered the tree said it was his last job before he would have to stop working or run out of gas, which was generally unavailable except at prices that amounted to grand larceny. Papá and Mamá were amazed that the man had kept on working anyway, and they tipped him generously with a box of hoarded canned goods.

The *ombú* was a native species of the Argentine pampas. When young, these trees looked like just a few stripped and spindly branches crowning a thin green sapling, with a rough bark that had the texture of pineapple skin. The seedling looked like a kind of pitiful reptilian stick that was improbably rising up out of a huge and heavy ball of roots. When the *ombú* grew, though it usually wouldn't get any taller than a midsized oak, its trunk could thicken to the size and bulk of giant redwoods or sequoias. Its twisting branches then spread out to form an immense umbrella that could be seen for a dozen miles across the flat grassy plains. One *ombú* tree could sometimes spread its leafy octopus arms out over a third of an acre of open space, covering it with a deep cool shade.

Mamá had long been planning a space for this particular seedling. There was a spot under the three tall pine trees of San Miguel. She was looking forward more than forty years to a time when the pines were sure to die from old age and the new *ombú* tree might replace their shade. The family followed the pickup truck as it moved out over the lawn to the place Mamá had selected. She looked around, thoughtfully paced off several lines from mysterious borders as if to make sure, then made a mark in the earth with the heel of her tennis shoe. It took all three men to drag the heavy wrapped roots of the seedling out of the truck. Papá followed the workman back to lock the gate behind the truck, then he settled down at an outdoor table to continue growling at his morning newspapers.

It was left to me to unwrap the burlap from the huge ball of roots. I saw that this tree would require a hole at least a meter and a half in diameter and maybe almost as deep. "That's right, a big hole," Mamá said. "The *ombú* is the national tree, you know. It likes to stand alone. And it needs room, because it's such a greedy tree."

"Are you sure? Here? Doubly sure? Certain?"

"Right here, I think," she said. "Then we'll see."

"We'll never be able to move this one," I said. Mamá just smiled, her eyes glittering. I shrugged. I started hacking furiously away at the ground with my shovel, tossing the rich dirt up in a black rain.

"We're grateful to you and to Betty Ann for helping us so much," she said. "Please don't think we're not."

"It's nothing," I said. "The way things are, I'm really glad for something to do."

The earth was flying now, and I was sweating. I accidentally tossed a shovelful across Mamá's white sneakers. She took a long step back. "Sorry," she said. She said it so softly that I stopped digging to ask what she had said.

"I said, 'Sorry,' " she said. "This must be hard on you and your wife, my son, to be out here. Maybe it would be much better for you both to move back to the apartment. There's really no need to stay at San Miguel. As for the men who followed your woman, that's nothing. No reason to be hiding yourselves out here, don't you agree?"

"No, really, it's much better to be shut in out here than in an apartment in the city, like so many people must be living. And if we can be more like a family . . ."

"You don't know," she said. "Before that happened to your wife, there were telephone threats for weeks. Don't tell your father, because I didn't say a word about them to him. Why bother? They were just phone calls. It's the way the military has of trying to get witnesses not to testify. The threats started coming the very afternoon they decided that your father's case had enough evidence to make a good argument at the trials. It's as if the very second the prosecutors made that decision, the military knew. We've often thought there must be informers in the human rights movement. Or maybe there are electronic devices planted in the offices of the lawyers and prosecutors and judges. Who knows? But that very same day, before Papá had come home and even told me that his case was going to be one of those presented, the telephone rang. I answered it and a man's voice said, 'If he testifies, we're going to kill you and your family.' Then he hung up. After that, once or twice a week, usually midmorning, when maybe they know that Papá is always at his office and I'm at home, the same voice calls me and says the same thing. It bothers me, surely, but I know that it's just something I have to live with. And why tell your father? What difference would it make to get him upset?"

"I don't know," I said. I stopped digging and caught my breath. "Have you ever thought that maybe, just maybe, Papá might be getting the same calls and not telling you?"

"Yes. I've often thought that," she said. "It may be a sort of service we do for each other, this screening of upsetting messages. But this is really nothing. Nothing at all compared to what we've already lived through. Sometimes I even answer the call and say to the man before he can finish, 'Come on over then, murder me, you'd be doing me a favor.' Then I tell him that he doesn't have the balls to keep his promise. Just like that. Balls. His own language. And I have the pleasure of hanging up on him.

"But it's really so absurd. They did the same kind of thing when I first joined the mothers of the Plaza de Mayo. I put on my scarf and made my sign with Alejo's picture on it and joined the other mothers for their marches. The telephone threats started. A voice said, 'We have him. We have your son. We're going to kill him if you don't stop.' You can imagine how I felt. It was only three years since Alejo disappeared. We didn't know for sure then that almost all those kidnapped were either murdered or let go during the first months. Those phone calls had the effect of making me believe what I wanted to believe, in a miracle, that Alejo was still alive and I could save him. So, for a time, I stopped making the rounds of the plaza with the other mothers.

"Then after a month or two, staying at home, feeling like a traitor, and worse, a fool for believing in anything they might say, I started back in with the mothers and worked even harder for their cause. After all, that was where I belonged. Right in front of the government house, raising my voice, right there where anyone in the world could see and hear about what had happened. That was real freedom. I didn't miss a single demonstration that year. And I was actually grateful to them, to those voices on the telephone. They made me learn that there are some things even more important to me than my child's life."

As she was speaking, I was listening and not listening at the same time, assaulting the earth in what had become my usual enraged and frenzied way. The hole was growing deeper and wider at a faster pace. I stopped again to catch my breath. I looked at the rough edges of the hole and measured it with the shovel handle.

"Not deep enough yet," I said.

"Let's try the tree now and see," she said. She tried to lift and drag the heavy seedling by herself until I had to jump up out of the hole to help her. Mamá Benevento knelt by the side of the hole. She watched me try to heft and drag the large ball of roots into the excavation, which was still too shallow. Without a word more, I set the seedling back by the edge of the hole and bent to work again. I hacked, dug, pickaxed with the shovel, using all my strength, dark soil flying up everywhere. I dug for a long time. Then, finally, I stopped. The hole was deep enough by then that it came up to my chest. Mamá and I dragged the seedling into the hole together, dropping in the heavy ball of roots. Mamá stood happily beside the tree, leaning out over the hole to hold it straight.

"This is such a beautiful tree," she said. "Now every time I look out at it, I'll think of you, my son, and remember this afternoon."

I started to shovel the dirt back into the hole, slowly and carefully covering the roots. Something moved in the loose earth under my feet. I jumped back a step. I looked more closely then and saw spatters of fresh blood on my tennis shoes. There was a trail of blood on the ground. Bright smears of blood spread out on the green seedling bark of the *ombú* tree. I panicked for a second, and looked down at my feet, thinking I must have cut myself somehow. It was then that I saw it, on one side of the hole, a toad nest I must have hacked through without noticing. It was a small underground passageway and cavern where the unfortunate little creatures had been living. And there, clinging to the side of the hole by its stubby arms, scrambling, bleeding, I saw an earth-colored toad about half the size of my fist. Both its hind legs were cut off. It was struggling to get up to the edge of the hole, trying to reach up and pull itself out by its arms. I dropped quickly to one knee and covered the toad with my pant leg. I pretended to be resting. "Listen, Mamá, I'm pretty thirsty. Could you go get me some lemonade or something? Water would be fine, too," I said.

"All right, my son. See how pretty? It's already standing on its own. I'll go now and get you some lemonade. Then I'll start setting the table for our lunch."

I waited until she was well across the lawn. Then I stood up again, feeling a little sick. That was followed by a sudden sensation that I was emptied, hollowed out, deep inside. The rage that had simmered all week long was somehow gone. It had given way to an immense, empty feeling of sad fatigue.

I took a long deep breath. I looked down at the toad. Benevolent and harmless in the *indio* mythology of the pampas, figures of toads had been fashioned out of clay with baby toads riding their backs. I thought of how they were given by the *indios* as tokens of a happy motherhood. I wondered if I might do something for the toad. But I had no choice. I raised up the shovel and put it out of its misery.

One afternoon, Papá and I were sitting alone at a table set for tea under the pines. The women were in the house, going through the stash of food, planning meals they could make from what remained of the stores.

"I've been thinking," I said. "Maybe I should take Betty Ann on a short trip into the interior. Just a few days, so she can see something. It might be good for all of us. I don't want her imagining Buenos Aires is the whole country. I was thinking we might even pay a visit to Tío Freddi," I said. "I'd like to see him again. It was an important time for me, the month I spent in the country. How is he, anyway? What news do you have from the family lands?"

"Nobody in this family has spoken to my brother in years," Papá said. He tossed what remained of his lemonade into the grass. Then he stood up too quickly, his teeth on edge, a muscle pulsing in his cheek. "But you go ahead. Visit him if you want. You'll have to make your own arrangements. As for me and my family, none of us is ever going to see him or speak to him again."

Papá Benevento took off across the lawn, fast, as though getting away before he said something he might regret. I jumped out of my chair and caught up to him.

"It's all right," Papá said. "Of course, you couldn't have known. . . ."

Papá slowed down a little. We walked together into the large stretch of lawn that used to be a soccer field for the boys.

"I don't like to talk about it," he said. "But I will now, because you must know. When the first squad of the military invaded our home, they crashed through the door in the middle of the night. They dragged your mother and me out of bed. One of them held a gun on us while the others went through the drawers and cabinets looking for what they could steal. The officer in charge slapped us around. Then he told us they were going to shoot us if we didn't tell them where the boys were hiding. We didn't know where they were living then, and we told them so. They threatened us some more, then they left.

"The next morning, I telephoned Frederico. He was a graduate of the military academy, and he had friends in the dictatorship. He was always bragging about his good connections. I asked him for help, to find out what this was all about. Why were these soldiers breaking into my house? Why were they hunting my sons, his nephews?

"Frederico and I had never been close. I had never asked him to help me with anything in my life. Still, we were brothers. He said he would do what he could. That night, he called me back. His voice was rough. He talked to me in an authoritative way, like an interrogator himself, so it was hard to believe this was my brother. He asked me, 'You live at Junín and Arenales?' And I said, 'Of course, you know my address. Don't be an asshole, you've visited me in this house a dozen times.' Then he said in that terrible voice, 'In the district of Junín and Arenales, there were no military actions last night.'

"I said, 'Freddi, what are you saying? Are you calling me a liar? There were soldiers in combat gear crawling all over my home last night.' And all my brother said, this brother of mine who had the good connections with the military, he said in that same cold voice, 'There were no military actions in your district. That's final. None. And you would be wise never to say another word about this, not to me and not to anyone. My advice is to tell your sons to turn themselves in,' he said. He hung up without even saying good-bye.

"A year later, after I was in a detention center, I discovered that my brother had managed to get all the titles to the family lands put into his name. Half of that ranch was mine. I had never had an interest in working the land. I had always left the business to my brother with blessings, never asking for a share in anything he earned. Still, half of that land was my inheritance. It should have been the inheritance of my sons. Well, he had the connections to the dictatorship. I don't want to get into exactly how he managed to steal the land from me and from his nephews just now, but that's what he did. It's all in his name. So, he can have it if he wants it that badly. The family land can go to the same shitpile that he comes from. He can go back to the whore mother who gave birth to him, for all I care—it couldn't possibly have been the same mother as mine," Papá said. "Now you go on and leave me alone, my son, with my apologies. I think I might mow the lawn now."

He didn't mow the lawn. He spent a long time in the utility shed, banging the machinery around, rattling paint cans, muttering under his breath. I strolled out on the grass for a few minutes, finishing my lemonade. I thought of the Benevento family history, and of the long visit I had made to their beautiful ranch in the province of Buenos Aires. I remembered learning to ride horses, helping with cattle drives, the time I had spent with the resident ranch hands who did most of the work of that valuable corner of the pampas, four square miles of this earth, half of which should have been, rightfully, still the property of Papá Benevento. It was hard to imagine what that loss might have meant to him.

The family history, as I remembered it, was that Grandpapá Benevento, around the turn of the century, was one of the wave of Italian immigration to Argentina. Laborers from strife-ridden and impoverished central and southern Italy got on ships, crossed the South Atlantic, and landed in Buenos Aires during the European winters just in time to catch the huge wheat harvests in South America. At the end of the season, they booked passage on ships back to Italy so they could work the harvests there. They were like swallows, transitory tramps flying back and forth, changing their nests, and so that had become the slang name for them, "the swallow immigration." Year after year, hundreds of thousands of European laborers worked in Argentina like this, living as transoceanic commuters. Gradually, some of them began to stay on in the country. The statistics were that for every five swallow immigrants to Argentina, only one elected to stay on and become a citizen. The rest returned to their European homes.

Grandpapá Benevento was one of the ones who stayed on. He worked hard, and saved enough money, at first, to buy himself a small seed and implements business in the remote pampas town of Henderson. Then he got the opportunity to sell the farm supply business and buy a piece of the rich dark land. Over the years, he added to his land. By the time he retired, he owned four large ranches that all formed one big place. He left the labor to hired managers and began living the good life in Buenos Aires with the wife he had brought with him from Italy. He raised his sons to become educated men. In the tradition of the era, one son would become a lawyer, a humanist, perhaps even a politician. The other son would serve in the officer corps of the military and then go off to manage the family land. And so it had happened. Papá Benevento went to law school. Tío Frederico finished military preparatory school but then never actually served in the armed forces. He went straight off to the family ranch and devoted his life to the land.

I thought back on my visit to Uncle Freddi's ranch more than fifteen years before. I remembered Tío Freddi as an outspoken, impulsive man. His wife was a devoutly religious woman, blind to his bouts of drinking and his excesses with prostitutes. He was like a king out there on his ranch. I remembered the dozen or so families of ranch laborers who lived in small cottages on Tío Freddi's place like feudal servants, doffing their hats and calling him *patrón*. Tío Freddi had wanted nothing more in his life than that the family land one day be transferred into his name alone. It was easy for me to imagine that he might have done anything to achieve that dream. Still, it was a shock to think such a thing could happen between two brothers.

Later that night, I recounted Papá's story to Betty Ann. We were holed up in the guest cottage, trying to keep a fire going against a wintry chill. We talked and drank wine, what was left of a cheap jug we found in the cabinet, until we could sleep. For a few moments, I suggested the possibility that the best thing I could do for my family would be to take them with us on the first jet home. Maybe there, somewhere else, the Beneventos could start to live again. They would no longer be trapped so much in the past, shipwrecked in it, hanging on to what they could from that past in obstinate survival. But that thought was impossible. Neither of them would agree to abandon this Argentina that they so loved. They were committed all the more to their nation because of their losses. And, in this country of unmarked graves, for what was still theirs.

A Robbery of Flowers

DURING THE YEARS of silence, after two of their sons disappeared and one fled into exile, Mamá and Papá Benevento slowly began to gather a new family around them. There were often four or five children from the shantytown slum at San Miguel that Mamá had collected in the streets. She established a regular custom of feeding them huge plates of beef ribs, potatoes, and salads every Sunday. Her good friends Beatrice and Amalita, society girls from the old days, one a rich widow and the other a spinster, came out to the estate and passed the long weekend days with her like sisters. There was an old handyman named Joaquín always puttering around, a worker who had for thirty years been a foreman in a paint factory that went bankrupt. The manager had stolen and squandered the workers' pension funds, a crime that became an easy and customary practice under the dictatorship. Papá

Benevento was trying to find the remains of any company assets and seize them in a lawsuit, at least to get Joaquín and his coworkers a settlement. In the meantime, the man was paid a small weekly sum to keep San Miguel in good repair.

In recent years, the Peluffo family were also regulars at San Miguel, among the first young friends of the Benevento boys to return from exile—El Gordo, his wife, Regina, and their three little girls. Then for the past four months since they had come home from Paris, there were Martín Segundo, his wife, Alicia, and their child, Graciela. Added to the growing family now were their yanqui son and daughter, who had also just returned to them from the years of silence.

Tables were set out in the shade of the trees each good-weather weekend. The smoke of cooking beef ribs, sausages, chickens, hearts, kidneys, tripe, and blood sausages, the traditional Argentine mixed grill, the fruits of the nation, seared and steamed and sent rich odors aloft on the breeze. As did any other Argentine family who could manage it, even during the economic crisis, the Benevento clan gathered together in the traditional weekend celebration of abundance and good fortune called the *asado del domingo,* the Sunday barbecue.

The second weekend we were in hiding at San Miguel, Papá somehow managed to come up with the meats, wines, and provisions, despite the crisis. The sun battled against the chilly rains of autumn and finally won a minor victory. Everyone was invited. The clan gathered on lawn chairs and lounges. We watched the children splashing in the swimming pool. As the barbecue was being readied for the feast, Betty Ann and I relaxed in the sun, sitting with El Gordo Peluffo and his wife. Both spoke very good English. It was like time off in paradise to have company, sipping wine coolers together in the sun, with Betty Ann included effortlessly in the conversation. We listened to Peluffo telling his story.

Peluffo had been a classmate of mine, and of Martín Segundo's, at Colegio San Andrés. It was strange to see him now. I had always remembered Peluffo on the thin side. Everyone had called him *El Flaco*, "the Skinny One," in those days. When the military dictatorship took over, El Flaco Peluffo was one math course away from getting his five-year degree in chemical engineering from the University of Buenos Aires. He had been active in the left wing of the Justicialista Party, one of the mainstream political organizations of the *peronistas*. Shortly after Alejo disappeared, it became clear to Peluffo that he, too, had become a hunted man.

He knew about San Miguel from the boys. He asked Papá Benevento if he and Regina could take refuge there. They were in hiding at San Miguel for less than a week before Papá Benevento arranged transportation across the border. The young couple escaped into Brazil in the middle of the night, hidden under the tarp of a truck full of grain.

Regina broke into her husband's monologue. She told the story of how El Flaco Peluffo began to gain weight his first days in exile. They were living a miserable life in Rio de Janeiro, without working papers or money. They made their living by odd jobs and even begging, moving from one cheap rooming house to another, pulling scams to dodge paying rent.

El Flaco made things worse. He sometimes earned money as a freelance tourist guide, mainly to North Americans, because of his near-perfect English. He began to spend everything he made on food, eating six or seven full meals a day. He was always eating, and rabidly, as his wife described him. He couldn't pass a vendor on the street without buying food. El Flaco ate his way steadily to becoming El Gordo in less than a year of the insecure life in Rio. By that time, they were terrified that the Brazilian military dictatorship would begin to sweep up Argentine exiles and ship them back to sure torture and death, as was happening in Uruguay.

El Gordo finally got some money sent to him by his family. He arranged a large bribe for immigration papers to Venezuela. He also bought himself a first-class forgery of a university diploma, a master's degree in chemical engineering, complete with a full set of fake credentials that would be forever on file with the corrupt institution. These arrangements cost his parents their entire life savings before they died.

"It was a difficult decision, what career I wanted in life," El Gordo joked. "There were many diplomas available for the same price. There was law, psychology, and mass communications. For a little more money, I seriously considered setting myself up as a psychiatrist, the highest-paid profession of pure bullshit there is, but I got scared at the last minute. Chemical engineering was what I knew. It was the degree I was unable to finish. So why not give myself a graduation party?"

El Gordo and Regina moved to Venezuela, where he found a good steady job in chemical engineering for an oil company. They settled down to a prosperous life in a nice home in a suburb of Caracas, and Regina gave birth to her three babies. Regina began to discuss the idea of their changing their citizenships to become Venezuelans, but El Gordo would hear none of that.

Six years passed. Then, as Peluffo characterized his country's history, there was the international shame of the Malvinas/Falklands War, a desperate move by the military to cover up its crimes and economic failures with a patriotic victory. After that humiliating, incompetent folly, that crushing defeat by the British, many savvy military officers and their secret police agents washed their hands of power. They quickly retired to their beach houses in Punta del Este in Uruguay, or to the Gold Coast in Spain, or to their villas in Miami Beach, carrying with them as much stolen cash from the national treasury as they could stuff into their suitcases.

As Peluffo told it, the more prominent of the military officers under the dictatorship had planned such escapes for years. During the whole sick term of the disastrous programs of the Economics Minister hand-picked by the military, Martínez de Hoz, they had been in a position to plunder cash steadily and launder it through foreign banks. "The only arrangements left for them to make were the reservations for first-class plane tickets," he said.

Argentina was left with an international debt of forty-five billion dollars. Fully half of that amount was mysteriously unaccounted for or finally untrackable through layers of dummy businesses and investment firms. One of the last acts in office of *presidente de facto* General Leopoldo Galtieri of the infamous Malvinas/Falklands disaster was to "nationalize" the outstanding bank debts of some three thousand such false-front businesses of dubious ownership and reputation. By that one decree, twenty-three billion dollars simply disappeared without a trace. The military dictatorship finally collapsed under the weight of so much corruption and indolence.

The interim regime of General Reynaldo Bignone, with its promises of free elections, was still very dangerous to returning exiles. But safe or not, El Gordo and his family were back in Argentina within a month of the new general's swearing-in.

"There was no other choice for me," Peluffo continued. "The country was getting ready for new elections. There wasn't anyone left to run the Peronist movement but the old union bosses, who were like gangsters, the same ones who had been stealing from health care and pension funds for years. The young people in the movement, the socialists and the leftists, like Alejo, they were all dead or disappeared, or still in exile. There were only two or three of my friends left alive among those who had fought so hard in the early seventies to bring Juan Perón back from Spain and to see him in power. What a farce that second government was. We felt betrayed by the cause, and by these right-wing *peronistas*, the ones who shut their mouths and went along with the dictatorship that followed the old Turk's death and the government of Isabel, who lost her mind at the helm. We lived with the memories of the most courageous in our movement, like Alejo, who had stayed right here. They were the ones who fought and died for *la lucha seria*, the serious struggle, as Perón once called it. . . .

"Being in exile does strange things to the mind. Looking back on it now, that was the worst time in my life, the most demoralizing, because it was clear what a failure everything had been. You begin to think that all your friends, the ones you have worked so hard and long with, they died for nothing. You start hating them for their senseless deaths. Then you start hating yourself for hating them. Most of all, you hate the way you're living. You've lost your country, your name, your identity. You're scared every time you step out of the house, even to go around the corner to get milk for your children. Sometimes we would run into others like ourselves, who would tell us stories about what was happening in Argentina that were never printed in the press. It became steadily clear to me that I had to get back to my country. I couldn't live with myself anymore. I had to get back into the movement, whatever way I could. So the first chance we had, that's what we did. Then we got here and found the best of us were gone. So the few of us who were left had to work all the harder, to organize, and to fight for a voice in the party.

"That's what we're doing now. We know it's going to take five years, or ten years, or maybe a whole lifetime. We're going to put up with a lot of interference and even violence from the *peronista* right wing. We're going to lose and keep losing, at first, at party caucuses and in the primaries. But we're not going to give up. We'll work one city block, one barrio and villa, at a time. We're going to work hard and keep on working for the cause, until the

Justicialista Party—or the Frente Amplio, my wing of the movement—becomes the party of social justice once again. There's no other choice for me. The best of us aren't here anymore. That means that the rest of us will have to work all the harder until we finally win."

"Don't listen to him, Diego," said Martín Segundo. "He's way too rabid about his cause." Martín brought a fresh bottle of wine out under the trees and filled our glasses. "Peronism is dead. It's all just nostalgia now. Posters of the old asshole and Evita. Maybe a few of the really good marching songs, because the people don't have the imagination to sing anything else."

"Martín is a cynic," El Gordo said. "It's what happens to these young intellectuals. Especially when they're lawyers, and have lived the good life in Paris. But don't worry. Martín is really a *peronista* underneath. In this country, there's no other choice. What other movement promises anything even close to a social agenda for the people? I'm talking about workers' rights, health care, decent pensions, education . . ."

"To the table! To the table!" Mamá Benevento called out from the sunny lawn. She repeated the call in English for Betty Ann, to make her feel welcome. Betty Ann got up from her lawn chair to help Mamá lay out the plates and silverware, and the abundant bowls of salad. Martín Segundo's little daughter, Graciela, grabbed Betty Ann by the hand. The toddler led her to a muddy corner of the yard, where a gang of children were making mud pies.

I was suddenly struck by the appearance of little Graciela. It was something about her eyes. They were the same deep brown, and had the same almond shape, as Alejo's eyes. When she laughed, her mouth took on the same lopsided grin that I remembered as belonging to Alejo. Her ash-blond hair was exactly the same color. There was the way she was moving, too, and how she seemed at times so lost in her dreams. It was like a sign, striking and hopeful, the thought that the Benevento family gene that had made Alejo had reproduced itself so completely in Martín's daughter.

Betty Ann was playing with the children. She helped them arrange their mud pies on a wooden tray. Then she led them ceremoniously across the lawn to the long table, where some of the adults were sitting down. The children began to act out serving the mud pies like a barbecue with a pair of tongs. There was a celebratory confusion all around. Beatrice and Amalita were talking at Betty Ann in their wooden English. Mamá Benevento was still trying to get everyone finally seated by pointing out places. By that time, the kids were laughing and scrambling under her feet and starting to toss the mud pies at each other. With Betty Ann's help, she managed to get all the children into chairs at a card table set for them.

El Gordo, Martín, and I stood to one side. We leaned against the trees, watching the merry gathering with a certain detachment perhaps known only to men. The world was a serious place for us. Such simple happiness as this weekend afternoon we were witnessing was a miracle in such a world. Happy voices and laughter rolled in under the trees. Children ran in ecstatic circles around the table. Papá Benevento had his sleeves turned up and was working over the hot barbecue. He sliced fat sausages and put them on bread to begin the meal. He wrestled huge strips of beef ribs off the grill and started cutting them up.

Mamá Benevento was an odd-looking sight. She stood at the head of the table, the matriarch of her patched-together family. When I was an exchange student, I never would have believed she could be dressed in such peasant clothes, in baggy pants and an old blue shirt, on her head a kind of short-billed cap worn by European factory workers. Her hands were filthy with garden dirt. The cap was tilted at a ridiculous angle to one side of her head. A lock of hair hung down over her face, and she kept brushing it aside with her hands, leaving smears of dirt. She had kept herself moving continuously all day. She replanted flowers again that she had just replanted the week before. She was on her hands and knees from one garden bed to the other, pulling up her failures and replacing them with cuttings. The intensity of her aggression was almost comic as she attacked her garden with rakes and shovels. "She's making war on her flowers again," Papá had said.

Mamá was a tiny, funny-looking picture in her peasant clothes. But for the first time, with her family around her, I saw that she was happy, shouting above the noise of those she loved, "To the table! To the table! Come on, children! Everybody sit down! To the table!"

Betty Ann suddenly appeared again with salad dressing from the house. She had made the dressing to go with her California salad, her contribution to the table, but had not found a container to put it in. She had grabbed up a *mate* tea gourd by mistake and had filled it with dressing. Laughter broke out at the table. Mamá quickly dumped the dressing into the salad bowl with an air of urgency. Then she was on the run back to the house to fill the gourd with *mate* tea and leave it soaking. Betty Ann didn't understand.

"The gourds for *mate* are like pipes," El Gordo Peluffo explained. "It takes weeks to break one in. You're lucky you're among friends. Filling one with oil and vinegar is a definite violation of local customs, a social *faux pas* of the highest order. It might be the clearest case I've ever seen of 'subversion against the Argentine way of life,' " he said. Everyone who knew English laughed, but there was a darkness in the sound. "My dear lady, we'll forgive you this time," he said. "Think no more about it. We'll no doubt drink *mate* later and you'll get the idea."

Beatrice and Amalita began to scold El Gordo in Spanish for making Betty Ann feel uncomfortable. Betty Ann found her place at the table beside me and sat down, her face red, clearly embarrassed by her mistake. The noise around the table rose again to its happy pitch. "Well, at least I'm trying," she said. "It's pretty tough, you know. The only people I can really talk to around here are the kids. They're teaching me Spanish. Let's see. There's *barro*. That means mud. *Perro* means dog. *Horno*, oven. And *pees* means piss. . . ."

Everyone laughed again. I took her hand under the table and squeezed, grateful she was trying so hard and pitching in, and for the devoted days she had spent with my family, settling into the new life, even now this life in hiding. We sat back and watched the big wooden trays passed around the table. We served ourselves portions of the feast.

Argentine beef is like no other. The grasses of the humid pampas are so rich that ranchers finish off their cattle not with grain in feedlots but with dry hay instead. Fat, grass-fed steers are then shipped off to market, extra prime. There is a special flavor to the beef not found anywhere else. The soil of the pampas is matched in richness only by portions of the Chinese coastal plain, and its natural condition of open grassland makes Argentina like the most immense and productive ranch in the world.

The *asado* of Sunday was serious business. The talk for a time was about the differences in the meats, the certain nuances of beef that perhaps only Argentines could distinguish. They discussed whether or not it had just the right flavor, if the blood sausage was well made, how to tell by color and texture a good *chinchulín,* or beef chitlin, and how the short ribs, though they were the toughest cut, were the best-tasting. The eating of meats and salads and bread could go on like that for hours. Kilos and kilos of beef were consumed, then chickens after that, washed down with dry red wines. I had read that heart disease statistics in Argentina were the highest on earth. It was easy to see why at a Sunday *asado*. There was no way not to eat pounds of this beef. Betty Ann and I were slicing off the tender rare filets from the bones, cutting the fat with generous splashes of Papá Benevento's sauce, called *chimichurri*. After a while, some of the family watched Betty Ann closely, as though her reaction to her first *asado* might be a question of national pride.

"My father believed in using the whole animal like this, too," she said. "He had a farm, when I was very young. This meat is making me remember him. The only time I've ever tasted anything like this was on his farm."

"Translate for Betiana that I think this national obsession with so much beef all the time is barbaric," Mamá Benevento declared. She had eaten only a small portion. Several voices began to protest. She cut them off, clearly enjoying getting a patriotic rise out of the others. "Tell me if what I say is not so," she said loudly. "Compare this to the refined cuisine of any really civilized country. Where is the subtlety? Where is there any art? Eating meat like this is savage and primitive. It's only one step away from the caves. Just butcher the whole beast and toss it over a fire. Nothing to it," she said.

"My opinion is that it's all delicious, and like so many savage things, it's irresistible," Betty Ann said. The two women exchanged a warm look across the table, as if their few days together had made them friends enough to disagree. Betty Ann went on with her appraisal of the meal. "Like primitive art, it's basic and simple," she said. She raised her fork and relished a small piece of red meat as if it held the flavor of a fine French sauce, a game to amuse the red-meat patriots at the table. "We could go to the most expensive restaurant in my country and maybe never find beef like this. We could pay seven dollars a pound in a market, and it wouldn't be nearly this good. I haven't been shopping since we had to move out here. I miss shopping. It's been my best way to get a sense of things. Do you mind my asking what you paid for this meat? How much does a steak cost this week in Argentina?"

"It cannot be said now what it costs," Papá answered, in English, then switched to Spanish for my usual translation. "With the inflation, and the new currency, the cost is really incalculable. Nobody knows. The idea seems to be to get rid of all the money in your pockets and to buy anything at any price. This meat I actually bartered for. That's a first for me. I traded the butcher an old lawn-mower engine I had stored away."

The meal was almost finished by then. Mamá rose from the table as if to help the children clear their plates, but also clearly to escape any conversation about the economy.

"The whole thing is madness," Papá continued. "It doesn't fit into my head anymore. Tell your woman that in this country, no one can be sure of the price of anything."

"Come on, this is the weekend," said Martín Segundo. "Nothing should get to us on the weekend. Let's just relax and enjoy ourselves." He turned to Betty Ann and said in English, "When we lived in Paris, beef was about twelve dollars for a kilo. It was a luxury. Here it is about one dollar a kilo for the best steak. About fifty cents for a pound. Very cheap, don't you think so?"

"The poor aren't eating steak today," El Gordo said. "Meat is now too expensive for the poor. Perón once said that the day the poor in Argentina could no longer afford meat, there would be a revolution."

It seemed the men at the table were about to launch themselves into variations of the three current themes of Argentine family men—politics, the economy, and soccer. At Papá Benevento's table, talk of soccer was discouraged when he was present. According to him, during the dictatorship, the military had used soccer games, including the World Cup celebration, as the Romans had used their gladiators. When the repression was worst, the generals ordered a doubling of the number of games, even encouraging public employees to take Wednesday afternoons off to go to the stadiums. It was bread and circuses, and Papá Benevento hated any talk of sports because of that. Knowing this, the men started to discuss more deeply the other two intense themes of the nation that Sunday.

The women gradually rose from the table and left it to the men. Only Betty Ann stayed on, trying to follow the conversation. But English was soon abandoned, arguments between El Gordo and Martín quickly turning to passionate exchanges of heated Spanish. Betty Ann picked up her plate and went off to join the card table around which the children had finished eating. They were now pretending to serve each other cups of mud tea.

". . . But on the subject of this national debt that the military left us saddled with," El Gordo was saying. He pounded the table with his fist. "Why should we pay back a single dollar? Why should we be the ones responsible to yanqui bankers who were stupid enough to hand billions to a bunch of criminal generals?"

"Personally, I'm for everyone not paying debts," I said. "At least I'm doing my best never to pay mine."

"In the next election, you wait and see," El Gordo said hotly. "Enough *peronistas* will go to the polls that we can tell the big banks to shove their debts where they belong."

"Don't believe it," Martín said. "El Gordo is still dreaming. He's like one of the victims in Sebreli's book. Do you know it? *The Imaginary Desires of Peronism*?"

"That's just a dirty piece of Radical Party trash," El Gordo said. "Martín is baiting me, Diego. He knows the only hope for this country is the *peronistas.*"

Papá Benevento broke into the conversation with a hard,

117

serious tone that silenced the others. "I don't know how many years I sat and listened to shit like this from my sons. Long enough so that we even voted for Perón, when he returned, convinced that would be a solution. But where did that get this country? What did that do for my sons? Juan Perón came back to power and handed everything over to a bunch of crooks and thieves and bullies. He was a coward, and it's famous, if you look into history. After the first coup, in 1946, he thought he had failed. He let himself be imprisoned by his own army to save his skin. Only Evita's speech to the crowds in the Plaza de Mayo gave him balls enough to come out of hiding and take the presidency. Perón turned into one big nothing once he no longer had the skirts of Eva Duarte to hide behind. Juan Perón was the biggest tragedy this country ever suffered, and the people who followed in his name are still suffering. The sad truth is that two of my sons ended up giving their lives for a man who was just a cheap opportunist surrounded by chorus girls. Juan Perón was never anything more than a criminal and a gangster and a coward. That's all I have to say. As for the rest of it, you can shove it up your ass. . . ."

Papá was suddenly up from the table, walking quickly across the lawn. There was a young boy from the villa at the gate, whom Papá had hired to push the lawn mower around. He busied himself fixing a plate of food for the boy. Then it wasn't long before he seemed happy enough again, cheerfully explaining to the boy how to start the mower, and how close he wanted the grass cut around the bushes and trees.

That left El Gordo, Martín, and me at the table, watching. Martín shrugged, then opened another bottle of wine. The talk changed briefly to rock music, to Sting and Madonna, and the huge concerts each was rumored to be planning in Buenos Aires. Then the subject changed to the Argentine national soccer team and why they were playing so poorly this season in their first eliminations for the World Cup. The sun was sliding behind the tops of the trees. Light was climbing down through the branches, the shadows growing deeper. A portable radio was turned on somewhere. Soft music floated in. The food and wine suddenly struck all at once, bringing on an irrepressible sleepiness.

I got up and found Betty Ann. She was sitting with Martín's little daughter, watching a pair of goldfish in a tiny stone pool. The two were carrying on a brief conversation in French, a kind of haiku exchange of baby talk in that language. I waited until they seemed to have finished. Then Betty Ann sent Graciela toddling off to play with the other children. I took my wife by the hand and we strolled off in the direction of our guest cottage in one corner of the grounds.

I pulled her down onto one of the beds. We kissed and held each other, and it was possible to imagine we had truly arrived in some exotic, pleasant place. We were alone together in a foreign land, secure and loving, without work or cares or worries. I was proud of her, and of the effort she was making with my family. I wanted to show her my gratitude with love and tenderness. We were suddenly making love without taking our jeans off all the way. But that seemed too quick and strange, and we were a little nervous about the chance that someone might walk in on us in the cottage. Besides, we were feeling too heavy with food and drink. We broke off, happily, then rolled to our sides and settled in. Slowly, we drifted into sleep to the rhythm of the sounds outside, to the noise of the children tirelessly playing, and to the voices of the women clearing the table and carrying dishes into the main house. Somewhere, Martín Segundo had tuned in the radio to the scratchy roaring of a stadium crowd gathered at a Sunday soccer game. Farther off, there was the low, insectlike humming of a lawn mower. For a long, sleepy, beautiful moment, the day was perfect. It seemed as if there were nothing missing.

I was awakened by a few gentle shakes and a voice whispering, "Shh! Don't wake her up! Come outside with me now!"

I carefully rolled over and sat up. It was Mamá Benevento. I saw that the strange-feeling hand touching me was wearing a gardening glove. Her other hand was clutching a small sharp shovel and a long knife that looked like a machete. With these, and in her cap and baggy clothes, she looked like a Basque peasant on her way to the revolution. "Hurry up," she whispered urgently. "There's not much time!"

I pulled on my sneakers and followed her outside. Beatrice, Amalita, and Regina Peluffo were waiting at the high iron gate of San Miguel with armfuls of burlap sacks. One of them gave me a shovel to carry. Then I sleepily followed the women out along a neatly graveled lane that bordered a neighboring estate.

"We're on our way to a secret place," Mamá said. "I've been robbing plants from the garden there for years. But don't say a word about this to your father. I like him to keep thinking I get my plants by buying them or as gifts from the neighbors."

"We're the four thieves of San Miguel," Beatrice said.

"One of these days we'll get caught at it," said Amalita. "We'll be the scandal of the neighborhood. This is what we do for excitement, Diego. We pull off a new and dangerous caper every weekend."

"For me, it's the first time with this gang," said Regina Peluffo. "And look at the risk to my political reputation. What would everybody think if we were caught with this yanqui along? Can you imagine the headlines? The imperialist yanquis are even out to rob our flowers?"

"Such a beautiful garden," said Mamá Benevento. "It's a shame it's been abandoned. For years, I've been trying to find out who owns the place. Either nobody knows or no one wants to say. I keep thinking maybe one of our friends would be able to buy it. We could start our own colony out here."

The late-afternoon light was beginning to fade into darker shadows along the lane. I could see up ahead, almost completely covered with a somber grayness, the outlines of a large, walled-off estate that took up about half the block. The whitewash had long ago chipped and faded from the brick-and-iron fences that stood as tall as a man. Through the spaces between the sharp spear points of rusting iron bars, I could make out a large, three-story, chalet-style house with boarded-over windows. Around it stood a stark, tangled mess of wintry bare branches from clinging trees. The roof of the house was nearly covered as though by a snowfall of rotting leaves.

We approached the gate, which was locked with a heavy, rusted chain. The driveway leading to the house was grown over and covered by wild brambles that crawled across it and then up the walls of the house.

"This is the place," said Mamá Benevento. She pointed out a break in the wall near the gate, hidden behind some thorny bushes, where the iron bars were bent back just enough. She led the way, pushing branches aside and squeezing through the bars into the wild garden.

The others stood back for Regina Peluffo to follow. She stepped in behind the branches and was about to slip through the fence when she suddenly stopped. She jumped back quickly into the grass, her face pale and with an expression as if she had just seen a ghost. "I'm sorry," she said, breathing hard, looking around at the others with frightened eyes. "I can't go in there," she said.

"Come on, don't be foolish! We were only joking about getting caught!" said Amalita. She tried to coax Regina back to the fence by taking her arm. That made things worse. Regina was really scared then, hopping away as if she had just stepped on a snake.

"Calm down, Regina. It's no big thing," Beatrice said.

"I don't know," said Regina. "You've been telling me about this place, but I just can't. Look, I'll be the one to stand out here on the road and keep watch."

"What's happening?" Mamá Benevento asked. She had stepped out of the bushes by this time, and was watching and listening through the gate.

"All right then, just stay here and keep watch," said Amalita. "Nobody's forcing you to do anything."

"There's something wrong here," Regina said. "It's just too sad, and I don't feel right about it. Who owns this place? Why aren't people living here? Maybe this house once belonged to a whole family who was disappeared."

"Sure, that could be true," Mamá said loudly. "But think about it, Regina. If that's the case, then who has more of a right to steal plants out of its garden than me?" Mamá Benevento waited for Regina to answer, but she only stepped back, still frightened, a little farther onto the lane. "Let's go then," Mamá said. "Regina stands guard. The rest follow me. Come on, thieves! We're losing our light!"

The backyard of the abandoned garden was a nearly impassable jungle of exotic flowering bushes. Mamá pointed out that there was also quite a collection of unusual cacti, and how here and there, under a thick mat of browning weeds, the outlines of what was once an aesthetic rock garden could be discovered. Mamá sent Beatrice and Amalita off to a flower bed on one side of the house to dig up autumn bulbs and to take clippings of a strange, bamboolike tree that was stripped of leaves but was still showing off thick clusters of tiny orange blossoms.

We were alone together in the jungle. Mamá made me lead the

way with the machete-like knife, hacking a pathway through thorns and brambles to a place in under the shadows of a huge, weather-worn tree. For a few minutes, we were surrounded by undergrowth. I had no idea where we were going or why, feeling Mamá Benevento's gloved hands urging me on to keep working our way straight ahead. Then I spread back some branches and it was looming right there in front of us, a weird, cactuslike plant that was as big as a compact car. Growing out of it in amazing ways and directions were arm-size tendrils. Each branch twisted up wildly into the air and at its end held out a deep scarlet flower like a clenched fist.

"I've been wanting someone to help me with this one," Mamá said. "Somebody strong enough to get in and dig up a big root. I mean a very big root. Here. Take my gloves for the thorns."

I forced my way in under the arms of the thorny green, monstrous thing. I squirreled my body into a kind of crouch in which I could use the shovel like a pickax to break through the ground. I dug steadily and surely. From time to time, I stopped at Mamá's instructions, reached down into the dirt I had loosened, and felt around for a large root. I found one, buried deep, and enough under the base of the huge plant that I couldn't really see what I was doing. Mamá passed me the machete. I began to use it like a hatchet as best I could.

"This afternoon, when you men were talking, I couldn't help but overhear some things," she said. "It breaks my heart to hear your father talk the way he did. He feels that Alejo and Miguelito gambled their lives away for nothing. I want you to know that I don't feel that way. Alejo and Miguel were heroes. Maybe Miguelito not so much. At the end, he really did gamble his life away. But that doesn't change the truth. They were both fighting hard for what they believed would bring justice to this country. Here. Let me see that," she said suddenly.

She was on her knees, scooting herself in beside me under the thorns and branches. She dug her hands into the small pit I had excavated and pushed back the dirt. "Look at this," she said. An orange-colored root the size and shape of a sledgehammer shone dimly in the black earth. "It's getting too dark," she said. "We should have started earlier. We'll take just this one piece of root here and see what happens. Cut it off as close to the plant as you can."

I continued with the job. The root was tough, and it was a tight squeeze using the dull knife like an ax to chop at it, trying to be careful not to do too much damage beyond the cutting.

"Miguelito was good at gardening," Mamá said. "He always liked it so much at San Miguel. Even later, when he turned so hard, he could be like a child again out here. It wasn't easy for him to be the youngest. He was the youngest but in his way also the proudest. I think he would have been good at working the land if he had ever had the chance. He might have made a very good rancher, or gone on to study agronomy, if he had ever settled down. Now Alejo was no good at all at working with plants and soil. He was like the other men in this family in that respect, no patience for it. He was the one always off reading or drawing. I'd want him to do something and he'd be hiding somewhere with his book. He was the smart and creative one. Too smart to gamble his life away for nothing."

I stopped working. I turned and faced her closely in the shadows.

"Please, Mamá, don't think you have to tell me these things," I said. "I remember how they were. Alejo was my best friend. He was a good person. One of the best people I've ever known in my life. He would never have been involved in anything wrong. And I know he was smart. Both of them were smart. I would never believe they gave their lives for nothing."

"I'm glad you think so, my son. It's very important for me to believe my sons gave up their lives for the right reasons. Now give me a cigarette," she said. "Let's stop now. The others are coming."

The three women beat down a small clearing and gathered around me to watch. The time had come for the big pulling job. It was cramped and awkward under the cactus tree, and the root was slick with a clear running sap and hard to get a grip on. I finally managed to close both hands around it. I leaned back and pulled. I let go with a loud and involuntary groan. I asked where we might borrow a team of horses.

I positioned my body again, more carefully, setting my legs just right on either side of the hole. I began to pull, using my legs and back like a weight lifter in a dead-lift contest, straining my whole body upward until all the air rushed out of my lungs in a gasp. A tangle of roots ripped free of the earth. The force sent me stumbling backward in a sprawling ridiculous tumble into the brambles, making the women laugh. Then I was lying there helplessly tangled in the bushes, looking up at them and laughing, too, holding out the prize for them to see. Mamá eagerly took the root from my hands and looked it over, this ugly orange arm of a thing with hairy bulbous branchings along its length. She shook the root clean of earth and showed it off to her friends, admiring the shape and size, then she carefully wrapped it in one of her burlap sacks.

It took all three women to pull me up out of the thorny bushes with minimal harm. Then we headed back through the garden with our arms full of roots, cuttings, bulbs, and flowers. The sacks were so bulky they wouldn't fit through the gap in the fence and had to be tossed over it to the waiting Regina. We strolled home along the darkening lane, smoking cigarettes, feeling the new crisp chill of the autumn twilight. The women were chattering on at Mamá Benevento, teasing her about where she planned to put her stolen plants. Was she going to dig up all the existing flower beds?

Or was she finally going to lay out a new garden that would take up the whole soccer field?

At San Miguel, the lights were on in the big house. We piled the bags of plants on the patio. Inside the house, everybody was awake from the siesta, eating sweet cakes and taking *mate* in front of the fireplace, which looked warm and safe and welcoming. I could see Betty Ann through the window, a shining nickel straw between her lips, the men enjoying watching her sipping the bitter tea from the gourd.

"Go on to the cottage and wash up first," Mamá ordered, in the doorway, just as I was about to clean off my shoes and step inside to the fire. The request seemed strange to me. I could just as easily have washed up in the big house. But I nodded once, obediently, and stepped back out onto the patio. She followed me a few steps into the darkness. She caught me by the sleeve. Then she reached up for my neck, pulled my face down close to hers, and kissed my cheek. She held her lips there, hard and intensely, then she let go. "Thank you, my son," she whispered. "Thank you for this day."

She went nervously to her big sacks of plants and began puttering over them, sorting out the cuttings.

I started off in the direction of the guest cottage. I found myself wandering across the lawn, hands in my pockets. The chill was sharpening, the air turning damp and cold. I was walking aimlessly around the wet mown grass, the dusk turning almost fully into night. I thought about all that had been said that day, the stories I had heard, the differing versions of what had happened. I remembered what I had said, and thought how I would keep saying whatever I felt my family wanted me to say. They had to believe what they believed in order to keep going. But this wasn't so within myself. The more I listened to their voices, the less clearly I understood the causes, and the less sure I was of the truth. I felt the anguished certainty that my family must be facing for the rest of their lives. With so much that had vanished, knowing what really happened was impossible.

I found myself standing at one end of the abandoned playing field. I leaned against one of the weathered and splintering arches of the goals. I stood out there a long time, cold hands pulled out of my pockets, twisting my fingers through the cold hanging strings that were left of the netting.

All at once, in the air around me, in the branches of the trees, the birds stopped singing. It struck me how I might not have noticed them at all and only could now because they had stopped. I might never have heard them but for their silence.

The Internal Exile

I DECIDED TO redouble my efforts to find out what had happened to my brothers. Mamá arranged a meeting with Jorge Gallo, who had been one of Alejo's closest friends in the student movement. I recalled the few times I had been with Jorge, the year I spent as an exchange student. I remembered a strangely loud and nervous kid at the fringes of a crowd that was heckling a military parade. Then there was the workers' strike and demonstration we had gone to together during the infamous *"Cordobaso,"* when hundreds of striking laborers in the northern city of Córdoba were killed or wounded. In Buenos Aires, we students had been tear-gassed and descended upon by cops wielding nightsticks.

The last time I had seen Jorge was toward the end of my year with the Benevento family. He invited me, Alejo, and Martín Segundo to watch the dawn from the balcony of his family's apartment. The balcony overlooked what appeared to be a quiet, tree-lined street. It was the day before a scheduled state visit to Argentina by the rich yanqui politician Nelson Rockefeller. We sat on Jorge's balcony, observing a supermarket of the chain called Minimax, owned by the Rockefeller family. Suddenly, just as the first rose-and-purple glow of the River Plate dawn was upon us, a bomb exploded. There was a bright flash. A muffled shock rolled up the street like a thunderclap. The doors and windows of the supermarket blew out in a rain of twisted metal and shattered glass. Jorge and my brothers were jumping up and down in celebration.

I remembered Jorge as an impulsive youth, always the first to take risks, a tall, skinny kid who seemed to be working out his rancor toward his aging, rich parents by his commitment to rebellions of all kinds, at school, with girls, and, finally, with bombs in the student movement for the return of Juan Domingo Perón to the presidency of Argentina.

"We've often talked with Jorge Gallo about the boys," Mamá had said. "We sometimes think that the boys first began to get involved in dangerous things with Jorge Gallo. My views are different from his. But don't take only my word. There's no reason to believe only your father and me. Go talk to him. Let him tell you the story of what happened."

I arranged to meet with him at a large restaurant on the border of the posh Barrio Norte, on the corner of Santa Fe and Pueyrredón. The place had an unusual location in that the entire second floor above it was a district campaign headquarters for the Justicialista Party. The windows of this headquarters were almost always thrown open wide. Loudspeakers blasted out recordings of the martial beat and rousing voices of crowds of thousands singing Peronist marching songs, a discordant music ringing out over the traffic of both avenues. I walked in through the revolving doors under the blue-and-white banners of Peronism, the oddly abstract and hollowly painted faces of Juan and Evita on flags unfurled over the balconies and lifting in the breeze. The slogans on billboards above the busy corner called for state worker unity, for resistance to the new economic reforms, for bread and for justice. They were the same words and images unchanged now for two generations of the populist delirium of the party.

The expanse of tables was nearly deserted but for Jorge Gallo, who sat in one corner, his back to the wall, darkly watching the entrances. I recognized him at once. He was clearly the same person, years older, but he didn't look well. He was thin. His complexion was yellow. His brown eyes were too deeply set. He had the look of someone who smoked and drank too much and rarely went outdoors. He wore a scraggly mustache and Che Guevara beard, giving him the appearance of an aging radical grown ragged at the edges. His eyes were quick, nervous. He had the jittery physical reactions of a man who had been pursued.

We shook hands. But before we sat down, Jorge wanted to clear up just who was going to pay the check for lunch. I noted the threadbare elbows of his rumpled tweed jacket. Buttons were missing on one sleeve. "I'm sorry to ask," Jorge said. "But with the way this new money is, and I have a wife and two children, and me only recently divorced . . . Normally, I don't even eat lunch. It's rice and spaghetti and beans for me, on a one-burner hot plate, you understand?"

"Of course the lunch is on me," I said. I reached into my pocket and pulled out a small tape recorder. I had decided to begin recording things, whenever possible, if only to keep track of what I was hearing. "You don't mind, do you?"

Jorge looked at the small machine sitting on the table. His eyes shifted quickly, his mouth twitching. He scooted his chair back away from the table.

"We might just as well have coffee," he said.

"Come on, don't be ridiculous. This is a celebration. Two friends having lunch and catching up on things. The recorder is because I have such a bad memory sometimes," I said. "Really," I said after a moment. "Look. If it makes you that nervous . . ."

"No! How nervous? It's all right," Jorge said. He pulled his chair back to the table and reached for a crumpled pack of cigarettes—Particulares of the cheapest kind.

"Good. Don't worry," I said.

"Let's order," Jorge said. "The waiters in here are ready to kick me out or die of boredom."

We fell silent for a moment as Jorge studied the menu the way a gambler looks at a horse-racing form. He must have been starving. I mulled over the prices, hard to figure since the money had changed. The banks were open again, and I had been able to cash in some dollars that day. The currency had stabilized on the black market to about three new australes to one yanqui dollar. Prices all over the city, and on the menu, had not yet caught up to that rate of exchange. I'd been lucky and was feeling gringo-rich.

The waiter approached the table. Jorge began to order everything he could think of, looking up from the menu after listing off each item and saying, "Pardon me," as though asking permission. He ordered a shrimp cocktail, a palm-heart salad in golf sauce, prosciutto and melon, broiled provolone, cold asparagus spears, and two ham empanadas. Those were just the appetizers. For main courses, there would be a roast breast of chicken in a mushroom-and-whiskey sauce, mashed potatoes, creamed spinach, and a side order of tortellini *à la bologna*. To go with his meal, he asked for a particular Chardonnay from *bodega* Navarro Correa that was one of the best and most expensive white wines in the country. He finished, gingerly setting the menu to one side. "And then, pardon me, we'll see," he said.

I asked for a beef Milanesa and a salad.

"Well, this will be an experience for me," Jorge said. "A little of the good life, the way only the rich in this country or you yanquis can live it."

I wasn't sure what he meant. The Gallo family had always had plenty of money, much more than even the Beneventos had once enjoyed. And here was Jorge now, his family's only son and heir, in rags, smiling across the table at me in an irritating way. It reminded me of how salesmen treated customers before picking their pockets.

Jorge's appetizers started landing on the table. It was impossible to have a conversation. I tried to start off by talking about my memories of the Cordobaso street demonstration we went to together, and the times we had gone out at night, spray-painting Peronist slogans on walls all over the city. Jorge nodded in response, chewing, grunting just loud enough to engage the voice-activation feature on the recorder. The cassette tape lurched ahead half an inch or so with the indecipherable mumbling, the single primitive syllables Jorge could get out between large mouthfuls of the food he was scooping up and swallowing as fast as he could. We settled down and ate then, together, saying very little. Only when Jorge had finished his second courses and a cigarette did he start talking, suddenly, all on his own. This caught me a little off guard. I had given up on prompting him with questions.

"The year you spent in Argentina, ah, those were really soft times," Jorge said. "The most they were doing back then was shaking us down every once in a while just to warn us. The generals back then, Onganía, Lanusse, and that other one, what was his name? Levingston? What ever happened to him? Anyway, they were really soft on us compared to what came later. I don't know how many times Alejo and I were arrested for painting walls. Six, seven times maybe. But it was like nothing then, just a few hours in jail and maybe a little bribe for the parents to pay and the police let us go. 1973 in Argentina was a lot like 1968 in Paris, or the antiwar movement in your country. There were demonstrations, and sure, some police riots when they came at us with clubs and tear gas. You remember one of the first of those. Later, the police let loose dogs on the crowds. But we were the ones who owned the streets in those days. . . ."

The red light glowed on the tape recorder. The tiny amp meter needle ticked up and back to just the right volume settings. Jorge had a smile on his face as he was speaking, though it didn't seem in any way an expression of contentment. It was rather an involuntary stretching of his lips, his stained teeth flashing, his dark eyes strangely lit up and giving him an expression of madness, or of delusion, or perhaps filled only with his memories.

"I remember once, at the Pacífico Bridge, in Palermo. It was the 11th of March, you must know the day. It was the day that dentist, Cámpora, was elected president in the name of Juan Perón. We all felt like we had won the war in the streets. Perón was going to return to Argentina, and we were going to see to it that he kept his promises for social reforms. . . ."

"This part is hard to understand," I said. My notebook was out now, and I was scribbling in a fast shorthand I couldn't figure out myself half the time. "How could any of you, especially someone as smart as Alejo, really believe that a fascist like Perón could bring about social change?"

"Ah, yes, surely," Jorge Gallo said. "You're talking about something basic to what happened, the imaginary desires we had for Peronism, which were totally wrong, of course. We were Marxists. We were communists. Of course we were. Our idols were Castro, Lenin, and Trotsky. But any real socialist revolution in a country as basically bourgeois as Argentina was impossible. So, we convinced ourselves that the workers' party of Perón was the

133

only way we could achieve a transition from an authoritarian to a socialist-democratic society. That was what the old Turk had promised us in his speeches from exile in Spain. We were idealists, and took him at his word. It was crazy. We had posters of Che Guevara on our bedroom walls with the slogan 'If I were still alive, I would have posters of all of you on my walls.' Can you think of anything more naive than that?

"Then after that dentist was elected in Juan Perón's name, tens of thousands of us gathered at the Pacífico Bridge to shout and cheer and sing our songs of victory. The police moved in. They fired tear gas. They used their fancy new tank with its water cannon. At one crucial moment, it was Alejo who stood at the head of the crowd. He was all alone up there, in front of everybody, facing down the police. He started shaking his fist in the air and chanting, 'Push them back! Push them back!' Then everybody all at once was storming across the police lines, throwing bricks and bottles. Alejo was leading us. We rushed the police lines. They broke ranks and started running away like whipped dogs. We thought nothing could stop us then. Perón was returning. And there were hundreds of thousands behind us. . . ."

"I once saw Alejo do something like that," I said. "You remember? The Cordobaso demonstration? Alejo raised up his fist and started shouting. I thought the whole crowd was going to follow him."

"He had balls, Alejo did," Jorge said. "He was very important to the movement. He was chosen as one of the chiefs of publications. He mainly wrote pamphlets and newsletters for the union action wings, also leaflets for public buildings and that kind of thing. . . ."

"What did he write? I mean exactly?"

"Oh, I don't know . . . whatever he was told to write. Solidarity with the union pieces, down with the fascists, that kind of thing. But he had this way of putting it. He would always dig up some great speech or poem from his books. Or some of them he wrote himself. Very patriotic words. But what Alejo wrote isn't the best part. It was the way he got what he wrote around. He would start out, and when he saw someone who seemed a likely prospect, he'd say to him, 'Take this. Read it and pass it on to your friends.' Or he just walked into post offices and telephone offices, right past the police, and left his sheets lying around on the tables. He did the same thing in buses, in banks, in large stores.

"But his favorite ploy, which was really a stroke of genius, was to utilize the government offices themselves. The public employee in Argentina has always been a good medium for spreading political news. It's because of his abysmally low salary, and the boring rhythm of his official duties, and because of the need for something exciting to break the monotony of his bureaucratic boredom. Alejo knew this from firsthand experience—he had worked as a public clerk—and he took advantage of it. He left his leaflets on the desks of functionaries, of clerks, in lunchrooms, on bulletin boards, right under the noses of the government. He got out some of the most important documents of the movement this way. Everyone knew about them almost instantly, like the first real call for a socialist revolution inside Peronism.

"Then came the massacre at Ezeiza Airport. It was the day we all went out there to greet Juan Perón on his return from exile. But the right wing of the party had it planned, with rifles, machine guns, even grenades. Perón landed at the city airport, in secret, while his right-wing elements opened fire on all of us. The whole thing turned into a bloodbath. To this day, there has never been an official statistic released telling how many of us died. Later, we knew it was Perón himself who had ordered this action. He wanted to purge us, the leftist students, out of his party, now that we were no longer useful to him. The AAA secret police was formed, and death squads within the army, all the basic structure that was later used by the generals. So what were we to do then? That was the question. What?"

Jorge stopped talking for a moment, his eyes glittering, his quick thin fingers nervously combing through his beard. He reached for the bottle of wine and poured the last drops of it in his glass. He raised the empty bottle toward me and said meekly, "Pardon me?"

"Sure, of course," I said. I waved my hand for the waiter and ordered another bottle. "What's hard to understand is why you didn't all just get out," I said. "Thousands were leaving the country by then. The Benevento family's deepest regret is that Alejo and Miguel didn't escape into exile."

"Think of it in these terms," said Jorge. "If your yanqui Constitution were suspended tomorrow and the army started sending death squads out to shoot people, wouldn't your first thought be to start carrying guns and shooting back? Wouldn't you consider the tactic of planting bombs? It should be clear to you that I say this as a nonviolent person. Alejo was also nonviolent. We were in one of the groups arguing most strongly against an armed rebellion. So how did we turn so fast to planting bombs that killed hundreds of innocent people? How?"

The waiter opened the new bottle of wine with a cheerful pop, then poured Jorge's glass full. Jorge watched it like a man contemplating an unexpected treasure. He sipped, tasted, relished, set his glass down.

"And so? How?" I repeated. "How didn't you have another choice?"

His expression changed. He looked over the wreckage of his plates, the chicken bones and crusts of appetizers heaped up in front of him, as if they reminded him of the ruins of a bombed-out building. His lips pressed into a sad, bearded shape, as if the good wine had soured.

"No one who didn't live through it could ever understand," he finally said. "I spent seven years living underground, in internal exile, under an assumed name and with fake identity papers. I ended up working in a factory just like any other *negro* on the assembly line. My wife and kids and I shared a miserable two-room apartment on the outskirts of the city. We lived as though we had been born into poverty. All that time, those seven years, I never did figure it out, and I still don't know why. No reason I can imagine now justifies the three bombs that I personally carried into public buildings. None of the bombs I planted ever killed anybody. One was a dud. The other two were just window-busters. But I was a *compañero,* you understand. Alejo and I both were *compañeros* of the very same ones who planted the kilos of plastic explosives that killed dozens of people in the Public Works Administration Building. And who were they? Who did we kill? Nobody special. They were secretaries, clerks, innocent people off the streets just trying to get their papers stamped and signed.

"After that, we didn't have much heart left for the struggle. But it was too late by then. Everything happened so fast. We thought we were victorious and accepted within the legitimate ranks of Peronism. Then, suddenly, Perón came back, and died in office, and we were being hunted down like rats. What would you have done? What?"

Jorge Gallo was leaning, intensely, across the table. His deeply set eyes looked like two tiny lamps had been lit inside them. He looked crazed, and like he was about to grab me, his long yellowed fingers about to reach out violently from the tattered cuffs of his jacket to shake some kind of answer from me.

"It's not my business to say," I said. "All I know is that Alejo was my friend, and my brother. To be honest, I still can't imagine that he was involved in any of it." The waiter was suddenly there, clearing plates. "Look. Order some dessert or something. Or a cognac or a whiskey. Whatever you want."

Jorge Gallo nodded yes, just once. He poured himself another glass of wine and seemed to calm down. He picked up the menu and inspected it quickly, then ordered two desserts, fruit compote and a caramel pancake, then a double cognac, asking the waiter to hold off on the cognac until he had finished the bottle of wine.

"Pardon me," he said in that strange way, after he had ordered. He reached across the table and shook another cigarette out of my pack, crossed his legs, then continued with his story.

"Maybe I can help you to see it then," he said. "This was our situation. Perón died in office. Isabel Perón took over the presidency. She went crazy at her desk and was under psychiatric care. Her chief minister, López Rega, took over control of the government. The whole country was in chaos. Death squads were sent out to hunt down elements of the left wing of the party. Orders came to us from the leadership of the militancy to strike out at anything connected to the government, at public buildings, at trains, at prisons and police stations. Some in the movement started riding around in cars, shooting even at lone policemen on their foot patrols. That wasn't Alejo and me, of course, as you well know if you knew him. We were scared, desperate and scared, by then, and forced into hiding.

"López Rega then ran off to Spain with all the money he could get his hands on from the treasury. The generals stepped in and took over the mess the death of Perón had left behind. Most people were really glad when they did. The generals promised an end to the violence. But they didn't end anything. They were even worse. The generals redoubled efforts to hunt down and find anyone connected to the movement, along with thousands of innocents, to crush out even the possibility of an opposition to their dictatorship. That was when Alejo disappeared. Our cell broke up in twenty-four hours. We all went deeper into hiding, or into exile.

"It was then that the real doubts came into my mind. We had been playing at revolution like children. We had wasted our lives. I was married by then, and I had my two babies. I realized that I had hurt more than my own miserable life on this earth. There I was, making my woman and my children suffer, all because of my stupid convictions that I might actually contribute to a movement that could change things in this country. Think of it. Believing in that, when the truth is that this country will never change. This is a country that is built on greed and corruption and influence, and on violence at its heart. It always was that way and it always will be. So then, that's my story. It's not very nice to tell and it's not very easy. Pardon me," he said.

He downed the rest of his glass of wine. Then he poured another glass and downed that one, too. He sat for a moment, breathing deeply, as though catching his breath. He reached across the table for another cigarette.

"Your Argentine mother wanted me to tell you about Alejo, not about my life," he said. "But the only reason I'm even alive to tell about it is Alejo. He knew where I was hiding. He knew the same about everyone in our cell, where we worked, when and where we were supposed to meet again. As far as I know, not one other person in our cell was disappeared. So he must have taken it, everything they did to him. He held out under torture until he died. Or at least he kept quiet long enough for the rest of us to get out of the country or do what I did. He was brave. He had balls. He was my best friend, and I owe my life to him."

"She says she's proud her son had such a devoted friend as you," I said. "She says that without you, she would never have known about what Alejo did or how he lived while he was in hiding."

"She's such a romantic, your Argentine mother. Such a pretty woman, too," Jorge said, and smiled. "Sometimes I call her up and joke with her. She asks, 'Who is it?' 'It's me, your secret lover,' I say. She laughs. Then she addresses me as 'my love,' with joy in her voice. She's really closer to me now than my own mother ever was," Jorge said. He leaned back a little in his chair and looked at the tape recorder with some suspicion. "I'm sorry. Suddenly, I don't like the idea that my voice is being recorded. Can you turn that thing off?"

"It is off," I said. I picked the small recorder up and showed that the red light wasn't glowing. "This side of the tape just ran out," I said. I quickly flipped the cassette over and slid it into the sprockets, ready to turn the machine on again. "What's the problem?"

"No problem," Jorge said. "It's just that maybe I should be more careful. And you, well, part of it is who you are. A North American, a yanqui. Even though you say I knew you once, and Mamá Benevento loves you as a son, it's hard to say these particular things to a yanqui. Call it years of psychological conditioning in the movement, pardon me," he said.

I didn't know how to respond. I looked for the waiter and ordered myself a whiskey. After doing this, I slipped the tape recorder into my inside jacket pocket. My thumb was on the voice-activation button, and for a split second I was just going to shut it off. Instead, I slid the button to its on position. I moved my thumb across the tiny control that turned up the recording volume on the machine. I made a show of doing this, making it look as if the recorder were turned off and hidden safely away.

"Pardon me," Jorge said again. "I know, in my heart, there's nothing to fear from you." He smiled again in that ingenuously humbled way. "You know, I was just thinking. You were talking earlier of that morning when we watched the supermarket bombing. It's strange. I think back on that and I don't remember you there. I don't really remember Alejo or Martín Segundo there, either. It occurs to me that I was with other people, but it could have been anyone and I wouldn't know who it was anymore. Isn't that strange? I had forgotten I even knew you.

"What's odder than that is that even though Alejo and Miguel and I went to the same school for years, I don't once remember meeting the Benevento parents or even going over to their house. I must have at some point, knowing Alejo as I did. It's like everything that's happened has caused these really strange gaps in my memory. It's like the experience of waking up after drinking too much, not knowing what happened the night before, only magnified many times over the whole course of my life before I went underground.

"In my memory, I didn't meet Alejo's parents until eight years after he had disappeared. That was only last year, though it seems longer than that now. It was one of the first days I had come out of hiding and gone into the city, after the election of this new democracy. I took a subway to the Plaza de Mayo to see the demonstration there that I had heard so much about. I was only going to take a look, nothing more, then be on my way, taking no chances. It was a big demonstration that day. The mothers and the families of many hundreds of the disappeared were there, marching around the heart of the plaza, carrying their signs and chanting slogans demanding justice.

"Then, suddenly, there was Alejo, a big poster picture of him carried high above the crowd. Isn't that strange? The very first day I had ever tried to observe a demonstration since I was in hiding, and there he was. The Beneventos were walking along at the edge of the marchers, holding up that poster of my best friend. I watched them for a long time. And I was scared, really terrified. In those days, rumor was that the military was still infiltrating the human rights organizations. It might be dangerous to go up to anyone and take the chance of declaring who I was.

141

"But then I kept watching the Beneventos, their faces as they marched, and I suddenly knew they were the real thing. So I did it. I went up to them in the crowd and marched beside them for a little while. Then I leaned in close to Mamá Benevento and told her that I had been a friend of Alejo's in the movement. She understood right away what it meant to say this to her. She put a finger to her lips, then told me her address and when to meet them. Later, at their apartment, I told them the whole story, and about Alejo, and how he saved my life. Ever since, they invite me to dinner two or three times a month. Or sometimes out to their country house for the weekend, giving me a place to take my children out of the city."

"That's the way they are," I said. "Once you have their friendship, it's forever."

"Sure, it's clear," Jorge said. "In my case, they've helped me to come out of hiding. Until last year, even with the new democracy, I was still hiding out. Papá Benevento helped me to get my real name back, and also a different job, one that pays more, even though it's tough to make ends meet. Sometimes I tell people that at the College of Law of Buenos Aires, my major was in street demonstrations and student politics. What an education, no? Really of marginal value, especially in these times.

"So Papá Benevento used his connections to get me a job selling condominium apartments. At least I was able to make enough to move my now ex-wife and the kids into the city, to get them out of the slums. I have enough left over to spend on my own tiny bachelor's apartment, a little food, subways, buses—never enough in my pockets for cigarettes. But I can't complain, not compared to how I was living. So my whole life changed as a result of knowing them. And I swear on my dear dead mother's soul that I will never again become involved with politics. That's the way it is with me now. . . .

142

"Say, one thing I was thinking, and maybe you can help me. What I would really like to do is to emigrate. I'm applying for a resident visa to get into the United States. They say it will take at least three years even to be considered, and probably they won't give me one even then. Do you have any ideas?"

"Never mind the immigration papers," I said. "Very few South Americans are approved through legitimate channels to get into the United States. You should do what everyone else does. Get yourself into the U.S. on a tourist visa, then start off by getting an under-the-table job. You start working for someone, for a building, a restaurant, things like that. Fishing boats in Alaska are a good bet. You do a good job. Then somebody sponsors you for a green card and that's it, you're in, after a long and terrible process. So my advice is just do it, get started, forget about the legalities and just get yourself north."

"No. I don't think that's for me," Jorge said. The cognac had been served. He picked his up, entranced with the snifter as he swirled the amber liquid around under his nose, breathing in the vapors like some long-forgotten pleasure. "No," he said after drinking. "I'm resolved now to be the most legal person in Argentina or anywhere else in this world. Look," he said. He reached under the frayed lapel of his jacket and brought out his wallet. He began to flip through the cards, holding each one up with a flourish as if he were showing off a series of magic tricks. "New driver's license, my own name. New federal identification, my real name. Real estate salesman's card. Library card.

"And this receipt here is very unusual. You can see that I paid my full share of income taxes, and a share of my company's value-added tax is taken from my commissions. You must know that almost nobody in this country pays taxes, especially not the rich. It's just about unheard of in Argentina to worry about paying taxes. But look here. I did. I won't do anything that makes me live in fear that someone is after me. No. Never again. Once on the run in my life was enough. So, I'll go legally or not at all, and that's the way I'm going to live."

"Well, then, it'll take years and probably not happen," I said. "You know, you might be one of the few people I've met in Argentina who doesn't have some kind of angle figured out. If not to get around the laws, then to make life a little easier for his family at the expense of the country or of someone else."

"Maybe so," Jorge said. He pushed his chair back a little and looked malevolently, darkly across the table. "This country has its faults, as you've pointed out. But at least in Argentina we don't have bloody aberrations like the repression in Central America and the war in Vietnam to look back on. We're not a capitalist giant controlled by multinational corporations that are the aggressive and uncaring agents of exploitation of the masses and of world imperialism. Unlike the United States, Argentina is not one of the most hated countries on earth for our wealth and our waste and our intolerable greed."

"I didn't mean to insult you and your country," I said. "I was just, well, asking about your reasons."

"No need to apologize. It's clear that I was the one trying to insult your country, pardon me. Another drink?"

His hand was up and waving for the waiter before I could decline. Jorge lit another cigarette, tossing the match into an ashtray already overflowing with what must have been two packs of butts. All the alcohol he'd drunk was getting to him, not in any effusive way, but in a steadily darkening, combative mood. I felt a bitterness leveled directly at me. His voice was taking on a tone implying a contempt that was growing close to hatred.

"You want to know how it was? Do you? Yanqui? Let me tell you then. This is how it really was with me. When Alejo disappeared, I was married and had two little baby girls. My wife and I were in love as only a couple of teenagers can be in love. After Alejo disappeared, I had to take my wife and my babies deep into hiding or we would face the same thing. Shortly after that, my parents died. First my mother, of a heart attack, then three months later, my father, of something like his tenth stroke.

"It wasn't safe to go to my mother's or my father's funeral. The death squads had my name on their lists. I couldn't come forward and claim my inheritance from the family lawyers, either, since they were all a bunch of fascists in with the dictatorship. I had heard from a family friend that they were waiting for me to turn up to ask about the will and they would immediately hand me over to a military action wing. Do you have any idea what happened to an inheritance under the military if no one claimed the property? It was confiscated by the government, with the lawyers, of course, collecting their fat fees. My family's landholdings in the interior, their stocks, their bank accounts, our home, everything just vanished. So my wife and I and my babies had to go on in hiding without a single peso. I mean, do you remember me? Do you? Really? From our student days? You visited me in my house and saw how we were living?"

"Yes, I did. The way I remember it, you always had money," I said. "We used to joke at school how when you were late, you always came in a taxi. When the others were short, you were the one who bought the Cokes and the pizza."

"Really? That's true?"

"Do you think I would lie about that? I even met your old mother and father. I made the mistake of asking if they were your grandparents," I said. "Look. Have you told Papá Benevento about any of this? He might be able to recover some of your family's money."

"The Beneventos can't even help themselves," Jorge said. "You should ask sometime what happened to their money. The military regime was filled with masters of thievery. Expert forgers worked at land titles and bank documents. What the generals couldn't steal by forgery, they took by other means. There are thousands like me in this country. But that doesn't really bother me so much. I ask you only to assure myself that you did know that my family once had money, you saw for yourself how well we lived. My wife and I came from very refined and well-educated families. So you can understand how it was for us, when, overnight, we were in the streets without a single peso. . . ."

Jorge talked nonstop, pausing only to toss down his snifter of cognac and then raise his hand for more with a now customary "pardon me," the tone of which grew more forceful, and more bitter. I could see he was getting drunk. The articulation of his words was growing steadily more slurred and stumbling in the pace of his Spanish until, were it not for the cassette tape in my pocket, I would never have understood all that he said. I played it over and over again later, spending hours deciphering his run-together words and making a transcription:

At first, I worked day jobs. Under-the-table things like washing dishes in restaurants. Or I unloaded vegetable trucks at the municipal markets. I shaved my beard and mustache off, and being dark-haired, somehow I blended in with all the other dark-skinned people who had come from the northern provinces to the city looking for work. Nobody asked any questions about those kinds of jobs. You didn't have to show documents. The pay was miserable, and just getting enough money together each day to get bread and milk was hard. Worse, for about five months, my wife and my babies didn't have any place to live. It was nearly impossible to rent an apartment without proper identification. In any case, I didn't have enough money from day laboring to get the deposits and rent together in advance. And there was the psychology of the situation. Each day was like our last day, that's how scared we were.

So why not spend all the money you can today if there's no promise of tomorrow?

Have you seen how all over Buenos Aires there are these transitory hotels? 'Half-hour hotels,' some call them, where men take their mistresses or their prostitutes? My family and I often stayed in the cheap ones. We generally checked in at ten at night and got out before six in the morning. We were scared of being turned in by curious managers or by customers who might wonder what we were doing. It happened like that a lot in those days. Someone asked a few simple questions about a person. The next day, that person disappeared.

So, there we were. While I was making my rounds in the streets looking for undocumented work, my wife, Elena, stashed our two suitcases and took our two babies in their stroller to one of the parks. Or she and the babies made the rounds of the cheap cafés if it was raining or cold. She waited for me all day, never knowing what might happen. Sometimes, if I hadn't found work, we slept in the park or in abandoned buildings. Or on a good day, I met up with her in the evening with enough money for food and maybe to hunt up one of the half-hour hotels where they would just take our money and nobody would ask any questions.

That was the way we lived, and Elena never once complained. We loved each other completely back then. Later, well, let's just say that this kind of strain has a way of catching up to people. We didn't last two months together after the swearing in of the new democracy. But in those days, when we were so low and poor and in so much trouble, no man in the world could count himself luckier than me with such a wife at my side.

One night, after about five months of living this way, we found one of the half-hour hotels. I had earned good money that day. We had spent two nights in an abandoned building and we all needed baths and rest, so we chose one of the nicer transitory hotels in Recoleta. We signed in.

Two or three fancy prostitutes and their men looked us over in the lobby, like what was this little family doing in a place like this? I never wore my wedding ring. She left hers on. I played an act in the lobby like I was Elena's illicit lover. I had just saved her and the babies from a jealous husband who was searching for them. That act always worked to explain ourselves. The trick was teaching the babies not to call me Papá when other people were around. We checked in.

The hotel room—like most rooms in half-hour hotels—had mirrors on all the walls and on the ceiling. You know the kind of place, really decorated like a bordello. There was a heart-shaped bathtub. We bathed the babies in the heart bathtub and then we took showers. We ate a little cold supper together at a real table. For a while, we felt like a family again. We put the babies to bed on this strange kind of couch that, by its shape—it had like a dip in the middle between two camel's humps—must have been designed for having sex in unimaginable positions. But it didn't make such a bad little bed for the girls. We were tired. Really wrung out and exhausted from the streets.

Elena put on her one nightgown, a long blue flannel one printed with white flowers. I put on my pajamas, which I always hated to wear, but a man wears pajamas when he sleeps in the same room with his daughters, no? So we climbed into bed together, really wiped out. We got ready to turn out the light to hurry up and sleep.

My wife lay back on the bed and looked up. She started to laugh. She laughed and laughed and wouldn't stop. It was loud and crazy-sounding, really a terrible laughter, then she was hysterical. It got so bad that I put my hand over her mouth, afraid we might draw attention to ourselves and the manager would be at the door. But that was no use. She kept pointing up at our reflections on the ceiling, and in the mirrors on the walls, all around that really tacky room. She was laughing so hard it sounded like screaming. Finally, she calmed down enough to say, 'Look! Look there!'

Then I saw it, too, just what she meant. Here we were, in this half-

hour hotel, a hundred rooms full of the history of only fucking, and we were probably the only people who had ever slept in this room wearing pajamas. She finally calmed down enough so that I told her I knew what she meant, and I laughed a little, too. Then we just held each other and started crying. We cried most of the night. We went back onto the streets the next morning more exhausted than when we checked in. That was when I knew we couldn't go on that way. We were ready just to turn ourselves in and die rather than to keep on like that.

Are you following all of this? Am I speaking too fast for you? I can slow down, if you wish. . . .

I shook my head. I had my notebook opened on the table. I was scribbling in my peculiar shorthand, making a show of it, as if this were the only record I would have of his story. I pretended to catch up to the words that I had failed to keep up with long before. I signaled that it was all right, he could keep going.

And he kept on talking, a great deal more, a steadily more incoherent and rapid stream of slurring Spanish until, later, even when I slowed down the tape, it was hard to understand him. What I gathered was that a factory manager helped him get a job under an assumed name. He moved his family out to a working-class slum on the outskirts of the city, where they blended in enough not to be noticed. They spent seven years in internal exile there, living so scared they hardly even associated with their neighbors. In their slum apartment, they practiced escaping police raids the way other families might have fire drills. As he talked on, his voice rose in pitch and volume ever more wildly, more out of control.

That's the way it was. Neighbors were afraid of neighbors. Husbands and wives grew so psychologically repressed that many couples started to give up making love out of the irrational fear they might somehow be discovered. It seems impossible to believe, but it's true. Nobody in this country has recovered. That's why you see so many young people now in the streets, kissing and feeling each other up so openly, in defiance of

149

their parents, and of the more traditional social rules. It's why the gay bars are so full. Why there's now so much pornography, and prostitution is all over the city. Do you understand? Do you see it? Do you feel how this country is trying in about two years to make up for all it has missed? Don't you see what's happening? How can people not try to find out the meaning of their freedom? How can they not? Tell me. That's what you should be writing down! That's what needs to be written!

One of his hands came down on the table so hard that his cigarette jumped from the ashtray and rolled off onto the floor. He was waving his smoke-yellowed fingers through the air in emphatic, wild gestures. He weaved around, and back and forth, in his seat, his speech thick and drunken. His voice had grown so loud he was almost shouting. I held up a hand as though to steady him, to calm him down, but it was no use. I told him to listen to me. It was all right now. If he talked any louder, we were going to be asked to leave.

That's what I'm saying! It's a free country now! Let them kick us out on the streets!

Jorge was shouting. The eyes of a group of waiters at the restaurant door turned away from us, the same way they might if they were witnessing a family argument. Jorge stood up then, suddenly, having difficulty keeping his feet. He leaned heavily onto the back of his chair to keep his balance. He started waving for the waiter in a crazy way. It was late in the afternoon. The other tables, never all full, were now long since empty of diners. The waiter was quickly at the table with a check on a plastic tray.

I stood up and reached for the check. Jorge lurched around the table and pushed me roughly away.

Thanks very much for the lunch. I hate to be the little bird that eats and flies away, but I'm late now. I have apartments to show this afternoon.

I tried to grab again for the check. But he held it tightly in his fingers and wouldn't let go. We struggled for a moment, pulling on the check between us. He started slapping at my hand.

That's all right! It's fine! Stop it! What is this? Don't you think I can be a host in my own country?

I let go of the check. Jorge took a long step back and grinned, drunkenly, as though he were holding a winning ticket at a horse race. He held the check up and looked at it without blinking. He reached into his threadbare jacket for his wallet. Loose cards and identification he had not properly fitted back into their holders began to flutter out of the wallet like so many falling leaves. The waiter was standing there again, close enough to jump in and pick up the cards and set them on the table. I watched, my mouth dry, and with an empty, sour feeling in my stomach. Jorge picked up his scattered cards and stashed them away. Then his fingers reached into the rag of his wallet and pulled out all the money there was. He tossed the few bills casually at the waiter, as thoughtlessly as if he were rich, and there was a good tip in there, too. The ragged flaps of his wallet clapped closed again on nothing.

There. That was a fine lunch. Good to see old friends, isn't that right? And maybe, someday, if I get lucky, you can host me for dinner in your country. What I'm saying is, maybe we'll meet again. Or maybe we won't. Either way, it doesn't make any difference. Are we agreed? Well? Agreed?

I said I agreed. I said I hoped he would make it. Then I didn't know what else to do but stretch out my hand. Jorge Gallo looked at my hand there for a second, not moving. Then he seemed to remember something, and he reached out and shook my hand just once, coldly.

Pardon me . . .

He pushed past the waiter, who moved a chair out of the way just in time. Then he weaved his way around other obstacles of

151

chairs and restaurant tables, staggering and pushing his way out the revolving door, and he was gone.

After he was out of sight of the windows, I reached into my jacket pocket. I pulled out the tape recorder and checked it carefully. The red light was off. The tape had run out. I wondered at just what point in his story the machine had stopped recording.

Archives

A FEW DAYS later, I again attended the trials. The tension was high around the Palace of Justice. A former *presidente de facto* of the nation testified against his colleagues in the military. General Alejandro Lanusse had been one of the more benevolent transition generals. He had governed before the first infamous return to democracy, when Juan Perón came back from his exile in Spain. From the witness stand, the general stated to his nation without once equivocating, *I cannot conceive of military groups acting outside of the law without the knowledge of the comandantes of the military junta.*

What he said was a damning piece of evidence against the latest tactic of the defense for the comandantes, that they did not know of the human rights abuses carried out under their command.

It was early afternoon when the session let out. I went across the street from Tribunales to the café Petit Colón, a famous place where lawyers, solicitors, and spies for the defense and prosecution compared notes and shared drinks and coffees. Around the tables, the talk was of nothing else but how the trials would proceed. With this unexpected, damaging testimony by General Lanusse, would the prosecution continue to be successful in imposing its unprecedented demands for a civilian tribunal without any last-minute surprises? Or would the defense, aided by the intense pressure from the armed forces on the new democratic government, even to the threat of letting tanks and armored vehicles loose in the streets, finally succeed in declaring any civilian trial illegal in favor of military courts-martial for men who were, after all, still generals and admirals of the nation?

I finished my own coffee, listening to bits and pieces of the conversations all around me. I reviewed my tapes of the morning sessions and tucked them in my shoulder bag. I stepped out of the elegant café into a day that had turned briefly and surprisingly sunny. Across the plaza stood the court building, its high white steps and polished columns gleaming in the sun, waiting for tomorrow's session of the trials to resume. Still, the streets around the Palace of Justice and the tree-lined plaza were like an armed camp. Police barricades were set up, blocking all approaches to the building. Dozens of federal police strolled around the plaza, patrolling back and forth along the barricades. Others remained positioned on the steps of the court building, standing guard in a bored-looking way.

I started off down the street, heading for the CELS offices, the Centro de Estudios Legales y Sociales. Papá Benevento's day in court was coming up soon. I was supposed to pick up passes for Betty Ann and me to sit with the family in the main gallery when that happened. My press pass wasn't good for the public sections. I left the plaza behind me, all but deserted except for police.

I didn't particularly want to visit the CELS offices that day. I had plans to meet my wife in the afternoon, after she had finished some shopping she had been wanting to do that had been delayed by our forced move to San Miguel and the economic crisis. She had been growing frustrated, as I was, feeling locked away behind the walls, and with little time to spend together. I had expected that the court testimony would carry over until afternoon and I would go directly from the trials to meet her. But the testimony had concluded early. I realized that I might have been avoiding a visit to the CELS organization all along, not wanting to confront the archives, and the dark news I felt sure I would find there. But I had to do it sometime, so I set off slowly, leaving the police and the barricades behind. As I walked along, I was suddenly struck by the welcome feeling of the sun on my face and neck. For a moment, I found my mind clearing of the sounds of my tapes, the sounds of so many words, and of too many silences.

The CELS was located in an old, run-down office building on Rodríguez Peña Street. The street was in a crumbling business district about eight blocks from the Palace of Justice and the Petit Colón. The offices of the CELS took up the whole second floor of the building. Looking up at the headquarters from the sidewalk, I saw that most of the windows were open. I wondered about this. It was an organization that had been under continual threats of violence. I thought how easy it would be to pitch a small bomb or a hand grenade through one of the windows from just where I was standing. After I entered the building, the only security for the human rights organization seemed to be a locked metal door to the entrance. The door had a tiny caged porthole in it, and there was an intercom speaker in the hallway.

I rang the buzzer. Part of the nose and one eye of a woman appeared in the porthole. I later found out she was one of the mothers of the Plaza de Mayo, a tough-looking, heavyset peasant woman in a common, frayed housedress. She looked as if she had just finished a load of laundry and was about to start scrubbing floors. She sized me up with a quick but careful inspection. I discovered that that was her job. She was a volunteer that day, one whose duty it was to decide who to let in or not to let in, and, in extreme cases, to call the police. I asked her how she knew who was who, especially with so many foreigners and unknown visitors to the offices. "Just an instinct," she said. "Don't ask me how. I just know."

The mother of the Plaza de Mayo led me through offices crowded with stacks of files. Cabinets spilled over with documents. The place was like the worst combined nightmare of at least a hundred clerks and secretaries. Folders of paperwork were stacked all around, rising up from the floor in columns so high they reached to my chest. In this sea of storm-tossed papers, there were about twenty islands of desks at which young lawyers, legal assistants, typists, clerks, and volunteers were busy in the production of even more documents and papers. The clattering of so many typewriters made a noise that people had to shout over to be heard. So, here it was. In these rooms were gathered most of what remained of more than ten thousand cases of the disappeared, and at least thirty thousand cases of illegal imprisonment, torture, and other abuses.

The CELS was like a miniature combination of the American Civil Liberties Union and the Nuremberg archives. In some sense, it was also like a police station. People came to its offices and turned themselves in, asking to give evidence and make statements. Lawyers and stenographers then led them off into small, brightly lit rooms for questioning. The legal staff took depositions, sworn testimonies, statements that would add to the volumes of paperwork and evidence that were being gathered for prosecutions. Three years had passed since the military regime had rolled up most of the razor wire from around their concentration camps, and still, each month, hundreds of scared and nervous people came in through the locked steel doorway, past its lone security system based on human instinct, willing now to risk their lives to give evidence about new or as yet undiscovered cases.

The staff of the CELS dutifully took down all the information they could gather. But there were already thousands too many cases to deal with in any detail, to investigate for the corroborative evidence necessary to "officialize" the numbers and add them to the tragic totals of the disappeared that seemed to go on mounting without end. There just weren't enough staff, enough volunteers, enough grant-funding and private contributions to do such an overwhelming job. Everywhere I looked, I saw scenes of young lawyers and their assistants treading water in this ocean of papers, just trying not to drown. The main job at hand was to look past the prosecutions of the comandantes, the generals and admirals, and begin to prepare the several hundred cases against lower-ranking officers in the military and the police who were guilty of human rights abuses. This was considered more dangerous work than anything the CELS had attempted so far. There were more than one thousand former torturers and murderers from the era of the dictatorship who were still on active duty. The new democracy's Senate had recently voted most of these former death squad officers pay raises and promotions.

After putting in his mornings at Papá's law office, Martín Segundo Benevento spent most of his afternoons working at the offices of the CELS, his meager salary paid for by a United Nations grant through the doomed agency UNESCO. Martín worked in a section that was busy gathering evidence about the locations of small concentration camps in the interior provinces of Argentina. He was helping the CELS to document the existence of more than one hundred illegal rural detention camps that had ranged in size

157

from a capacity of five to as many as fifty prisoners at a time. These camps had certain design features in common. Each was equipped with an interrogation room that had a metal table with leather straps, and an electric device of variable current and amperage that ended in a long, slim metal prod. Generally, each had its cramped concrete cells. Each had its killing room, with running water and a hose handy for washing down.

As Martín Segundo informed me, the camps had individual methods of disposing of bodies. In the early days, many were shipped off in army or navy airplanes and then dumped off from thousands of feet into the River Plate. Disemboweled corpses then washed ashore in Uruguay, including the bodies of three boys under the age of fifteen. This carelessness by the military resulted in an international incident that even reached the back pages of the newspapers in North America, and so the methods changed.

In the provinces, the bodies of the disappeared were customarily tossed into unmarked trenches, long shallow holes dug by the victims themselves, then they were shot in place and covered with lime. This procedure followed an instruction pamphlet distributed to district commanders that had been drawn up exactly following the techniques of mass murder invented by the SS Einsatzkommandos in the early years of World War Two. At some of the larger camps, where such open shootings might have drawn too much attention, the bodies were dragged out to specially designed steel trash bins at night. They were cremated among piles of used tires, so that the pungent black smoke of burning rubber might mask the smell of burning flesh. The ashes were then hauled away in trucks of garbage. Some of these large camps, such as the one at the Campo de Mayo army base just outside Buenos Aires, built crematoriums out of red bricks, very similar in design to the ovens at Dachau, but smaller in scale.

Then there were other camps that were so bold in their methods that they simply loaded the bodies onto army trucks and drove them to established cemeteries. There were differences in the kinds of mass graves that were being found. The ones that were dug by army soldiers had the bodies tossed into them every which way. When the death squad soldiers were too lazy to dig their own holes, they simply roused the cemetery grave diggers in the middle of the night and ordered them at gunpoint to dig the graves with machinery, put the corpses in them, and keep their mouths shut about it or else. The mass graves dug by the grave diggers and later located and denounced in testimony by them had the bodies all laid out neatly, hands crossed, eyes closed, all of them facing upward in the earth. "Interred with some decency," stated one of the workmen, "so we wouldn't carry any of the blame, then be pursued by their unquiet spirits."

I stood by Martín Segundo's gray metal desk, watching him reading quickly through folders of testimony. Martín was relieved to have a visitor to break up the monotony of his painstaking chore of sorting through the scattered mountains of papers piled around him. Today, Martín was working through dozens of folders of testimony and depositions, trying to combine elements of them into one big file that would contribute to a case the CELS was planning to bring against the adjutant commander of a concentration camp in the mountainous jungle province of Tucumán.

"At first, my job was to work on cases relating to what happened here in Buenos Aires," Martín explained. "But I kept running across the names of my friends. That was just too depressing, so I asked to be transferred to our project for the provinces. It's still a shitty job. But this way, at least it's more professional. I can be more objective about what I'm doing."

Martín gestured at the piles of folders on his desk. He shrugged his shoulders in a way that showed that what he was trying to do was impossible.

"Today, we're going after one Comisario Inspector Roberto Heriberto Albornoz. He was a provincial police inspector in Tucumán. He allegedly helped to make a detention camp out of his own central police headquarters. An army officer came in to oversee the tortures and murders of at least eighty people we know about up until now.

"Do you understand how this works? It's not Albornoz we want. This police commissioner was probably not the actual guy who turned up the voltage on the electric torture machine. He may not even have wanted his headquarters to be a camp. He might have been ordered to do it or else. But we're going after the police commissioner in order to get at the army officer, who was a lieutenant colonel. We think we've got enough evidence on Albornoz that we can force him to break his silence and agree to testify against the colonel. We've got a lawyer going up to Tucumán the day after tomorrow to see how many witnesses have the courage to give depositions against their own commissioner of police. It's the shits in the provinces. It's so much harder to convince witnesses that they're going to be safe. Now there's even a rumor that this new democracy is going to cut off the trials after the nine comandantes are convicted. That's the real trouble with this kind of work. We're never sure anything we're doing is going to have results.

"And now, because you yanquis are pulling out of UNESCO, the grant funding for my miserable salary here will probably be cut off. That's the way it is. On the other hand, personally, I'll be glad enough to get out of this. I'd rather be in commercial law anyway," he said. "In this country, commercial law is the only way to make any significant money."

Martín Segundo took a break from his desk and showed off the offices of the CELS. In an adjoining room of desks that looked very much like the one he worked in, save for a different messy arrangement of columns of paperwork, Martín introduced me to a young lawyer from Alabama. The yanqui was managing to get along rustily in an odd Spanish that had a marked southern drawl to it. He was on a grant from the American Bar Association to study human rights cases in the Third World. He would spend three months in Argentina and then move on to Sri Lanka.

"Here. Dennis, Diego, my brother," Martín introduced us in English. "You two should get together sometime and compare notes on your work for the Company," he said.

"What's this shit about the Company?" I asked in the hallway. The hallway was so packed with stacks of paperwork that people had to walk up or down it in single file.

"It's just our little joke," Martín said. "The CELS has long suspected that the CIA has sent agents here. Not so much now, but when the organization first started working, when Reagan was elected president and before the military regime was driven from power. Any North American who comes here is immediately burned by the joke. It's just office policy. Our way of letting the yanquis know that we don't care, and that what's strange is that while we're sure there have been spies sent here, why bother to send them? Almost anybody who wants to can come in openly and look at anything he likes if he only asks us in the proper way. We've got nothing to hide here." Martín stopped in the crowded hallway and turned to face me. He sensed how irritated I was at what he had said.

"It's just a joke! Don't get all heated up!"

"Okay, forget it," I said.

"We've got to do something to cut through the boredom," Martín said.

He opened the door to a big room at the end of the hallway. Two women clerks were sitting at a long table, looking like cataloguers in a library. They were selecting certain cards from boxes, then transferring information from them to other cards that were in their typewriters. Around them, on all four walls, the room was lined with filing cabinets.

"This is the main file room," Martín said. "Over here," he said, gesturing to one full wall of cabinets, "are the files of people who have been officially declared as disappeared. This section of files that covers two walls are the other cases, the twenty thousand more we suspect are disappeared but as yet don't have enough evidence about to make their names official. Then in these other cabinets are the names of those confirmed as dead, like the ones who supposedly died in gun battles. You'll find Miguelito's case in there, the original file. Papá said that he brought the copy home for security reasons. He said he was going to show it to you."

"I haven't seen it yet," I said. "He's been working in the city. And we've been out at San Miguel, as you know."

"That's maybe best," Martín said. "Take my word for it. Showing it to you himself would be too hard on him."

"Understood," I said.

"It's a simple system. All the files are alphabetical, except that section of the unknown and unconfirmed, in which we have only denunciations by eyewitnesses of unknown persons who were carried off. Those files are organized by dates. Here," Martín said. He moved quickly over to one of the tall banks of drawers and slid one open. "This one. This is Miguelito's case," he said, stepping back from the open file drawer a little too quickly. "But I want you to know that I don't approve of Papá testifying. Or if he does, he should not do so in Miguelito's case. I feel this way not only on personal grounds. It's just that we have stronger cases. Papá was not being objective to push so hard for this one. There are some things in Miguelito's file which could cause us problems."

"Are you sure?" I asked. "How could the family rest without trying to bring his case out in the trials?"

"Legally speaking, I just think it's a waste," Martín said. "More, it's a total disaster for the family. The first question the Examining Magistrate is going to ask Papá is if he knew of Miguel's involvements with the militancy. What's Papá going to answer but the truth? Then the defense will use the Nuremberg argument. The death squad that shot and killed Miguel was only following orders in a war against so-called subversives, and the comandantes were justified in time of war. That's what they'll say. So it's not the ideal kind of case to use at the trials. But Papá will testify, and we'll be there, of course, supporting him. I tell you, I can't wait until all of this is finished and we can get back to some kind of normal life again in this family. Not that that's ever really going to be possible, but you know what I mean."

"Sure," I said. "You don't have to explain."

"Here. Give me the passport numbers. I'll get you both registered for passes to the trials. Then I've got mountains of work to do. Let's see each other on Friday. We'll take the car. Alicia and I will pick you up. We'll have a night out on the town, *che*, drinking and dancing, just the four of us, for a change. You can't spend all your time just thinking about all of this or you'll end up going crazy."

I agreed. I thanked him. I said we'd look forward to going out with Martín and his wife on Friday. Then Martín hugged me around the shoulders like a brother, and started on his way out of the room. He stopped in the doorway, turned, and said, "Alejo has a file in there, too. It's in the big cabinet marked 'Disappeared without a trace.' But there's nothing to his file. Just a name, a date, his photograph, and various declarations Papá made in front of judges."

He gave me a quick wave of his hand and went back to his desk. I faced the archives. The women at the long table in the middle of the room kept sorting through their cards. The keys of their typewriters were clattering. They had hardly glanced up from their work during the conversation, as if such talk in this room were nothing unusual. I turned to the cabinet drawer Martín had left open. I let my fingers glide over the packed stacks of file folders, then they stopped. I pulled the folder out. It was in my hands. For a long moment, I couldn't open it and look inside. I only stared at the typed name, BENEVENTO, Miguel Angel. Beside that, there was a date, in parentheses, with a question mark after it, (8/12/77) ?

I opened the folder. The first thing I saw was the black-and-white police photograph of a Miguelito I had never known. It was the frail, lanky body of a youth who was skin and bones. His limbs were spread out with odd angularity over the pulled-back and very clean white sheets of a single bed. There were six bloodless bullet holes in his chest. His hair was ragged and messy. The face had a beard that looked like black moss growing across the starved bones of his skull. His eyes were closed. They looked blackened, cavernous, the head turned to one side on the mattress, and at an odd angle as if the neck had been broken. There was something else that was strange. The body was dressed in clean boxer shorts that looked some off color, maybe olive green, and the same cut as standard military issue.

I felt queasy suddenly. I couldn't look at the photograph anymore. I hid it in some papers at the back of the file. I took a deep breath. Then I went on, looking over some of the testimony. The point of most of the depositions and declarations was that Miguelito had been seen in the detention center called the Club Atlético. Two prisoners who had been tortured, then identified as "parsleys" by the interrogation squads, the military's code word for the ones they tortured and then let go, had positively identified Miguelito from photographs. One of them had overheard Miguel shouting out his name until the noise was stopped. There was a small note in the file that stated, "accompanying testimony, Martín

Alejandro Benevento, father." I searched through the file for those pages but couldn't find them.

There were numerous other documents. Some of them were forensic reports on Miguelito's body. They were written in complex medical terms, a kind of Spanish that was hard for me to fully comprehend. The gist of them seemed to be that there were significant signs on Miguelito's remains, which had been exhumed. Both his legs and his pelvis had been broken. The bones in the legs had started to heal but the pelvic bone hadn't before his death. There was also some question about the gunshot wounds. I wondered what that could mean.

I paged through to the official story, a series of cold, factual statements from the Buenos Aires federal police. According to police reports, they were called about shots being fired, and responded. At the scene, they saw men with guns jump into a car and speed away. They entered the apartment and stated they found Miguel's body just as it was shown in the photograph. The death was classified as "killed in a gun battle with persons unknown." The apartment was rented in the name of one Juliana María de Martínez, "whereabouts not known." End of story. There was an added comment from an investigator at the CELS. It stated that a young woman with the same name and address was included among the unconfirmed cases reported to the organization as "believed disappeared without a trace."

I had read enough. I replaced the file gently in the cabinet and shut the drawer. I was about to leave, but then stopped. I crossed the room quietly. Neither of the two file clerks seemed to notice I was there. I went to the larger bank of files of the confirmed cases of the "disappeared without a trace." Even among the nearly ten thousand folders, Alejo's was easy to find. It was so thin. Almost empty. Reading the name on its small typed sticker, *BENEVENTO,*

Alejandro Martín—19-11-76, had a numbing finality to it that felt like ice inside my chest.

Inside the folder, there was a small photograph of Alejo. It was a snapshot copy of the big blowup that Mamá had tacked to her sign for the Plaza de Mayo. Alejo was shown in three-quarters profile, his sharp nose raised as if sniffing the good air of San Miguel like a Sunday gentleman. The shape of his mouth looked as though he had just finished a big laugh, his eyes full of life and of amusement, his gaze directed a little to one side as if he were still sharing a good joke with someone off camera.

It was strange, and affecting, to see this photograph of Alejo so reduced, to be able to hold this last image of him in the palm of my hand. I searched, numbly, through the few other pages. There was a list of declarations in front of judges. There was a page that referred to other files of supporting depositions from the family. The only other document was a note that read, "Last whereabouts confirmed by telephone call the afternoon of 19/11/76—re: Benevento, Martín Alejandro Segundo."

I dropped the photograph back in the folder. I closed the thin file and replaced it, carefully, in the crowded cabinet. Even with the noise of the typewriter keys behind my back, I felt how quiet the two clerks were being, and how silent I felt inside myself. The four walls with their thousands of names were watching in silence. I had come here looking for news of my brothers. I had found it, a few papers excavated from a mass grave of papers. It struck me then. That was all there was. That was all we would ever know.

I met Betty Ann at a small café on the Avenida Santa Fe. She had a new hairstyle, cut as short as though it would soon be summer, the color changed to a more auburn shade of blond. She was seated at a table next to a big window that looked out over the tiled walks of the avenue, which was like a Parisian boulevard.

She was writing postcards as she sipped from a glass of wine. She didn't see me until I was next to her at the table. She stood up excitedly and threw her arms around me.

"Here's the plan," she said happily. "I left word with Mamá that we're staying in the city tonight. I booked us rooms at the Plaza Hotel. You said that was the best hotel and I just went there first thing and got us a suite, sweetheart! What do you think? Don't we deserve a touch of luxury?" she said. "Honey? What's wrong? Sweetheart?"

"Nothing," I said. I forced a smile. "A long day . . . How . . . ah . . . never mind," I said.

"My hair? I had to do something to get all the paint out of it," she said. "Come on. What do you think?"

"Really fine. It looks great," I said. I was fighting to contain a sudden panic about how much money her plan would cost. She could hardly know that it had been two months since I had made the payment on the American Express card. I wondered how close to the limit we were on our other credit card. Short of a small miracle, we would soon run out of cash. But she had done what she had done, and it was too late. I reached into my pocket and tossed a few new crisp bills on the table to pay for her wine.

We walked through a blustery evening wind coming off the river. Off across the Plaza San Martín with its famous statue of the general on horseback leading his troops across the Andes, his arm raised and gesturing toward final victory, the elegant Hotel Plaza stood with its flags of many nations whipping colorfully in the wind. Going through the doors was like a plunge into the luxury of another era. Heavy brass fixtures gleamed. There was rich, dark red carpeting, crystal chandeliers, clerks and bellhops in starched uniforms as striking as full livery. The people milling in the lobby were prosperous-looking, in tailored suits and designer fashions, fur coats, walking on glove-leather Italian-style shoes. Crossing through so much ostentatious richness after where I had been that day did nothing for my mood.

Betty Ann proudly unlocked the door to the large two-room suite, showing it off. She moved her hips and shoulders with seduction. I saw piles of bags and boxes spread out on the bed and looking like Christmas. She began to chatter away about all the bargains she had seen that day and hadn't been able to resist. I sank slowly into a heavy French chair that was covered with brocaded silk. The feeling of that chair made my back and shoulders stiffen.

Betty Ann showed off her purchases. There was a hand-knit angora wool sweater for Heather, deep burgundy ponchos of alpaca wool for each of her four sisters, tooled leather handbags for both our mothers, two kidskin jackets of a modish Italian design from the Marisol shop, one for her and one for me, a pair of patent-leather sling heels from Botticelli, a pair of knee-high calf-leather boots she had bought for herself at Ferraro. The quantity and quality of the other items she was spreading out all over the room seemed to multiply before my eyes, lingerie trimmed with Spanish lace, perfumes and colognes, wood and pottery souvenirs. My panic was growing. I didn't want to look at anything else. Money. It was the one topic between us that could always lead to raised voices and then hurt feelings that lasted for days. She had spent far more than she realized. But that was her way. Whenever she felt repressed, trapped, boxed in, she got out the credit cards and the checkbook and simply let loose. I was about to say something. I knew better. I just lifted a hand up and shielded my eyes.

"What do you mean?" she said. "These boots only cost us eighty dollars. Where could I get a pair as nice as these anywhere else? And at that price? Don't you see we're really saving money?"

I nodded my head, slowly, afraid to speak.

"Look. Try a little romance for a change. Some of this is especially for you," she said. She held a wine-colored lace pegnoir and negligee up to her body. I glanced at it quickly and nodded my head. "I get to feeling happy for once, even excited to be in this country, and look what you're doing," she said. "I need a drink."

She left me alone in the bedroom, on her way to the bottle and ice in the elegant sitting room. What she had said was true. When it came to money, I was definitely unromantic. I was self-concerned, unappreciative, blind. I was rotten, imposing, oppressive. Worse, I was cheap. Telling her that we were shorter on money than she knew, under these circumstances, would make me even cheaper. I heard her angrily rattling the ice in her glass. I was imagining the accusations she was thinking up to hurl at me, and I admitted to myself they were true. Without saying a word, I was guilty as charged.

She came back into the room, her drink in hand. She had thought to make one for me, and she set it down on the antique table next to my chair.

"I'm sorry," I said. "It's been a hard day. Thank you. Thank you for thinking this up for us."

She raised her glass at me and I raised mine, declaring a truce. Then she spread her arms out and whirled around a few times, marveling out loud about the elegance of the hotel, ending her graceful dance by taking flight toward the big four-poster bed. She landed on it like a diver breaking water. "Look! Look at this bed! Real down pillows! Do you realize that we haven't had a decent bed since we got here?"

She rolled over and stretched out, primping up her new short hairstyle and giving me a look that invited sex. She lay back there, happy in her surroundings. The thought struck me that she had saved up months of her part-time teaching checks just to be here, only to end up suddenly in hiding with my family. And she had hardly complained as so many cold, dark days were rolling past into little or nothing. "Come on. Admit it. Isn't this wonderful? Right here? Isn't it fantastic?"

"Sure it is. And so are you," I said.

I tossed my drink down and lifted myself out of the chair. I started for the bed, meaning to climb in next to her and give her a kiss.

"First help me pull off these new boots," she said.

We made love. I wanted to concentrate my mind and energies only on her, losing myself in her arms. But there was nothing I could do to get over my distance. I had always had a good memory for photographs. Some, from newspapers I might have seen twenty years before, I could still envision exactly. The photographs that now rose up startlingly like flashes going off in my brain, the ones of Alejo and Miguel, I couldn't get rid of for more than a few seconds. Love, laughter, forgetting was impossible. Twice, she pulled away, breaking off, pushing me up enough to look into my face. "What's wrong?" she asked.

"Nothing," I said, the first time. The next, I shook my head, pushed my lips against hers, and continued, sadly, as best I could.

Later, she got up to run a bath, and went into the next room for the bottle of scotch. I rose from the bed and sat down in the silk-covered French Provincial decadence of the suite. I was spooked by it. With every move I made, I was sure I would topple the antique lamp, drop a lit cigarette on the chair, spill something unremovable on the Persian rugs. I wasn't made for a room like this. I felt as uncomfortable and as at a loss as the one or two times in my life I had rubbed elbows with the excessively rich, feeling small and inferior to them, and always judged by them, despite knowing better. I felt the same way about this room.

I went into the gilt-fixtured bathroom, where Betty Ann was indulging in a perfumed bath. Her drink and an ashtray were balanced on the ledge. I sat down on the edge of the tub, took up a sponge, and started scrubbing her back. There was a strange pressure in my hands, an eerie sensation that I was somehow not quite attached to them.

"Are you all right?" she asked.

I said yes, I was fine.

"Listen, I was planning to have dinner sent up to the room. But what do you say we dress and go downstairs? Later, we'll order champagne and really enjoy this place."

She dressed in a gauzy strapless gown I had not seen before. I put on my good suit, which she had packed for me. It was just a little too large, blue and three-piece, and made me look, I thought, like a no-longer-young banker who had just run through his luck.

We rode the liveried elevator down to the lobby. I watched her striding through the lobby in her heels. Her body was held gracefully erect, posed as though there were an elegant crowd that was noticing her. The restaurant was one of the most expensive in Buenos Aires. Under the crystal chandeliers, surrounded by the candlelit silver place settings, formal waiters strode back and forth under trays of artful French cuisine. I ordered a Bordeaux, a good Saint-Emilion, without looking at the price. I avoided the rest of the prices on the menu by handing mine to her and asking her to do the ordering.

She smiled, gladly. She struck a casual, luxurious pose for me across the table, reading the menu with a carelessness she must have imagined was characteristic of the wealthy. She felt and looked more at home at that moment than at any on our journey. We were in another world, sealed off from the city, in a place where she could feel intimate, safe, and rich. It was clear that she wanted me, all hers, in this dream.

After marveling like a schoolgirl at the luxury of our surroundings, she changed the topic, trying to draw me in. She asked me about my day.

"Let's not talk about it," I said.

"Come on, sweetheart, tell me what happened."

"The same, you know, only maybe worse," I said. "I saw Martín at the CELS office. He showed me the files, Alejo's and Miguelito's. I saw the photographs of Miguelito's body. That's all that happened."

Something was thick in my throat. It was hard to speak. The last words came out in with a hoarse, scratching sound. I reached, quickly, for my wine. Betty Ann started to get up from her chair to go around to me.

"I'm okay," I said. I swallowed several times. I cleared my throat. I started to say something more but couldn't find my voice. I was having trouble seeing across the table, making out only sharp, glittering refractions of disorganized light. I brought my napkin up and tried to clear my eyes. I made involuntary sounds. My shoulders began heaving as if someone were shaking them. "I don't know," I managed to say. "I don't know . . ."

She stood beside me. Her hand reached down to the table and rested on mine, which was gripping the edge, trying to hold on.

"They were my brothers," I said. "And Alejo. Alejo. Alejo . . ."

She saw we were drawing attention from neighboring tables. The maître d' was on his way toward us across the room. She tried to help me out of my chair. I was out of all control by then. It must have felt to her as though some huge brute wrestler had clamped her husband in his arms and was shaking him up and down. She finally stopped that by holding me tightly. She managed to cancel our orders, sign for the wine, then get me up and out of the restaurant. I carried my napkin with me and buried my face in it.

In our rooms, I gave in to grief. She pulled the covers back from the pillows. She undid my tie and laid me down in the bed. She climbed in beside me and held on. It was a long time before I stopped. She coaxed me up and into a sitting position. She found a box of tissues and passed them to me.

"It's okay. I'm okay now," I said. As soon as I said that, I was knocked back again as if I had been kicked in the chest. "I'm sorry. . . . Sweetheart," I said, and then I was useless again.

"Quit this. That's enough now," she said.

I stopped again. She took me by the shoulders and gently lifted me back up into a sitting position on the bed. I blew my nose and wiped my eyes. I reached for her hand.

"I'm sorry," I said again. "This is your night, and look what I'm doing. Wait just a minute. We'll head downstairs again."

"We're okay right here," she said. "When you're ready, we'll call room service. The guidebook says that the room service here has five stars from the society of the best hotels in the world. This is my first time, you know," she said. She laughed sadly. "I've never been in one of the best hotels in the world."

She smoothed my hair back. Then she reached over and hugged my head to her breasts. I closed my eyes. I breathed in her perfume. I pressed my cheek into that deep warm place. A moment came when I could finally pull my head away and straighten up. I cleared my throat. I smiled, and kissed her cheek. I braced my arms against the bed and started to lift myself to my feet. Then it happened again. I couldn't stand up. I was lost, floating, gone, as if a huge breaker had crashed in without warning and knocked me right off the beach.

"Dear, dear," she said. "Oh, my dear. . . ."

Tango

THAT WEEK, THE internal caucus was held by the Unión Cívica Radical—the Radical Party, the party of the new president—to choose candidates for the congressional elections. The new democracy was less than two years old. The nation looked on, thinking of its future, as the president opened the sessions in the provincial capital of Santa Fe. On the second afternoon, seen on televisions across the land, the caucus suddenly broke up in disorder. With angry shouting, politicians in the hall rose up out of their seats. Several contending candidates for the primaries then pulled revolvers and started shooting at each other.

The talk in the streets of Buenos Aires that day was filled with comment on the vulnerability of elections to this faster, more final method of selecting candidates. There was a dark mood of insecurity and fear, and an outrage that such a thing could happen yet once again, as in the 1930s, when the old Conservatives sometimes acted like gangsters, shooting at each other or at their enemies. The new Radical Party was supposed to be more civilized. A resignation was setting in among the people that such was the nature of the political process. Even the supposedly most liberal, humane, and democratic of their political parties was tainted by a heritage of violence.

The Justicialista Party, the coalition of Peronists, which had gone down to defeat in the first election after the dictatorship, began to celebrate this ultimate failure of words by its enemies. Peronist leaders dominated radio and TV broadcasts, shouting insults and shaking their fists, taking oratorial potshots at the Providential President for not being able to keep order in his own house. This, when the Peronists had become world-famous in past eras for knocking each other off, especially inside the huge labor unions, engaging in blood feuds that resembled mafia wars.

That night, Martín Segundo and his wife, Alicia, picked us up at the Hotel Plaza for a night on the town. Like almost everyone in Buenos Aires, we talked about the situation. Maybe it was really a conceptual problem, I offered. I went on to explain that by conceptual problem, I meant the fact that in Argentina, and perhaps generally in Latin America, the idea of compromise has always been equated with defeat. "As far as I know, there isn't even a word in Spanish that means 'compromise,' at least not in the sense it has in English," I said. "What would it be? *Compromiso?* Which means an obligation, a duty, a necessary appointment, a place one has to be in, or a position one's forced to take whether he likes it or not?"

"Forget that idea, yanqui," Martín Segundo said. He was at the wheel of his little Renault, the two of us sitting in front, our wives in back. "This government is self-service, not civil service. What's at stake is the right to rob from the treasury. It's no wonder politicians are ready to shoot one another for the chance to get filthy rich."

It was a Friday night. We were all riding in Martín's little car, bouncing along over the part-pavement, part-cobblestone boulevard that ran along the port into the district of the city called La Boca. Alicia had recently been in a fender-bender with the small car. It was still drivable, but the two women had to squeeze in tightly against each other to the right of the backseat, leaning their weight over the right tire. If they moved too far to the other side, the left rear tire would scrape against the dented fender, the car filling with the smell of burning rubber. Even leaning to the right side like that, when the car hit a bump or a pothole, the tire hit the fender, squealing. Martín laughed.

"He's just not practical," Alicia said to Betty Ann, but intending to be overheard. "We could just as easily have taken a taxi," Alicia said. "But nothing was going to spoil it for him. He wanted to take us for a drive."

Martín turned in the seat and asked Betty Ann in English, "Aren't the lights of this city fucking wonderful like this, in this fucking car? Fucking right?"

"They really are," Betty Ann said.

"When Martín wants something, he just does it," Alicia said. "In Paris, I used to have to watch out. He might spend all the money in one night. Once, they closed our bank account. So I started writing the checks. He's lucky he found me to take care of him," she said. "Isn't that right, fatso?"

She leaned a little forward in the seat and socked him, hard, on the shoulder. The tire squealed underneath us, a blue smoke cloud trailing behind. Martín laughed.

"I'm the one who's impractical in our house," Betty Ann said.

"I'm the one who bounces checks. Usually it's when Mr. Cheap-skate here starts to gripe about money. It's really the only thing we ever fight about, how cheap he can be sometimes."

"I know what you mean," Martín said. "I remember that about this yanqui. Always the last to pull his money out when we were students. We say here that such people have crocodiles in their pockets. *Un cocodrillo en el bolsillo.* Get it? The big lizard bites your hand if it reaches for the money? And how did you call that fuck-ing thing? A cheapskate? Does that make any fucking sense? It's a strange fucking language, this fucking English," he said. "But it's clearly better to say fuck it all and spend all the fucking money you can than to feed it to the fucking crocodile. . . ."

"Just listen to this fatso's English," said Alicia in Spanish. "Swearing all the time. I hate it."

"What did she say?" asked Betty Ann.

"She said that I say fuck too much when I speak English," Martín said. "You have to forgive me. It's because I learned so much fucking English from your fucking yanqui movies. Aren't they always saying fucking this shit and that shit and all kinds of fucking things? You know what the fuck I'm saying?"

Everyone laughed. Martín then changed his parody, toning it down to the occasional off-color word, showing off his good Eng-lish for Betty Ann. We drove on into the port district of La Boca, the tire squealing as we made a hard turn. We entered the night.

"There's La Boca," Alicia said. "You see how the city becomes in-dustrial? You see the old port? Look at the colors of the houses. . . ."

"Tin houses," Martín said. "All painted blue, yellow, orange, very bright colors. The immigrants getting off the boats took boxes and crates from the port. They used the wood and tin to make these houses."

La Boca was gaily colored. The two- and three-story wood-and-tin buildings were leaning, cockeyed, some of them looking as if they might come tumbling down into the streets.

"This is where the tango singers started," Martín said. "We'll pass by the street in a minute named for Gardel."

The street named after Carlos Gardel was in total darkness. So was the famous Caminito Street, about which Gardel had sung such a nostalgic tango of homesickness and lost love. It was strange not to see the street lit up like a fiesta, the sidewalks filled with artists and musicians. I remembered there was a theater company that sometimes closed off the street and gave its plays using the cobblestones as a stage. The families who lived in the rickety tin houses set up chairs and sold tickets for their balconies and windows.

The whole of La Boca was almost deserted that night. As Martín cruised around, his spirits sinking, the car passed only a few local couples walking hand in hand. There was a bewildered-looking tourist or two, sitting behind the brightly decorated restaurant windows on the Calle de las Cantinas. The Calle de las Cantinas was one restaurant after another, red checkered tablecloths set up and waiting in almost all of them. Bottles of wine stood on the tables, with no one gathered around them. Normally, three- and four-piece tango bands would be playing away on a weekend night until dawn.

"What is this fucking shit?" Martín said. "Why is there nobody here?"

"Look. Even the boats are sinking," Alicia said. It was true. Among the old, leaning pilings of docks that jutted out into the dirty brown port canal, there was a rusting hulk of a steel cargo ship, listing over and ready to go under. Farther down the row of pilings, closer to the shore, at least two drag seine fishing boats were up to their decks in water. They must have been sitting on the shallow bottom. The dozen or so boats that were still floating looked as if they hadn't been painted in years. I remembered the port district as something very different. It was a loud, happy place the times I had been there.

"There must be something wrong," I said.

"Can it be it's just an off night?" Betty Ann asked.

"That's impossible," said Alicia. "When did we ever hear of a Friday night that was an off night in La Boca?"

"It must be the situation," Martín said. "It's the last weekend before the end of the month, when almost everybody gets paid. Even then, with this new money, who's going to go out and spend their penguins until they're sure they can pay the rent?"

"La Boca's not like this," Alicia said. "This isn't the Boca we know."

"Well, this is the fucking place," Martín said. He pulled the car over onto one of the side streets off the Avenida Pedro Mendoza. The curb stood about a meter and a half high. The sidewalks were raised because the streets flooded like canals when the river rose during storms. We got out of the car in front of a small, faded yellow sign that looked at least as old as the neighborhood. The sign was swinging gently in a light breeze. It hung from a rusty metal arm attached to the building under rows of broken and burned-out lightbulbs meant to show it off. The sign read *Club Alicia Duncan* and hung over a red-painted door. The door was closed. Behind the dirty curtains of the one small window, the place looked dark. "Could it be there's nobody fucking here?"

Martín tried the door, and it opened. We watched as he pushed his head and shoulders inside for a moment, then turned to us with a dejected look. "The place is open," he said. "But there's nobody here. What do you want to do?"

"Let's go anyway," said Betty Ann. "We'll have the place to ourselves."

"Sure, let's go," I said. "I need a fucking drink."

There were three other people inside the club—a piano player, a woman in a drab, funereal black dress who looked as though she had been wheeled in from a nearby nursing home, a bartender who was a stooped, elderly gentleman with stains on his tie and a look in his eyes as if he hadn't slept in twenty years; then there was Alicia Duncan herself, brightly painted, dressed in a glittering pink evening gown like a showgirl of another era. Sequins and rhinestones flashing, she stepped with energy toward the door and greeted us like a hostess. "Welcome! Come in! We have a great tango singer from the neighborhood tonight! Are you foreigners? English? Yanquis?" She started leading us over to a small table near the piano. It was covered with a yellow plastic tablecloth. A candle at its center had long ago burned into a puddle. "Don't I know you?" she asked Martín, sitting everyone down.

"I used to come in here," he said. "About ten years ago, this was a place I brought my girlfriends for a good time."

"Ah! You're such a love to come back!" Alicia Duncan leaned down and gave Martín a big hug and a kiss on the cheek. There was something very obviously obscene in the way she rubbed up against him. She turned her face toward Alicia and Betty Ann as she was doing this. "He's such a handsome boy, isn't he?" she said.

On closer look, Alicia Duncan must have been about seventy years old. Her face was all paint, makeup caked and powdered, her blond wig slipping a little as she left another lipstick smear on Martín's cheek. Then she stepped over, leaned down, and did the same thing to me. She pressed her body against my side, bumping and grinding me with her hips. Her hands slipped in under the table. She gave me a quick squeeze between my legs, right on target, so fast I didn't even have time to jump. Then she planted a kiss on my cheek and stepped away. "Come on, loves! Let's make a night of it! Whiskeys!" she called out to the old, tired man behind the bar. "Humberto!"

"I remember now," Martín said. "She'd do that to me when I came in here. She checks out the cock size of every man who walks into this place."

We all shared a laugh at the table. Then we watched the bartender shuffling toward us with great effort. The tray he was carrying trembled so much the ice cubes were rattling in the drinks. Martín pointed at his feet. He was wearing bedroom slippers. We struggled hard not to laugh at him as he served the drinks, so slow and shaky and decrepit in his movements it was a miracle none of them spilled.

"Alicia Duncan used to be a famous radio star," Martín said. "During the forties and fifties, the era of Juan Perón, she was a big personality. She was a singer and a sex symbol. She was famous for her love affairs, almost every one of them ending in a scandal. Some politicians spent more time in bed with Alicia Duncan than they did in office," he said. "When she got older, she started this club. She was still a great singer, when I used to come in here. The place was always packed. Never tourists, but the real people from the neighborhood. Now look at it," he said. "What a shame it's so empty now."

We looked around at the deserted tables. The place was in nearly total darkness, and there was a claustrophobic feeling. Looking out across the room was like looking into the depths of a cave. At the bar, Alicia Duncan sat on a high stool, in candlelight, sipping a drink. She waved at us with a big smile. We waved back. Then she slipped off her stool and stepped over to the piano, her movements rock-solid in her high heels.

"Music! We have music now!" she called out. She clapped her hands as if getting the attention of a crowded room. "Ladies and gentleman," she announced. "Our piano player is Rosa María Gultielli! She's the best barroom piano player in La Boca! Let's give her a hand!"

Alicia Duncan led the applause. We clapped loudly at our table, and again struggled to contain a kind of contagious fit of giggling among ourselves when Rosa María stood up from her piano bench and took several bows, even to various parts of the empty room, as if she were ready to give a concert at the Teatro Colón.

"Where are you people from?" Rosa María asked, after her bowing was finished. "North America? Ah, but how much I love all the old North American songs! What do you want me to play?"

"How about 'Green Dolphin Street'?" Betty Ann asked.

Martín translated the request into Spanish.

"I don't know that one," Rosa María said, unfazed. "But how about if I start with the theme song from the movie *Casablanca*?" She nodded her head at us and smiled as though we had enthusiastically agreed. There was a sudden expression in her eyes that made it clear she was either completely insane or drunk or probably both. She sat down behind her piano and started to play. "This song is called 'Como el tiempo pasa.' Can you listen to it the right way? It won't come out of the piano properly unless the audience knows the right way to listen."

"What's the right way to listen?" Martín asked.

"She is crazy," Alicia said. "A poor old crazy woman."

"She means when people are dancing to the music, they're listening in the right way," Alicia Duncan said, approaching our table.

"What did she say?" asked Betty Ann.

"She wants us to dance to it," I said.

"How is it possible to dance to 'As Time Goes Fucking By'?" Martín said.

"Let's go then." Betty Ann stood up out of her chair and pulled me to my feet. "Come on! Let's make them happy!"

"You tell him," Alicia Duncan said. Rosa María started off into the slow, dreamy melody of the song. I put my hand behind Betty Ann's back, leaned my cheek in against hers, and began moving my feet. Then Rosa María began to sing the words. They were strange in Spanish. Doubly so through that voice that was something between a coffee grinder and a basso kazoo. Martín clapped his hands and let go in a fit of laughter. Betty Ann and I shuffled across the gaudy linoleum dance floor. A lone and partly shredded red paper lantern dangled overhead.

"Dance! Enjoy yourselves!" Alicia Duncan called out from somewhere behind us. "That's it! The way you're listening is making it sound pretty good!"

Rosa María knew all the old cornball songs, "Stardust," "Sentimental Journey," "Moon River," "The Sunny Side of the Street," and others of mixed eras. Most of them were nearly impossible to dance to, but Betty Ann and I kept it up. We began to enjoy ourselves by at first acting out with each other and for Alicia Duncan that we were enjoying ourselves. Then we were holding each other tightly, totally gone into the slow dancing.

"So how come you two don't get up and dance?" Alicia Duncan said to Martín and his wife. Martín's wife, the other Alicia, didn't want to. Alicia hated to dance unless she could blend in with a large group of dancers. Martín made it up to Rosa María by having a whiskey sent to her piano.

Rosa María took a break from playing, and to rest her cement-mixer voice. Betty Ann and I sat down again and ordered more drinks.

"For me, this place was so important," Martín said in a quiet moment. There was an expression on his face that made it clear he was seeing this club the way it had been years ago. He would hold hands with his girlfriends, kiss them in the dark corners, draw them away and out the door to find a place to make love.

"The trouble was just starting to happen in this country. Our first friends were disappeared. Alejo and I had just gone underground. Sometimes, just to get away, that's all, I would catch a bus and come down here, alone or with a girl, in the middle of the night."

We sat for a while, quietly, drinking our whiskeys. Alicia Duncan was sitting at her bar, also drinking. It seemed hours had passed and the woman had a fresh drink in her hand every ten minutes. Then all of a sudden, there was a loud noise in the doorway, a whirling of coats and scarves and hats being taken off. A group of middle-aged people began taking seats at several tables. Alicia Duncan took one of the women by the hand and led her over to our table. "Do you remember this one?" she asked Martín. "This is the great Lucía Beruti, our best tango singer! Better even than me! Our program has changed! Listen to these tangos, my loves, and tell me if they aren't the best in the world!"

The tango singer looked old, worn out, her graying red hair clinging to her head in a messy home permanent. When a spotlight was switched on and found her next to the piano, it revealed a deep scar on her cheek that ran all the way from her left eye to her chin. Martín remarked that he was sure that some sad night in the past a husband or a lover had slashed her face with a knife. A small, gray man in a rumpled black suit, who had come in with her, suddenly pulled a chair up and unpacked an accordion-like instrument. He sat down, fading into the background save for his jumpy, manic half-dancing as he bent and bounced the unusual instrument over his knee, his *bandoneón,* a kind of combination of a concertina and accordion, filling the room with a sound of plaintive sadness.

The piano player jerked and swayed, attacking the keys in accompaniment to the accordion's minor chords of the first tango, quick and jumpy, then leading into a slower rhythm. The tango singer began to sing. She sang the lyrics with her whole body, pumping her arms and spreading them out dramatically. Her voice was magical, powerful, amazing, the kind of voice that made the whole room feel her sad vibrations. She stepped forward, opened her closed fists, punched the important words. The song was about a man who had left her behind, a man who had wronged her. There were places mentioned in the lyrics, street corners, bars, and houses in the neighborhood of La Boca that lived on in the song with the full force of passion and of tragedy. The lyrics were in a dialect called *lunfardo.* That was the language of the Italian immigrants to the port district who, in the first generation off the boats, began mixing their words with Spanish, then turning certain phrases around, inverting words even, peppering them with new slang expressions that rose up from the streets. The slang of her songs was so thick that even Martín couldn't understand it completely.

There was no question that this was a great tango singer. And these were no traditional tangos she was singing, but original songs and music, most of them, or tangos that were so much a part of an evolving neighborhood that the versions of them she sang no longer resembled anything that had been recorded. The people of La Boca must have known she was singing. Either that, or there really was a magic about her that moved out through the closed red door and past the darkened sign into the streets, drawing people in, first singly, then in small groups, until by her third sad tango, there were at least fifty sitting at the bar and at tables in the club.

The tango singer made the walls sweat and tremble and cry. Alicia Duncan was moving from table to table in her glittering gown, a joyous queen of her dark, smoky palace, laughing, ordering drinks, leaning over to kiss and touch all the men. There was no music I knew that was sadder. How strange that it caused so much happiness.

"This is more like it," Martín said. He slapped the table. "Fuck it, man! This is really a fucking good time!"

On an impulse, Martín jumped up out of his chair and put his arms around Alicia Duncan. He pulled her out onto the dance floor. Rosa María and the tango singer changed songs. The accordionist launched into a rapid, dancing beat that carried Martín and Alicia Duncan along in aggressive, quick tango steps. People around us began to clap their hands and cheer them on. Martín dipped the woman passionately at the end of his tango slide; she curved her back and thrust her breasts up against his body. Then she took over, moving him backward with a bold look of lust and desire. One of her sharp-nailed hands was digging into his flesh, then it moved over his body as if it couldn't get enough of him. Her steps and movements were smooth, graceful. She was on her toes, then she spun around in his arms with a speed and agility that seemed fantastic, considering her age. The tango ended on its final two accordion chords of sadness. Martín leaned over Alicia Duncan's body in a long, low dip. Then suddenly he French-kissed her and held the kiss romantically. The club was loud with cheering and applause, both dancers gone into their kiss, their eyes closed, a sense about them that they were traveling back over the years, lost in time, escaping everything.

Later, the four of us staggered out into the street, arms around each other, drunkenly trying to sing out lines from a tango. No one was in any condition to drive. Alicia—Martín's other Alicia— took the wheel, and we sped off toward the city. The rear tire screamed and burned against the dented fender. We laughed. We kissed and hugged each other. Martín and I gave each other knuckle punches on the shoulders as we did when we were kids.

We called each other "brother," riding through the wet deserted streets, looking out the windows from time to time as though we were no longer a part of what we were seeing. The world outside passed by in the windows like it was nothing more than a movie that was mostly darkness. Inside, we laughed. We hugged each other again. We kept on singing.

Miguelito

WE MOVED BACK to the confinement of San Miguel after our night of tango and our three-day weekend at the Plaza Hotel. We felt low and depressed. The reality struck home that we had spent in a few days more than the spare money we had left. Worse, we were avoiding each other, as though guiltily, waking up each morning just to get through the day. Betty Ann stuck close to Mamá and helped with domestic chores. I was in the small cottage most of the time, reviewing tapes, taking notes, waiting for what more I might learn at the trials. The weather changed. Temperatures dropped to freezing. Most days were misty, with a low covering of dark clouds. Looking out through the high iron fences of the estate, broke and irritable, we felt as limited and enclosed as if under house arrest.

The Sunday barbecue was held as usual at San Miguel. Even in the cold, the family set up tables under the trees. The Beneventos and their guests ate their meats and salads and drank their wine bundled up in sweaters, jackets, scarves, and hats. Jorge Gallo and his two young daughters were there. His girls cried easily. Any kind of brattiness was tolerated by their father, who was drinking too much, letting them run around, screaming, out of control. Jorge was in one of his more abusive, dark moods. He started ranting about yanqui exploitation of the world, forcing every country it could into "obscene consumerism." He directed his remarks straight at me, across the table. I gritted my teeth and pretended to ignore him. Only once did I ask a question—if he hated the United States so much, why was he trying to get a work visa and go there to live?

After the meal, Mamá and Betty Ann did winter chores in the gardens, mulching the flower beds. Papá and Martín retired to one of the bedrooms in the main house to review some legal papers for the trials, then sleep a siesta, while Alicia tried to quiet the children enough for a nap. Jorge staggered off to the guest cottage, appropriated my bed, and passed out cold.

That left Amalita and me still at the table, getting reacquainted. Amalita was a spinster, a close friend of the family. We called her Tía Amalia, like an aunt. I had vague memories from my year as an exchange student that this woman had been at family gatherings, holiday tables, even at graduation from secondary school with Martín Segundo. She was shy, had turned gray at a young age, and was so quiet and in the background most of the time that it was as if she wished no one would notice her.

It wasn't long before we were driven out of our chairs by a cutting breeze. We walked around the grounds briskly, clapping our gloved hands together to stay warm. We found ourselves walking in circles near the corner of the garden that Mamá had reserved for brown failed experiments with tropical plants. There was a particularly unfortunate banana tree there, its long boats of leaves yellowed by frost, hanging like limp shredded rags.

Amalita talked about her life. She described her mainly solitary existence without sorrow or regret, her small apartment, her nights spent reading and knitting, her days at her good job as a laboratory technician for a large medical practice in the city. She reminded me that she had been in the room or at important events during the year I had been an exchange student, and all through the years when my brothers were growing up. "Nobody realizes in this family that I was actually very close to the boys," she said. "That was especially so with Alejo and Miguel at the end. Except for Martín Segundo, I was the last one to see either of them alive."

"When was that?" I asked.

"I don't like to talk about it," she said. "It's been the main topic around here far too long, in my opinion. Those were terrible, terrible years. But that's over now, God willing. There are thirty million Argentines who have to go on living. The best thing is to put those years behind us, to get them over with once and for all so this country can function again. Isn't that what people are supposed to do when they wake up from a nightmare?"

She pulled a pack of cigarettes out of her jacket pocket. They were the cheapest brand available, a kind that smelled like burning sawdust. I took out a good American brand and offered her one. We fumbled, clumsily, with gloves and matches and cigarettes.

"I don't agree with the family on this subject, as you can see," Amalita continued. She smoked in short puffs, without inhaling, like someone unaccustomed to smoking. "I have a very different view of what happened to the boys. They were running with a very bad crowd. Colonel Dipaoli, you remember him? He had a son who went to school with you and the boys. The colonel visited Martín at his law office. He warned him, 'Watch out for your sons. They're running in very dangerous things.' But what did

Martín do? Oh, maybe he tried to persuade them to stay out of politics, but he clearly didn't do enough. None of us did. We should have knocked them over their hard heads and shipped them out of the country before they woke up. It was hell in Buenos Aires by then. Bombs were going off everywhere, and there was shooting in the streets. Do you know what happened to Miguelito? The story of how he was expelled from school?"

"No," I said. "The family doesn't talk much about him. I keep thinking it's because Papá is going to testify about him, but I don't know. . . ."

"Come on, Diego, seriously. They avoid talking about Miguelito because of what he did. Getting expelled from school was just the beginning. Miguel ran with a gang of the militancy among his classmates. They packed pistols, showed off their guns in the hallways. They were wild, and nobody studied. Miguelito was suspended for being caught painting slogans, 'Down with the dictatorship,' on the walls of the school in broad daylight. The family had lost all control of him by then. Martín was desperate. He talked the administration into giving Miguel one more chance. Then he was with the group of boys who rebelled during a chemistry exam. Like it was all a joke, they drew out their guns and shot up the lab tables, the blackboards, the windows.

"That's about the time Alejo and Martín Segundo moved out of the house, for good reasons. They weren't concerned only for themselves, but for their parents. By that time, Miguelito was in thick with the worst of the militant gangs. They planted bombs. They shot people. Even though I'm like an aunt to this family, at a certain point, it was too much. I grew afraid to have anything to do with him. I shouldn't be talking about this. My God, I'm getting upset now."

We were strolling back from the brown corner of the garden and found ourselves near the tables. There was a large bottle of wine left there. I found two glasses, picked the wine up by its basket handle, and poured them full. Amalia shook her head once, no, then reached out and took a glass.

"Those boys were the closest I ever knew to having children of my own," she said.

We sat down and drank together in silence. I was unsure if that was all she was going to say, and I didn't feel it was the right moment to press her for anything more. There was a far-off look in her eyes as she stared out across the cold landscape into the trees.

"One of my cousins, on my mother's side, had a job in the Public Works Administration Building," she said after a while. "The building was bombed. My mother's family is from Córdoba, and they didn't have much money. I was the closest relative to this cousin in the capital. He was new to the city, happy about his state job, and he would come over to dinner once a week. After the bombing, naturally, I was the one they called to identify his body. Then before his body was shipped home, there was a mass memorial service, and I stood in for my mother's family. Coffins were set up on stands, with flags draped over them. I'm not the kind of person to be at that kind of service. I mean, what's the point? What was the military trying to say?

"Still, I stood by my cousin's coffin, facing crowds of people and the press. Comandante General Videla was there with all the other important generals and admirals. Videla gave a speech that declared war on the urban guerrillas. Thousands of people cheered him on. Then the general marched down the line of coffins and shook hands with the families of the dead. He got to me. I was face to face with him. He seemed very polite, a very sincere and caring man to me then. He reached for my hand and I felt his mustache when he kissed my cheek. It was then that I said to him, 'Find out who did this. Find out who killed my cousin and punish them.' He answered, 'Don't worry, señora, I'll see they are punished.' God forgive me. But nobody knew how far he would go. Nobody knew."

Amalia stopped talking. She reached up and rearranged some messy ends of white hair sticking out from under her stocking cap. She looked at me strangely, as if she needed reassurance about what she had said.

"I don't believe that nobody knew," I said. "I've been finding out since I got here that plenty of people must have known what would happen."

"In this country, nobody ever knows what's going to happen," she said. "Think about the 1950s, when the generals threw out Perón. They were far less bloody than the elected government had been. Think about that and tell me who knew."

"Alejo knew," I said. "Miguelito probably knew."

"Miguelito didn't even know how to make his own coffee," Amalia said sharply. Her tall body stiffened. Two thin, blue-veined hands came up out of her lap suddenly and pressed against her cheeks. She looked away from me, her mouth tightly closed, trying to avoid an argument.

"I appreciate your telling me what happened," I said.

"I'm telling you because someone has to tell you. I'm only sorry it has to be me," she said. "Everyone else in this family is living in a delirium. Here. Give me another cigarette, please."

As I was removing my gloves, taking out my pack and matches, and lighting one for her, she said, "Actually, I hate smoking. I do it because I grew up thinking smoking might make me more attractive to men. That's the way it was then. Just look at the movies from that era. Men and women smoked first and then they kissed. Now look at how the world has changed."

She drew in one of her short, mouthy puffs, not really smoking so much as nervously playing with her cigarette. We sat for a long moment in silence.

"The best I can tell you is how the boys were, the last time I saw them," she continued. "A few days before Alejo disappeared, his mother got a message to him that he could meet me at a theater, so I could pass him some money, and some clothes and things. She couldn't do that herself for fear the death squads were watching the house. I got there and saw Alejo standing at the edge of the crowd in line to buy tickets. This was at the San Martín Theater, inside, in the lobby. Alejo didn't see me coming. I walked up next to him and touched his shoulder. I'll never forget the way he jumped. He turned and gave me such a frightened look. It's clear to me now. He must have known how close they were to catching him. Oh, he recovered, it took just a minute. You know Alejo, how he had such good spirits.

"I had bought us both tickets to the play that night, thinking how much he always liked to go to plays and movies. He was surprised that I had done that, and he thanked me, then said he couldn't. He had to be somewhere. We hugged and kissed in the lobby. I passed him a small tote bag with the money and things his mother had given me. He melted away into a line of people who were leaving the theater. I went in to see the play alone. But I didn't stay. That look he gave me when I touched him was as if I had poked him with the point of a knife. I told his mother about it. She and Martín were busy trying to make arrangements to get Alejo into exile. They were too late. Except for Martín Segundo, that was the last time anyone in the family saw him. Excuse me," she said.

Amalia began fumbling around in the pockets of her drab camp jacket for a handkerchief. Her mouth was trembling, her eyes watering. I thought she had started to cry. I fished around in my own pockets for tissues but couldn't find any. I picked a linen napkin off the table and held it out for her.

"It's all right," she said. She pulled a dainty lady's handkerchief from her pocket and waved it once at me in irritation. "I'm all right," she said again, sharply. "Call it allergies. It happens every time I come out to San Miguel. There's something out here that makes my nose start running. I turn into a mess."

She blew her nose and dried her eyes, turning away from me so I wouldn't see. When she looked at me again, she had a hard expression on her face. Something in the set, unmoving wrinkles around her eyes and mouth, and her eyes that seemed now a darker shade of brown, made me think of Spanish widows who dressed in black for the funeral mass, resolved never to wear colors again for the rest of their lives.

"The case of Miguelito is different," Amalia said. "After he helped to shoot up the school, he went underground. He told his mother and father not to worry if they didn't hear from him. If anything bad happened to him, he didn't want them to know. This was shortly after Alejo disappeared. Miguel was a self-centered, uncaring boy, really, to say such a thing. Martín tried to stop him. He had everything in place to get the two sons he had left across the river and out of the country. The times Miguel did get in touch—oh, maybe once a month he would turn up out here on a weekend—the arguments the two had about saving him were terrible. Miguel grabbed some food and money and just took off for the train station. This went on for almost a year. . . .

"One night, Miguelito turned up at my apartment. It was late, almost midnight. He was soaking wet from a rain, and he was dragging his right leg. Of course, I let him in. He was wounded. I tried to put him on the couch, but he refused to lie down anywhere but on the kitchen floor so he wouldn't get blood on anything. I tried to get his pants off but ended up cutting them off. He had several very deep wounds in his thigh, bleeding badly, and black at the edges like burns. I asked him what had happened. He said, 'I was just fooling around with some friends.' He laughed through his pain. He was doing everything to pretend it didn't hurt him. And why had he come to me? He knew I worked for a medical practice and had things in the house to give first aid.

"He tried to keep me from using the telephone, but I did. My friend Dr. Giezeman came over, the same doctor who had been with the Benevento family all the boys' lives. We put Miguel up on my dining room table, which I had prepared. Dr. Giezeman gave him local anesthetics. Then he worked for more than an hour taking pieces of shrapnel out of Miguelito's leg. When he finished, the boy looked about done for. He was so thin, and he hadn't shaved. His clothes were filthy. He smelled like he had been living in the subway.

"Dr. Giezeman bandaged him. Then he told Miguel that this was the last time he was going to treat him for anything. He wasn't going to waste his time sewing up anyone fool enough to play with hand grenades. I tried to reach Martín on the telephone but remembered the family had left to go out to San Miguel, partly in case Miguel might turn up out there again. In those days, they had the phone here disconnected for security reasons. Miguelito sat up on the table. He let himself down, and was already trying to walk on his wounded leg. Dr. Giezeman threw up his hands and told him he was impossible, he was going to rip through his stitches and start bleeding again. Miguel insisted that he had to go, walking or not. Dr. Giezeman gave some pain pills to him. Miguel didn't take them. He dropped the pills in his dirty T-shirt pocket. Then Dr. Giezeman went home.

"I tried to get Miguelito to spend the night at least, so he could get some rest and food. What was his hurry? When I saw he meant to leave anyway, I really got mad. 'Why can't you stop?' I shouted. 'What can you possibly gain now by gambling with your life?'

"Miguel just stood there, testing his leg. After my shouting at him, he was looking at me with this infuriating smirk. Then he asked me for his clothes. The doctor had made him take off most of his filthy clothes before he worked on the wounds. Miguel was in his underwear and a T-shirt. I found the rotten bundle of his clothes, opened the balcony window, and tossed them down six stories. I shouted that if he was planning to leave my apartment before his parents talked to him, he was going to have to do it naked. He laughed at that, and at me. Oh, how he laughed and laughed. It was a bitter, painful, terrible sound. 'Don't you know your father could have you on a boat to Uruguay by tomorrow?' I shouted. Miguel turned serious then. 'My parents can't do anything for me, and neither can you, because I'm not going. That's final,' he said. 'What kind of a hold do they have on you?' I asked. 'Are you afraid of someone? Or are you doing this for something so foolish as a feeling of loyalty?'

"He looked at me then with this terrible thing in his eyes. The pain in his leg was there, but that wasn't it. I still dream about that look sometimes and wake up with a shout. It was hatred, pure hatred, hatred of everything. I felt then all that he must have suffered, God knows, the way he had been living. 'I don't care anymore,' he said. 'I've made my decision. I'm going to keep fighting. Please, Amalita, go get some food I can take with me.'

"What could he possibly have been thinking? He would have thrown a coat over his underwear and walked out that way if I had let him. Don't ask me to explain, but there were some men's clothes in the apartment. They were too big for him, but he could still manage in them, and anything was better than the ones I had tossed out. I helped him into the clothes. I gave him one of my sweaters, which fit him. I started to fill the pockets of his coat with food. He stopped me. He took this big black pistol out of one of the pockets. He checked the pistol, cocked it, I think, then shoved it under his belt. It makes me shiver to think of it. Here he was hardly a man yet. That gun looked so big in his hands. It was like watching him as a boy, playing cops and robbers. You knew Miguel then. You knew how he always got into trouble. Maybe he would have been just as wild anywhere else in this world. In your country, he would probably have been in trouble with drugs. There he was, with that gun he carried. I could see he knew how to use it, and the most terrible thing was that he was proud of himself with it. Just by the sure way he handled it I could see what he thought of himself. . . .

"But what was he fighting against? Over the years since it happened, I keep telling myself that whatever he ended up doing, no matter how many crimes, he must have started out feeling he was doing it for something good. Don't you see? All his life, he was the youngest, not as good at things as his brothers. He had trouble in school. He was always getting into trouble at home. He must have started off in the militancy thinking that now, yes, he was going to show everyone. He was going to be a guerrilla, a soldier, the best fighter of them all. And I think about what he had come to by that night. I think about that look he kept giving me, the one so filled with hatred. Only someone who has seen it knows what I mean. There's no other way to say it. It was the cold hard look of a killer. He had killed people. And he was going to leave my apartment that night so he could keep on killing.

"So, there it is. Am I saying he deserved to die? Maybe even the way he did? No. I'm just telling you what I saw. I loved Miguelito. Maybe he was the one who needed my love the most and I hadn't given enough to him, or the right kind, when he was growing up, and then it was too late. That night, I emptied out all the money in my purse for him. I found my big black umbrella that he could use as a cane. I hugged and kissed him in the doorway. I sent him off into the night, praying to God to keep him safe. No one in this family ever saw him alive again.

"The next day, I took a train out here. I told his mother and father what had happened. Martín Segundo was with them. We were all upset, out of our minds with worry. Then the three of us ganged up on Martín Segundo and begged him to go into exile. He kept saying, 'Why me? Why would they be after me?' He had quit all his involvements since Alejo had disappeared, and enough time had gone by that he was starting to feel safe again. Can you believe it? He still didn't want to go. . . ."

" 'Go!' We told him. 'Go! Go now! Go!' And that day, it worked. He finally said he would go. His mother and father had him packed up and ready in about thirty minutes. You know the story. He was sent across the river to Uruguay that evening, in a tourist boat, under a false name. Later, arrangements were made for him in Rio, and then he was able to get to France and he was safe.

"You said before that you don't believe that nobody knew. I'm telling you that we didn't know, or at least not what it meant, that young people were being tortured and disappeared. It was just too unimaginable for us that here, in Argentina, there were concentration camps. The day Martín Segundo went into exile, we even believed there was a good chance Alejo was still alive, maybe in some kind of secret prison. Or it might be that he had been hurt so badly he didn't know who he was. He was being taken care of in some hospital until this nightmare was over and we could find him. We talked about the wildest ideas, still looking for some hope.

"And just you consider the way Martín was thinking. He should have known better than any of us. Still, he had the idea that the death squads would leave him alone. Does that sound to you like someone who knew what was going on? I'm telling you. Nobody knew. Or nobody really knew. I'm just grateful for the rest of my life to Martín that he made his decision. We can all thank God that at least one of them had enough good sense to save himself and escape."

Recruiting the Enemy

LATER THAT WEEK, I attended the testimony given by a retired naval captain. The captain had not been an important man in the military. His area of expertise was procurement and supplies. He stated that during the dictatorship, he was careful to avoid his usual cocktails at the posh Club Naval in Buenos Aires for fear he might hear loose talk about the "clandestine operations," from which he meant to distance himself. He was painstaking in ducking assignments and conversations that might involve him in the "state of war," as he referred to what had happened. He was a midlevel functionary, or so he said, just trying to survive in the armed forces long enough to collect his pension.

One night, his daughter was visiting a girlfriend from secondary school. They were doing innocent things, playing with hairstyles for an upcoming *fiesta de quince,* a coming-out party for one of their friends. The parents weren't at home. A death squad kicked in the apartment door. The maid witnessed the ransacking of the place, the way the death squad carried off the stereo, the TV, and a few other valuable things. They found the two girls hiding in the bedroom. They slapped them around and accused them of being "guerrillas." When the girls wouldn't stop screaming, they knocked them unconscious and dragged them out into the hallway. According to the maid, the death squad dragged the girls out of the apartment by their hair. They were never seen again by their families.

Aside from the facts of his daughter's disappearance, the point of the testimony by the naval captain concerned the many efforts he made to find out what had happened. The captain drew a picture—an organizational chart—of the many lines of command within the Argentine navy, how the "action wings" were organized into "task forces" with districts, streets, certain blocks of houses and apartment buildings defined as their exclusive territories. Within these jurisdictions, in cooperation with the federal police, any "task force" or *grupo de tareas* had absolute power of command and control. The navy's main torture center and concentration camp was located inside the ESME building and compound, the naval engineering school, where as many as 140 prisoners were held at a time. The facility was located near the river, in the heart of Buenos Aires, a place that a million people drove or rode buses past every week.

The naval captain interviewed many of his colleagues who were responsible for the "task forces." For months, his efforts to locate his daughter, taken by mistake, as his fellow officers to a man agreed with him, continued to lead him nowhere. Finally, he managed to get an audience with Admiral Emilio Massera, allegedly the commanding officer of the Argentine navy's "war against subversion."

Admiral Massera was a man very close to the military junta. He had by most accounts a charming personality, and was often chosen by the junta to act as liaison and information officer to foreign embassies, including the embassy of the United States, during the many inquiries about human rights abuses. The admiral served on the equivalent of the joint chiefs of staff of the nation.

It took two months before the admiral would even meet with me, the captain testified. *He treated me like a boot camp seaman. Me, with the rank of captain.* His voice grew weaker in volume the more emphatic the point he made, as if he still felt some sense of shame to be who and where he was, an officer of the armed forces now testifying against the branch of service to which he had devoted his career. *The admiral said to me that none of this affair was my business, and that my inquiries about my daughter should cease at once. He told me nothing I did would get my daughter back. "We are in a state of war,"* the admiral said, *"and we are officers. We officers must make some sacrifices for the good of the nation."*

The captain then told the story about how, two days later, he received a request from the naval command to put in for early retirement at a reduced pension. Several of his colleagues telephoned to warn him that if he didn't resign from the service, *it will not go well for you and your family.*

He resigned from the navy. He waited six years until he could testify about his experiences. His testimony was part of a tide of evidence that was overwhelming Admiral Emilio Massera's defense, which maintained the admiral was innocent because he did not know what was going on in his own command.

The afternoon session broke up in a slow, undramatic way. By this stage of the proceedings, the retired captain's story was being treated as routine—just one more victim paraded before the court to say his tragic piece. I wondered why his words weren't given more attention. After all, he was among the mere five or six military officers willing to speak out with inside information. But I could also imagine the response by military spokesmen assailing the captain's character, a story I would read in the papers the next morning, claiming he was an incompetent at his job and was now seeking revenge against his superiors for getting rid of him.

The television crews had recorded only a few minutes of the testimony, then they packed up and left the court. I found myself virtually alone in the press box except for an Argentine reporter I had never noticed there before. I rewound my tape and gathered up my notes, waiting for the crowd of spectators to file out of the room. The other reporter slid into the chair beside me and thrust out his hand. He introduced himself as Carlos María Facuña, "the military correspondent for *La Prensa*."

I had heard of him, and had read a few articles written by him in that fading relic of a newspaper. In saying "military correspondent," Carlos Facuña was telling me two things. He wrote about military matters for his newspaper, that was true. But his main occupation was the other way around. He was a reporter *for* the military at public functions, at government press conferences, anywhere they paid him to go and at which the presence of an officer in uniform might appear tasteless or out of place. Carlos Facuña introduced himself, shook hands stiffly, then said in perfect, unaccented English, "And you're with a Public Broadcasting program in the United States, isn't that right?"

The fact that this reporter knew who I was made my mouth go suddenly dry. Almost no one in the press had even cared to ask my name, let alone who I represented, not even any of the U.S. reporters. The only correspondent from the United States who had even said hello was Anderson, of *Newsweek,* who, as it turned out, had read one of my books, or at least said he had. Why would Carlos María Facuña, military correspondent, make an effort to introduce himself? How did he know and why did he care who I was?

"Don't worry, I'm just saying hello," he said, easily reading my thoughts. He was a short, thin man in a dark brown double-breasted suit. His hair was closely cropped on the sides. With a pair of epaulets on his shoulders, he would look like an army officer. "You know, the people I work with are interested in your program. They tell me that it is very popular in Washington."

"Technically speaking, I'm here on my own, freelance," I said. "When it comes down to it, the program doesn't give much of a damn about the trials."

"Yes. So it is," Facuña said. He smiled. He pushed his wire-frame glasses a little higher on his nose. "You could hardly call the program 'mass media,' now, could you? It has, what? About four million viewers? But it has its influence in the right places, or so I'm told."

"I guess that's just about right," I said.

I turned away from him, busying myself with packing notes and the tape recorder into a small shoulder bag. Facuña continued talking to me as though he hadn't noticed the brush-off. "Let me get to the point. Some people I'm close to are very interested in your program, and also in you. Could we perhaps work together on a story?"

I had just started to stand up and leave and was about to sit back down again to hear him out. But I thought for a moment. Then I turned to Facuña and said, "You've got the wrong guy and the wrong program. I'm sure not going to be used by you people. And no matter what you have, I don't think you could get ten seconds out of the producers. So let's just say no, Carlos, and no thanks. You can spread your poison somewhere else."

"No hard feelings," Facuña said. He had stood up beside me. Suddenly, he reached out and put a hand on my shoulder. "Even you must know that there are elements in the armed forces who are, well, shocked and embarrassed by what's happening here.

They want nothing more than to put these trials behind them," he said. There was an eagerness in his voice, and a false quality to it like that of a high-pressure salesman. "Those are the people I'm proposing to you, the officers who fought to try and stop what happened. This might be an opportunity, really, for you and for your program. That's what I'm saying. At least think about it. Think about it overnight," he said.

He offered his hand to shake again. I looked at it, shook it once, coldly, then took a step back and started out of the press box. "Do you know the Florida Garden?" he asked. "The café on the corner of Florida and Paraguay?"

I was slipping past the disordered chairs set up in the press box. Then I was down the two wooden steps, on my way out the side door of the court. The court was deserted now except for a team of security guards going over the seats and aisles in their twice-daily search for bombs. I left Facuña calling out in Spanish behind me, his voice full of friendship and persuasion, "Think it over! Change your mind! Tomorrow at four. The Florida Garden!"

It was on a last-minute impulse that I packed my shoulder bag at San Miguel and caught the train into the city. And I wasn't sure I wanted to make the meeting. But at least the train ride was bright and pretty, the open landscapes of the flat green pampas giving way to rich suburbs with swimming pools and walled-in gardens. The train continued on through the vast system of parks in the northwest district filled with families and children on such a sunny day in winter. Finally, the train pulled in at Retiro Station, at the foot of the clock tower that was an imitation of London's Big Ben, in what was once called the English Plaza, now renamed Air Force Plaza after the British defeat of Argentina in the Malvinas/Falklands War.

It was only a short walk up the hill to the Florida Garden. I strolled along toward the Plaza San Martín, keeping a leisurely pace in the fresh breeze and under a clear winter light that held all the promise of spring. I crossed the Plaza San Martín and entered the narrow mouth of Florida Street, closed off to all traffic but pedestrians. Ahead, there was a long file of news and souvenir stands. Racks of papers and magazines fluttered in the breeze. I walked at an easy pace along the tourist shopping street, looking around at the bright windows full of expensive clothing, shoes, furs. I saw, about a half block ahead, at the corner of Paraguay Street, the bright sign that advertised a large, split-level café and bar, the Florida Garden. I slowed down, dawdling at one of the newsstands. I checked the doorways and street corners in front of the café for signs of a stakeout, which I spotted immediately.

Kitty-corner to the double glass doors of the entrance to the café there was a heavyset man who had a haircut shaved close on the sides. The man was leaning against the large window display of a men's clothing store, watching the street. He wore a heavy over-coat that was buttoned to his neck, much too warm-looking for the temperature. One of the pockets of the coat bulged a little, and the man had his hand plunged deeply into it—I guessed it contained a radio and he had his finger on the call button. The man wore sunglasses of the kind that could easily be masking a small earpiece. He was an undercover cop of some sort, if I had ever seen one. On the other hand, he was so obviously conducting surveillance that I had a hard time believing what I was seeing.

I took my time at the newsstand, looking over the many foreign newspapers available on the tourist street. I felt watched from the corner. I looked up above. There were several windows with partly opened French blinds that could be second and perhaps third positions. I picked out a copy of the *Süddeutsche Zeitung,* only one day old from Munich, and paid the newsstand man. From his covered booth, he said a thank you in German, which I returned, wishing him a good day in that language. I folded the paper under my arm and walked quickly across the street to the café.

Martín Segundo had told me about the Florida Garden, then given me some commentaries to read by the writer Jorge Asís, who allegedly had once worked for the secret police. Asís wrote that between three and five in the afternoon, the Florida Garden was a meeting place for intelligence agents. During the last months of the dictatorship, there had been so much uncertainty among the ranks of secret police forces that the army intelligence service had agents watching agents from the navy, the navy was following and recording conversations of the air force agents, and the SIDE, Servicio de Inteligencia del Estado—like an Argentine FBI and CIA combined—was watching all the others. Some agents had recently participated in the tortures and murders. Others had stayed away as best they could.

But the problem then wasn't so much a fear they might be found out, charged, and tried for crimes against humanity. It was that so many agents were certain they were soon to be unemployed. They were scrambling around between the various military wings and Ministry of Interior services, trying to follow every inside lead they could get and planting favorable lies about themselves and their friends. Each agent was on his own, trying to figure out how to enter the new democracy still on his feet and with his job. Then the hard times crashed down on them. As soon as the newly elected president was sworn in, as many as a thousand former agents of the military intelligence and secret police services were given their walking papers. Asís maintained that for months after that, the CIA had a man often stationed at one of the café tables at the Florida Garden, taking applications from unemployed agents for possible duty in Central America. And from above, with all their high-tech gear, they were busily recording everyone who was recording everyone else.

Inside the café, there was an atmosphere of frantic noise, hard voices, mixed with the thick smells of coffee, smoke, and sweat. It was a busy place, filled with men dressed in off-the-rack suits who were leaning in close to one another over their double espressos, cigarettes sucked down to the filters in intense conversations. Many of these men were bureaucrats for nearby government agencies. Many others were unemployed agents. I could make out several men who fit such a description, their expressions filled with sad, disillusioned nostalgia for better days under the dictatorship, men who were hanging around morosely over their drinks, waiting for the winds to change. On my way to a table at the back, I caught the drift of just that kind of conversation, a few quick, encouraging words from a more fortunate colleague to another who was unemployed. I looked over the faces of the crowd for Facuña.

I sat down at a table. I came to the conclusion that what I had read was true. And along with the unemployed spies, I saw men from government offices who had managed to find jobs, who were engaged in their daily meetings over whiskeys and coffees, and others, too, who looked comfortable, who projected a sense of immense good luck, the fascists who had landed on their feet in this unsteady and unpredictable era of constitutional laws. I also noticed the stony faces and unmistakable haircuts of military officers out of uniform. Many of their bulky briefcases probably contained their uniforms. The trials of the comandantes had so aroused people in the streets that military officers were now afraid to wear them. They carried their uniforms around in bags and briefcases while dressed in civilian clothes, then, in the men's rooms at their offices—or when they got where they had to go—they changed into them.

Looking through the smoky haze of the café, I also saw a few faces I recognized as belonging to reporters, openly trading gossip and information back and forth. And why not? Didn't such a place make sense? Wasn't having somewhere to meet and exchange information a help to avoid tragic mistakes? After all, spies must be in many ways just like anyone else. Why shouldn't they have their union hall, their watering hole, their nice friendly place to buddy up?

My table was inconveniently located, the waiters rushing back and forth down the open aisle that ran beside it. I ordered a coffee and looked at the clock. It was five after four. I searched the crowd again for Facuña. Suddenly, I wondered, why meet at this place? Then again, this would be the regular spot for Facuña. This would be his crowd, a place he went to every day to gather and spread the kind of pro-military propoganda he made his living writing.

My coffee arrived. I sipped at it. Suddenly, from somewhere to one side, I heard the click and whir of an automatic camera. Two tables away, a large, heavy man near the Paraguay Street windows was rattling something off in French, gesturing to a woman who looked like his plump little wife. He appeared to be telling her to position herself for a snapshot. The man raised the camera and shot several more frames. But he did it too quickly, I thought, much too quickly for a tourist. And why so many pictures? A tourist would take one or two snapshots at a time. Also, why would a tourist use a film so fast he could take pictures inside a bar without a flash?

The thought struck me that my face and profile were directly in the man's viewfinder, just in back of his wife. The camera was a Minolta, the kind with automatic focus and an electronic zoom lens. The length of the lens setting didn't look just right to me, not that I could be sure from two tables away. I raised an open hand up as though to brush my hair back. I leaned my forehead against my fingers in a way that was sure to cover one side of my face.

The camera clicked and whirred. Smiles from the man, a kiss for his wife, then the couple sat down again.

It was four thirty-five. I ordered another coffee and waited, opening the German newspaper and reading some of it. It was hard to concentrate. I waited until five o'clock with a growing uneasy feeling that I should never have come into the city that afternoon. I was just about to leave when Facuña came breezing in the side door. He raised a hand and waved at me. On his way to my table, several people greeted him. Then he was standing over me, out of breath, apologizing for being late, on Latin American time, he joked, late to everything. I asked him to sit down. He said he had to hurry off to another appointment. He reached inside his suit jacket, pulled out a business card, and handed it to me. "Tomorrow, three o'clock, it's all arranged," he said. "Brigadier General Manuelo María Cruz will be waiting. Do you know how to get out to San Isidro?"

"I'll manage," I said. I looked at the card. It had a familiar off-white color and texture, and the address and telephone number looked strangely as if I'd seen them before. "Say," I said. "How did you figure to arrange a meeting when you weren't even sure I'd turn up?"

"Just go there. Maybe he can tell you something," Facuña said. He shook my hand quickly, and was just as quickly threading his way through the crowded tables and out the door. I sat for a moment, staring at the business card with an eerie sense of its familiarity.

Breathing in the fresh, crisp air outside was a relief from the noise and smoke. The sun was nearly down, the city covered with a gray light fast turning into darkness. I started up Florida Street. I stopped in front of the Lincoln Library, a bicultural center supported by the United States Information Service and the U.S. embassy. Inside the doors, there were two armed security guards.

Young students were filing past them, through metal detectors, giving over their bags and purses to be searched for bombs.

I turned to continue up the street. Behind me, I saw a man in a heavy overcoat, the one I had noticed an hour before. He was a few store windows away, dawdling there as if he were window-shopping. I slowly walked a short distance, then turned my head and saw him there, still behind me, ambling up the street, his hands thrust deeply into his pockets, moving along as remarkably slowly as my own casual strolling and with an expression on his face as if he were just killing time. I walked, faster, to the corner, my heart pounding. I held my hand up into traffic and hailed a cab.

I told the driver to take me down toward the river and along the Avenida Leandro Alem, then the Paseo Colón, then up the Avenida Independencia into the district of San Telmo—exactly the opposite direction from the train station. Once we were in San Telmo, the driver gave me dirty looks in the rearview mirror as I asked him to circle around a few blocks near Mexico and Peru streets, a run-down neighborhood, some of the buildings abandoned and taken over by the poor, who lit kerosene lamps inside them and hung their laundry out to dry over the balconies. I pretended to give up trying to find an address on Mexico Street and asked the driver to take me to the Plaza Dorrego.

I got out of the cab there. The bar and music club scene hadn't begun around the plaza. I sat down on a wooden bench, alone. A man with a guitar was singing a tango in the distance across the plaza, a few people gathered around him and tossing money into his hat. I kept searching the plaza, trying to force my eyes to see more clearly into the shadows surrounding the few pools of light made by the streetlamps, which had just come on. I didn't notice anything unusual. A cab let some people off in front of one of the bars. I rushed over to catch it and we sped away.

212

I had the taxi let me off a few blocks from the train station. I walked along, fast, nervously checking behind and ahead. Nothing. I joined the crowd inside Retiro Station and wandered around for a while. I found one of the bars and ordered a whiskey, turning on my stool so I could look out over the vast space under the high-domed ceiling for anything at all unusual. I checked my watch. I had about an hour to wait for the next train. Suddenly, I missed my good German newspaper, realizing I must have dropped it somewhere without noticing. I loosened my tie. I breathed in the good warm vapors of the scotch and began to relax a little. Everyone in my family had to be careful getting to San Miguel. Often they took roundabout ways to get to the train station. Still, this afternoon had been ridiculous. I felt like a fool that I had run so scared this time, convinced I was being followed.

San Isidro was one of the most expensive, exclusive suburbs of Buenos Aires. The general lived in a house set in the middle of some wooded acreage, its red tile roof visible a long way off through the trees. The cab I was riding in turned through the open iron gates onto a neatly trimmed lane. Just outside the general's gate, I noted another of the empty steel pillbox structures that were set into the middle of many of the streets in this paradise for the wealthy. During the dictatorship, they had been filled with soldiers standing guard over the rich estates.

The house had seen better days. Though it was large and magnificent, two stories, the balcony on the second floor looked in bad disrepair, and there was a peeling row of Greek columns in front. In back and beyond the house, a green line of eucalyptus verged off into blackness, their tops looking like the crests of dark mountain peaks against the sea-blue sky. I told the driver to park down the lane and wait for me. There wasn't any other vehicle in sight, and nothing that resembled a garage. As I mounted the steps to the front door, I noted a feeling of absolute quiet, far from any traffic noise, the surrounding trees pressing down in the silence. It looked like there was nobody home. I rang the bell and waited. Not certain the bell worked, I knocked on the door. Then I tried the bell again.

As I was about to leave, the door was opened by a maid. Behind her was a familiar face surrounded by perfectly styled, strawberry blond hair, smiling at me and singing out a greeting. It was Ana María Cruz de las Heras, the owner of the art gallery where Mamá Benevento had shown the slides. The thought struck me, of course, that General Cruz would be her father. Ana María was elegant in a gray wool dress cut to show her figure. She rose up on the toes of her Italian shoes for an exchange of friendly kisses.

She led me down a hallway toward the back of her father's huge house. I could see into rooms overcrowded with baroque antiques. She chattered away at me with small talk, saying how happy she was I could make the appointment, and wasn't this visit so nicely arranged?

"Why go through Facuña?" I asked. "Why not just reach me through my family?"

"Your family's not exactly easy to reach these days," she said. "Facuña is a friend of the family and said he knew who you are. Besides, you might not want them to know you're doing this," she said. We stopped in the hallway. "I'm sorry about what happened to the Benevento family, as I'm deeply moved and sorry about what happened to so many others. But that doesn't change the fact that I'm also proud my father is a general."

Ana María led me into a library room, filled on all sides with high cases of dusty, leather-bound editions that looked as though the pages had never been cut. A gallery of photographs stared down from the shelves. There was a desk at the center of the room, also dusty, on which there were several neat stacks of file folders. I noticed a photograph on the desk. It was of Ana María in a crowd of reverent-looking military officers, standing at attention next to a gray-haired general with a thick mustache who was surely her father. She saw me looking at the photograph and picked it up to show me.

"This is recent. It's not only the mothers of the Plaza de Mayo who've lost loved ones. We families of the military also gather in a vigil, respecting and protesting the deaths of our soldiers and police during the war against subversion. That's one of the stories that almost never gets told in the foreign press. Maybe you can help to do something about that," she said.

I held my breath, not answering. In the photograph, I had suddenly recognized another face, not far from Ana María's. The face belonged to Teniente de fragata Astiz, of "the case of the flying nuns." In the background, there was also the former *presidente de facto* General Jorge Rafael Videla, weighed down by his gold braid, looking on at the memorial mass with a resolute, unrepentant expression. I fought the urge to turn on my heel and get out of there. I felt tricked into wasting time and money coming all that way just to see what amounted to a small trophy room of the dictatorship. Who did this woman think she was?

Still, I said nothing. I followed Ana María out a glass door from the library and down two steps into a large solarium. The place was a greenhouse, messy with untended plants. Among the tangled, dead flowers and creepers, some kind of black insects zoomed around through the dying leaves and yellowing stalks. An old dog was dozing by the door that led outside. We carefully stepped over him without his twitching so much as an ear. We reached the end of a strangling corridor of plants. In a clearing among them was General de Brigada Manuelo María Cruz, retired.

The general was in a wheelchair. His white hair and mustache were yellowed, a tone which matched the waxy yellow color of his skin. He was a terribly thin man, his cheeks sunken. The hand he raised up in a weak greeting looked like a pack of loose bones in an old yellow coin purse. The general was covered to his chest with red plaid blankets, as if the temperature weren't already like a tropical hell under the sun-drenched glass. I could feel my shirt soaking through under my jacket. There was a drink cart nearby with bottles and an ice bucket. Ana María poured us both a whiskey, then excused herself and went back into the house.

"You may take off your jacket," the general said.

I stiffened at his tone of voice, as if he were granting some kind of favor to an orderly. I took off my jacket and loosened my tie. I took out my tape recorder and a notebook, glad to have them, as if they might somehow assert my own authority. We sipped at our drinks for a moment. Then I pressed the record buttons and started with some questions. Why had I been invited out here? What did the general have to say that might be of interest to the press?

Don't talk to me about the press. Hang the press. I can get all the press I want with a couple of phone calls. This has nothing to do with the press, it's a favor for my daughter. She says you came here looking to find out what happened to your family. Well, I can't tell you that, not specifically. But there are some of us who were never the cruel, unchar-itable sons of bitches we're painted as being. To convince you, I'll tell you what I can about the way it really was. . . .

I waited to say something. I wanted to put it to this old goat sharply. Did he mean to say that he had had nothing to do with what had gone on? Or was he going to try to put over on me the same defense for himself that other officers were using, that he had only been following orders? I cleared my throat and started to ask that question.

Don't interrupt me, sir. . . .

I sat back and listened. The steaming atmosphere in the solarium was getting to me. It was as if a hot fog were rising behind my eyes and filling my head. I reached for some napkins off the drink cart and wiped at the sweat rolling down my face.

. . . *Here's what was happening. Our army was seething with dissatisfied officers. No point in my giving you the whole and why of it, the perpetual mess with the Peronists and their unions. But the notion of absolute rule, and their seeing recent military coups, those in Chile, Peru, and Brazil, had gotten many of my fellow officers wondering if this country might not also be ripe for a dictatorship. In any case, that's been the tradition in Argentina. You're more likely to end up president as an officer in the army than going into any other profession. Isn't that true?*

I nodded, yes, it was true. I also gave the general a bored, impatient look, letting him know he was telling me nothing new. He continued without registering the communication.

It's been the tradition that the officer corps in Argentina will consider almost any kind of idea for a coup, as long as the generals in charge can show that they're organized. The officers were fed up with democratic theories, including legislative representation, which had been a complete failure. It's always been the same, since the first coup d'état I took part in, the one in 1930. Do you know Roberto Arlt? He was a great writer in those days. He had a friend, a major, who was also a friend of mine. His name doesn't matter now—he long ago came to nothing. But take a look at Arlt. This major, this friend of mine, was like a prophet about the coup of 1930, and about every coup that's happened since. He laid it out this way. Ninety percent of our elected officials are less educated than a first lieutenant in our army. And as far as running the country, a politician accused of having a hand in the murder of a union boss put it like this: "Running the country's no big deal— no tougher than running a big ranch." . . .

The general's voice was taking on a different tone. It sounded lost in reflections and memories, most of which seemed as though they pleased him. I stopped taking notes. I was about to reach over and stop the tape recorder, too, but left it running out of a sense of politeness. I served myself another drink, the general giving me no sign he even noticed.

It's just like the major said . . . before 1930 . . . and before the action we took in this latest one in 1976. . . . The army represented an elite group within an inferior society, since we were the country's real strength. And yet we were at the beck and call of government. And whose government? . . . The legislative and executive branches, men chosen by some half-assed political party. . . . And who do they pick? To land a seat in Congress you have to go the whole route of double-dealings, smoke-filled rooms, wheeling and dealing with shady characters and payoffs, until your whole life is nothing but crimes and lies. I don't know if that's the way it is in countries more civilized, shall we say, than ours. But in our two houses of Congress, we had accused loan sharks and murderers, people on the take from foreign companies, and others so grossly ignorant that the legislature had turned into the most banal kind of farce that could possibly disgrace a nation. What party politics in this country really boils down to is a contest to see who can sell out the country and get the best price for it. So, then, what were we to do? What would you have done in our position?

Bare branches of a tree outside moved against the windows of the solarium, a stark web outlined against the clear afternoon sky. I looked out at it for a moment, thinking that I hadn't really come here with any expectations. "General, forgive me," I said. "But I don't see how your telling me this is doing either of us any good. I'm sorry," I said. I started to reach for the tape recorder to turn it off, getting ready to leave.

Not yet. Sit down and listen. This next part should interest you. Two years before, when that son of a bitch Perón and his cohorts came back to stick their snouts in the hog trough, our officers were already making their plan. The younger generals agreed to back them up. It was exactly the same scheme as in 1930, but so far more effectively accomplished. I was in the office of strategic planning, and I'm proud of our efficiency. Just as Arlt wrote about the conspiracy of 1930—which really lays out how it happens all over this miserable continent—the idea was to make it look like a totally communist plot. The trouble with that was there was no real communism in Argentina, not unless you wanted to count some bunch of soreheaded students who sat around playing Che Guevara and being rude on principle. Now, we knew that every secret plot is a cancer on the host society. Letting it be known there was such a plot would inspire fear that the whole system would be disrupted. So we infiltrated every leftist organization we could find, putting our own people in strategic positions. We then made sure that those organizations looked in every way like a unified communist scheme. . . .

"Hold on a moment," I said. I was back in my chair again, reaching for my notebook. "You're saying that you, in the military, were actually the inspiration behind the leftist guerrillas?"

Guerrillas? Guerrillas? I wouldn't even honor them with the word. If you're talking about really dangerous leftists—ready to pull off terrorist acts for a cause—you could probably have rounded up all of them and you'd have maybe three or four busloads. And that's exactly what we did. We had killed off or driven into exile almost all the really dangerous people before the coup even happened. You know Firmenich? That double-dealing son of a bitch who was supposed to be the leader of the Montonero group?

"Sure," I said. Firmenich was allegedly the worst of the leftist leaders, and due to be prosecuted for leading the wing of the Montoneros which planted bombs, robbed banks, pulled off prison breaks, and generally created an atmosphere of terrorism just before the comandantes took over the government. "Look," I said. "Do you have any proof of any of this?"

The proof is in how it all worked out.

"What does Firmenich have to do with this?"

Firmenich was our boy. Or at least he turned into our boy once we killed off most of his friends.

"Really? Firmenich? You can prove this?"

Shut up for once and listen. Firmenich was like one big turd in a whole shitpile. We had almost everybody at the top. The point is how it all worked. The many leftist facades we created, or infiltrated, since they already existed, immediately made groups such as the Montoneros, the People's Revolutionary Army, the many socialist labor groups, all very attractive to idealistic students and crackpots of all kinds. The ranks swelled. Then came the terrorist attacks, the prison breaks, bank robberies, everything. We stirred up a widespread agitation, which was exactly our plan. Everybody in this country felt the change. Newspapers kept the pot boiling. The cops did their share by arresting innocent people and roughing them up enough so that they came out of it as real revolutionaries. Believe me, people woke up in the morning even eager for some fresh news of violence, hoping it would be worse than the last one so the military would have to react. There were some hotheads out shooting policemen, then labor got into the act, calling strikes right and left, and all the while this loose talk of revolution and Cuban-style communism kept the country in a constant state of both fear and hope.

So, then, after the bombs started going off all over the city and people had read these wild leaflets, many of which we had written ourselves and be damned and to hell with the Peronists, just when the prerevolutionary state was just right, that's when we stepped in, the military. . . .

"But can you offer me any proof?" I asked again. He had paused to catch his breath. His lips were covered with some kind of dry white substance. He took a sip of his drink and cleared his throat. "I've got to have proof before I can use anything."

Just look at what happened! Think about the plan! It's just as the major once said it was—the military steps in, saying that, given the government's inability to defend the nation, free enterprise, and the

family, we're taking over the reins and declaring a temporary dictator-
ship. It's very important for all dictatorships to say they're temporary.
Saying it's temporary has such a reassuring sound. Then bourgeois cap-
italists, and, especially, conservative foreign governments, like that of
the United States, immediately salute the new state of things. Our gen-
erals say it's all the fault of the Cuban- and Soviet-inspired communists
that we have to crack down and shoot a few poor slobs who've confessed
to planting bombs. We tie the hands of the legislature. We make big cuts
in the nation's budget. The running of the state is given to the military.
The nation will be on its way to unprecedented heights of glory. And
isn't that just how it happened? Tell me, isn't that true?

"I don't know," I said. "I'm not sure what to believe anymore.
But I do know you can't call thousands of the disappeared just a
few poor slobs who were planting bombs."

That part of it got out of hand. And you can see how it would. After
all, we had the lists of names, almost every one of them, in the leftist
movements. Our generals took over on the pretense of a war against
subversion. They and the younger officers took that position seriously, as
if forgetting their own part in starting it all. . . .

Look. The principle is very simple, and it's all over the continent.
You're afraid of a certain political movement coming into existence. So,
you create that movement yourself and let everyone attracted to it join
in. Then you systematically destroy it and arrest everybody associated
with it so that the movement will never exist again. But in our case this
last stage of the process just went too far. And that's when I could no
longer keep in the thick of things. What I saw going on was just too
much.

A group of officers and I went directly to the junta and consistently
argued against so many abuses. We wrote position papers on strategy.
We leveled protests. Our point was, sure, round up all the politicos and
leftists and put them in prison. Go ahead and even shoot some of the

leaders. But why not do it all within the system of military justice? Why not do it right out in the open, which would show that we had nothing to hide?

In the end, we just weren't strong enough to persuade the junta. They were wild with their own kind of Gestapo program by then. I applied for a transfer from the office of strategic planning to a teaching post at the military academy. I got it. Then I found that the place was being used as a concentration camp and a mass grave. The cadets were encouraged to sleep with photos of Adolf Hitler over their beds, who was a military failure if there ever was one. I applied for another transfer, as a military attaché out of the country. Ana María and I spent a wonderful year in South Africa, really a very beautiful country. It was fairly calm with the blacks then, too. That job was like cocktails around the pool and tennis courts all day long. By that time, I was ready to put in for my promotion to brigadier general and for retirement.

And here we are now. But think how well our plan worked. Seven years in power, the longest-lasting Argentine government since the first regime of Perón, and who knows how long it could have survived without the disgrace of the Malvinas War? And you still need proof? You want evidence? We'll see. . . .

The general reached painfully over to the drink cart and rang a bell. The maid and Ana María came into the solarium quickly, as if they had been hovering just outside the door. The general directed the maid to wheel him into the library. Ana María and I followed. She kept asking me in a whisper how things had gone. I nodded my head foggily and said nothing. She remarked how tired the general looked. With each bump of his wheelchair over the steps, his head bobbed around like an old gray melon on a stem. I agreed how bad he looked, knowing my interview had come to an end.

Stepping into the library after the heat of the solarium felt like walking into a freezer. The maid wheeled the general to his dusty desk, and he began to go through his file folders, muttering to

222

himself, searching for some papers. Ana María began to pull photographs of the general's military career from the bookshelves. She showed me one of a young lieutenant in riding boots and jodhpurs on top of a sleek chestnut mount—the general's first command in the aristocratic Argentine cavalry. There were other pictures of his rise through the ranks, promoted to captain after the coup of September 6, 1930, when he was twenty-three years old. During the shakeups of the 1940s, he was seen at the side of a young, dark-featured colonel, Juan Domingo Perón. Then there was a notable absence of photos until the coup of 1956, when the general reappeared again, promoted to lieutenant colonel, this time at the side of General Aramburu after his coup d'état that overthrew the Peronist government and established yet another military dictatorship. The effect of the pictures was clear—the general was a pragmatic man who had always managed, somehow, to land on his feet on the side of the cadre of officers who had taken power.

"Here. Here it is," the general said from his desk. He picked up a fountain pen and with great difficulty removed the cap and positioned it in his fingers. "This should be enough," he said as he wrote something briefly, then signed his name. "This should put me on the record," he said. Then he dropped the pages into an envelope, his knotty, arthritic fingers barely able to seal the string clasp. He held the envelope out to me. "I could give you hundreds of similar reports," he said. "Our office prepared these every day or two for our network. Firmenich was one of the names on our list. After all, how can you be an effective terrorist if you don't know what's happening in your country?"

I took the envelope and thanked him. He waved a hand through the air weakly, in a gesture of dismissal, and as if he didn't have the strength to hold it up again. The maid took this as a cue to wheel him out of the library, presumably to his room to rest.

He said a few terse words of good-bye. Ana María continued to show off his things. "This is the sword he was given as a commander of the presidential honor guard. These, his silver spurs from the cavalry command. . . ."

"I hope you don't mind me asking," I said, "but your family, and you, are clearly very wealthy. This house, your gallery, your apartment in New York . . . how was it all managed on a military salary?"

"Oh, no, surely it wasn't," she said. "My father was never good with money. His salary for a year wouldn't have covered two weeks of what our family spends. The money comes from my mother, from the de las Heras family. Did he talk about her?"

"No, not a word," I said.

"It's no wonder. She was always off in France, or in Spain, while he was serving his country. She died almost twenty years ago, of a bad heart. This is the house she bought for him. You should have seen it once, with a full staff of servants, the stables filled with prize horses. Her family continues to send us her share of the inheritance."

"Inheritance from what?"

"Haven't you seen the avenue in Buenos Aires that's named after us? The de las Heras family has so much land that no one has ever been able to say how much we own."

"Really? That much?"

"I'll show you," she said. There was a giddiness in her voice, and a sense of playfulness as if she were letting me in on a secret. She led me to a medium-sized globe that stood in one corner of the library. It was the kind of globe that spun freely, like a ball on a cup, supported by a polished wooden stand. She put her long red fingernails on the ball. She turned the globe, tipping it over to reveal the southern hemisphere. In the middle of the long lines that defined the map of Argentina, someone had drawn a rough rectangle about the size of a fingertip. The rectangle marked off an area that was bigger on the globe than many countries, far bigger than some of the smaller American states. "There it is," she said. "This much of the world belongs to my family."

Not long after that, I was able to leave, with the general's envelope tucked under my arm. Ana María had wanted me to stay for tea, clearly implying there would be just the two of us. I made excuses, declining the invitation. She changed the subject to how much she liked spending the autumn months in New York, and gave me a card with her address and telephone number there. I said I would get in touch sometime.

She took my hand and led me out a side door and then the long way around the house, through an overgrown garden. For a moment, it felt very nice to be walking this way, with a beautiful, elegant woman on my arm, even if she was a general's daughter. She was clearly available, and rich beyond anything I could imagine, a fact I couldn't get out of my mind any more than I could get her perfume out of my senses. She only once asked me about my interview with the general. She asked in a way that implied she thought the news media in North America would be greatly interested in whatever he had said. I told her I wasn't sure the general had really told me anything beyond some interesting speculations that would be hard to prove. But I promised that I would write up a summary of the interview and send it to New York, which I later did.

I signaled for the taxi, which I was relieved to see was still waiting. Ana María Cruz de las Heras then rose up on her toes and kissed me, again, the same way as the first time, boldly and quickly, leaving lipstick on my mouth that I kept tasting on the ride back to the train station.

As the cab turned out of the gates of the general's aging estate, I was having a hard time with myself. I was married, true enough, but I had rarely in my life felt so married. Along with this, I kept thinking about the writer Roberto Arlt, and how the general had quoted him. Something I had read by Arlt sounded in my head: "Even if I had a silver boat with golden sails and marble oars, and the ocean were to turn seven splendid colors, and a millionairess were blowing me kisses from the moon, I would still be unhappy. . . ."

I turned my attention to the envelope the general had given me. I opened the string clasp and spread the few tissuey-thin pages in my lap. At the top of the first page, the general had written, *Report delivered to Firmenich from my office,* under which he had signed his name.

26 March, 1976—army intelligence services—federal district headquarters—classified:

The military junta that took control of the government in the coup d'état of 24/3 elects Lieutenant General Jorge Rafael Videla de facto president of the nation. Ex-President María Ester "Isabel" Perón continues under arrest in Neuquén province. The military junta has consolidated power and there appears to be little resistance within its ranks. Cleanup operations of some guerrilla strongholds are planned for the coming week.

The banks and schools reopen after the military actions of the preceding two days. A new "Advisory Legislative Council" is named by the junta and will set up its jurisdiction in the National Congress. The ex-Secretary of Sports and Recreation, Adolfo Phillipeaux, is arrested while trying to flee into Chile. Ex-members of the National Congress turn in their weapons to police, including some machine guns. Union leader Lorenzo Miguel and others are confirmed to have been arrested and detained. Discussions are underway among the junta to declare wildcat strikes in the form of absenteeism from factories and jobs as a crime against the state. Previous agreements with supporters and negotiators

226

of and with the National Institute of Compensation, Productivity, and Participation are abolished. (See special report of 9/2.) Only the 20 percent uniform raise in basic salaries will be granted by the junta, according to decree number 906.

In response to these measures, the International Monetary Fund confirms the granting of an emergency credit of U.S. $127,600,000 to the new government.

Hurlingham: Two bodyguards of a Ford Motor Corporation executive are assassinated, César Iglesias and Osvaldo Notario.

Córdoba: Three guerrillas are killed in a gun battle, two of whom are identified, José Luis Nicola, 25, and Vilma Ethel Ortiz, 22. Four guerrillas, two men and two women, still unidentified, are killed while trying to rob a truckload of milk products. A worker for the Materfer company, described as a "random sniper," is killed by an army patrol. One Josefina Aguiar de Gambanto is killed while trying to avoid a military checkpoint.

Banfield: Police sergeant José Cristobal Armando Pizarro, 42, is assassinated.

Chubut: One Myrddin Evans, 58, is accidentally shot and killed while passing through a military checkpoint.

Buenos Aires: The newspaper La Opinión publishes a story which states that during a military task force action breaking into a local office of the Communist Party, two men were killed, as yet unidentified.

Thirty-six countries around the world have so far granted recognition to the new government of the military junta.

The ex-president of the Senate, Italo Luder, calls for a new chapter in the life of the nation.

De facto President Lieutenant General Jorge Rafael Videla assures foreign ambassadors and embassy officials that he will maintain both security and calm, and that he will tell the people of Argentina, "A historical cycle has been closed and we will now begin a new one."

Spoils of War

THE NEXT MORNING, the day before Papá Benevento was scheduled to testify at the trials, news broke in the papers that the wife of a witness named Muralles had been kidnapped. She was standing out by her front yard gate, picking up the mail, when a black Ford Falcon with four men inside it pulled to the curb. She was jumped on, blindfolded, wrestled into the car, then driven out into the country. Her clothes were removed in the backseat. Two men took turns burning her body with cigarettes. One of them kept telling her repeatedly, *If your husband gives his evidence tomorrow, you know what we'll do. We'll come back for the both of you and you won't get off so lucky.*

Señora Muralles was fifty-six years old, the newspaper stated, as if that somehow made a difference. She was dumped off into a ditch by a highway leading to La Plata, naked, her body burned

228

in more than thirty places. She staggered along by the edge of the highway, waving at the few cars that passed, but none of them stopped. She found a farmhouse, little more than a cement-block shack. The humble people inside took her in, found her some clothes, and sent for help.

Papá and I sat over coffee and rolls, reading the story in the newspaper *Clarín*. We were at a table on the patio at San Miguel, having breakfast under a bright morning sun and in a crisp winter air that had the effect of making the story even more shocking. We passed the pages of the paper back and forth, reading and rereading them.

Mamá Benevento was inside the house. She had the radio turned on loudly. She was listening to the witness, Señor Muralles, being interviewed just before going up the steps of Tribunales and into the courtroom to give his evidence. The scratchy sound of the man's voice echoed out onto the patio. He was making a stand. He and his wife were agreed that such tactics of fear were not going to deter him from testifying.

Most of what he was going to say was already available in depositions. The newspaper summarized his testimony. Señor Muralles was going to speak out against General Ramón Camps, who, as a colonel working under the orders of the dictatorship, allegedly had been the chief of many action groups working in the province of Buenos Aires, and had been an administrator responsible for numerous torture and detention centers. Colonel Camps had later been promoted to general for his "valiant service to the nation." The connection of the activities of General Camps to the trial of the comandantes would serve as one more argument to knock down any claim of legitimacy by the dictatorship that they had been fighting, exclusively, "a war against subversion."

Señor Muralles was the retired president of a bank in the city of La Plata, the provincial capital. He had been rich, powerful, active in Rotary Clubs International, a solidly established, influential man in the business community. Two of his children, a teenaged boy and girl never involved in any way in political or subversive activity, were kidnapped by a "task force" allegedly under the orders of Colonel Camps. Military men in civilian clothes then brought tape recordings of the children's voices to the Muralles home. They demanded almost everything Señor Muralles had in his personal fortune except for his house if he wanted to see his children again. The man emptied his bank accounts, sold stocks and properties, cashed in insurance policies, and handed over, in cash, an amount that was equivalent to about half a million U.S. dollars. The soldiers of the "task force" took the money and drove off.

The Muralles family never saw either of their children again. Over the years, soldiers in civilian clothes had turned up at their door a few times, demanding more money and saying the children were still alive, though Señor Muralles no longer believed them. Since the new democracy, the family had been left alone by the army "task forces" until yesterday, when Señora Muralles had been kidnapped and mutilated.

The voice of the banker on the radio floated out the open door and over the breakfast patio at San Miguel. It was echoing, distant, surrounded by a scratchy static that made it seem thousands of miles away. *The tactics of fear employed by the forces of repression yesterday prove their guilt as does no other action. The irony of this is that too little has changed in this country despite the new democracy. Accounts have yet to be reconciled. The nation is doing nothing to restore our grievous personal and financial losses at the hands of these common gangsters, men who robbed us as if they had a right to whatever we owned as spoils of war. . . .*

The head prosecutor, an attorney named Strassera, then took his place in front of the microphones. He complained that his office had received three new bomb threats that morning. He made a plea to the press and to the people to urge the government to increase security at the trials, and, finally, to provide police protection to witnesses scheduled to testify.

Betty Ann came out to the patio, bringing a tray of fresh hot coffee. "We've got to buy Mamá a decent radio next chance we get. She's all hunched up like a monkey on a grindstone over that little transistor."

She sat down beside Papá, who was still buried in the newspaper. I explained the day's events and the Muralles story, and showed her the front-page photo of Señora Muralles being helped through the doors of a hospital, a blanket wrapped around her shoulders, her neck and face burned. The words hitting the sunny air in my own language made the witness tampering seem at once more real and more outrageous. Betty Ann was sobered, her happy mood of the day changed by the photo of Señora Muralles. I looked around the estate at San Miguel, noting how flimsy the wrought-iron gates and fences really were, thinking how easy it would be for a Ford Falcon to drive right through them. I thought of how remote and isolated we were, surrounded by large country estates that were virtually deserted except on weekends.

"Maybe they've gone too far again," Papá said. "The best face this news can have is that people will see the courage of this man Muralles and his wife. They'll know we have to clean out the police and armed forces of everyone who was involved."

A car horn honked at the gates of the estate. It was the same taxi that took Papá to the train station and off to work each morning. He excused himself, took a last sip of coffee, and went into the house for his briefcase. From inside the house, Mamá's voice sounded, raised, nervous, scolding her husband for even thinking of going off to work today. "You're asking me to wait out here not knowing what to think while you're off in the city where anyone could get his hands on you?"

Papá insisted. He reminded her that they had decided long ago not to live in fear. The front door of the house opened. His quick footsteps sounded on the stones of the walk, then there was the sound of the iron gates squealing open and closed. The rattling taxi drove off down the lane trailing clouds of blue exhaust. Mamá came out onto the patio and sat down at the table. She asked Betty Ann for a cigarette, though she hardly ever smoked. "Sometimes your father can be as crude and insensitive as a wheelbarrow," she said to me. "You see how he is? How he drives himself when there's no need?"

I was about to say something in his defense, then stopped. I nodded my head, agreeing with her. Betty Ann needed no translation. She raised a thumb in the air and jabbed it in my direction.

"Men," she said in English.

"It's clear," Mamá answered in Spanish.

I shrugged, guilty as charged. I rose from the table, cleared some cups and saucers, and went off into the house. Behind me, the two women smoked with wounded resignation.

I was filling the sink with hot water and dish soap, doing the breakfast cleanup, when I heard a car pull up by the gates. The gates opened, fast, with a loud shriek of iron hinges. I opened the door and looked out. It was Papá, hurrying up the walk. He called out in a loud, excited way to his wife.

Mamá ran around the house, answering him with alarm, and met him on the walk. I watched as they discussed something urgently which I couldn't make out. They came to a fast agreement, Mamá nodding her head once, then rushing back toward the house. She brushed past me in the doorway and hurried into the bedroom.

Papá came in after her, gestured toward the sink and my apron, and said, "I'm afraid there won't be any need for that today." He was smiling, and there was a cheerful tone to his voice, but it sounded forced. I untied the strings and took off the apron. "Your mother and I have decided that it might be best for us to leave San Miguel right now."

"Leave? Right now?"

"Well, yes. It's probably not important, but there were some unmarked police cars at the station. Let's just say I didn't like the look of things. It's most likely only a bad feeling. Who knows? But as Dr. Mignone says at the CELS, when we get a bad feeling, well, why be such a fool as not to do something about it?"

"The day before yesterday, I had the same kind of feeling." I told Papá what had happened outside the Florida Garden, and how I had thought I was being followed. "Of course, it was nothing," I said.

"You did the right thing being careful," he said. "There are too many times when your mother and I haven't been careful enough. God knows they could have followed us out here and found out about this place. But we've never been bothered here, not once. There's really no reason to think they would bother us now. Only just in case . . . well, you get my meaning." He smiled, gave me a sound pat on the shoulder, then went off to the bedroom to help with the packing. "No need to take everything," he said on his way. "It's at most going to be for a couple of days."

I went out to the patio and told Betty Ann.

"I think they want to do this pretty fast," I said.

"Let's get on it then." She was up out of her chair and off to the guest house fast, but too fast, I thought. I could see her experience with thugs in the unmarked police car coming back to her. In the guest cottage, her clothes were flying across the room as she tossed them messily into an open hanging bag.

"Hey, slow down," I said.

"Just hush up and get your own things together. Jesus," she said. "When the hell is this going to end?"

I looked at my heaps of notes and papers. There were about ten shopping bags full of them by now. I was stunned for a moment, realizing it would be impossible to take them with me. Then I was at a loss trying to think of a safe place to put them. I got down on my hands and knees and began rifling through each bag for cassette tapes, pulling them out of file folders of their accompanying pages of notes and documents. I worked fast, scattering the cassettes out behind me on the floor, going through the bags just once, and not sure I got all of them. By that time, Betty Ann had already zipped up and gone out the door. Mamá began calling to me from the house. I found my suitcase, gathered up the tapes, and tossed them in. Then I got down my one good suit from the closet, my good shoes, two clean shirts, and a quick and disorderly handful of things from the dresser drawer. Papá was in the doorway then, looking flushed and out of breath. "Ready, my son?" he asked.

"Just a minute," I said. I grabbed up my suitcase and the small shoulder bag with my tape recorder, addresses, current notes. I thought for a moment about the laptop computer, then, on second thought, I decided to shove it and the shopping bags of notes under the boards of one of the built-in beds, out of sight. Papá saw what I was up to and helped.

"By the way, how are you fixed for money?" he asked. "It was my day to go to the bank to get money for the month. I'm afraid we'll need some for this taxi to take us all the way into the city, since we won't want to use the train. I've only got about half the fare. . . ."

I checked my pockets. I realized that in my hurry, I had almost left all the rest of the money I had behind, stashed in a dresser drawer. I pulled a thin sheaf of U.S. twenty-dollar bills from out of a ball of socks. "Will this do?"

"Just until I get to the bank," he said. "Let's go then. If we pay him in dollars, I'm sure our driver will take us for a twenty."

We rode into the city in an overloaded taxi with bad springs and bald tires. With each acceleration on the four-lane into Buenos Aires, the engine made a high, whining sound as if threatening to explode. The first few times it made that noise, Mamá grabbed at her throat and took in a deep breath. Papá was also nervous, keyed up, looking out the back window frequently to check what was behind us. He tried some cheerful small talk for a few minutes but saw that wasn't working. After a while, he pulled some papers out of his briefcase and began reading them in a distracted silence.

I was in a dark mood. I went over in my mind what I had packed, knowing I was missing something I would need. I tried not to think about it. I looked out the window. The flat and seemingly endless ranchlands stretched out on either side of the highway, the pastures still green in winter, fat cattle grazing in the yellow sun.

The engine of the taxi made that loud siren sound again. Mamá jumped. She slid closer to Betty Ann on the seat, put her arm around her, and said she was sorry. Betty Ann squeezed her arm and told her not to worry, but Mamá wouldn't stop. She broke into the grim silence of the ride and said again that she was sorry, so sorry. I turned away from them, trying not to listen. We reached the outskirts of the city. It struck me then. We were running. It was as simple as that. And the fact that we were on the run was by now so acceptable that I hadn't asked and no one had even said where we were going.

Testimony

APPREHENSIONS ABOUT FAMILY security grew in the wake of the Muralles kidnapping. Papá telephoned Martín Segundo and Alicia to join the rest of us, and to leave their baby with friends. We checked into a third-class hotel. The family shared a small suite of three rooms on the hotel's top floor, with a kind of sitting room in between that had a few pieces of scarred and dusty furniture. We spent a bad night. There was a strong stench of insecticide. The mattresses felt as if they were stuffed with packing straw. The damp beds crackled under our tossing bodies. We awoke with little time. We rushed through the motions of swallowing aspirins, taking quick showers, sipping at hurried cups of bitter coffee sent up to our connecting rooms.

While the others were dressing, I took the stairway down to the lobby. The men had agreed over a dinner no one could eat that the family should take every precaution. I was chosen as the logical one to go through a security drill in the morning.

I came out of the stairwell and into the lobby. I stood to one side, near the check-in desk, looking around for anyone who might be loitering there. The lobby was empty except for an elderly couple getting ready to unload their heavy bags onto an abandoned bellhop's cart. They looked like pensioners on a tour of the world they had saved for all their lives. But they had been steered into a wrong turn, landing at this hotel. Or maybe it was just dawning on them what was in store for them on their inadequate budget. Here they were, after a long and uncomfortable night flight on a charter, now at the mercy of a bad hotel in a strange country, caught there, unsure, wondering whether to wait any longer for the boy in his greasy uniform to appear from his languid cigarette break in the coatroom or simply to carry their bags up to their rooms by themselves. I passed near the couple on my way to the hotel doors. Both wore the sleepless, pursued, fearful expression of people who found themselves trapped.

I stepped outside. The weather was wintry again, with a low cloud cover pressing down on the city. I started checking up and down the street. I took quick imaginary photographs and reviewed them in my mind, watching for any sign of stakeouts. I saw nothing unusual. I pulled my coat collar up to my ears, turned, and walked up the street one block. It was a sad little street. The sidewalk tiles were upended and broken. There were deep holes dug into the sour earth under the tiles every few meters, exposing buried drain and water pipes that had been repaired and then abandoned that way. I moved along, stepping gingerly around the sharp, broken tiles and open trenches, scuffing my polished shoes.

The cold was momentarily refreshing, waking me up more fully from a bad sleep. Then the humid chill of the river breeze cut through my overcoat and suit jacket with such numbing penetration that I almost let loose with a small moan at each new gust of wind. It was just before the morning rush hour. Small groups of bus riders were stamping their feet to warm them in the rubble of the busted walks. I continued up the street, passing the people at the bus stop. I bared my ears to the cold and looked over my shoulder to see if anyone was following me.

I stopped, turned at the corner, and crossed the street. I walked back down the sidewalk to the next corner, squared off, and crossed the street again. I loitered a moment to look into a butcher shop window with its hanging slabs of beef. The chalkboard prices looked as though they hadn't been changed for a few days, which I took as a good sign—the delirium of the hyperinflation was finally abating. I searched again up and down the block. Nothing had changed, not even the lone taxicab that was waiting in the loading zone in front of the hotel, its driver scanning the sports pages of a newspaper. There was no sign of any danger.

I crossed the street and went through the revolving door into the hotel lobby. I crossed the worn red carpet with its fraying pattern of golden laurels. At another time, I would have stopped to take closer note of the architecture. The hotel was an aging, crumbling overstatement of optimism and pretension from another era, a relic of the 1920s, when baroque facades were drenched in coats of gold paint and halls of mirrors went up everywhere. Argentina was imagined to be one vast and endless fiesta, and each new building was meant to be a palace. Buenos Aires was a "city of white Caesars," as Christopher Leland described it, rich and limitless, indulging itself in wine, tangos, and arrogance. I walked through the lobby of that old hotel called the Ayacucho Palace. On either side of me stood two fat Romanesque columns covered with marble-patterned wallpaper, paper that was peeling off in large dangling folds. The columns looked like ancient scrolls stood on end, ready to unravel over a sad, nostalgic emptiness that seemed to me, under this morning's circumstances, nothing less than blessed.

Papá Benevento had been right, as usual. This hotel was the perfect place for family security. No one would think of looking for us there. The elderly couple was gone. The lone night clerk had his back turned to the check-in counter. He was busy adding up receipts, waiting for his shift to end, puffing on a black-tobacco cigarette that produced a thick cloud of greasy smoke that smelled like organic fertilizer. I picked up the telephone receiver on the desk. The mouthpiece had its tiny holes so filled with grime that it was hard to believe it could transmit any sound. I asked the crackling voice of the hotel operator to ring the family's rooms. Papá answered. "All ready now," I said.

The family came down in shifts. Papá and Mamá were together in the creaking elevator with its sliding cage door. He was dressed in his best three-piece blue lawyer's suit, his thinning gray hair slicked back, his mustache perfectly trimmed and combed. He tucked his leather portfolio under his arm, pulled the cage door back, and like a gentleman made way for his wife. He escorted her through the lobby. There was an eagerness in his stride, as though he were on his way to accept some great honor or prize. Mamá Benevento was slowing him down, stopping him while she arranged her black wool scarf around her neck. Then she pulled on her black leather gloves. Her face was pale. She had a distracted, reluctant expression, like that of a distant relative on her way to a funeral.

Coming down the stairs, Martín Segundo and Alicia were chatting in a cheerful-sounding English to Betty Ann, who, like Mamá, was also dressed in black. She looked around nervously as she stepped out into the lobby. When she finally saw me, I caught in her eyes an expression I knew well.

We had lain awake most of the night. She had sat up on the

239

edge of the bed, chain-smoking in the darkness. When she was nervous or frightened, she had this way of drawing so deeply on a cigarette that with one long inhale half of it was ash. Sometime in the night, we heard a quiet weeping. Betty Ann was the one who got up, and with her few words of Spanish, she persuaded Mamá to lie down on the couch in the connecting room. She massaged Mamá's tiny back and shoulders, kneading out the tension and pain. There was a low whispering between them, words in different languages neither could fully comprehend but which they understood at some deeper level of tone and intention and intimacy. The two of them finally fell into a tender dozing together on the couch.

Now here was Betty Ann, looking barely awake, startled out of sleep. With all the rush, without time even for a full cup of coffee, she was up and moving by the force of nervous tension alone. She knew the dangers—knew that the wife of the witness Muralles had been tortured, burned all over her body with cigarettes, then dumped naked into a highway ditch. Still, she knew the least about the reasons or what might happen. Papá Benevento assumed the attitude, even in the worst moments of his family's hiding out, that he wouldn't dwell on the darkness of our situation. He withheld all talk about the grim possibilities with the same cheery, euphemistic style he used when he avoided unpalatable subjects at a dinner table. He expected the same of everyone else, which could leave too much to the imagination and only make things worse. I could tell with one look that my wife's nerves were shot. She was the most alone of all of us, doing her best, but the least connected to what was going on.

I was about to go over and take her arm when Papá pulled up short beside me. Papá looked out the big window at the street. He made a small shifting of his eyes at the one waiting taxicab. I nodded, just once, the order understood. I pushed out through the revolving door and stepped off the curb into the oncoming traffic. I raised my arm, hailing a cab. I marveled, as always, at how Buenos Aires was like a New Yorker's wildest dream when it came to taxis. Any time of the day or night, even during rush hour, all I had to do was raise an arm or even so little as point a finger into traffic and a cab pulled over in no more than a minute.

We would need two cabs. Papá was in the street beside me, also hailing a taxi. In a few seconds, two fresh taxis pulled up in front of the hotel. The driver who had been waiting in the loading zone put down his paper and began angrily honking his horn. Papá gestured in the cab's direction. I understood. I would play the role of the family enforcer this time. Papá helped Mamá into the taxi he had randomly hailed, and it quickly sped away. I pulled a few crisp new bills out of my pocket and waved them near the window of the angry driver. The driver suspiciously unrolled the glass a few inches. "Take this and quit complaining," I said. "Go on. This should buy you enough gas to take your taxi somewhere else."

I shoved the bills in a small wedge through the crack. They fluttered into the driver's lap like colorful litter. The man tried to scoop up the money and shove it back out the window, but I was already walking away. The driver shouted after me in an angry rattling of Spanish. He made an "up yours" gesture out the window.

Martín Segundo had already seen the women into the other taxi that had pulled up. He was standing at the open door, waving at me to hurry. I trotted down the sidewalk and slid into the front seat. I took one more quick look ahead and behind, and through the glass of the hotel window. The cab lurched out into traffic. I leaned awkwardly over the seat just enough to take Betty Ann by the arm and squeeze it once, as though asking her how she was doing. The eye contact said that she was holding her own. I pulled my arm away. She lit another cigarette and drew on it deeply.

"To the Plaza of Justice," Martín said. "Take the Avenida Las Heras, the long way around."

Only when the taxi turned out into the smoky and anonymous chaos of the traffic on the boulevard did we feel safer. Alicia leaned back beside Betty Ann and relaxed the tense severity her tall body assumed whenever she was around her mother-in-law. She talked in English to Betty Ann, complaining about the bad night, the terrible beds, how no one had slept. She yawned. "If only this day were over," she said. She said it as if she were talking about making it through a Sunday barbecue with unpleasant relatives. "Just one more day," she said. "We get through this, then maybe we can get on with our lives."

Easy access to the Plaza of Justice was cut off. There were as many as a hundred police behind steel barricades. Martín had the taxi approach the plaza behind the main courthouse building. The cab stopped in a traffic jam. We searched the small crowd at one of the corner barricades for Mamá and Papá. We spotted them, standing off to one side. A police officer with a machine gun slung over his shoulder was checking through their papers as though he might have singled them out of the crowd. We ditched the cab in the middle of traffic and hurried up the street.

"It's all right, children. No need to rush," Mamá said. "We thought it best to start with the red tape before you arrived. Here," she said to the police officer. He was a young man with a dark, *indio*-looking face that seemed too youthful for his authority. "These are the others in our group," Mamá said. "Come on now, children. We'll need your identity cards and passports."

So it went. Mamá Benevento handled the necessary papers, incongruously, considering her small size and the fact that she was a woman dealing with armed police in a culture which automatically deferred such matters to men. But she was effective, getting her family through the first police check ahead of the crowd, using a tone of voice to the various police officers as if she were praising a group of schoolchildren. Still, there was something unsettling about her being in control, a reversal of family rituals. Normally, it would have been Papá Benevento making his lawyerly demands, coming to agreements, pulling his wallet out either to offer proof of his civic position or a small contribution to a police unit's beer fund. The police were being extra careful and official this morning, in the wake of the Muralles kidnapping. Even to get near the main courthouse, there were outdoor checks, one at the barricade entrance, then another at the long steel crowd-control gates set up at the foot of the high steps that led into the building.

Mamá's black-gloved hands were full of our cards and passports and official papers. She was even the one to take Papá's leather portfolio and zip it open for inspection as he stood by, calmly watching. He looked as if he might be feigning helplessness, giving things over sheepishly to his wife, I thought. That was hard for me to imagine. Mamá got her way easily with the armed guards, now treating them like helpful ushers in a crowded theater. It was strange how the police guards snapped to so willingly at the sound of a mother's voice.

Her family was let through, one by one. Mamá marshaled us past the police barricades and up the steps into the courthouse as if she were leading a tour group into a museum. That was only the beginning. Inside, there were electronic searches, X-ray machines. Officers seated at tables double-checked lists of names of those to be allowed into the courtroom against the names on passes and identity documents. Farther on, a group of special service police was leading a pair of German shepherds, brought in to sniff at purses, coats, and briefcases pulled at random out of the crowd. Papá Benevento seemed calm enough, even cheerful, though every few minutes he reshuffled through his leather portfolio a little anxiously, as if he might be missing something. He had been going over his notes for days, as though committing them to memory. He, too, had been up most of the night. One would never think he hadn't slept by his appearance, his good pink color, his eyes that were so sharp and clear and awake. He checked his watch again. The searches were taking too much time.

Many people were taken aside and frisked. The last electronic gate was so sensitive that my belt buckle kept setting off the alarm. An officer stepped in and used the wire stock of his machine gun like a goad to cull me off to one side. I took off my belt. Then I had to take off my shoes with their metal zippers, my watch, my rings. I was pushed farther off into a small group of people who waited there with me, also stripped of their jewelry, their pockets turned out. We milled around in stockinged feet, meekly holding up our trousers, until we were finally let into the hallway.

It was eight fifty-three. Papá was due in the witness room in seven minutes. One of the prosecutor's assistants stood by in the hallway leading to the courtroom. With him there was a group of friends of the family. El Gordo Peluffo and his wife, Regina, were waiting with open arms for us to get through security. Off to one side, leaning against a wall, Jorge Gallo was smoking. Mamá's best friend, Beatrice, was also there. It was the whole crowd from San Miguel. Only Tía Amalita was missing. As soon as Papá Benevento was through the last security gate, they surrounded him like a family. The prosecutor's assistant stepped in, gesturing at his watch in agitation. Papá hugged each of his children quickly. We pounded him on the back, gave him the thumbs-up sign, wished him luck like an athlete before a race. He hung on for too long to Mamá, then kissed her on both cheeks, embracing her once more. "Go with God," she said.

The prosecutor's assistant stepped in and urged them apart. The portfolio had been left partly unzipped somehow. Pages spilled out and scattered. We were all on our hands and knees for mad desperate seconds, gathering up his notes, shoveling them in disorder back into the portfolio. The assistant and Papá then rushed off down the long hallway, turned a corner, and were gone.

The family waited in the large outer corridor. It was like the entryway to a neoclassical palace but smaller in scale. The long angles of the hall's perspective and the spacing between the thin columns seemed manipulated, the proportions scaled to reduce the impression of individual size of anyone standing there. People seemed to grow smaller as they crossed under the square Roman arch over the doorway and entered the courtroom. Though there were increasing numbers of people let through the security checks and crowding into the corridor, their footsteps and voices echoed with a steadily more hushed and lonely sound. Over the entrance to the main courtroom was a sign that read: *By order of the authorities, once you enter, if you leave for any reason, you will not be permitted back inside.*

Martín Segundo pointed out the sign. The family crowded around an ashtray near the center of the corridor and smoked voraciously, even Mamá. The cigarettes were passed out among us with a quiet and pensive grimness.

A few meters away, there stood a small booth with caged windows, painted brown, like a ticket-selling pavilion at a fairgrounds. Mamá took a few steps toward it, tapping the ashes of her cigarette into her open palm. While Martín Segundo and El Gordo were talking over what was going to happen, I followed her around the small structure. I saw that she was counting off the ticket windows until she found a particular cage. "I didn't think of this until now," she said in a dreamy, distant voice. "This is the booth where Alejo worked. This was his first real job. Here, three days a week as a federal clerk for the courts while he was going to the university. He sat right there. He stamped and filed papers. He collected and counted fines."

"He hated that job. It bored him out of his mind," said Jorge Gallo, who was suddenly standing just behind us. Jorge tapped me rudely on the shoulder. Without his saying anything, I held out my pack of cigarettes. He shook out a handful and dropped them in his pocket. "Pardon me," he said.

The three of us stood together for a dreamy moment, looking through the mesh into the cage that was suddenly filled with an illusion of Alejo, his hands stained with ink, dust covers on his sleeves, his intelligent, good-humored face looking bored. Then the booth was empty again.

"He never wanted to study law, you know," Mamá said. "He went to law school and took this job to please your father. If I'd had my way, he would have been long gone to Paris to study letters or painting. Alejo should never have been here. Now look," she said with an edge of bitterness. "The very place he worked is in sight of where they'll take evidence in the case of his brother."

"It's always the same in this country," said Jorge Gallo. "The guilty are set free and the innocent are forgotten."

The noise was steadily growing around us. On either side of the office booth, groups of well-dressed spectators were beginning to pass by, their voices as subdued as though they were entering a church. As they moved past the final table of guards and on into the courtroom, the sound of their voices and footsteps was echoing and then diminishing into what seemed a limitless emptiness.

I reached over and took Mamá's hand, spilling her ashes. She gripped my hand back, hard. She sucked in a deep breath and held it for a long time. Martín Segundo was suddenly beside us. He put his strong hands on our shoulders and started to move us along. "Let's go now, people," he said. "They're ready to begin."

"Are you all right, Mamá?" I asked.

She let go of my hand and let out her breath. She pulled away from Martín's urging and stopped moving. She stared off through the wire mesh of the empty cage.

"Mamá? Are you okay?"

"Your father and I have been waiting for this moment for seven years," she said. "In all that time, he hasn't told me exactly what he plans to say. Not that I don't know. I mean generally. I'm the one who has spent so long doing interviews and taking notes on what happened to other families, and your father thought he was being kind not to tell me the details of what happened to my own. Only now, I'm not sure that I want to know."

"Come along, Mamá, please," said Martín Segundo. "He's going to need us in there, and you've got all our papers in your purse."

"Of course, my son," she said. "Let's go in now."

The courtroom where the comandantes were being tried was surprisingly small. It was said among the press corps that such a forum had been chosen by political design to make it impossible for large numbers of the public to attend. The courtroom looked like a neoclassical chapel. A congregation of about eighty people was cramped into hard wooden pews that faced the long bench of the magistrates, the defense and prosecution tables, and the lone witness box set up so that testimony would be given directly addressing the judges. At most, the backs or profiles of the witnesses would be turned toward the public and to the press. Above the main floor, rising up on either side of the main gallery reserved for official guests and dignitaries, there were two narrow balconies of steep benches for the general public, from which they could look down on the proceedings. About another eighty people could be crammed in up there, packed in shoulder to shoulder. To get a pass to the public seats required waiting in line long before dawn or even camping out overnight as if for tickets to a popular concert in front of a special, auxiliary building of court offices. There had been times when the street had been cleared of those waiting for passes because of bomb threats. Once, in the gray of dawn, from a black speeding car, there opened up a burst of machine-gun fire that had miraculously not injured anyone.

Underneath the overhangs of the public balconies were the press boxes, one side for newspapers and radio, the other side for television crews. Most of the seats in the press boxes were empty. On the newspaper side there were four reporters with tape recorders and notepads sitting in their laps, sleepily waiting for the testimony to begin. As usual, I didn't see any member of the international press corps present. Several had turned out the opening week. They scribbled a few notes and had all they could use. Anderson from *Newsweek* made a quick television appearance on a Buenos Aires talk show to discuss the issues as though he were an expert. The *Los Angeles Times* and, after them, the *New York Times* had done the best job of coverage. They had Buenos Aires correspondents who dropped by regularly. But most of the international reporters took airplanes home after the first week to file stories that were six or seven column inches at the most, the majority of them buried on the back pages.

In the television box, one lone crew from an independent channel in Buenos Aires was setting up a battered tripod and camera. It would be the same as usual. There would be a few quick shots of the major witness for the day, fifteen or twenty seconds of tape, then another twenty or thirty seconds of the prosecutors, the defense attorneys, the judges, going through their motions. Then a correspondent would do a summary voice-over and a stand-up commentary in the hallway or back outside on the courthouse steps. That would be it, a wrap. Each evening, the trials were given barely two or three minutes of the news on Argentine television.

National TV coverage was scanty for good reason. During the

years of dictatorship, no media so supported and spread propaganda for the military as television. Most of the correspondents and people in charge of the three major channels at the time still continued in their jobs. Only one international television crew and reporter had done more than show up for the first week or two of the trials. VISNEWS, out of London and Amsterdam, had faithfully stood by in the courtroom, day in, day out, hour after hour recording the most important moments. There was talk of an extensive documentary. Then the crew had been suddenly pulled off the story and sent home. For their hundreds of hours of hard, full-time work, I guessed that no more than fifteen minutes of reporting about the trials had been viewed so far on television in the rest of the world.

Here it was, I thought, the first time in the history of the world that a country had decided to put on trial its former government for human rights abuses. When had that ever happened before? When had any other country so turned in on itself in shame, grief, and resignation, exposing its past crimes, uprooting its own honor and beliefs, and at such great risk of military reprisal and violence from within? Yet the press boxes were empty. So much for the real story, the one that wasn't known before. Now, long before it could ever get out completely, the editors had made their cuts and gone on to something else. Producers told directors to go to a wipe and fast-forward on the switching boxes. The world turned but briefly a faint interest to a story and then it was forgotten. The story went on. But from the news it simply vanished.

Mamá Benevento led the way into the courtroom. She stopped at a long pew near the back, exchanging quick words with Martín Segundo, and with El Gordo, who wanted to sit farther up front. They agreed to find seats toward the back, near her. "Let me sit in the aisle—explain to your wife," she said to me. She took my hand again and squeezed it hard.

"You don't have to explain," I said.

She let go of my hand. I slid to my place near one end of the long bench. Martín and Alicia and the others sat in the pew just in front, craning their heads around, unhappy at how far they were from the witness box. I looked at my hand. There were deep red marks where Mamá's nails had dug in. Betty Ann sat down beside me. Next to her, Mamá remained standing, uncertainly. Other people were pushing past her to take seats, convincing her finally to sit down. When she did, she put one of her small arms over Betty Ann's shoulders. The two women leaned into one another in a kind of embrace.

The courtroom was full. From the public galleries above, voices joined the rest like whispered prayers before a mass. Above the high judges' bench that rose up over the court like a medieval altarpiece, there was a colorful painting on the wall that seemed meant to be worshiped. At a level just above where the judges' heads would reach when they were seated, there was an ornately lettered motto, *Afianzar la Justicia,* "To Uphold Justice." In a billowing white cloud rising up out of the motto, there was an elongated figure that was a bad copy from the paintings of El Greco of a merciful Christ with both arms spread wide. Above the head of the Christ, hovering over him and lit from within, there was a stained-glass window that depicted the great seal of the nation. Two strong arms were extended into a sky-blue oval of glass. The arms were clasping hands around the blade of a sword. Covering the gilded handgrip and part of the hilt was the red stocking cap of liberty with its republican rosette made famous during the French revolution. Above this there was the face of a golden sunburst, the rays extending from it in dozens of sharp bayonets of glass, the sun symbol of the nation. On both sides of this national seal, in a position above it and the Christ and the clouds, painted larger than the other symbols, there were depicted two helmeted knights in full armor, heads bowed, praying over the hilts of their drawn swords.

Under these images more military than merciful, the bailiff and groups of attorneys entered somberly and took their places. Everyone stood. The lights in the courtroom grew suddenly brighter. The glare was almost too bright to look past or through and see the tall judges' thrones with any clarity. Off to one side, through an open doorway, smoke from a cluster of policemen's cigarettes drifted in and covered the front of the courtroom in a haze.

A line of judges walked in, single-file, with thin leather briefs under their arms. They were young-looking men, all six of them. They wore no robes, only conservative business suits, white shirts, ties, an air about them more of a corporate board meeting than a courtroom. The largest of them was a heavyset man with a black mustache, flanked by his colleagues on either side. He sat down first, in a seat which appeared a little higher than the others. In the glaring haze of light, seated as he was just under the painted wall, there was the bizarre effect, a momentary optical illusion, as if he had suddenly taken life from the painting or was wearing it like a crown. This was the president of the court, who generally served in the capacity of an Examining Magistrate. He was, in the end, the judge whose motions and questions mattered more than anything else.

The stenographers waited, hands poised over their machines. The prosecutor was catching his breath. He was straightening his tie with one hand and riffling through what looked like a cluttered mess of papers with the other, his assistants helping him. The defense attorneys sat with a bored-looking reserve and appeared at any moment as though they might fall back into an interrupted sleep. They were curiously inactive, as usual, given that under the Napoleonic Code upon which Argentine law was based, the accused were considered guilty until proved innocent. The burden of proof rested not with the prosecution but rather with the defense. The accused could choose either to be or not to be present at their own trials. They could refuse to answer questions, in person, put to them by the prosecution, except for their initial declarations of guilt or innocence, which could be delivered to the court in writing. In the cases of the comandantes, former *presidentes de facto* and commanders in chief of the nation, the generals had decided to abstain from the trials. They had other teams of lawyers moving with appeals and Supreme Court petitions to declare any civil trial illegal in their cases, arguing that, as military men, they had the right to military tribunals. So it was a crucial defense strategy not to recognize the legality of the charges against them in the civil cases. The defense lawyers deported themselves as if their clients did not exist in fact but in name only, mere technicalities in a process they regarded as meaningless and absurd. There was no place reserved for the accused at the defense tables.

The court president who acted as Examining Magistrate was the chief questioner in this system. He and his five colleagues would decide the verdicts. The prosecution and the defense attorneys could mainly present written arguments, depositions, declarations of evidence. They could bring witnesses in to answer written questions submitted to the Examining Magistrate, to be asked or not by judicial discretion. The prosecution and the defense could cross-examine, argue before the bench, deliver their summations. So it was the Examining Magistrate who had the power to lead the trial wherever he wanted. He coughed once, cleared his throat, and said to the prosecution, "You may bring in your first witness."

A thin youth with long, wavy hair, effeminate in his movements and dressed in a brown suit about two sizes too large for him, was led in from one side of the courtroom. He seemed to wilt as he became aware of how many people were watching him. Even from a distance, his dark eyes could be seen shifting around in a jumpy way, like a frightened bird's. The bailiff swore the youth in. His name was Gustavo Nino. He faced the Examining Magistrate and took his seat in the witness box. He sat so that his back was mostly turned to the crowd. The microphone let loose with a shriek of feedback. The youth shifted his position, experimenting with the microphone until he was so bent over it that his lips must have been touching it as he spoke.

The Examining Magistrate began with his usual question. "Have you ever been a member of or in any other way been associated with a political group that was enemy to the defendants?"

No, the witness answered.

"Have you ever known or been associated with anyone who is a member of such a group?"

No, he said again, more reluctantly.

"Do you know of anything else that would prejudice your opinion of the defendants?"

No, the witness said.

"Would you then describe for the court the events of the 8th of December, 1977, and those of the following day?"

Betty Ann was squeezing my arm, pressing for a translation. The witness was hard to hear. His voice grew steadily lower in volume as he told his story, and with a manner as if he were revealing intimate and embarrassing secrets. Still, he spoke too fast for simultaneous translating. It was hard to get across the main gist of each statement in English without losing too much of what followed. I began to get behind the witness after a few seconds. I had the sense of words coming to me through the whistling microphone like the playback of a cassette tape with bits and pieces of it erased.

. . . three in the morning . . . two carloads of men . . . jungle fatigues . . . pistol to my mother's . . . They pulled me out of bed by the hair. . . . older brother . . . address . . . I don't know why. . . . tied my

253

*wrists with wire and put a hood over my head. . . . their car, a green
Ford Falcon . . . kicked me and shoved me into the trunk. . . .*

"What's he saying?" Betty Ann still had an arm around Mamá.
She had to lean over awkwardly and whisper into my ear. "Is this
about your brother Miguelito?"

"He's saying the death squad came to his house. They beat him
up and made him take them to his brother's address."

*. . . my brother and his friend . . . in the car following the car I was
in. . . . There was this little hole in the trunk, made by a screw that was
missing. . . . I got my blindfold partly off and could see out this little
hole. . . . We turned, sped up, slowed down. It was a long time before we
stopped. Then I could see where we were. That's how I know it was the
corner of Paseo Colón and the Avenida Juan de Garay. The car my
brother and his friend were in was gone. Nobody in my family ever saw
them again. . . .*

I stopped translating. Nino's voice was so low by then it was a
barely audible, hoarse mumbling. The shoulders of the youth were
hunching like an old man's in the witness box, as if he were trying
to make his body smaller. He looked and sounded so small and
remote it was hard to believe the sound was even coming from his
direction.

"Come on, please, tell me what he's saying."

"He's talking about how he was taken into the basement on a
certain corner he knew. They laid him out on a metal table and
tortured him."

The Examining Magistrate's voice boomed out over the quiet,
rasping sound of the witness. "What is it, exactly, that you mean
when you say that they tortured you?"

*. . . the electric prod . . . on my stomach . . . on my arms . . . on
my testicles. . . . I told them everything but that was nothing because I
didn't know anything. . . .*

"Honey, what's happening?"

254

"I don't know. Please. I can hardly hear what he's saying myself, damnit," I snapped.

"While you were a prisoner in the building later identified as the Club Atlético, as in your previous depositions, did you in any way see or speak to with positive identification one Miguel Angel Benevento? And if so, could you please tell the court how you came by this identification. How are you sure?"

There was a gentleness in the magistrate's voice, as though coaxing the witness, reminding him of some crucial evidence he might have overlooked.

. . . clear, from photographs, later. And from his nickname there, Tato, which I heard some of the other prisoners using. . . . small groups for the showers . . . they took our hoods off while we were waiting. They made him crawl past the rest of us so we'd see what they would do if we caused them trouble. The guards emptied our slop buckets over his head. He couldn't walk. He was dragging his legs. He pulled himself across the floor with his arms. . . .

Mamá was suddenly out of her seat and into the aisle in a rush. The violence of her quickness drew attention from the galleries. She was running down the aisle as if fleeing a fire, then was out the door and gone.

"Go after her!" Martín whispered urgently.

Alicia and Regina were on their feet and starting to work their way down the pew. Betty Ann stopped them. "It's okay," she said. "I'll be the one to go."

People were beginning to shush us. It wouldn't be long before the bailiff would notice. I grabbed my wife's wrist and started to offer to go myself. Beatrice was standing by Betty Ann by then, gesturing for one of us to come with her. "No, really," my wife said. "I've seen enough."

I wanted to say something, but she was off into the aisle and on her way, following after Beatrice to catch up to Mamá. Alicia sat down again, her face showing concern. Martín shrugged his shoulders. He gave me a look to say there was nothing we could do. The family had been expecting this possibility. For seven years, almost every Thursday afternoon, Mamá Benevento had tied a scarf on her head and had taken up her sign. She had walked the rounds of the Plaza de Mayo with the other mothers. She had met with them, organized, listened to their stories. For the past three years, she had worked as a member of the National Commission on the Disappearance of Persons, the CONADEP. She had logged, compiled, sorted, catalogued, collected depositions, edited and revised hundreds of thousands of terrible words, always the stories of others, then she had signed her name to the final reports. All of this she had accomplished without tears, without cracking even once. But when it came to such words about her own son, she couldn't even begin to listen.

The first witness concluded his testimony. Neither the defense nor the prosecution added any questions. A commotion broke out in front of the bench. The prosecutor was asking the court if he could make a statement about his next scheduled witness, who had failed to appear. The defense attorneys were suddenly on their feet, declaring that the prosecution had no right to explain. The Examining Magistrate was about to sustain the objection when the prosecution shouted at him hotly, "He's been threatened! Men have assaulted his aunt in the streets! I beg the court to read into the record the prosecution's strong protest of this continuing and insufferable tampering with our witnesses!"

"What about our witnesses?" shouted a defense attorney. "What about bomb threats?"

"That goes on both sides!" an assistant prosecutor joined in. There were outbursts of loud argument from both defense and prosecution. A few scattered flashes went off from the area of the press box, as if this one event would become the news of the day.

The Examining Magistrate raised his hands in a gesture of frustration. He looked toward the bailiff in an exasperated way. Then just as suddenly as the commotion began, both teams of lawyers were quiet again, standing there, waiting. "Enter into the record that both the prosecution and the defense register complaints of threats against their witnesses," the Examining Magistrate pronounced. "Let us proceed."

I noticed a smile under the gray bush of mustache on the face of the main prosecuting attorney. It was as if he had won some kind of victory, though I couldn't figure what that might be. For the rest of the court officials, it seemed nothing unusual had happened. The attorneys took their seats again.

One of the assistant defense lawyers pulled what looked to be a box of cough drops out of his pocket. He passed the box around the defense table. Colorful wrappers were dropped to the floor in a sparse confetti. Then, amazingly, the box of cough drops suddenly sailed through the air across the wide space of aisle between the defense and prosecution tables. One of the assistant prosecutors caught it. He shook out a few for his colleagues and passed them around, then slipped the box into his pocket. Nothing more happened for a long moment. The two tables of attorneys just sat there, calmly sucking on their candies.

The next witness was a forensic scientist who worked for the CELS group, the Centro de Estudios Legales y Sociales, the Argentine equivalent of a Civil Liberties Union. His name was Dr. Eustacio Alvear-Simms. Many articles had appeared in the more liberal newspapers about the man's activities. He was a bone specialist, primarily. I saw a short, mop-haired, spectacled man with slumped-over, ruined posture.

Dr. Eustacio Alvear-Simms had once been a faculty member of the medical school at the University of Buenos Aires. He had spoken out against the dictatorship when he saw that his students

257

were disappearing by the dozen. He was arrested briefly, then allowed to go into exile. He spent his exile studying as a postdoctoral fellow at the University of Texas, where he had learned his new trade. He was taught by the world-famous Dr. Clyde Snow, forensic anthropologist, who later came to Argentina to work with Dr. Alvear-Simms and others in the training of investigation teams.

It seemed incredible to me, from what I had learned the military surely knew, that the death squads had let a man like this one go into exile. They should have seen what a dangerous weapon he would become, a scientist who not only could determine by the smallest chips of bone a cause of death, a specific trauma, but could also extrapolate his many findings into a detailed story of the victim's life and death. For three years, Dr. Alvear-Simms had spent his days and many nights, his face wrapped in an odor-suppressing mask, digging through the mass graves, unscrambling the mixed-together corpses, painstakingly laying out remains on dissecting tables in a large, cooled warehouse building on the outskirts of the city. So far, of the hundreds of bodies that he and his staff had been working on, after thousands of hours of laboring with bones and dental records and genetic matching techniques, Dr. Eustacio Alvear-Simms had established the certain identities of thirty-two of the disappeared.

I followed the man's swearing in and the first robotic motions of his questioning as though through some kind of dense and confusing fog. It was as if thick layers of mosquito netting had been tossed over the courtroom, and I could hardly see through them into a gauzy light. My ears were plugging up with an intense inner pressure. My head began to ache. There was a thumping pain in my eyes and ears until I suddenly had to put my face in my hands. I pushed with my fingers against my eyelids and temples to try and stop the pounding in my head.

I couldn't listen. All I could think of was the image of young

Miguel, kneeling over toy soldiers spread out on the floor of his bedroom, arranging them like two opposing teams in an imaginary soccer stadium. A tiny ball of paper sailed through the air between the plastic players as he made low, breathy noises to imitate the sound of the cheering crowd at a soccer game. I thought of the boy who pocketed candy bars from the corner cigarette stand and then ran off with his friends. It didn't matter what he had done later, what he had become. After his brother Alejo was disappeared, he became bitter, violent. He joined the militancy. He carried a machine gun. He planted bombs. But I only heard the happy voice of the boy who had been the first to call out to me each time I came home from school, during my year with the family as an exchange student. There was nothing I could do to stop the memories. He was my kid brother. I had lost control, and any objectivity. I was fighting to get it back again, but it was no use.

. . . *the sacrospinous ligament and the lesser sciatic foramen . . . the cartilage of the ischial rami . . . showing evidence of trauma prior to the official date of death so mentioned . . .*

Photographs of the evidence were making their rounds on the bench and on the attorneys' tables. The prosecutor from time to time held up a large color print or X-ray plate for the judges, and the public, to see. I raised my head and looked a few times. Then I could no longer bring myself to do it. I listened, vaguely, my eyes focused intently on the stitching of my shoes.

. . . *irregular healing of multiple fractures of the ischium and pubis for at least two weeks . . .*

No one had told the family this would happen. Papá must have known, but had said nothing. He had thought to spare his family. He had harbored this sadness all alone. In the years after Miguel's body had been discovered, identified, buried, it must have been he alone who had attended the exhumation, who had observed the ritual of the body's reduction and numbering and

259

recomposition as though it were so many shards of shattered pottery being catalogued from an anonymous tomb. His many absences during the evenings of the past year must have been spent reviewing the facts and photographs and plates to give his approval. His nights of acid silence as he wandered the tiny apartment in a delirium of insomnia were stripped down at this moment to this single, primary cause. These were his bones, the bones of his son, spread out before us.

. . . fractures to both the right and left femurs in the area just above the medial supracondylar lines. . . . we must conclude this is of secondary importance. . . . evidence of massive hemorrhaging in the region of the internal and external iliac veins, and the obturator, gluteal, and rectal plexus the probable cause of death. . . .

The defense attorneys rose to cross-examine. Their voices were monotonous and wooden. They were reading from statistical charts, citing other authorities, trying to discredit the probable accuracy of the doctor's conclusions.

Martín Segundo whispered to me. He asked if I was all right, but there was a shaky quality to the question that made it clear he was also asking it about himself. I raised my head and drew in a deep breath, and we exchanged looks at each other that shared both our pain and a grim, weak, resigned satisfaction. The case had been made. Miguelito had not died in a gun battle, as the federal police and the military claimed. He had died of other, more terrible causes. The dictatorship had surely lied to cover up in his case. Still, even if that truth had been confirmed, the family had learned nothing really new. We had been sure of the truth all along. And I kept thinking, why bother then? What good was any of this doing?

I felt the sudden and overwhelming sense of the smallness of such proceedings. Nothing really mattered here, in the individual cases, in Miguelito's or anyone else's. Day after day of the trials, it was the gradual and accumulating weight of so many hundreds of similar accounts, the building and powerful mass of them combined into a unified, unstoppable force, that had already decided the outcome. The conclusion had already been reached from the first day, from the very first moment this court was called into session. Guilty until proven innocent, the comandantes were already convicted before this trial had even been allowed to begin. Justice was a rigged game. These trials were a public show in which all of the movements were known. That was why the world had turned its interest away, why no editor or producer so much as blinked. The suspense had gone out. The conclusion was foregone. Unlike the slow, tense building of the acts of a popular drama, the trials were no longer news. There only remained the sad denouement of testimony and conviction. So why not go home now? Why not withdraw right now to some safer, healthier, more healing place? Why put ourselves through any of this? Why should the family suffer any more?

"Martín Alejandro Benevento," the bailiff announced.

Papá Benevento was slow coming through the witnesses' door. This morning, he had seemed in possession of an eager energy, and now, each step closer to the witness box seemed to age him. His face looked colorless, washed out under the lights, blank of expression. Only his eyes seemed alive at all as they searched through the court quickly, not finding where his sons were sitting. I had to control my impulse to raise my arm and wave at him.

Papá was looking downward by then. His movements were careful and stiff, as though he were somehow too frail to make his way up the short steps into the witness box without looking down at his feet to keep from falling. He stumbled anyway. The sound of his shoes clopping on the step was loud, like a pair of bricks dropped on a wooden drum. He turned his back to the crowd, facing the judges. The bailiff swore him in. For a long moment, Papá didn't sit down. He was busy with the quiet shuffling and rearranging of his pages of notes.

"What are those papers you have brought with you?" the Examining Magistrate asked. The judge's voice was kind in an exaggerated way, as though addressing either an invalid or a child.

Just some insignificant scratchings, in case I lose my train of thought. It is not unheard of, Your Honor. With the court's permission . . .

One of the younger defense attorneys rose to his feet. "I object in the strongest terms," he said. "This witness should know better. He is an experienced attorney. He should answer direct questions without the aid of notes or prepared statements."

This is not a prepared statement, nothing of the kind. I know the laws, and this is not in any way . . .

"May I remind the witness that it is the prosecutor who is conducting this case, not you," said the Examining Magistrate. A nearby sector of the courtroom broke into tense laughter. Papá turned his head quickly to look at the crowd. His hands were shakily clutching at his sheaf of notes. A single, thin page escaped him. He stood up partway, reached out for the page, and missed. It drifted out into the air and to the floor. The Examining Magistrate looked on in disbelief. He said in a scolding tone, "Sit down, please. We direct the witness to answer questions without reference to any notes."

Under strong protest . . .

"Very well then. Your protest will be entered into the record. Now may we proceed?" The Examining Magistrate paused for a moment, waiting for an answer that Papá Benevento didn't give him. The judge cleared his throat and rattled off in a quick and dismissive way, "Have you ever been a member of or associated with a political group that was an enemy of the defendants, or have you been associated with anyone who is a member of such a group, or do you know of anything else which would prejudice your opinion of the defendants?"

That is not a fair question, and I would like it so entered into the record. Whether the answer is yes or no, there is still no justification for the crimes that have been committed.

Now three defense attorneys were on their feet with loud objections. "The witness will answer the question," one of them said. "Either that, or we demand that his testimony be disallowed on the admission of prejudice."

"Please answer the question," the Examining Magistrate said. "Let's not be difficult. It's a long enough day."

Not that I knew about then, no. But I wish it entered into the transcript that I give this answer only with extreme protest. Such a question of me and other witnesses at this trial is a clear violation of our rights guaranteed under the restored constitution.

"Acknowledged," the Examining Magistrate said. He continued in a bored, distracted way, "Now, if you please, Dr. Benevento. We all know very well what we're doing here. So let's get this over with." There was more nervous laughter from the front of the courtroom, a restrained but incredulous sound. "All right now. Dr. Benevento, can you describe for the court what happened to you on the date in question, the 8th of December, and the significant events leading up to that day?"

The second-eldest of my three sons was Alejandro Martín Benevento, who was the first to disappear, on the 19th of November, 1976. On his behalf, I presented a plea for habeas corpus on, let me think now, one moment, yes, the 12th of December of that year. In the following months, I made many appeals to the federal police and to each branch of the armed forces, including an interview with General Roberto Viola on the 20th of February, 1977, without resulting information of any kind. . . .

One of the defense lawyers rose to his feet again. "The defense objects on the grounds that it is difficult to see how any of this is relevant," he said. "The case we are hearing today makes no mention of any other Benevento family member but Miguel Angel Benevento. Certainly testimony concerning him has so far not brought up or provided any grounds for the defamation by hearsay of the good name of my client, General Viola."

"The court has asked Dr. Benevento to describe the events leading up to the 8th of December of 1977, and that is what he is doing," the prosecutor answered.

The Examining Magistrate leaned to one side and consulted a colleague for a moment, accepting some whispered remarks. "I order all references to the name of the defendant General Roberto Viola in the last statements of the witness stricken from the record," he instructed the stenographers. "This court allows unusually ample leeway in the presentation of testimony, as is consistent with our established policy for these trials. However, may I please remind both the witness and the prosecution to be as brief as possible. We are running late enough as it is. It's nearly time to break for lunch."

"Thank you, Honorable Judge," the prosecutor said.

Papá didn't speak for a long moment. By the quick shifting movements of his back and shoulders, it looked like he might even be glancing down at his pages of forbidden notes. The notes still lay open in their leather folio, balanced on the railing of the witness box. He cleared his throat a few times. He drank from his glass of water. He closed the leather folder and pushed it to one side.

Excuse me, he said. He coughed. *To continue now, about the events leading up to the 8th of December, let me summarize that four times during the year following my son Alejandro Martín Benevento's disappearance, gangs of men dressed in jungle fatigues broke into my home. They held guns to my head, in front of my wife. They smashed our fur-*

niture, ripped down our paintings, and went through our belongings. *They carried off anything they could find that was of value. During three of these break-ins, with a pistol to my head, which was a nine-millimeter Beretta, the same kind that is standard issue to the military and to the federal police . . .*

He saw the defense attorneys beginning to object again and he stopped talking. He covered his mouth and coughed once more.

. . . I'm sorry. I know. You may disregard that, of course. Pardon me. . . . In any case, each time they broke in, they questioned my wife and me as to the whereabouts of our youngest son, Miguel Angel Benevento. They threatened to take the life of his brother, Alejandro Martín Benevento, who had disappeared, and who they said was in their custody, if we did not or could not tell them where our son Miguel could be found. On the fourth break-in and questioning, they no longer asked where our son Miguel could be found. They did not once mention the name of his brother, either. They blindfolded me and tied my wrists together with wire. My wife screamed at them to stop until they silenced her. They kicked me down the stairway of our building and out into the street. That was the 8th of December, at about three in the morning. They arrested me illegally, and brought me in the trunk of a car to the torture and detention center called El Club Atlético. . . .

"Excuse me," interrupted the Examining Magistrate. "Could you please make clear to the court how you know you were taken to the Club Atlético?"

Yes, of course, pardon me. I should have my notes. I knew it later, after I was released. I was part of the tour conducted by the National Commission on the Disappearance of Persons. My deposition is on file with them. A copy has been made available to this court. I recognized my cell, by feeling inside it, along the walls. There were so many individual marks there, scratched into the cement, by prisoners before me. Wearing a blindfold once again, I was able to count the exact distance in paces down the hallway. Also, the number and size of the steps to the torture room. There was a particular damp smell I immediately recognized. So I could say with all certainty that I was imprisoned in the urban concentration camp that was known as the Club Atlético. But for that one fortunate tour, it would be impossible to say now for certain. The Club Atlético has been demolished. So many of the urban concentration camps were condemned and torn to the ground before they could be used as evidence. . . .

I know, yes, and I'm sorry. I ask the court's patience. That is a statement that should be established by other witnesses. If I could only be allowed to refer to my notes, for the orderly sequence of events . . . But of course not, that's clear, and I apologize again. . . .

To continue, there were no formal charges against me. That was what I was mainly concerned with when I was arrested that morning. What were they charging me with? No answer from them but another kick in the side. So, very well then, I was at least charged with something a year later, during my second arrest. They called it "Illicit Association." Keep in mind that I was never arraigned before a judge, and those charges were never formally submitted. But at least the second time, they gave me something I could go on.

That was after the police contacted me and said that the body of my youngest son, Miguel Angel Benevento, was in the central police morgue. They stated that he had been killed in a gun battle with other so-called subversives. They had kept his body for a year, and under conditions in which it had been allowed to decompose. I filed a civil lawsuit against the federal police over this matter and was in the first stages of it when I was arrested again and taken to a precinct jail, where I was told I was charged with "Illicit Association." You can imagine my reaction. They were charging me with associating illegally with my own two sons, one of whom was a corpse, and the other, Alejandro Martín Benevento, long after he was disappeared and tortured and probably executed. . . .

"These statements are inadmissible!" The chief defense lawyer was on his feet now, shouting. "No one has yet established that this other son of the witnesses is even dead! He could be on the beach in Rio for all we know!"

"Please, gentlemen," said the Examining Magistrate. "I order the witness's last statements to be stricken from the record. Dr. Benevento, you know that this trial is not an open forum for you to express your personal opinions. You must realize how tolerant and broad is the testimony to be considered here. It is unprecedented in the legal history of this nation. But you go too far. I will no longer allow you and the prosecution to play with the few limits that have been set down. I ask you not to insult me, or this court, or your profession any further. Take this as my final warning. I will cut you off at the first opportunity. What you have come here to say will be finished."

Papá Benevento coughed, and shifted in his seat. One hand came up and rubbed the back of his neck as if to release the tension there. He coughed again, stalling for time. He looked at the chief prosecutor, who simply nodded once, as though the two men shared some sudden agreement on how to proceed.

It suddenly struck me that the prosecutor had very little to say. The man was leaning back in his chair, apparently unbothered, his legs stretched out under the table. His hands were folded across his middle in the posture of someone sleepily digesting a heavy meal. It was Papá who showed all the nervousness, so uncharacteristic of him, even down to the hesitant, apologetic tone and direction of his voice. Here he was, a lawyer with thirty years' experience in courtrooms, acting in some ways as if he had never been in one before. Each time I listened to his wavering, uncertain voice, I felt a sour, empty burning in my stomach, and a deep humiliation for the family. It was as though after all the days and months and years of preparation, the coming in late at night with his salmon-pink legal folders full of pages on which he had carefully prepared the details, the facts to be presented, the exact words he considered using, Papá Benevento had suddenly become unhinged, broken, and with every sentence he spoke was at the point of being unable to continue. But was that what was really happening? What was the story underneath the story? What was he really managing to say?

There were facts, events, places, names being spoken that appeared at first to be the confused mutterings of a pitiably unprepared and pressured old man. But beneath that first impression, there was so much else that was being allowed to get through into the record. Papá had not, I realized, even really lied about his knowledge of Miguel's involvement with the militancy. Three or four times, he had even managed to get written into the official transcripts the name of his other son, Alejo, which might one day be further grounds for the claims of and prosecution for his disappearance, should other evidence ever turn up about him. There were large, broad statements of condemnation that had somehow been passed over for objection by the defense. They went farther than any I had heard or read about before in the official record of the trials. Was this an act we were witnessing? Was every line and movement blocked, staged, carefully directed? Was there a larger, hidden design to what he was saying?

I should never have imagined anything else of Papá Benevento. Not after what he had survived, not after the acid and patience of the crumpled time he had voyaged through to arrive, finally, here, at this one moment, this single event that would record in a manner unchangeable and forever what had been so far taken from him and his family and done away with, vanished, disappeared.

Accept my apologies, again, please, and my request for the court's patience. Know that I do not come before you in the capacity of my profession as an attorney, but rather as would anyone else, that is to say as any other father, and as a father of but one of the many thousands of cases of the murdered and disappeared to be considered, and in this case, that of my youngest son, Miguel Angel Benevento, as has been stated. This is a hard thing for me, and I beg the court's indulgence.

For my own part in it, as to the events of that morning, the 8th of December, it has been over seven years that I have been waiting for the opportunity to speak out before a court of conscience. That morning, I was taken from the car in which I had been kidnapped. I was led blindfolded into the detention center called the Club Atlético. They took me up some stairs into a small, tiled area that looked like it had once been a shower room. My blindfold was removed. I was strapped into a metal chair, around the legs and chest, so my arms were free. Across from me was a very bloodstained foam mattress on a metal table. It was the same kind of table used for massages at the athletic club. There were two guards who brought me in, and they wore ski masks.

They left me alone for a moment. Then they came back in, dragging a young boy between them, whom they laid out on the table, on his stomach. The boy was naked but for the cloth hood over his head. Another guard came in, a large fellow with dark skin, a heavy growth of beard, and a very full mustache, whom the other guards called by the name of Turco or sometimes Captain Turco. They addressed him always like soldiers, with military respect, though he wore no uniform, only blue jeans and a flannel shirt. This man did not wear a ski mask, and he did not seem to care if I could see his face. That led me to believe I was living through my last hours on this earth.

This man Turco was the one in charge. The guards did everything by his orders. They spread the legs of the boy out and tied them wide open, to the table. They tied his wrists down also. This boy was not making a sound. He was cooperative, not once resisting. The one called Turco came over to me and pulled my head back by the hair. He called me by my name, and my title, Doctor. He said he wanted me to watch what they were going to do to this boy. "This is a Jew boy here," he said. "Pay attention to what we do to this Jew boy, because this is what we are

269

going to do to your son Miguel, your Tato, if you act like a Jew with us."

Then one of the guards gave this Turco a folder of papers and put a pen in my right hand. He held the papers out and ordered me to sign them, one by one. I did not get a very close look at these papers, but I could see enough to guess what they were. They were bills of sale and legal titles. As I later learned, there was one for each of my two cars, one set of papers for the sale of my apartment, and insurance documents for my wife's jewelry, which had already been stolen. There were authorizations for money transfers from two of my bank accounts, and from my stock market account, and there were some other legal papers. Prices were listed on some of the documents. I could see that the names of the receiving parties, or the so-called "buyers" on the paperwork, had all been left blank. In this condition, they were demanding that I sign them. Copies of some of these papers have been recovered. They are on file with the court. Most of the rest were probably so changed and transferred through the legal system, from one false owner to the next, that by now they are impossible to trace. This is a matter still pending legal disposition. . . .

Yes, of course, please, there is no need. I'm off the point now, I agree. To get back to the events of that morning, I was understandably shocked and dismayed by what this Turco was asking me to do, and I refused. My thoughts were that they were going to murder me in any case. I stood to lose nothing by saying no. They slapped me around. But that wasn't much. "If that's the way you want it then," this Turco said. "Do you see what you are going to force us to do? Didn't I warn you what would happen if you acted like a dirty Jew with us?"

I told him my family is as Catholic as the Pope's. Then the two guards started working on the boy. One of them had a piece of steel pipe. He hit this boy behind the knees with it and made him cry out. Of course, I was willing to sign anything then, and was shouting at them to stop, and that I would sign. But it was too late. The Turco slapped me across the face and stuffed a rag into my mouth. "Here is what we are going to do to your son Miguel, you rotten Jew," he said.

He made a signal to the two guards. One of them grabbed the boy by the legs and spread them wider. The boy was screaming and trying to kick at them, but he was helpless. The Turco grabbed me by the hair and made me watch. The other guard took the steel pipe and rubbed some kind of grease on it. He spread the boy's cheeks and shoved it up his . . . his rectum . . . more than halfway. There was a terrible sound, a cracking, the sound of bones breaking. The boy screamed and heaved up once and then he was quiet. One of the guards left the room. The Turco was still holding me by the hair, calling me names, making me watch.

The guard came back in, carrying a shoe box. The Turco let my hair go. He opened the box and took out a small rat. He held the rat out, by the tail, so I could get a good look. That was enough. I was moving my hand through the air like it had a pen in it, frantic to tell them I would do it now, I would sign anything they wanted. It was no use. The Turco went over to the pipe. He fitted the rat, head first, into the open end, and it was gone. One of the guards screwed a cap over the pipe.

There was a terrible noise. The boy woke up screaming and trying to throw himself around. He went into convulsions, and passed out again. They slapped his face. They sprayed him with a water hose. He came to again, and the same thing happened. It was terrible. I don't know how long this went on. The Turco held out the papers for me, set by set, and I was signing my name to all of them. I signed and kept signing, as fast as I could, begging them to stop. The two guards just stood by, over the boy, watching him. Then they didn't watch him anymore. It was all routine for them. They lit cigarettes and talked about the new football season, the World Cup tournament.

I finished signing the papers. As I said, they were the titles and bills of sale to almost every article of property that I owned. The Turco checked the papers over and put them into a briefcase. "You've been a Jew with us anyway," he said. "You can be sure we're going to do the same thing to your son." He left the room. One of the guards strapped my arms to the chair, and then they left, too.

The rest of that night, a long time, I don't know, I was alone in there with the boy. He would wake up, make horrible sounds, fight against the straps, then he would finally pass out again. It went like that. I sat there and watched him bleed. Or I turned my head away and tried not to watch. There was so much blood that I couldn't breathe for the terrible smell of it. I vomited and nearly choked to death myself because of the gag. There's no way to tell how long I was in there, or we were in there, the two of us. Finally, the boy didn't wake up anymore. He stopped breathing.

Other guards came in for me. I think it was in the morning. I was blindfolded, beaten with nightsticks, then dragged down the stairs and thrown into a tiny cell. I won't describe the conditions there, it's common knowledge, sleeping in the stench of my own urine, being forced to my hands and knees to eat cornmeal from a dish like a dog, all the same way as they treated so many thousands of others. I was there for eight days. Or at least it was eight days later that I was taken away from there, put into the trunk of a car, and driven to the outskirts of the city. They dumped me off in a ditch by the Pan American Highway.

When I was found and then untied and could get back to my home— and this matter is hardly relevant, I mention it only to describe what happened afterward—I discovered that my wife and I had already been served an eviction notice by a real estate company that now owned our apartment. Our cars were gone. Most of our money was missing from our bank accounts. Worse, the law firm where I had worked for twenty years served me notice that my services were no longer desired. There was almost nothing left even to get moved out on, to try and put together the most minimal existence. But, as I said, none of that matters here. What is important here is that no one in my family ever saw my son Miguel again. The men who detained me and tortured me knew he existed, they even used a nickname his mother and I had once called

272

him when he was a very little boy. How would they possibly have known that if he had not been their prisoner? As to the cause of his death, from other testimony here, it seems to add up to a manner very similar to the one they threatened. Let me ask you what other conclusion . . .

. . . It's clear. Yes. I beg the court's patience once again. What I mean to say here is that to the end of my days, I will never understand how this could have happened. I have been a loyal and patriotic citizen. I have spent the best years of my life in the legal services, believing in a system that in the end is right and just and which I have dearly loved. . . .

. . . Is that not to be allowed? No? . . .

. . . All right. No need. You don't have to tell me. They can sit down. The defense lawyers are correct, and you can surely strike that from the record. This is almost over now for them. It's nothing. The lives of my sons mean nothing to them. They're brilliant lawyers. They're sure to make names for themselves. Defenders of the former de facto presidents of the nation. Their offices are going to be full of rich clients from now on, you can be sure. . . .

. . . All right. I know. You don't have to say any more. This is almost done now, and you can all have your lunch. . . .

. . . I'll be leaving now. There will be no more disturbances. Just let me say, in conclusion, to this court, to this official and legal record of the nation . . .

. . . Yes, all right, yes. . . . My sons may not have been angels. But they deserved at the very least what you have here, a trial, the chance to defend themselves. . . .

. . . Laws? You refer to laws? It seems to me that no patriotic citizen can rest until all those responsible are tried and punished under the laws. . . .

. . . That's it then. That's all I have to say. You don't have to tell me, not me, Honorable Judge, when my testimony is finished.

Last Rites

SMOKE ROSE UP in black, funnel-shaped clouds into the gray sky over San Miguel. We could see it from the private cars, driven by El Gordo Peluffo and by Beatrice, that drove our family home after the morning testimony. There wasn't a thought that it would be the Benevento family estate that was burning. Not until, at the end of the paved lane that led to it, Martín Segundo looked up ahead to the roadblock of fire engines and a crowd of people from the neighborhood and said, "Oh, no. No, please, no . . ."

Mediterranean houses burn up, they don't burn down. Because they are built with so much brick and plaster, with very little wood but the beams supporting the roofing, flames leap up from the inside. The fire blasts the windows out from within, sucking in the glass, spewing it upward in a roil of heat and smoke and pressure, leaving them looking like scorched black eyes that stare out from walls that almost always remain standing. The roof then explodes, up and out, like the lid blowing off a pressure cooker, scattering pieces of charred beams and sheets of red-hot zinc and tin into the yard around the building. Everything left inside is baked, melted, reduced to a thick layer of black ash inside an immense brick oven.

That was what happened to both houses at San Miguel. The family stood at a safe distance from the intense heat that cracked the windshield of a fire engine that was parked too close. The power wires melted, then swung crackling to the lawn in a shower of sparks. We watched in stunned disbelief, helpless to a force of nature. The pitiful and inadequate volunteer fire brigade from the town did a heroic job of spraying two thin, weak streams of water at the blazing houses that did little more than raise clouds of steam.

It was all over just before the sun went down. By that time, Papá and Mamá Benevento were searching through the hot ashes of the big house, hand in hand, as if they could find anything.

"At least they didn't touch any of my gardens," Mamá said. "We'll have to plant new flower beds around the house, of course, but see how the trees are only scorched? They should make it just fine."

"The foundation still looks good," Papá said. "I don't see any cracks. With the insurance, who knows? We'll have to see what trouble we have collecting because of the arson, but we had always planned on expanding the big house."

They were touring the wreckage of the estate they had owned and kept so proudly so many years as if it were now a virgin parcel they considered building on. They decided where they were going to put the new dining room. An extra bedroom would go where the old utility shed had been. The fireplace, this time, was going to be built just right, with its back facing the southeast, the direction of the worst winter storms. Less than an hour after the last flames were out, they were keeping their sanity by making plans.

Martín Segundo and his wife, Alicia, sat in shock and tears out on the lawn. He kept going over what had happened with El Gordo Peluffo and the rest of us, angrily pounding his fist into the grass. *Hijos de puta,* he kept saying.

We repeated it after him, helplessly, not knowing what else to do. He swore he would get back at the people who had done this. If he had to, he would spend the rest of his life finding a way. He resolved from that day on to give up everything else and get himself into the government.

The story of what happened was brought to us by Joaquín, the family maintenance man, who had gathered several witnesses. Late that morning, they had seen two cars, both Ford Falcons, one black and one green, parked in front of the gates. Guards with machine guns were posted at either end of the paved lane. Witnesses saw men in business suits and with cans of gasoline in hand forcing their way through the iron gates. The whole operation took less than five minutes. The two cars drove off with the first columns of smoke rising up behind them.

I walked off, in a daze, across the lawn to the guest house. I rolled up the cuffs of my good suit pants and waded through the black, gummy sludge left after the fire hoses had finished. Through the scorched doorway, there was nothing left but an uneven landscape of charcoal and ashes. The dresser and closet where we had kept our clothes, our gifts, everything my wife had purchased, were reduced to a single, indistinguishable heap of charred remains. I waded through the wet, sooty pile to the built-in beds, nothing left of them but a few melted scraps. Under them, I couldn't find anything that looked like my laptop computer, not one piece of it I could identify, not one circuit board or silicon chip, not one backup disk. I kicked and cursed myself for not shoving my boxes of disks into my bag when we had made our move into the city. Nothing remained. Everything I had written for months, every note I had taken, every word, had been vaporized, turned into smoke and ashes. Here and there, I could see a few white bits of paper, bizarre and indecipherable ink-scratchings on them, all that was left of my handwritten notes. A few of my books were strangely, not completely, burned. Ragged, fire-browned pages crackled when I opened the ruined spines. Then they fell to pieces in my hands.

Sometimes, now, not so many years later, in the shadows of the night, I awaken suddenly and listen for the sounds of my step-daughter breathing in the next room. Not able to hear her, or sense her there through the layers of darkness between my bed and the hallway night light, I toss back the covers and quickly pad over the cold floor and across the hallway to her room. I push the door open and stand there for a moment, looking in on her calmly sleeping. I'm always relieved to find her there. I see her as a young woman, just now reaching the age when my two brothers disappeared.

I remember that winter of the trials and our last few days in Buenos Aires. We were all still in shock from the fire, and from the testimony. The family gathered that last Thursday afternoon in a silent vigil, our ghostly, quiet footsteps circling the Plaza de Mayo in a march with the mothers of the disappeared. We walked, arm in arm. The only noise was the crowd of footsteps on the plaza tiles. By that time, my wife and I had both reached a cold stage of alienation from our surroundings. We were experiencing a numbed and deadened feeling that was worse in some ways than what we had felt before. We were looking only to the plane flight home. We stepped reverently on the stark, white outlines of conceptual human beings that had been painted on the plaza to symbolize the disappeared. I would never again know a Thursday when I didn't think of the mothers marching there. There would never be an ending.

After a rushed and tearful send-off from the family, with the few scraps of baggage that we had left, we were soon on an airplane, heading north. The feeling of relief after the flight took off is hard to describe. On the trip home and for a good while afterward we carefully avoided mentioning my family, or what had happened to them, or the grief we felt for them and for what they had lost.

We wanted to be alone and set free. There was something inevitable about what happened. It was only natural, this reembracing of our lives. We were teaching ourselves to care and not to care. After all, we were the ones who could travel on, far away from what we knew and no longer wished to know. We even felt it was like an imperative of our nationality, of our station in this world. We could abandon the memories and the bitterness, leave the devotion to causes to others. We could learn both never to forget and how not to remember. We could kiss the ground when we got back to the United States. We were the lucky ones. We were Americans. We could shut the doors behind us and go on living, even happily, for a time.

Four years later, the Providential President and his Radical Party, largely made up of businessmen and the oligarchy, abandoned the government of Argentina amid scandals and charges of corruption. A new, Peronist president was elected. Carlos Saúl Menem took the oath of office six months ahead of time, during the national crisis of inflation, torpor, and indolence brought on by the collapse of the previous administration. One of his first acts in office was to begin the process of laying down pardons for the military officers responsible for human rights abuses and for the disappeared. He said he wanted to set to work repairing the economy, unifying his people. His justification for the pardons was "national reconciliation."

Five of the nine comandantes were convicted of crimes against humanity at the only trials that were ever held. They were Teniente General Jorge Rafael Videla, Almirante Emilio Massera, Teniente General Roberto Viola, General de Brigada Orlando Agosti, and Almirante Armando Lambruschini. Four other comandantes were set free on technical and evidentiary grounds that amounted to mistrials. Also set free were two top commanders of the federal police. The five comandantes who were convicted were sentenced to terms ranging from four and a half years to life in prison. The longest term actually served by any of them was a little more than six years. The comandantes were then set free, publicly unrepentant, to live out their lives in luxury.

Strongly influenced by the Argentine experience, proposed trials for crimes against humanity committed by the military in Chile, Brazil, Uruguay, and El Salvador were abandoned.

Over the years since my wife and I returned from Argentina during that winter of the trials, we exchanged many letters with my family. We telephoned regularly, too, at first. Then I resigned myself to the fact that I could never convince Mamá and Papá Benevento that the placing of international calls was cheap and easy from the United States. They would ask in alarmed voices what was wrong, going through such attacks of fear when they answered that I finally contented myself with the three to five weeks it took for letters to reach them. Sometimes we made tape recordings and asked the same of them, so we could at least hear their voices. Their questions were always the same. *When will you come to visit us again? When will we be able to see you?*

We were able to make three more trips, in the next five years, back to Argentina to see them. Money was always the problem. One trip we made out of my own pocket, another on assignment for a travel magazine. The last trip was on a government grant from the Fulbright Commission. The last time we saw them, Mamá and Papá were fading under the strain and pressure of their lives. The family had just finished the quiet reburial of the remains of their son Miguel, which had been kept for years as possible evidence for new trials that had been planned. On weekends, Mamá and Papá supervised the slow and costly rebuilding of their house in the country. Five years after the fire, it reached the stage when the new roof would keep out the weather.

Martín Segundo and his family were managing to hold on, and were even prospering. After the winter of the trials, he gave up his work for human rights and his father's practice. He devoted himself to one of the liberal wings of the Justicialista Party. With the new Peronist president, he landed a government job, becoming an undersecretary in the Ministry of Foreign Relations and Culture. He and Alicia had another child, a second girl, and were making plans for more.

Still, judging by what I saw on my visits, the country and its economy were continuing to fall apart, only to rebuild, then to fall apart again, then to have a period of stability—an endless cycle, or so it seemed, that hadn't changed in decades. New slums grew out along the tentacles of open brown canals that flowed toward the river from almost every direction around the city. Inflation again reached the delirium of 1,000 percent. Then a new period of economic stability followed, more permanent this time. Yet another new currency was issued, the old peso reinstated, and Buenos Aires suddenly became what was said to be the third most expensive city in the world, after Tokyo and Paris. The Menem government declared this a victory.

Papá Benevento was forced to work hundreds of hours of

overtime at his commercial practice just to make ends meet. I tried to persuade my family to make a trip to the United States. I offered time and again to buy their tickets. They always said no. They were too proud to take gifts from their children. And there was too much to do. There were new trials to prepare for, and the fight against the pardons. There was work to be done for human rights.

I remember a visit before the new government, when they were fighting the law of "owed obedience." There had been uprisings among the military with the threat of new trials. Army bases were taken over. Tanks rolled through the streets. The Providential President, Raúl Alfonsín, had finally caved in. He signed legislation affecting the legal status of the hundreds of torturers and murderers among the military and the police who were due to be tried next for crimes against humanity. The law effectively laid the groundwork for their defense that they were "only obeying orders," and the later pardons of the comandantes.

Mamá Benevento responded physically to this news. She began experiencing dizzy spells. The spells could last for days. She was so sick with spinning that she couldn't leave the house. When that happened, it was an effort for the whole family to try and make her stay in bed.

I sat beside her bed one afternoon, during my last visit. I brought her tea and kept her company. She talked of the past when I had lived with them as an exchange student, of how happy and complete her family had been, of the hopes and dreams she had had for her children. Then her thoughts returned, as always, to her cause. She experienced another attack of vertigo. She closed her eyes and I held her hand until it passed.

"This government has committed a cowardly act by passing this law," she said. "We can see how it's going now. The trials of the others in the police and military we have worked so hard to see will be suspended. But there's something else that bothers me even more. Secret gangs of the military and the police have begun repressing information about what happened. It's now very difficult to find copies of the book *Nunca Más,* you know, the report of the National Commission on the Disappearance of Persons, in bookstores, or even in our libraries. Copies are being removed from the shelves. Videocassettes of the films that have been made about the history of repression are also vanishing. We are entering a dark era in which the military and the police are trying to erase from history all evidence of their crimes. We run the risk that a whole new generation of youth in this country and in the world will not have the opportunity to know. The world will forget. The cause to which we've devoted our lives, that of 'Never again,' will be changed into the lie 'It never happened.' "

Papá Benevento was busy that week having new doors put on their apartment. They were no ordinary doors. The brick-and-wood doorframes were knocked out with sledgehammers, then replaced by hardened steel structures that were bolted into the concrete pillars that supported the whole building. The steel frames were then nicely plastered over, painted, and finished. The day came when the actual doors arrived. They were thick oak slabs, reinforced in the middle with hardened steel sheeting at least a third of an inch thick, so heavy that it took three men, straining, to lift them up and hang them on carbon-steel hinges. The heavy doors were oiled and adjusted until they opened and closed easily. The family would now need three keys to get through these doors, one for each of the two-inch deadbolt locks that secured them into the steel frames.

Papá showed off the new doors to me in a mood of celebration, repeating the family joke about them, "It's no longer just an apartment. It's more like a bank vault. See?" he said. He took two light, dancing steps from the hallway into the apartment, shut the door, and turned the three keys. "We're in the vault now," he said. He turned the keys and opened the door, then gingerly stepped out into the hallway. "We're outside the vault. Inside, outside," he said, repeating the steps with a proud grin. "It would take an artillery shell to get in here," he said. "And maybe that wouldn't be enough. . . ."

Later that afternoon, I wandered along the banks of the river. I was due to leave Argentina again the next day. I was thinking about what Mamá had told me, and about the new doors for the apartment. I leaned out over a port railing and looked out across the moving water.

There it was, Paraná Iguazú, the *indios* had called it, "the river as big as a sea." I wanted to get lost in it suddenly. I wanted to dive in and drown, forget what I knew. I had read in Faulkner that memory believes before knowing remembers. And so, I thought, that was the way it was. Human experience was finally reduced to the lie that we think we know what we have forgotten.

While staring out across that vast, muddy, sun-stained body of water, it was clear to me that even the river forgot its banks and its sources. It changed, constantly, as it kept spilling like a great muddy sea into a shock of ocean blue. The river had no single color that could be accurately described. Especially this was so on maps and charts and by other designations of man. It was as though the river had been given its name according to that first basic principle of forgetting through lies in calling this red, muddy tide, this concatenation of waters and soils, sediments and the dreams from half the continent south and east of the Andes, the Río de la Plata, River of Silver, like a gleaming promise of riches and light. This, when it was red, as red as the color of blood mixed with earth.

The waters of the river washed down from the rust-colored hills of the high plateaus of Bolivia and Peru, through the scrub brush jungles of Paraguay and southern Brazil, the earth eroding away in a slow wash of pride and of destiny and of lassitude beyond even the terms of human imagination. And in the end, the water was red. I thought of the eulogized actions of the Spanish conquistadores that stretched back through history along its banks clear to the mountains. The waters were as red as all their executions and injustices combined, the murders of thousands, the abandonment of millions more to misery and to disease for His Holy Majesty the King of Spain and in the name of his Holy Church and for boatloads of silver and gold and the sanctuary of heaven.

The river didn't care. It remembered but knew nothing. Both contained and uncontainable, its waters went on rolling now as carelessly as ever through the generator drums of the new hydroelectric stations financed by the International Monetary Fund, but so tired and so slowly that, as though in its apathy, the river sometimes left the country in darkness. Knowing what their vision had been for Buenos Aires, the city's millions of descendants from Spaniards, Italians, Germans, Jews, and mixed-blood *indios* had failed in their mission. This land was never meant to be Europe. It was common wisdom that empty pockets had no room for such dreams.

So, the river was constant in forgetting, like the country it flowed past. Tradition and reality would clash heads like two pampas bulls. The cycles of power and cruelty would come around again. The recent memories would be erased, the tens of thousands gone, my own two brothers among them. I saw it then, clearly, captured in liquid hands. The newest soldiers of the *conquista* would march once more into the past. Everything would happen again. The River Plate was red, not silver, a sickly, rusted, decaying red, a wash of red as from pre-Columbian human sacrifice, a dark, sad red like the mood of a tango of abandoned love. The river was as red as in the beginning and always. As red as the last light of the southern sun on a land of vanished and forgotten graves.

—1985–94: Buenos Aires, Syracuse,
Montevideo, San Miguel,
Las Vegas